ROBERTA CRUSOE

Her Shipwreck and Return

ROBERTA CRUSOE

Her Shipwreck and Return

by

Corless Smith

To Alleah,
Enjoy!
Corless Smith

Design Consultant

Ann Decker

ISBN 978-0-615-97557-3

For Harriet R. Smith, my mother,
seamstress extraordinaire.

Chapter One—I Am Lost

I opened my eyes to a light so bright it hurt. My head was half jammed into a mound of wet sand, its grit riming my lips, my nose and eyes. I heard the soft cadence of waves upon a shore and the cawing of a water bird. Suddenly, into my waxing awareness sprung the vivid nightmare to which this dawn was the sequel.

The sailing ship on which my mistress and I had been riding to the new world had come on foul weather. In the morning it had been calm enough that we'd answered the invitation of the ship's captain to escape our cramped cabin for a stroll on deck. I quickly gathered our bonnets and parasols and we went up top, our russet puppy Roger happily trotting behind us. "Oh look, Roberta!" my mistress cried, pointing to a black form arcing into the air from the water's surface and back again. "It's a dolphin, milady," said the Captain. "Keep your eyes open and you will see more. They travel in groups and sport about as if on purpose to amuse us." In my mind I formed the reply that "The dolphin's porpoises were mysterious," to play on the Captain's "purpose," but did not say it aloud as he would have thought it odd to hear a joke proffered by a maid. The puppy frolicked a bit and leapt up to inspect the Captain's leg. "Oh

Roger," my mistress Leora scolded, scooping up the puppy, "Behave yourself!"

Off in the distance loomed a band of ominous grey sky that seemed to my eyes to be widening. The Captain was regarding it attentively as well. He hollered a command to the crew, each of whom hollered it on to another until at the end of the string, the immense white sails were noisily reassembled in a new formation.

"I think it's blowing up a storm on us, ladies," the Captain said, " so you'd best return to your cabin to ride it out." "Oh no!" my mistress cried out, "Couldn't we stay? It would be so romantic!" Getting battered about and soaked to the skin was not my idea of romance, but then I was two and twenty and Lady Leora de Robideax Hordley was seventeen and had had no adventures until this sea voyage out to Virginia to be married to a planter and take up residence in the American colonies. I had had no adventures either, but I expected none.

I had been ladies maid, housekeeper and all-around factotum to her mother, Lady Evelyn, for seven years, and she had sent me over the sea to look after her daughter. Though neither my permission nor opinion about this uprooting was ever asked, I felt it as an opportunity, perhaps even an escape, though from what and to what I had no idea. I did know it was a great compliment that Lady Evelyn was sending me with her beloved young daughter, and, in fact, it was a double sacrifice for her— her daughter and me. "Oh, Roberta, how shall I get on without you?" she'd said, and I certainly wondered that myself, seeing as how she could hardly brush her own hair. Lady Evelyn's common sense ran in a very narrow vein; she spent most of her mental energy deciding what was and wasn't ladylike, the highest value in her universe, so I often found myself consulted on the many topics outside the realm of the ladylike that usually make up no part of the maid's duties. She was advertising now

2

for an estate manager who would take my place as all-around advisor, though I doubted that like me he would dress her hair as he gave his advice.

I'd said goodbye to my five brothers and pointed myself towards the new world with a great deal of curiosity. My young mistress was curious too, but hers ran always upon her husband to be. She quizzed me as she played with the puppy, her blonde head and the russet puppy making a pretty picture bobbing up and down together: Would his house be to her taste? Did I think he preferred dark or light eyes? Would they have a grand coach? Would he like Roger? I entered into these questions as well as I could, wanting her to be at ease in her mind and yet ready for the inevitable strangeness she was bound to meet in her new home. The bridegroom would be a beast not to like Leora, and I was sure he would like Roger, who was a dear puppy and gave promise of being a stalwart hunter and friend to man.

"Do you think my husband would find me brave to have stood on deck during a storm?" my mistress asked as we stumbled below deck to our cabin, an awkward descent through a small opening for women encumbered with yards of skirts and petticoats. I had no idea how the man would regard such behavior, but I said, "I think he would rather you were prudent and stayed out of it, so that you'd make it safely to him." In light of what followed, it would not have mattered if she had strapped herself to the boat's prow as a living sculpture, spume making a halo about her head. In fact, I almost wished I'd counseled it so that the dear girl could have had the thrill of doing such a thing when she had the chance.

As it was, we'd no sooner reached our little cabin than the wind's roar rose, and the ship began to roll from side to side so that we were obliged to hold on to the posts of our bunks in order to avoid being thrown violently against the plank walls. "Roberta, I'm frightened," Leora wailed. I clutched her to me and she clutched Roger, who squirmed and whimpered at this treatment, "Be calm, my dear. We must ride it out," I murmured, as we rolled back and forth.

Just then we were wrenched violently apart and thrown around the cabin like dice shaken in a box by a giant gambler. Water was running steadily under the cabin door, which worried me a great deal. Having had no previous experience on the sea, I didn't know if this were common during storms or a sign of disaster. As I weighed what to do, I realized that Leora had grown quite still, and as this was generally the case only when she was asleep, I quickly turned and saw her stretched across the chintz-covered bunk, limply rolling with each reel of the ship, Roger licking her face. "Leora!" I cried, lightly slapping her, but she did not respond, and I thought she must have struck her head against the wall or fainted.

Meanwhile, more and more water was pouring under the door, inundating the small braided rug that had given the cabin a semblance of home. The water had risen well over my ankles, so I determined I had to get Leora out of there if she were not to meet a quick, watery end. Leora was elfin and I quite sturdy, but still, heaving her over my shoulder was most difficult. I had no idea how I would carry her up the narrow ladder to the deck nor what to do when we got there, but I knew anything would be better than to sit in our cabin and be drowned, no matter how ladylike a course that might have been. So I opened the door and lurched towards the ladder. Luckily, a young sailor passing the hatch saw my plight and dropped down to help us. He lifted Leora off my shoulders and took her aboveboard. I went back for Roger, tucked him under my arm and scrambled after.

Up top it seemed a bad day in hell. The wind screamed against a roiling sky. The ship was rolling up onto a mountain of dark water and sliding down the other side, sluicing the sailors back and forth across the deck like so many rag dolls. Some of the crew were unlashing a lifeboat, and the sailor was bearing Leora towards it like a heavy sack over his shoulder. "Get the women into the boat," the Captain shouted above the din, and I felt the puppy yanked from my arms and myself lifted over the keel and shoved into the boat's bottom. Leora lay beside me, still unconscious as the boat descended into the violent sea. As we went down the Captain's shout of, "God bless and keep you!" was braided over the wind. How quickly things had changed! It seemed only moments since we had strolled the deck, watching dolphins leap above the calm sea.

In the boat were ten sailors, we women, and a large wooden box. The little boat went at each colossal wave, mounting one only to meet another. I wanted to help, but I had my hands full holding Leora's head above the water that was rapidly filling the little boat. Over and over we climbed wave after wave, the sailors rowing and bailing, rowing and bailing.

I do not know how many hours we went on like this, continuously lashed by the water, gasping for breath and soaked to the bone until one by one the men tired and abandoned any effort to control the boat; so that at last it tossed willy-nilly across the water's rolling turmoil.

When Leora finally opened her eyes, their blue depths immediately registered the terror of our situation. "Oh Roberta! What has happened to us?" she screamed. "The ship was about to go down, so the Captain sent us off in this lifeboat. Calm down, milady. We can ride it out," I said, knowing no such thing. "Where is Roger?" she asked plaintively. Before I was obliged to explain that Roger had been left behind, the boat plunged into a vast watery ditch and could not mount the next wave, spilling us all screaming into the sea

"Leora! Leora!" I shouted before I went under the churning water. Bobbing back up, choking and sputtering, I saw the wooden box that had accompanied us in the boat. I lunged for it, grabbed with all my strength and hung on as hard as I could, trying to hoist myself up to see if I could find Leora as the ocean chivied my box hither and yon. The waves tossed me up and down, sickening me and driving me ever further from the boat. I could see men flailing upon the water and some figures grabbing on to the boat, but I could not make out Leora among them, and I could not hoist myself upward again as it took all my strength to cling to the box as it tossed about on the waves. For what seemed like an eternity I clung on, wrestling for breath, trying to keep my head above the ocean waters that continually slammed over me.

Gradually, the sea grew calmer, and I fell limply over my raft of a box. I was cold, but as we were in the Tropics, I knew it was not the cold that would kill me, but the water. I floated over the sea for many hours, my arms clasped around the box and my legs dangling in the sea. As the day fell into night my aching limbs forced me to change position, so I curled into a little ball atop the box.

At last, the storm cleared off completely, and I lay a tiny human presence under a starry sky whose beauty I could not help noting in spite of my dire circumstances. I sorrowed for Leora and for her mother and for myself as I was surely going to die, but eventually weariness overcame me. As I felt sleep steal over me I thought how odd it was that in such a predicament I had not even the power to prevent myself from falling asleep. Such are the demands of the body.

The next thing I knew I was lodged in the sand as I told at the beginning of my story, somehow having been deposited on a beach.

Warm water lapped around my ankles. I dragged myself to my knees, and as I tried to stand I found I was enormously sore, as if I had been beaten all over, but that no part in particular cried out in greater alarm than another. In short, I stood and found that though pounded and weak, I was sound and on solid ground, a miraculous circumstance given my certainty that I would die, so I looked around at where I had landed as one newly born.

It seemed like a page ripped from a fairy story, so unlike England was it. The beach was golden, and palm trees riffled lightly in the soft fragrant breeze, but I was struck with a dreadful thirst, so the beauty of my landing place receded before my need for water. I staggered along the beach a good ways, hoping to find some sort of fresh water stream feeding into the ocean. My boots were waterlogged so I pulled them off. I had not had the pleasure of walking barefoot on a beach since I was a girl, but now my parched throat and cracked lips made me oblivious to its glories. After half an hour of painful tramping I came upon a gentle flood flowing from the land towards the sea, so I turned inward and followed it until it narrowed into a rill, whereupon I sank to my knees, cupped my hands and scooped the cool, clear water into my mouth and drank deeply again and again. How elementally satisfying it was! When I had had my fill I lay back on the grassy bank and fell into a stuporous sleep.

When I awoke I was confused, then again amazed at the manner of place where I had been thrown up by the sea. As I looked round I wondered if there were any danger from man or animal here and, more pressingly, if there were anything to eat. As before my thirst had prompted my wandering, now it was hunger because I had not eaten for many hours, though I could not calculate how many. In trying to do so, I had another wrenching thought of Leora and hoped that somehow she had been saved.

The sun was high overhead and I realized I would soon be quite redly roasted, so I tore off a piece of my petticoat and fashioned a scarf with a short projection over my face, covering my neck and bosom and holding back my hair which was a combination of tangled clumps and salt-stiffened strings. Thus I initiated the mufti garb that would often characterize my appearance in this place. I walked further up the stream, taking a mental inventory of my knowledge of tropical foodstuffs and what I might reasonably expect to find. There would be fish, but how would I catch them? And exotic fruits, but how would I know them when I saw them and which were safe and which poisonous?

As I walked inward, the land rose and grew steadily greener until I reached a small ferny glade overhung by cliffs strung with vines and studded with delicate cream and purple flowers. Over it flowed a waterfall into a small pool below. So lovely was it that I gasped and quickened my step. Then for an Englishwoman, I did a scandalous thing. Without considering yea or nay I stripped off my salt-stiffened clothes and slid down into the cool luxury of the water. I paddled slowly across the pool towards the waterfall. The mist around it reflected the sunlight so that the air shimmered.

I thought then that perhaps instead of surviving my drowning, I had, in fact, died and gone to heaven. However, my idea of heaven was not so solitary. Here there was not the white-robed greeting party Sunday school leads one to expect. I had to laugh because, in truth, I did not believe in heaven. This, nor anything about my religious life, could I have told anyone of my acquaintance as it would have been shocking and caused unhappiness, to me perhaps most of all, but here I was alone, and there was no one from whom to hide my true belief, or lack of it. I climbed out of the pool much refreshed and put my clothes on, all except for my stays which I saw no reason to force myself into, so I left them there and, prodded by the complaints of my stomach, pressed on to find something edible.

Suddenly it occurred to me that some of the ship's crew, or even Leora herself might also be cast ashore as I was, or that there might be a passing craft that I might hail to rescue me, so rather than going further inland, I took a course parallel to the beach so that I might have a view of whatever was happening on or near it. The sand was also easier on my feet, which were loudly protesting their unfamiliarity with pebbles, twigs and grit.

Such was my hunger that I more busily scanned the trees and ground than the sea. Beneath the lavish fronds at the top of the palms I saw what I took to be coconuts, whose sweetness of both liquid and meat had been described to me many times by our neighbor Samuel Smallwhite who had gone as a sailor on a Caribbean voyage as a young lad. This sweetness remained theoretical for me, however, because the nuts were far above my head, and, though I had climbed many trees as a girl, they all offered more hand- and footholds than these trees, whose great sweeping trunks offered none. Luckily, my search beneath the trees revealed some fallen fruit, but their greenish-brown rinds were very hard and thick and I cast about for a way to open one.

I felt as if I were a new Eve, set out in a garden that presented itself as a puzzle I had to solve to feed myself. I must regress to the primitive and take up the customs of my ancestors if I were to eat, so I looked about for a rock big enough to crack the coconut, but not so big that I couldn't carry it. Having found a likely candidate about the size of a sheep's head, I held it aloft and crashed it down on the nut. To no effect whatever! I thus pounded the coconut many times, but it refused to yield. Then I took up an opposite strategy, and by this I don't mean I subjected the coconut to diplomacy instead of violence because I was certain that it was inaccessible to reason, as, in my experience, are many people, whose heads might well have been made of coconut shell. Instead, I picked up the coconut itself and dashed it sharply down on the point of a small rocky projection from the earth. This strategy eventually succeeded, and the coconut shattered into several pieces. The liquid was lost, but I quickly chewed into the waxy, white meat and found it good indeed. As I dug this meat out with my teeth and munched away, I was unreasonably proud of my victory over the coconut. I smiled to imagine what Lady Evelyn would think of me, as for her, eating a coconut would probably require the use of a several implements of tableware.

I determined to go further, and since the coconut trees were plentiful, there was no need for me to encumber myself by packing along any of their fruit. A shady grove some distance up from the beach caught my eye, so I pushed my way up into it and found attached to its tall trees a fruit that I had never seen nor heard of. Curved greenish-yellow tubes about five inches long hung in immense clusters. These also were well beyond my reach, but not so high as the coconuts.

I searched about for something with which I might knock them down and after a bit of scouring found a dead branch that might do the job, so I hauled it up and started to whack away at the clump. Eventually, several subclusters fell at my feet. I detached one of the tubes from its mates and tore it open; indeed, it seemed packaged to invite this sort of unwrapping. Inside was a brilliant white fruit with small ridges along its sides. I broke it in two. Should I eat some? I turned this over for a few minutes, debating the alternative of a diet consisting entirely of coconuts versus the possibility that I might be about to eat something poisonous. At last, my curiosity, the heavenly odor and a certain intuition of safety overcame my prudence, and I bit into the white fruit. Oh my! It was good—sweet and of a texture something like a pudding. I put a few of the yellow cartridges for which I had no name into the deep pocket of my gown and went back towards the beach.

I was now rested and had both eaten and drunk. So I sat down beneath a palm tree on a small rise above the sandy beach, looked around me and considered my situation. I had little idea where on earth I was, somewhere in the warmer sections of the Atlantic was all I knew. I had as yet no idea if I were marooned on an island or if my location were part of a larger continent. If the latter, I might walk the beach and eventually come upon other humans. I might also do this if I were on an island. In either case, I was in peril. Could I be rescued? Probably no one even knew I was missing. It seemed that my best course was just to try to stay alive. I had food and water, though nothing else besides the clothes I wore, which consisted of a blue woolen dress, a white undershift, and a petticoat, from which I had already ripped a big piece, and, of course, the whale-bone stays I had discarded by the waterfall. I was of a good height and hale in body. I was utterly alone, but I had been on my own in my mind for many years, so I was not as bereft as I might otherwise have been. Thinking of this, however, reminded me of Leora and my brothers, especially my youngest brother, Richard, who was most dear to me, and all the other people I might never see again, and I remembered the terror of the storm, and at last I broke down and cried, rendering my own storm of great gusty sobs. For a long time confusion and hopelessness flooded me with an acid misery. When my tears finally receded, having changed my situation not one whit, I reminded myself that I was young and strong and had my wits about me, and that there was food to keep me alive until some rescue came, and so my misery ebbed for the nonce.

The slant of the golden light told me the afternoon would soon slip into evening, and I had better find some sort of shelter for the night. I thought of the grotto with the waterfall, but its dampness decreased its desirability as a bedroom, so I scouted about my seat just above the beach and found a hillock nearby with a better overhang. It was nowhere near what one would call a cave, more a scalloped out closet. I gathered fallen palm fronds from under the coconut trees near the beach and in several trips dragged them to this little closet. Some I lodged into the overhang to extend it a bit, and the rest I mounded on the ground together with some long grasses that grew nearby to make a bed. I went once more to the stream for drink and brought into my closet some of the yellow tube fruit. Just as I had finished with the construction of my room, a small shower erupted, but I was dry enough under my palm porch and soon fell into a slumber that roiled like the ocean that had flung me into the unknown. I clutched in vain for something familiar.

Chapter 2 — Misery and Acquisition
or The Odd Bazaar

I awoke scratching myself vigorously. I itched everywhere, and was covered with small red splotches. I'd noticed a number of insects the previous day, but so focused was I on the brute necessities of water and food that I'd given them no thought. They, however, had attended to me much more carefully and made of me a vast meal.

I emerged into a day as peaceful as I was agitated. The sky was utterly blue, and there was no evidence of the evening's shower; thus began my lesson in tropical weather, where showers arrive almost every afternoon but go as quickly as they come and leave little evidence other than a daily freshening of the landscape and a moistness in the air that is quickly dissipated by the constant gentle breeze that blows in off the sea. My circumstances were perilous but the stage upon which they were unfolding was very lovely indeed.

As I stood scratching and scanning the beach I was much startled to see rising in the distance an immense dark hulk hanging off a rocky spit I had noted the previous day. I was astounded to realize that it looked to be the very ship on which Leora and I had sailed. I ran down the beach and up the spit towards it, scrambling over the rocks as far as I could, my sore feet protesting all the way, but I was still a hundred yards from the vessel. "Hello! Hello" I yelled again and again, hoping that someone might yet survive aboard her and I might gain a companion.

I searched the surroundings to see if there were not some way I could get closer and noticed that the sand on the beach showed both a drier and a wetter portion, indicating that the tide was either coming or going, as, of course, it always is. It would take some time to tell which it was. In about twenty minutes it became clear that the tide was going out, and if I were patient I might well be able to get much closer to the ship, close enough that I could swim to her. I was good enough at swimming, having learned at an early age in the pond near our farm, and I had some experience of struggle in the water too, having been the object of my brother's dunkings many hundreds of times. They were protective of me, but made sport of me just as often.

By now avid scratching of my insect bites had begun to draw blood, so I resolved to bear the itch until it abated, a model of the forbearance I had many times to invoke in the coming days as my English body encountered the tropical climate. Now, as I waited for the water to recede and forbore from scratching, I occupied my mind with what I would do if I were to gain the ship, how I would board her and what I might find there.

I noticed near her a sort of floating lagoon of detritus, some of which I could identify as spars and mere pieces of wood, some as boxes and casks, even some things that could be chests or trunks. This sped my heart as these might well be the very trunks that Leora and I had brought on board with us and which contained many household items that would be very useful to me right now.

I decided to swim out as close to these as I could, hoping that I might be able to tow them in towards the shore, wait for the water to rise and tow them in further. To do this I had to rid myself of my dress as it would be a heavy prison to swim in. As for my shift, it might also entangle my legs, but I wanted its protection from the sun on my shoulders, so I tore it off right above my knee and left the remnant in a heap with my dress. I braided my unruly brown bush of hair and tied it with a string from my petticoat. Then I waded out into the water, which was pleasantly warm and calm, though the salt sorely stung my insect bites.

Ocean swimming was more strenuous that what I'd done in the pond, but I churned my way out and first came upon a short plank that I then used as a float as I kicked my way towards more interesting quarry. I soon reached a trunk that was not one of ours, so I thought it must belong to one of the officers. A bit further on I was delighted to see the oxblood leather surface of one of Leora's trunks. I swam up to it and grasped the side handle, hoping to begin towing the trunk towards the shore, but the awkwardness of the grasp made it difficult to swim. I needed a rope. Kicking my legs to hold myself in place above the water, I took off what remained of my shift and tore it into strips, which I then tied together to make a primitive rope, one I might have used to escape a prison had I been in a fairy tale, though I myself seemed to be in an adventure story. I tied this rope to the trunk and found I could swim and tow much more easily now. I even had enough rope to tie Leora's trunk to the unknown one and thus tow two at once, though the swimming was then even more strenuous. When I reached shallower water, I stood up and tugged the two trunks as far forward as I could, at last untying them from one another and dragging one, then the other as far up the beach as I could. I did not want them floating away again when the tide turned.

Meanwhile, the water had receded further, and it looked like I could swim to the ship, but the sun's position told me it was just midmorning, and yesterday's ordeal and the hard swimming of today had much sapped my strength. I was tired out by my towing trip, and also hungry and thirsty, so I decided I would make a short walk up to the stream to refresh myself, and then try a trip to the ship. Of course, I did this naked, but since there was no one there to see me, I thought it was not so great an offense against modesty, unless the bite of the sun on my skin was some sort of cosmic rebuke. My breasts were rather flopping about so I took one of the strips I used as a rope and bound it around my chest. I would need to cover myself more completely soon, as I could feel my body slowly roasting under the sun's broiler. To shield my lower quarters I dragged the blue dress over my head and made a sort of pantaloon out of the skirt by wrapping the strips torn from my shift between my legs and around my waist.

Eating two of the yellow tubular fruit and a bit of coconut stiffened my resolve, but also made me hope that I would find some other sources of food soon, for even after eating my fruit I remained hungry.

I went back to the beach and found that the tide had further ebbed and I could walk over the wet sand much closer to the ship before I would have to swim. It occurred to me that I should open the trunks I had already retrieved to see if there might be in them some tools or some rope that might aid me, but I decided I wouldn't burden myself and would consider this trip one of preliminary exploration, as it had not yet occurred to me that the ship could disappear from this close mooring as easily as it had come. So I waded as far as I could and then plunged ahead into the water towards the beached leviathan of the wrecked ship, which rose larger and more menacing the closer I got. How haunted was its air! Great gashes wounded its sides and rigging hung chaotically off broken spars as if hell's washerwoman had hung a ghastly laundry.

I had wondered how I would mount when I reached the side of the ship, but this turned out to be elemental as I saw a rope ladder hanging over the side and there was attached to the ship's side a series of wooden block steps that I was able to grasp and upon which I could pull myself upwards little by little, until I could take hold of the ladder that, I surmised, was the very one that Leora and I had descended into the lifeboat.

I dragged myself over the rail and fell in a heap on the ship's deck, tearing the sleeve of my dress and etching long red scratches on my arms. When I regained my breath and looked around me I saw no person, and probably if I had done, he would have been dead. The ship was lodged upon the rocks at an angle and the deck was canted so that I walked uphill across it to look below. A foot of water lay down there, but it seemed safe to descend. I looked into all the cabins and into the hold where the seamen slept but found no one amidst the chaos of clothes and shoes, pipes, buckets and hammocks all twisted together in a forlorn stew.

When it was clear that no people to hail or help were on the ship, I began to look amongst the chaos for things that might help me in my own solitary situation. In the galley I found a number of water-soaked items, gloppy masses that had once been food, but also several casks of the crackers that pass as ship's bread, several jars of pickles and other sealed casks whose contents were not apparent. I resolved to haul the casks back with me and to take some of the cooking utensils that were lying about as well. I particularly looked for a knife, a flint and steel for making a fire, and for something in which I might carry and store water, finding a large pot and several covered jars that would serve this purpose well. Near the stove I found a six-inch knife and a larger one of about ten inches. I also took a fork, two spoons, a tin plate and a cup, all of which I wrapped in rags and put into some coarse tow sacks and hauled them up to the deck, then continued my tour of the ship.

In the Captain's cabin I found a spyglass and a number of waterlogged books and maps strewn about. I was also glad to see hanging from wall hooks some clothing that appeared to be sturdy and undamaged. I unstrapped myself from the contraption I had made of my dress, now dripping heavily with water, and pulled a soft white shirt over my head and fastened it around my waist with a great leather belt. I shoved two more shirts, a pair of buff-colored britches and a navy great coat into my sacks, which were now grown so heavy that I began to consider how I would haul my treasures back to the shore.

I had as yet gone into only a few of the cabins nor had I scouted the deck very well either. It was most clear, however, that there were many things here that could aid my survival and that I should make a great effort to retrieve them for my use and comfort. The sense of housewifery I felt in provisioning myself combined with the eeriness of the deserted ship to present this scavenging in an odd light.

As I thought on this I was most startled to hear a faint whine from the direction of the Captain's bunk, a whine which grew louder as I eagerly approached it. I pushed aside the soggy bedclothes and there in the corner shivering and whimpering was Leora's puppy Roger. "Oh Roger!" I cried. How glad I was to see another living creature of my acquaintance! The puppy eagerly crawled towards me, whimpering in a more pleased key, and awkwardly mounting up to lick my face. I held the trembling caramel creature and caressed him. "Oh, Roger, dear pup, you made it." The puppy collapsed against me in a sort of ecstasy of recognition as I rubbed his ears and plushy head. I was sure the poor dog must be hungry and thirsty but had no way at the moment to care for him other than to assure him that he was safe.

As Roger and I reestablished our connection, I began to consider how I could transport him to shore along with the useful things I'd found aboard the ship. I concluded that I must build a raft and that I must build it in the water beneath the ship. I had observed my brothers build a number of flimsy rafts at the pond, but had never built one myself, though doing so now seemed just another part of the extreme improvisation of the day.

Carrying Roger, I began to go back up top, when I heard yet another faint bleating sound that seemed to come from the hold beyond the one where the sailors slept. I put Roger down on the deck, where he whined pitifully at my leaving, and went back down to investigate. The ship's tilt made wading through its lower depths very challenging. The bleating grew a bit louder as I slogged towards the far hold, where, inside a pen, standing miserable in a foot of water were two shivering goats, a dark brown buck and a tan doe, both crying piteously and louder as I came nearer. I knelt between them in the water and held them to me which seemed to ease their distress a bit. A length of rope was attached to their ship's pen, so I laced them together and led them splashing and bleating back through the hold. I went up top and gave a yank to the rope whereupon the two goats quite lithely scrambled up.

In light of these new arrivals my mental image of the raft-to-be grew larger. I scanned the floating lagoon beneath me, spying two rounded beams that might have splintered off the main mast. I thought these might be overlain with the several planks that floated with them if there were something to bind the whole thing together.

Leaving the goats to their own devices, which were scant as they were hungry and thirsty, conditions whose cure would have to wait, I went in search of the ship's carpenter's store, Roger tripping after me. Had I been rational in my search, I would have started out at the carpenter's room, for I soon found there a well-furnished alcove whose array of tools had been preserved from the general chaos by their having been fastened down against the wall with metal hooks or rawhide ropes. I took a hammer and shoved it in my belt. From a cask of four-inch nails I took a handful, emptied them into a rawhide pouch and tied it to my belt too. "This should suit us well, Rog," I said, and he did not contradict me.

I took several lengths of rope and looped them over my shoulder, then remounted to the deck, went down the ladder and lowered myself into the water. I winced as the salt attacked the new scratches on my arm and made yet another assault on my rash of insect bites. At the same time Roger went crazy with a sort of grief-stricken barking, perhaps imagining that I would leave him alone again on the ship. "Roger," I called. "Hush, I'll be back," and as I stayed beneath him and did not move very far away, he soon calmed down and closely inspected my work, occasionally making little barks at the cowering goats.

Immediately on entering the water, I grabbed my floating spar, and it was a good thing because my carpentry tools weighed me down and made swimming so difficult that at first I went under and swallowed several choking gulps of salty sea water. When I regained my balance, I gathered the two beams I had seen from above, and holding one close to the other, in a very haphazard manner I tried to nail one plank to the other, using the ship itself as a solid surface against which to drive the nail. The awkwardness of this maneuver can scarcely be exaggerated. The nails kept falling into the water before I could sufficiently lodge them in the wood, and, of course, I landed a hammer blow on my finger that brought tears to my eyes, as much from frustration as pain.

At last I did join the planks to each other, and I then extended out from the plank, carrying the other beam with me and nailed the other end to it with only slightly less trouble. Because it was beastly hard to do such nailing floating in water, I was not able to sink the nails to their hilts. However, I was grateful that having grown up with five brothers I had many times watched carpentry work and had often tried my hand at it so as not to be outdone, especially by the younger ones. Life with these five brothers had disinclined me to seek a marriage, but it had prepared me for practical building tasks. To further strengthen my little barque, I ran rope over and under the planks and tied them together as closely as I could, leaving long lines so that I could pull the raft and also tether it. Every once in a while Roger would bark and I would reassure him, "Be patient. I'll soon fetch you down."

Eventually, I went back up the rope ladder and again threw myself over the ship's side to Roger's frenzied elation. This time I scraped my thigh against the rough wood, but did not stop to attend to it; it simply joined my other wounds in hope of future salve. I retrieved the sacks and threw them down upon the raft. I wondered if I threw the food casks into the sea if their contents would be spoiled. I decided upon an experiment of sorts, I threw down two of them and put one in a sack that I strapped to my body and took down the ladder.

But how was I to bring off the two goats? My solution was to fashion a sort of sling out of canvas and rope and in it to lower each of them down to the raft, an awkward task that strained the limits of my strength. One of them nipped at me and left more bloody marks upon my arm. Reaching the raft, the goats balanced uneasily upon it and bleated mightily, but their delicate, deft little hooves served them well.

Then I went back up and fashioned another sort of sling out of the remaining sack, scooped Roger into it and wrapped it around my body so that Roger was immobilized and transportable. He seemed alarmed by the procedure but did not complain unduly, perhaps sensing that this constraint at least meant he was not being left alone. Reaching the sea I hauled my casks up on the raft and then spent a moment contemplating my return trip to the beach loaded with a small menagerie, Roger hugged to my breast and looking up at me as if to say, "What now?" I set the bagged Roger down and slipped into the water with some trepidation, expecting the sting of the wounds on my thigh and arm.

While I was foraging on the ship, the tide had apparently reached its lowest ebb and seemed again to flow in towards the beach, so I needed to make haste to take advantage of it. The raft was too heavy for me to tow by swimming, but I was able to push it along until I got to shallower water where I could then more easily drag it forward onto the sand, which I did as far as I could.

I was exhausted and hungry, and bleeding a bit from the scrapes on my arm and thighs, but knew I had to stay on the beach and continue guiding the raft up to the shore as the water flowed in or I would lose all I had gained. I grabbed one of the sacks, that with the knives and the flint, and splashed up to the beach with it. I set it down and unbound Roger from his cloth restraint and set him loose on the beach. He was delighted, ran about a bit, then, as I had done when I first rose from my own landing on this beach, he went in search of water. I saw him heading down towards the stream, so I turned to attend to the goats who were loathe to jump into the sea. I pulled one and then the other terrified creature into the shallow water, where they first churned about in anguish but then found their feet and went towards the beach, where I tied them and led them towards the stream so that they might have fresh water.

I tethered them in a shady spot where they immediately tucked into the tender grass while I went back to the beach and lay down on the damp sand, my chest heaving from exertion. With the captain's shirt splayed out around me I must have appeared a great jellyfish as I lay there considering how I ought to proceed. I could have taken everything off the raft and lodged it further up, but I did not want to lose my raft, and so I had to let the water bring it close enough to moor it on the nearest suitable rock

It was now late afternoon. The wounds in my arm and thigh smarted, my bites itched, and my skin was dryly puckered from my extended stay in the water, but my day's labor was not yet complete. I was hungrier than ever, so I took my hammer to the cracker barrel and pried off its top. There were ugly specks of incipient worms in the ship's bread, but it still looked mighty good to me and I made an immediate meal, nits and all. Soon Roger trotted back and leaped at the bread, so I gave him a hearty portion that he chewed into eagerly. Strengthened enough with rest and nourishment, I began to carry the goods back to my little closet under the overhang, Roger ever at my heels. As sorely as I wanted to open the two trunks that stood tantalizing me, I thought it best to stow my tools away and see if I could start a fire and get some water. My feet were now complaining against the sharp pebbles, so I again put on my boots.

I went first for the water with my bottles, noting that the goats were calm and pleasantly occupied nibbling on their surroundings. I gathered dried grass, twigs and larger pieces of burnable stuff. In front of my closet I made a small enclosure with rocks and then repeatedly struck my flint near the tinder, which at last obliged me by smoking and then making a tiny flame, which I fed with the larger pieces I had gathered. As soon as I had accomplished the making of the fire I wondered why I had done it. I had as yet nothing to cook and it was not in the least bit cold, and, if there were a chill, I had furnished myself with the Captain's greatcoat to withstand it. I concluded that I had made the fire because it was the human thing to do.   I needed to establish a hearth. It gave me strength and hope. Roger seemed to agree as he formed himself into a ball, snuggled close to me and went to sleep, for all the world as if we were by a warm kitchen fire in Shropshire. In a bit I tried my big knife on a coconut and found that a hammer's blow on top the knife split it easily, so I feasted on coconut, yellow fruit and ship's bread.

It was still some hours until night, and I was determined to open the trunks I had dragged in, so despite my weariness, I took my hammer and returned to the beach.   Roger seemed not so eager to be up and about again, but he followed me dutifully and this set the pattern of our life together ever after—wherever I went Roger followed. He became my faithful confidant and, though our relationship was quite one-sided, I doing all the confiding and he doing all the listening, I hope I repaid him by always looking out for him and being very grateful for his companionship.

Leora's trunk was not only locked, but sealed all around with wax as well, which made a good guarantee that its contents would be dry, but also made entry into it more difficult, so I decided to open the other one first, which, though it was locked, was quite easily pried into. On top lay a yellow oilcloth Macintosh in which was wrapped a violin case from which I surmised this to be the trunk of Lt. Swarthmore, who was in the habit of playing music to the captain of an evening. I opened the case and gazed upon the lovely instrument.   I plucked its strings, producing a mournful sound that brought before my imagination a picture of my youngest brother, Richard, playing a dirge at our father's funeral the winter I was fifteen; he was a wizard upon the fiddle even as a young boy. This vision was like to throw me again into the profound misery of the previous evening, so I put the violin aside and delved further into the trunk.

I found there another selection of men's clothing—shirts and britches and a blue satin waistcoat, white linen stocks and hose. Deeper down there was also a pair of soft leather boots. I pulled these out and found wrapped in a kerchief beneath them a pair of spectacles, a Bible, and a tiny oil portrait of a brunette woman and two children. I looked at the portrait and thought of this woman who had not yet heard the fate of her husband. I hoped that she could go on for some time thinking that he was safe. It was not impossible he had survived and would someday return to her. At the bottom of the trunk there were several bottles of ink, a good deal of paper and a handsome pistol. It made me wonder what sort of situation might arise here in which a pistol would be useful. Of course, I would need powder and balls with which to load the pistol and in thinking of where I might locate these I considered what other weapons the ship might provide.

I made several portable bundles of these things from Lt. Swarthmore's trunk and then turned to Leora's chest, which after a good long time eventually yielded to my scrapings and pryings. Opening it I knew at once what I would find within it, for I had packed it myself. It was one of the secondary trunks, not that containing her ivory satin wedding dress and trousseau.

I pulled out an initial layer of fine but sturdy bed linen and a woven coverlet in blue and white. There were three lengths of fabric, a heavy red and yellow striped damask that was meant to become drapes in Leora's new home, another piece of fine dark blue wool for a bridegroom's coat, and an enormous length of sprigged calico in blue and yellow, future summer dresses for Leora. There were smaller lengths of other stuffs as well as many skeins of fancy yarns for embroidery. There were also the tools to work these textiles—needles and two pairs of scissors, which when I viewed them now seemed to me quite glorious in their fine precision, but which I had scarcely noticed when I'd packed them. I was struck with how material objects take on their character entirely in relation to human needs and locations. I also drew from the trunk three cakes of scented soap, two silver brushes and a comb, a packet of mother-of-pearl buttons, and Leora's extra stays, which looked as if they had been made for a doll. It struck me as bizarre that custom decreed a sylph-like girl such as Leora should be trussed into this uncomfortable device. It was one thing for me, who had a shelf of bosom to contend with, but it was inexplicable applied to her.

Further down in the trunk I found three of Leora's gowns, a cape and a pair of wee boots, all too small for me to wear but made of serviceable fabrics that I might use. Their colors and patterns so strongly brought Leora herself to my mind that I was again threatened with weeping so I set them aside. Close to the bottom was a bundle wrapped in yards of heavy black and white ticking that Leora had bade me pack without looking into it. I happily beheld the ticking itself as auguring a mattress for myself, and I wondered if I would betray Leora's trust by looking into the packet. I decided that the strangeness of my current circumstance created a special situation in which I could be excused from many offenses, and so I looked inside. There lay Leora's own christening dress and cap, delicate white creations with bands of lace and embroidery along their edges. The sight of them struck at my heart, as I realized that Leora had brought these items in hope that her own future babies would wear them. I could not this time evade my misery and was once again overwhelmed with sorrow and loneliness and wept noisily for a long time, until Roger nudged me as if he were curious what more the trunk had to offer and so brought me back to the moment.

At the very bottom of the trunk was a bundle the sight of which was able to lighten my spirits: it was an oilcloth packet containing smaller packets of seeds, both flowers and vegetables and also of herbs and medicaments that had been given to me by Mr. Chalcote, Lady Evelyn's groundskeeper. He was the kindest person I've ever known, and I loved listening to him talk about growing things in ways that extended his meanings beyond plants. I had little free time, but I spent all of it with him until Lady Evelyn forbade it as improper. I protested, "But, milady, he is an old man!" "It is not his sex that is at issue," she said, "but his station. You are a ladies maid. He is a groundskeeper." To me this seemed a distinction without a real difference, especially now as I knelt on faraway sand rifling Leora's trunk.

I had reached the bottoms of these trunks that increasingly took on the character of treasure chests, so I gathered my bundles in transportable groups and trekked back up to my campsite, Roger ever at my heels.

Now I was well and truly exhausted, sore and aching, and made no effort to arrange these goods, because I had another task before I could rest. I had to pull my raft further toward the beach and unload the rest of its contents. I was so deadly exhausted that this was utter drudgery, but I tried to keep before me the idea that my work was contributing to my survival and rescue and this kept me going.

At last I trudged up to my camp with the last cask, and made my leaden arms spread the ticking out upon the fronds and grasses I had mounded for my bed, hoping to protect myself from further insect incursions. I put the coverlet at its foot and dropped down; Roger immediately snuggled at my side as if to say, "It's about time!" I hoped the goats would be safe by the stream as I could not summon enough force to bring them closer.

I was so sunburned that I felt enclosed in a warm poultice rent by raw sores, and despite the warmth, I shivered from time to time and pulled the coverlet up over me. I looked out at the darkening sky, its rose and lavender descending to purple, each new star seeming a brilliant bangle. I thought over my day. How strange the empty ruined ship had been! The whole crew had certainly left her, but had they been rescued or had all perished in the sea? My thoughts traveled into gratitude that I had gotten off the ship so many useful things that could prolong my life, and I was even more grateful that my previous life had been one of hard work because it had made me capable and strong. Certainly today I had worked as hard as ever I had in England, and, uniquely, it was not at the behest of anyone else but on my own behalf. So, odd as it may seem, anxious and sorrowful as I was and scored with an array of small wounds, I felt some pleasure and satisfaction as I fell asleep, further pleasured by running my hand over the silkiness of Roger beside me.

Chapter 3 — Roundtrip Retrievals

wakening on my third day in the wild, I was stiff and my skin was a field of scabs, but moving about soon eased me. I smiled to imagine Lady Evelyn's disgust if she were to see me. I doubt my circumstances would have mitigated the verdict one whit. It then occurred to me that I ought to keep track of how long I stayed here, and so I chose a nearby palm and with my small knife made three small nicks in it to mark each day so far. Then I breakfasted on ship's bread, and the native fruit and gave some to Roger as well, though as we sat there he sensed something moving in the grass beyond us and took off after it. If I had been at home I would have thought it were a rabbit or a mouse, but here it could be some animal I'd never seen before. Soon Roger returned without any prey and looking a bit crestfallen. He was still a puppy and not yet as swift or skillful as he would soon be. "That's all right, Roger," I said. "You'll be getting them before long."

I tore off more of my petticoat and bound up the blisters on my feet so I could put on my boots again. Then we visited the goats, who came eagerly towards us, hoping, I suppose, that I might have something for them to eat besides the grass that surrounded them. I patted their heads and was struck by the asymmetrical shapes of their deep agate eyes. Roger practiced barking at them, at which they looked suitably disturbed and backed off, which seemed to recompense Roger for his earlier failure to run his prey to ground.

As we walked back to the campsite, I set myself to consider how I ought to conduct my work this day. I had already decided that I would go back to the ship and bring off her as much as I could and that I should continue to do this until I had exhausted her help in furthering my survival. I ought also to make a pen for the goats so that they might have a wider range of forage. But I also considered where I had set up my camp and if it were in the best place. If I decided to move my site, it would be better to decide now and not have to haul things more than once, nor would it make sense to position the goat's pen before I knew where my own camp would be. Since I had not explored my location except in the smallest degree, I had no basis upon which to decide where to install myself more permanently, though I still hoped that I would soon be rescued and that "permanently" would turn out to be a very short time. At first glance it seemed that it would be better to be somewhat further from the sea than I then was, but I would need to explore the terrain more thoroughly before I could make a decision. For now I would maintain my current camp.

Remembering that yesterday when I had finally reached the carpenter's alcove it struck me that I should have gone there first, I thought now about what I might look for when I reached the ship today. It would be good to have a proper hat to shield me from the sun and any kind of wheel would be a great boon for with it I could construct a cart, instantly leaping eons in my facsimile of the progress of human history. I thought I would bring back whatever spirits I could find too, not because I was accustomed to taking spirits, but because I anticipated further injuries such as the bites and scrapes and blisters I'd accrued the day before and these could be cleansed with spirits.

With this preliminary shopping list in mind, I put on a pair of the captain's breeches, hoping to protect my bottom which had gotten a bit roughed up the day before. The breeches were much too big so with the larger scissors I cut them off above my knees and tied them on with a strip of my now decimated shift. Again I donned the captain's shirt, belted round with my hammer shoved into it, and went down the beach to untether my raft, pausing to drive in the nails I had sunk halfway the day before. Pushing the raft before me into the water as far as I could while standing, and then paddling along with it in front of me, I again approached the ship, which now seemed less ominous though more forlorn as this time I knew there was no one alive aboard her.

I went up the ladder more adeptly than I had the day before and threw myself over the rail with somewhat more grace. Now I saw more clearly the devastation the storm had wrought upon the ship because I was not looking through it for human beings. All the neat arrangements of the vessel were thrown down in ruin as if to mock human enterprise, and my scavenging felt like that of a bird taking twigs to build a tiny nest from the limbs of a great fallen tree.

In the cabin of the doctor, who was wont to wander about looking at botanical specimens, I found a large woven hat with a wide brim, just the sort of hat I needed. I strapped it around my neck so it dangled down my back by its strings. Back in the cook's galley, I found rum and in the captain's cabin I found brandy. In the various niches and alcoves that honeycombed the ship I found some great lengths of canvas, a number of leather bags, more useful tools such as a saw and an adze and a whetstone, which, though quite heavy, I determined to wrestle back to the beach. Try as I might, though, I could find no wheel or anything wheel-like enough to serve me. The cannon rested on carriages atop small wheels, but the cannon being so immensely heavy, I could not remove the wheels no matter what method I tried. I could not exert enough leverage to move a cannon. I hoped this would not be a metaphor for all my efforts.

It occurred to me that since the ship had visited one port after we had come aboard and had taken on cargo there, it would be sensible to inspect the cargo and find out what it was. So, hammer in hand, I went into the hold and there found a number of large barrels still in an orderly array, so heavy that they had not been dislodged by the ship's foundering. I set myself to work with the hammer and soon had one opened. It was entirely filled with very small, hard black berries of a type I had never seen before. I bit into one and found it very bitter. It struck me that this must be a coffee berry, the source of the brew that kept the London men up talking all night, and I decided to take some of them with me. Perhaps I could make a drink of coffee, but then who would I talk to?

As I was filling one of the bags with a few handfuls of these berries I heard a series of faint cries behind me and whirled around in great surprise to see sitting on a ledge near the hatch a bedraggled grey kitten. The poor kitten must have taken to its perch to escape the water, but could not now get down, and being so weak had not been able to make me hear it before. I climbed the ladder and reached over to get it. It was sorely frightened but could struggle little. On deck I searched for some water to give the kitten and found what I took to be the run-off of the morning's dew on a piece of torn sail. As soon as I set the little creature down it began eagerly lapping. I also gave it some cracker to which it eagerly applied itself as well. I then put it in a small bag to take it back to the shore, wondering how Roger would welcome it.

When I had gathered as much as my raft could carry and I could propel towards the beach, I went back down the ladder, the kitten mewing lightly at my breast. My energy had been flagging, but now I felt myself strangely invigorated and energetic and wondered if the berry I had been sucking had anything to do with it. I set the kitten in a box on top the raft and lowered myself into the water to paddle it back to the beach. Roger had apparently waited there for me and started to cavort about in welcome as I waded into the shore, the kitten again inside my shirt against my breast.

"Oh Roger," I said, "we've got another member of our exile band, and I want you to be very nice to her." I sat down on the dry sand and pulled back my shirt to reveal the kitten's soft grey head. This intensely interested the puppy, who sniffed all about her, which the kitten tolerated a bit fearsomely. Soon we all went up to my little camp where I built a tiny enclosure of branches so that the kitten would be confined for time enough to grow used to Roger and me and not run away into the interior.

For the next week I made two trips a day to the ship, hauling away from her good amounts of timber and metal work and all the tools I could find, even if I didn't know what they were for. I also brought off those books and papers I found in the Captain's and the other officer's cabins though most had already been ruined by the water. Even those that remained were much waterlogged, but I laid them out to dry around my camp, choosing shady spots so that the paper would not dry so quickly that it would crumble. The constant breeze made a good drying oven, and each day for many weeks I went round and turned a page in each volume and eventually dried out my library. I had two Bibles, Bunyan's *Pilgrim's Progress*, *Piers Plowman*, and book on tropical vegetation. I was struck with the irony that with one exception they were religious volumes, when I myself was so uninterested in religion. Nonetheless, they formed an important part of my new life for they were my only source of human language, and for this purpose they were splendid companions.

I also brought off all the muskets and the powder and shot needed to shoot them. I had shot muskets a few times with my brothers, who gave me some rudimentary lessons, a fact of which my father remained ignorant for had he known he would have forbid it. I knew how to load and fire the weapon, but at what I would fire it I had no idea as I had yet to see any game, nor had it occurred to me that I might need to protect myself from other humans. At this time, so eagerly did I wish to see some that they appeared in my imagination only as friendly saviors. I had explored only my tiny spot, however, and resolved to get a better sense of this place as soon as I could. It seemed negligent though not to take as great advantage as I could of the treasure chest represented by the ship, so my exploration would have to wait.

The kitten needed a name and as I cast about for one, I remembered an acquaintance of Lady Evelyn who had salt and pepper grey hair and blue eyes quite like the kitten's. Her name was Miss Sophia Higgins and so, as an amusement I named the kitten Miss Higgins. Roger got on well with Miss Higgins and sometimes assisted her in her catly play. The awkwardness and charm of these young animals gave me much enjoyment, and I could have borne my solitude and frustration much less well without them. As it was, I descended into melancholy at least once a day, often as I nursed my array of wounds, crying as if I had become the human counterpart of the daily bout of tropical rain.

One evening several weeks after my arrival, the rain came down much more heavily than usual, and gusts of wind tore noisily among the tops of the palms. Roger and Miss Higgins were uneasy and so was I, as it seemed a large storm would hit us. I gathered the goats into our little alcove and hung a piece of canvas from the top of my overhang to protect us from the blowing sheets of water. At the last minute I remembered the books lying outside and ran to gather them before they were further soaked. I had already stowed and covered most of the trove from the ship.

We seemed safe enough; so, snuggled all in a heap, we listened to the storm hiss and smash about us. How it brought back to me the events that had landed me here in so strange a situation, and for the thousandth time I wondered if it were possible Leora had survived. At last I heard the kitten purring, was comforted and fell asleep.

The next morning I flung back the canvas cover to discover the world made shiny and peaceful again, though the seascape that formed my view had radically changed—the ship was gone, only a few spars and bits of wreckage floating where she had once been. I reasoned that the storm's violence had dislodged her remains from the rocks and set her carcass once more adrift, perhaps to fall to the bottom of the sea. After returning the goats to their enclosure, I made one more trip to gather the lumber that remained, and thus werc my days as a ship's forager brought to a natural end.

That very afternoon I began to explore my locale. I considered two strategies: going inland towards higher ground to see what was there and also to put myself in position to better view the extent of my new country or following the coastline as far as I could and back. Lunching on my steady diet of yellow fruit and ship's bread, I decided on the former course.

I had taken a knapsack from the ship, into which I put more yellow fruit, my hammer, a knife, the Captain's spyglass and a few of the berries from the ship's cargo. Sucking upon them had become a habit because they seemed to invigorate me. I then considered my feet. I had been mostly barefoot on the beach, wearing my own boots for working on the ship. As a result of frequent dunkings and hard wear, they were quite worn, so I retrieved the soft leather boots I'd found in the officer's trunk and tried them on. They were much too big, but I found that a bit of moss stuffed into their toes made them fit quite decently, especially with the addition of a pair of the gentlemen's stockings, and my blisters were much comforted by the moss. I tied on my hat and cooped up the kitten in her enclosure, not wanting her to follow me, but Roger I invited along. He had quickly gained strength over these weeks, and he bounded along in front of me, zigzagging across my straighter path in a kind of ecstasy of movement. Perhaps he was glad I was not going onto the sea where he could not go with me.

I took a path up past the waterfall and the little pond I had found on my first day, but resisted the impulse to stop and bathe. I was still in profound enough anxiety about my situation not to afford myself much leisure, but it did occur to me that at some future point I might do so. This was a milestone of sorts because it meant I had resigned and accustomed myself to the possibility that I would be here for some time, that I would not merely stop at this place, but would inhabit it.

And what sort of place was it? In general, as I have described, it was tropical, but this generality contained a multitude of specifics I had not yet attended to. Besides the coconut palms and the yellow fruit trees, there were numerous lower lying trees and shrubs, some with leaves like enormous aprons. There were grasses of green and purple hues amidst the rocky outcroppings and small culverts humming with insects both flying and creeping. There was a natural path formed by the run-off of the daily rain that was quite muddy in the lowest places, and many times I had to haul myself up and over tree roots or even whole trees that had fallen across the path.

As I struggled forward I was beset by various insects who would have feasted on me if I had not covered myself more closely than the warm weather required. While I was generally rising upward as I walked, there were also moist hollows and dales punctuating my ascent. I heard skittering and scuffling on the ground and in the trees that told of animal and bird life, and, indeed, I caught a glimpse of a large red, yellow and green parrot, a very colorful and miraculous creature. Perhaps I could lure it into acquaintance and teach it to speak, as I had heard sailors say they had many times done.

After three-quarters of an hour I reached a clearing where I saw vines laden with bunches of opalescent purple fruit that I took to be grapes, so I ventured to try them and found them sweet indeed. I celebrated finding another food source and determined to load my knapsack with these grapes when I descended. Beyond the clearing the vegetation thinned a good deal and at last I found myself on a small, lightly forested plateau, much dryer than the lower regions. A promontory rose above it on which there was no obscuring vegetation and that offered a fine vantage point for inspecting a great distance, so I eagerly scrambled up it with Roger at my heels.

I pulled myself up to the very highest point, rose and looked around me. What a revelation! I slowly turned completely around and saw through the crystalline atmosphere a vast stretch of land bordered everywhere by water. I was indeed on an island. I dropped down atop my rock to think. It was a large island for one person (as far as I knew I was the only person there) and would require some days to explore it, but there was no chance of walking down the beach eventually to find civilization. I could leave only by the sea, and I had no way to do that. I found this a grim realization as I had harbored a hope that I was on the mainland. Now this hope was gone.

I heard in my mind the voice of my eldest brother Tom, always an optimist. "Just think how lucky you are, Roberta! You've been shipwrecked on this beautiful island with food and drink and safe lodging. You could have been marooned in the Arctic where you would have died in hours. Thank God for your good fortune." I did smile then, not in gratitude to God, but to the memory of this familiar voice. Of my brothers I loved best Tom, the eldest, and Richard, the youngest. Tom was always kind and cheerful. George and William were rougher and given to practical jokes. Arthur modeled himself on them rather than Tom. Richard was a very sweet little boy, and I played with him often until the older boys' teasing drew him away from me. Despite Tom's kind character, however, I could not accept the theology implicit in the speech I had invented for him, for if I had God to thank for my good fortune, who was I to blame for the bad? This seemed to me one of the troubles with God, but I resolved not to go into my theological musings at this time. Nor did I want to think long on my brothers as their loss pained me greatly, especially that of Richard. I was on an island in every way, and I could only make the best of it.

I brought out the spyglass and took a closer look at the coastline. I resolved to pay better attention to the direction from which the daily rains came, so that I could be sure to make my permanent station on the leeward side.

I wended my way back over the same path on which I had come, stopping only to stuff my sack with grapes. At the waterfall, I took off my clothes and slipped into the water, thinking that next time I would bring the soap I'd found in Leora's trunk, especially since my hair was by now quite awfully dirty and tangled. What a fright I was—a dirty, sunburned, wild-haired woman dressed in tattered men's clothes!

As I regained my little campsite I scooped Miss Higgins from her enclosure and reassured her of our return. As I petted her I reflected that I had not looked at the passing surroundings with enough view to a more permanent habitation and resolved to do that the next day. I also resolved to try my hand at fishing as I had a continuous hunger that the fruit was not satisfying and I was, I thought, losing flesh. I would need to maintain my strength if I were to survive. Of course, I could not think of slaughtering one of the goats until they had produced some offspring. How I longed for some English roast beef!

Chapter Four—I Become a Householder
and Am Laid Low

The next day as I went for water, sucking on another of the coffee berries upon whose invigorating effects I'd begun to rely, I looked much more carefully around me with a view to establishing my homestead. The previous evening I'd determined that indeed I was already on the leeward side of the island, so it would not be necessary to go round the other side to find greater protection, though I resolved to go there later to explore it. My current alcove was quite comfortable, but not big enough, especially in light of the need to store many of the goods I'd brought off the ship.

I strayed off my regular path to the waterfall several times to examine promising overhangs that might conceal a useful cave. Nothing suitable presented itself, and I had turned to regain my beachside closet when I noticed some twenty yards to the left of the falls an opening in the vegetation which seemed to issue an invitation, so I hiked over to it and passed through to find a clearing of sorts on the left of which was a shadowed copse against a large hillock. I pushed my way into the copse and found at its back rocky walls enclosing a space some twenty feet by twenty feet at its mouth and narrowing as it went further into the earth.

I went warily into this cave and found it entirely dry, and, as far as I could tell, uninhabited by any animals, though I did see traces of scat that told me some creature had found refuge here.   Having no light, I could not explore further back into the cave, so I exited, worked my way back through the copse and climbed up on top of the hill into which the cave burrowed.   I was much amazed and pleased that the trees were so arranged that from this perch I could see the whole beach. Right then I decided that this would be my new camp. I could remove many of the trees forming the copse so as to afford more light to the front of the cave, though it also occurred to me that the trees offered some protection. Water was quite near and the cave's mouth faced away from the direction from which the rain blew. Roger had thoroughly sniffed the locale and had lain down contentedly in a spot of sun that penetrated to the cave. I took this as a sign that he felt as at home here as I did, and so I resolved then and there to move our ménage to this spot. I found myself savoring as ironic that I was so pleased to have found a dusty cave to live in, for all the world as if it were a pretty cottage in Cornwall.

I was eager to move house. Though this would entail a lot of work, I looked forward to it as most women do to creating a home, and since I had never had even a small room to call my own, I can perhaps be forgiven for finding a cave so delightful. I tripped back to what I immediately began to call my "old" camp in a happy frame of mind and began to plan my move. How I wished I had found some usable wheels! I thought that I might at some time try to make some, but my move could not wait for that.

I went back up to the site with my hatchet and plied it in among the copse, at last hacking an angled path towards the cave's mouth to maintain some of its secrecy. I cleared out the brush just in front and also chopped out some of the trees to expose the cave front to more light, though I left the trees that overhung from above and even imagined I might build out further with palm fronds to give myself more protection from the rain.

I made a circle of rocks near the mouth to serve as my fireplace, hoping that the pattern of the breezes would not bring the smoke back into the cave. My first fire would tell me. I saved out some straight branches to use in making a litter with which to aid my transport and piled the rest of the foliage and bracken I had chopped into a heap to use later to feed my fire.

It grew dark before I finished and returned to the old camp, very weary in my arms as I had never plied an axe for so long. I had also accumulated a further panoply of scratches and cuts on my arms and legs, which had not yet healed from my exertions upon the ship. I should dress more protectively for this building enterprise, I thought, as the lighter garb necessitated by swimming or protection from the sun no longer suited. As I lay down to sleep, profoundly weary, the kitten and puppy at my side, I realized that I had entered a new phase of my life on the island. I was to be a householder here.

Next day I carried out my plan to further and reinforce the overhang of my cave. I gathered great armloads of palm fronds from beneath the beach's trees and dragged them up onto the hillock. There I determined that my design was insufficiently ambitious to give me the protection I wanted, so I conceived a simple frame for the front of the cave and dragged forth some of the lumber I had foraged from the ship with which to construct it. It was a structure consisting of three sides of a rectangle with small braces forming triangles at the corners for strength, a three-sided square arch. I made three of these using the saw and the hammer. I dug holes in which to sink the ends of these frames so that they would stand upright until I could bind them into a free standing structure by nailing cross pieces on them, which, having no ladder, I had at first to do by leaning down from the overhang, a precarious position indeed, and I succeeded in straining my back so that I had to walk gingerly for some days, though I kept working. When my frame was built I overlaid it with palm fronds and thus had a good roof for the mouth of my dwelling. As I labored I thought of how my brothers would respond to my building efforts. There would be much ridicule, but later, in private, one or the other of them would come to say "Not a bad job, Roberta."

I knew my building had a frenzy to it. I wanted to keep busy so as not to fasten my mind on the depth of my plight. Nonetheless, from time to time, when I was forced to rest, I sensed how near despair's dark void lay, how easy it would be simply to lie down and await my fate—to rest, to die. It was Roger who fetched me from these moods by always acting as though everything was normal. So I would turn my mind again to practical matters, and that was my salvation.

For the floor of my dwelling I considered if I should bring in sand or gravel or even flat stones, but finally decided that as the dirt was well-compacted it would serve well enough for now and that later I might refine it as materials to do so presented themselves.

Several natural ledges were available as shelves within the cave, but over the next few days I also constructed some wooden shelving and a primitive bedstead whose mattress would be the ticking I had found in Leora's trunk, filled and refreshed with grass from time to time, though later, as I will in time relate, my bedding improved due to a providential find.

In rest periods during my building I tried my hand at fishing. With line and hooks drawn from the ship I sat on the rocks of the spit and fished, but as I had no good bait, the fish being uninterested in grapes, I had no luck. I did, however, see upon the beach the telltale breathing holes of clams and dug down to find them. I celebrated this as a major event and boiled them up for a wondrously satisfying meal. That I had noticed the evidence of the clams' existence so long after my arrival made me reflect again on the selectivity of perception. It seemed that as I calmed down and felt less shocked and desperate I could see more. If this were true, I wondered what more I might notice in the future which I had not the eyes to see now.

As I was abuilding Roger was transformed from a puppy into a young dog. He made countless field trips around the site, chasing through the brush and bounding back and forth along the beach amidst the waves. On one of these occasions he returned to the camp and greeted me with a strange kind of bark. When I turned around he flung at my feet the body of a mouse. "Oh Roger! You're a full-fledged hunter! What a good dog!" I praised him and rubbed his head, and he accepted my homage very happily. Thereafter, Roger assumed his own provisioning with only a bit of supplementing from me, and he grew into a beautiful russet spaniel.

At last my new home was ready and I began hiking back and forth to carry my goods to it, acting as my own ox, dragging my litter to and fro, though I left a good deal of the timber and metal I'd brought off the ship in my original shelter as it was a good storage space. When all had been neatly installed and my bed prepared, I took the length of red and yellow damask from Leora's trunk and draped it from a rock outcropping at the top of the wall over my bed. It gave a gay and sumptuous look to my décor, and made me consider how I might further furnish my cave apartment. I felt a twinge of guilt about expropriating to adorn a cave what had been meant to grace a parlor, but this twinge passed quickly. As yet all I had were a bed and some shelves. I had retrieved several boxes from the ship, but these were too small to serve as a proper table and so I cast about for the materials to construct a table and a chair. For the nonce, I used my bed as my sofa and spent much time sitting on the rocks I had drug to make a circle round my fireplace.

I began to experiment with cooking as well. I had by now learned how to penetrate a coconut shell with my awl so that its sweet milk was not lost in its opening, and I used this milk to stew my clams, adding some of the coconut meat as well. I tried adding the yellow fruit to this stew, but did not like the gooey consistency that resulted. In hopes of adding to my diet, each day I inspected the doe goat to see if she were in season. I thought she had been, and sometime later she began to wax large in her belly, so I looked forward to goat milk and perhaps cheeses as well in a short time. I chuckled to think that I could use the captain's stockings to strain my curds. I felt some unquiet about the doe's delivery, but I had seen many animal births on the farm and trusted I would remember what to do.

I also was in season, as it were, as my monthly bleeding came and went in its usual way. I had not the customary supply of rags, so I had to use the least desirable of the shirts I'd brought off the ship, which I rinsed and dried and used again and again just as we do in England, though I made no effort to hide them as is the women's custom there.

I had fetched a lantern off the ship, but as I soon ran out of oil, it became a useless ornament. I wondered much about how I might provide myself with light in the evening, besides staying very close to the fire, which was often excessively warm. For now my life followed the sun: I arose when it did and lay down when it set. Before sleep each night I mingled thoughts of the day's activities with memories of home. I discovered that these memories could either fill me with a hopeless nostalgia or be a fire to warm me. I tried to will myself towards the latter with varying success.

One morning on my way back from collecting water at the spring I felt quite dizzy and had to sit down by the side of the path that my frequent comings and goings had created between my cave and the spring. I rested for sometime with my whirling head between my legs, but at last made my way back, feeling worse with each passing moment. As this sickness overcame me, I compounded its dizzying effects by the sudden terror of being alone with no one to look after me. Back at my camp, my hands shaking, I took out the packet of medicines that I had found in Leora's trunk and put to boil in water several lengths of willow bark, so I could reduce my fever.

I began to sweat heavily and yet also felt quite chilled, so I set the pot of brew beside my bed and wrapped myself in the coverlet. Still I shivered, so I pulled the Captain's greatcoat over me as well. There I lay, alternately burning up or freezing, sipping the willow brew whenever I gained enough consciousness to do so.

Strange images and shards of conversation rotated through my mind, and I conducted several heated conversations with various of my brothers on subjects that seemed of urgent importance, but which I could remember little of later. It occurred to me several times that I could easily die, but my fever did not allow me to dwell much on this possibility as it kept me busy churning broken but very vivid scenarios through my mind. One of these involved a bird pecking at my intestines, looking up now and again to say, "Oh yes, you're an odd one, all right!"

I could hear Roger's whine now and again as he inquired of my state in his own way. I also heard my mother repeating over and over as she looked down on me, "Don't, Roberta, don't!" I didn't know what it was she was telling me not to do, but the aura of disapproval and warning was very great and but an exaggeration of the attitude with which she usually regarded me. I loved my mother very much and her attitude towards me was kind, though she seemed often to treat me less as an individual and more as a member of a class which she pitied—that class being women, the class to which she herself belonged. That she would hold such a sentiment was, I think, based on the pain and labor of bearing twelve children, only six of whom lived. She herself died of the last one. No doubt it was her example, combined with my experience of five brothers that determined me to go into service and not to accept whatever marriage the meager dowry my father could offer might attract. My parents' own marriage offered no enticement into that state as they were only occasionally affectionate. Though he owned his own plot, my father was a poor farmer who worked very hard to feed us all and dropped into his chair each evening with little to say. He was never brutal with us, nor was he warm except very rarely if angered. He died shortly after my mother, so perhaps his love for her was greater than I could see.

Lest it seem that I am cold and unfeeling, I must say that I also loved my brothers very much. Their lusty energy and good humor, so in contrast to my father's taciturnity, were most endearing. But especially the older ones were also incessantly demanding and took for granted that my job was to wait on them. They would fiercely defend me if someone from outside the family in any way affronted me, but within the family I was their drudge, no matter how much I protested this role.

The cooking and cleaning and washing and sewing and mending never ended, especially after my mother died. I was attracted several times to men outside my family, and they were very persuasive in kissing and caressing me, telling me my hair was like gold and my eyes like emeralds, but I had always my mother's example before me, and I never yielded to their desire, or to my own. In short, I was a virgin old maid. My brothers were much angered when I went into service with Lady

Evelyn, I suppose because they had assumed I would always be their beloved slave, even after three of them had married and brought their wives onto our farm. These women not only wanted me to attend to them, but were also jealous, wanting to run the household themselves. Only Richard was truly grieved to lose my company and I to lose his.

Going into service actually relieved me of a good bit of toil. I had been noticed by Lady Evelyn's steward when he had come to our cottage to inspect our linen weaving, perhaps to buy some for the estate. He looked about very superciliously, then said, "A tidy house. Who keeps it? I had understood there was no wife here." "I keep the house, sir," I said. He looked me up and own. "You might well do as a domestic for Lady Evelyn Hordsley." He gave my brother Tom two sorely needed pounds and bid me pack my things. As I did so, Richard ran to me. "Oh Roberta, how shall I get on without you?" he cried. "You shall be fine, and you may visit me at the hall." At this prospect his sobs abated, but I often remembered his affection for me as the warmest part of life at home. Tom stood gaping as I rode away in the stewards's trap, while Richard ran after us for a good distance.

I had originally gone to Lady Evelyn's manor thinking that I was fit only to be a scullery maid, and this is where I began, but within a year, after frequent conversations and noticing my "skill and efficiency," as she said, Lady Evelyn brought me upstairs as her maid and, eventually, I acted as her secretary, especially after the steward who had brought me to the manor left, unable to tolerate Lady Evelyn's eccentricities.

I had been to a dame's school for only a few years, but I had to attend Leora's lessons with her and was much more interested in them than she was. Her tutor, a distant relation of Lady Evelyn's, was a learned man in his fifties whose deformities, a clubfoot and a stammer, had debarred him from the career his intelligence might have procured him. He encouraged me as a conversational companion and began to address his teaching to me, though from time to time he seemed to pull himself back from our communion when he remembered my role as maid and feared Lady Evelyn would rebuke him. Despite his hot and cold treatment of me, I learned a great deal from him about many things, especially history and geography. He also taught me simple mathematics so I was soon attending to the estate's accounts, which Lady Evelyn found fatiguing.

I slept upstairs in a room with two other girls and had one small chest as my private domain. I was paid three pounds a year except for the first year as my wages had been paid in advance to Tom. Each Christmas I was furnished with a sturdy blue fabric suitable for a dress and a cape. I was also welcome to whatever wool was produced on the estate and then spun by the cottagers, and so I knitted myself several stout shawls and scarves. I also received six yards of linen with which to make myself aprons, caps, nightdresses and shifts. My boots came once every two years from the village cobbler.

I had a good deal of time to reflect on my earlier life, for when my illness at last receded, I was too weak to move for many days. I lay in my bed, grateful for the warm presence of Roger and Miss Higgins. Through the hours of my rest, I also frequented the byways of my memory, visiting the events of my life on the farm and then on the manor, and as the sickness in my body cleared off, my mind grew clearer as well, so that I found myself making judgments and drawing conclusions in a way that I had never done, probably because my life was one of constant work and I had never had the time to do so.

I turned over in my mind one incident that I came to see as a defining one in the formation of my character. I had been with Lady Evelyn for two years and was 16 when her husband's nephew, a handsome young man of 20, paid a visit. He had failed to apply himself at university and had been sent down to his aunt and uncle to consider of his ways. It was punishment by boredom. He paid assiduous court to Lady Evelyn, but mocked her behind her back in order also to court the servants. Had he not been very kind to Leora who was ten at the time and regarded him as a god, I would have disliked him entirely.

To amuse himself he plied his charm not only upon Lady Evelyn, but on all the women of the house, assessing each one to decide upon his approach to her. To me he was very polite and assumed a complicit attitude that seemed to say, "We've found ourselves in this provincial situation, and though we are larger than it is, we will be patient and allow it to entertain us in its paltry way." I cannot say that I was wholly immune to the compliment implicit in his projection of me, a country maid, and he, a scion of a noble house, as superior mates, but I was mostly very suspicious of him and tried to avoid him.

One day I was descending the stairs to the garden when he suddenly appeared going up them. Later I realized that he had lain in wait for me. "Ah, Mistress Roberta," he said, blocking my path, "I have so longed to see you without others about us," at which he gave me a look in which his eyes shone with a sincerity whose practiced character fertilized my own cynicism. "Excuse me, sir, I must be about my work," I said and tried to go past him, at which he moved forward and pinned me against the wall with his whole body. "How warm and lovely you are. Your hair is a miracle," he said into my ear as if to caress it and fingering a curl that peeped from beneath my white linen cap. "I simply cannot resist you and I am so starved here," he went on. "Then it would be well for you to go to the kitchen and find some bread," I said in as even a tone as I could muster. Then his hand went to my breast; he pinched my nipple and pressed his mouth to mine, at which I brought my knee up sharply between his legs. As he screamed and fell backward, Lady Evelyn appeared at the top of the stairs. "Roberta!" she said very sharply, as her nephew knelt in pain on the stairs. "I had not thought you were this kind of girl," she said. "I'm very disappointed in you. Go to your chamber immediately." As I turned to go I saw her lifting her nephew to his feet, cooing her concern and apologizing to him for my barbarous behavior.

I marched upstairs burning with the injustice of my being blamed and his being comforted. I dragged forth my little bag and angrily stuffed into it my few belongings, certain that I would soon be summoned to a sacking. Yet no such summons came, and later that afternoon I saw the young man mount the coach with his own luggage in tow.

In the evening Lady Evelyn sent for me. She was seated before her looking glass and glanced up at me. "Please brush my hair, my dear," she said. I lifted off her wig, unwound her plaits and began to run the brush through her thin hair. "Ah, that's nice," she said. I was very puzzled that she said nothing about the incident with her nephew, so I broached it myself. "Lady Evelyn, I must tell you that I did not invite your nephew's attentions to me. I inflicted injury on him only to defend myself." "Yes, of course," she said, as if there had been no question about this at all, and as if she had not berated me before him. "Then why were you so angry with me?" I blurted, though this kind of questioning of one's superiors invited more censure. "You had to be blamed, Roberta, because the young's man's station and relation to our family demanded his innocence." "But what of justice, milady?" She made a flicking gesture with her hand, but said no more. She certainly did not apologize to me; in fact, she acted as if I had had a lesson that I needed. I went away in a welter of feelings and thoughts, one of which was that Lady Evelyn's nephew had not been the only one to see that I was not entirely at one with my station.

As I lay in my sick bed, I felt how this incident had further pushed me into solitude. I realized that though I had always been surrounded by people, I had been lonely. The other girls in service to Lady Evelyn came and went very quickly and were often very unserious creatures, and I made no true friend but Mr. Chalcote. Perhaps the only place I could have solitude, privacy and justice was in my own mind, which necessitated not sharing it with others. I had made myself self-sufficient and mentally isolated so as to have an inner refuge.

Little by little, in another week I had regained my health, though I was quite depleted and had to go slowly for a while. However, the introspection I discovered during my recuperation stayed with me. Now that I was on an island, in fact as solitary as could be, I found myself enjoying the freedom to work according to my own needs and desires and that my privacy was absolute and limitless. My moods of despair became fewer. While this was a great relief and helped me reconstitute myself in a different way, it also starkly externalized my loneliness, which began to pain me here as it never had before, for now I recognized a possibility that before I had not, that the desirable opposite of solitude and loneliness could be intimacy, which seemed to me a continent more foreign and unexplored than the great one off which I presumed my island lay.

Chapter 5--I Plow and Am Plowed

I don't mean to say that I became a great thinker, for in fact I worked hard most of the time and my mind was taken up in the tasks. I would not have had to work so hard if I had been content to eat only the fruits the island provided, but my life had always been one of work and I derived great satisfaction from it. This was especially true now that I was directing my own work and had no one telling me what to do. I even thought that I might add my bit to this part of the world through some cultivation. It was wondrously lovely already, but I might make its beauty even more various.

Once my basic shelter was built, I examined the seeds that I'd found in Leora's trunk. Mr. Chalcote had been very fond of both Leora and me, and in giving these seeds he had offered us what was most valuable to him. When I first found them, I had not looked very closely to see what sort of seeds were included, but now that I could give effort to planting them I looked them over with an eager eye. There were carrots, lettuce, turnips and what I took to be two kinds of beans, string and white. Having been so long without them, my mouth watered just thinking about this humble fare, and though I was sorely pressed to eat the beans there and then, I held off. There were also seeds for flowers-- pinks, marigolds, daisies and even four bulbs, one of daffodil, one of iris and one of tulip, and, I saw with delight, three of onion. There was also a packet of flax seeds. All these plants were suitable for cultivation in the often rainy climate of Britain, but I had no idea if they would thrive or even grow at all in this tropical one, given the daily torrents that buffeted it, but I determined to try and gave thought to how I might prepare the soil in such a way as to improve their chances.

For my garden I chose a level spot some fifty yards from my cave that offered trees as protection on two sides, but which remained sunny throughout the day. The ship's spade was my tilling implement and I plied it mightily for many hours, often resorting to the hatchet and the axe to break through roots. I removed many rocks, attempting to pile them around my plot so as to make a primitive stile. This was very hard, hot work, and both Roger and Miss Higgins lounged in the shade regarding me with what I took to be curious wonder.

The work went very slowly, but I had the time to invest in it, and went frequently to drench myself in the cool waters of the falls and wash away the grime that encrusted me as I sweated into the dust aroused by my digging. I truly wished I had some sort of oil to rub into my hands, which were very red and blistered but at last got calloused into good workman's hands

At night I experienced the heavy relaxation that rewards physical labor, and I began to read my little library, the red-bound *Piers Ploughman* and the green-bound *Pilgrim's Progress*. It struck me now very forcefully that a work on how to achieve salvation made its chief character a plowman and cast Christ as a plowman working in the field of the soul. It was a fetching idea, though the rest of Piers dwelt far too much on the author's distrust of friars and his endless metaphoric conceits. The worst was how very bad both Bunyan and Langland believed human beings to be; whereas, I thought them more foolish than evil. On the whole, since I cared little about the idea of salvation, I felt like someone making a trip to France who'd been provided only with books about India. And yet these books contained beautiful language and became my beloved companions, like relatives with whom one always contends.

At last I had cleared my plot of about 50 square feet and broken up the ground to the depth of a foot. I recalled that my brothers left parts of their fields to lie fallow and used manure upon them, and Mr. Chalcote made other applications as well, such as ashes collected from the house grates. I wondered how I might strengthen the soil and resolved right then to save the ashes from my fire as fertilizer. Mr. Chalcote also told me how the Irish hauled seaweed up to their fields, and I thought I might do that too. I figured some sand would be useful and wondered how I might recoup the goats' excrement and my own as well. I found myself chuckling at this notion because I imagined that Lady Evelyn would have received it as the epitome of unladylike thinking. I was, however, no longer in the realm of ladies, and in fact, had only ever been tangential to their world, though compelled to acknowledge its often capricious dictates, just as I never felt part of the endless religious goings on but had had to acknowledge their dictates as well.

In the first few days on the island I had relieved myself indiscriminately, but soon I had dug a series of latrines so I might patronize them in sequence and thereby reduce the odor accompanying them. I had also established a midden for my food scraps and clam shells. With some addition of leaves and turning, I could feed my garden upon this, just as we did at home. All these plans were aimed at the future, and I sometimes felt that planning for my future here militated against my rescue, but this superstition yielded to my pleasure in making the garden and what is a garden after all if not a faith in the future? Now, however, I could do nothing for the soil but add some sand, which I dragged up from the beach in tow sacks and spread around as best I could without a rake. I began to wonder how I might make a rake, as it would be a most useful tool.

At last my field was ready and so I planted my flowers and vegetables in neat rows that I marked with sticks. I planted the marigolds at intervals around the plot, hoping thereby to repel some animal and insect invaders in the way I had seen Mr. Chalcote do. If I had had more than three onion bulbs, I would have planted them around the perimcter as well. I hoped very much that the onions would thrive so that I might use their protection on what I hoped would be future crops. I was very concerned that the birds, mice and rabbits would makc quick work of my seeds and their progeny, so I set up a rough scarecrow with a shirt on the cross piece and attached to it red and blue ribbons that I took off of Leora's gowns. I hoped that the fluttering of these in the breeze might scare off predators. At least they gave an gay aspect to the plot.

As for watering the seeds, I trusted that the daily rains would perform this task and, I hoped, do so without washing the seeds away, the prospect of which had made me plant them a bit deeper than I would have in England.

For the next several weeks, I stayed close to the field to guard it and used my time there to build up my stone wall. Had I invested a great deal of effort into gathering stones I could eventually have built a low wall entirely of stone, but the prospect of such arduous labor led me to consider alternatives that later I tried. At the time I didn't know from what exactly I was protecting my garden, of course. I wondered if the island's plentiful grasses, reeds and palm fronds might be used to construct wicker bulwarks that could be braced between piles of stone.

So I gathered a stock of reeds and spear-like leaves from around the waterfall pond and, whilst guarding the field, set about experimenting.

I had spun and woven frequently at home on the farm, though never with the stiff materials I was now using. I first laid out a horizontal grid the length of the average reed, about four feet long with five inches between each green spear. Then I interwove a more pliable spear between them, starting in the middle. This was very awkward as the spears refused to stay put, so the result was all askew and quite unsatisfactory until I hit upon the device of dousing the spears with water to keep them pliable as I worked. This also proved useful in that when the reeds dried they molded to each other. I also worked from the middle out which proved more efficient than the top to bottom pattern I'd grown up with. I made many of these mats and when they were dried I wove in grasses to fill the gaps between the spears. At last I had a series of straw panels to place between my stone steles. As I worked I wished that I had paid more attention to Mrs. Laughton, who wove most baskets in our neighborhood, but she was so given to inveighing against sins and giving previews of hell that I avoided her company.

As I worked on the panels, the seeds began to sprout. How I rejoiced to see the tiny green shoots break through the ground, some bearing the seed coat itself as a kind of hat! The beans came first; then the lettuce and carrots and flowers made velvety green lines on the earth.

On the third day after the first sprouting, I was dismayed to see that many of the seedlings looked wilted and borne down, and I realized they would need to be shielded if they were to survive the tropical sun. I brought out from my cave the great length of yellow, blue and white sprigged cotton meant to be a dress for Leora and stretched it over crude frames I made from stout saplings buried in the earth and shored up with rocks. When I was finished the field sported the gay appearance of a bazaar, and my seedlings stood up under the shade of their awnings. Now, however, they were less accessible to the rain, so I dug a series of trenches among the rows hoping to route the afternoon showers through them.

Full of optimism about my farming efforts, one morning I went to the field with a plan to make poles for the beans to climb upon, but even from far off something struck me as askew, so I quickened my pace. I arrived to find a devastating scene--the lovely order of my young garden was now a muddy chaos, a shambles, the awnings torn down, trampled and strewn about, the ground much trodden, and many of the sprouts ground miserably into the earth. The churned soil showed marks that looked to be the hoof prints of a pig, and I concluded that there must be wild boar upon the island. It or they had made quick work of my wicker panels and though there was nothing as yet for them to eat in my garden, they had certainly established their presence as if to put me on notice that altering their natural order would not be an easy task. "Damnation!" I shouted, uttering the first curse of my life and stomping my foot.

I threw my spade as far as I could and then cast myself down on the ground much angered, chagrined and saddened. I felt very small, and my aloneness bore down on me like a stone. I supposed this is the usual life of an agriculturalist; I tasted the bitterness that is the other side of the joy I felt to see the seedlings. Though my spirit was cast down, I set about reckoning up the damage and wearily salvaging what I could, setting up my awnings again and redredging my ditches. The afternoon rain came as I was so engaged, but I kept on working, the water running down my face and arms, runneling trails on my dusty skin and making my braid a heavy tube down my back. When I had done what I could, I reckoned about half my crop had been lost.

In the cool calm after the rain I sat forlornly by the field in my sodden clothes, wondering how to prevent a similar incursion. I determined that I must reinforce the garden's enclosure and that I would need to sleep by the field to run off intruders if I wanted to see any fruits from my work. I thought of using the muskets and the pistol to scare off or even kill invaders and was filled with distaste at this prospect, but I also remembered the many days of work I had put into making the field and how good it would be to have more foodstuffs, and decided I would do whatever was needed to preserve my garden. I felt discouragement pulling at my spirit, not only because of my loss, but also because of the disquiet created in me by the presence of large dangerous animals as malevolent companions on the island.

I set about making another fire circle and gathering wood to stoke it and spent that night and many following on a rough pallet beside it. I fetched two muskets and the pistol from Lt. Swarthmore's trunk, as well as the powder and shot to load them, and practiced shooting several times. I set up a target about 15 yards away, and though I wasn't scrupulous as to my aim, I did manage to hit the target once, making an infernal din in the process.

At home hunting had fallen to my brothers for whom it was great sport, especially when they poached upon the lands of the local squires, which they did to thumb their noses at these worthies as much as to get meat. I was allowed to tag along from time to time to act as witness to their heroism and on rare occasions allowed to shoot, my own ineptitude acting as a comparative backdrop for their skill. Now I would have improved if I had practiced more, but I was loathe to use up my store of powder, and also the fierce report of the gun made my shoulder hurt and my head ache.

To pass the time by the fire and take my mind off my problems, I brought up some of the silk embroidery threads and a piece of linen upon which I thought to amuse myself by sewing a pretty scene. With a light thread I lightly sketched a picture of the little stream by my childhood home, with the trees and flowers of England around it, and the thatched roof of our house showing through. I then filled it in with the darker threads. I kept up this embroidery after returning to the cave and made many more pictures of home that acted as a memory album for me. Sometimes I put people in the scenes and thought of them as my brothers, Mr. Chalcote, Lady Evelyn or Leora. My favorite was one of Richard when he first picked up the fiddle as his look of wondrous pleasure was deeply engraved on my mind.

During the days I applied myself to fortifying my fence. I chopped down many saplings in the surrounding brush and stripped off the greenery and small branches. I sharpened the ends into points until I had a series of staves that I pounded into the earth on both sides of my wicker panels. In this way I created a very strong wall indeed, and, in time, many of these green staves sent out roots and branches and further reinforced the wall until it became a dense hedge that I was obliged to trim regularly. I had no more visits from the boars, but their presence produced an awareness that I ought not to be too casual about my safety on what I had thought was an uninhabited island.

As soon as my fence was sufficiently reinforced I returned to the cave, glad to sleep in my more comfortable bed. This also pleased Roger and Miss Higgins who had dutifully kept vigil by me at the fieldside fire but now jumped eagerly back onto the bed and nestled into its softness.

One evening while we were still by the field I heard the little doe goat bleating pitifully, so I hastily grabbed up the pistol, thinking that the boars might be attacking the goats. When I arrived at their enclosure, I found the doe on the ground in the throes of giving birth, having nearly accomplished the full expulsion of her babes. I helped pull them the last little way out and tore off the bloody sac enclosing the two kids. Their mother did not like my interference and began licking them proprietarily. In a very short time the kids struggled up on their spindly legs and inspected the world, which they did not seem to find too astonishing. They quickly sought their mother's teats and began to feed.

Over the next few days, they grew apace and I had much pleasure from petting their silky infant bodies and watching them gambol about their pen. I also began to milk their mother for myself and enjoyed her lovely milk as a most wondrous addition to my diet. She produced an enormous amount of it, and so I resurrected the cheese-making skills I had practiced on the farm. The cool dark of the back of my cave made an excellent aging cellar. I gave both Roger and Miss Higgins milk and cheese, and Miss Higgins especially seemed to regard it as a special ambrosia. Her muzzle coated in white, she looked up at me dreamily, then set about licking her chops and cleaning her face with her paw.

It occurred to me that I could slaughter one of the kids for meat, and that at some point I would have to do so, especially should my little herd exceed my ability to milk them, but I was enjoying the kids too much to dispense with them now, and I had clams for meat. I reminded myself that it would not do to be sentimental about animals that were not pets, and I did not name my goats because of this, but still I liked them very much, and when the time came that I did kill them, I did so with a heavy heart and with much more awareness of them as fellow living creatures than I had had back in England.

Midwiving for the goat had greatly stained my clothes, and I had to labor mightily in beating them clean against the rocks below the falls. I had previously determined that I would reserve my tiny cache of soap for my own body until I could find the means to make more, but I found increasingly that stains did not bother me so much, and that making soap was not my highest priority.

With my own little farm and household established, I decided it was time to further explore the island. I had many times gone back to gather grapes at the furthest point I had reached on my earliest foray, but had not gone beyond. I again gave a good deal of thought to whether I should forge on overland or follow the coast. It seemed to me that overland I could reach the other side of the island in something like two day's hike and that, if I were adventurous, I could then walk back on the coast, and it was this course I resolved upon.

I packed my knapsack with cheese, what was left of the ship's bread, a bottle of water, some powder and shot and the book on tropical vegetation. I had taken to wearing trousers exclusively in my work and I thought this would be good hiking garb too. I also characteristically wore a shirt belted round in which I could put tools. I wrapped my large knife and put it in the sack and put my hammer, hatchet and pistol in my belt, so I was quite weighed down. I wore the leather boots with moss-stuffed toes and my broad sun hat.

As I passed the pond and looked down at my reflection I saw that I looked like no female I had ever seen before and thought how shocked Lady Evelyn would be at my appearance, though I knew her as a kind woman beneath her obsession with propriety and her allegiance to the cruelties of her class, and I hope she would understand that I had now to fit myself to a life utterly unlike that I had known in England. One might wonder how I could be concerned with the views of someone so far distant. I suppose I used Lady Evelyn as a measuring stick whereby I judged my ever-growing departure from what I knew as conventional life. It was also a sort of conversation, the only sort I had.

I soon gained the grapelands, as I called them, and then set forward into new terrain. In character it was, of course, more of what I was already familiar with—palms, lower-lying trees with grey-green leaves whose names I didn't know, and some with dark leaves as big as napkins, grasses and rocks with various little valleys and hillocks. Half a day's walk I found another small spring and splashed my face and hands in it and refilled my water bottle.

Roger raised a number of rabbits and little by little I gained sufficient resolve to try to shoot one of them for our supper. I tried the pistol three times with nothing to show for it but powder smudges and the shock of the explosion, and was about to give up, though I thought that Roger was looking at me as if to plead for a chance to retrieve a hare. "All right, all right, I'll try one more shot if you can rouse another," I told him. He did so in a short time, and eons of instinct led him to run the hare for a good ways across my view so I sighted and finally let off a ball. Not by aiming, but entirely by accident, I caught the rabbit in the head, a very desirable accident that preserved the body intact.

Roger brought the poor hare to me in his mouth, dropping it dutifully and triumphantly at my feet. "What a good dog!" I exclaimed to please him. I grabbed the hare by its ears and put it in the extra bag I had brought. In a few hours when I determined to stop for the night, I brought it out and skinned it, a procedure I had performed many times at home when my brothers brought home game. I built a fire and spitted the carcass to roast it. The skin I scraped with my knife and rolled it up back into the bag.

When the rabbit was cooked, I cut off a good chunk of the flesh and fed it to Roger, taking for myself the legs as more easily consumed without utensils. I wrapped what was left in large leaves and kept it for our breakfast.

As I slept in the wild that night, I felt nourished as I had not since leaving the ship, and it seemed a good idea to sharpen my hunting skills so as to hunt more meat or to reconsider my decision not to slaughter a goat.

As I walked along the next day I had set myself the task of trying to match the plants that surrounded me with those pictured in the book as belonging to the tropics, but the process of checking through the whole book with each specimen was so time-consuming and tedious that I decided to approach it from the other way around, that is, in the morning before setting out, I pored over the book to find pictures of those plants that might be useful to me so that I could particularly scout for those. I hit upon sugar cane and a root called taro to look for especially, as these would be good food; the taro root was called the "potato of the Tropics" and might be more substantial, but I was greatly hoping to find some sweet cane. The book said the cane leaves were "much like blades and about five feet high", while the taro leaves were "arrow shaped of one to two yards." The engravings of these plants were rather crude and their sojourn in water had wrinkled and shrunk them a bit, but I thought that if I came upon possible candidates, I could taste the stalks of cane to check for sweetness and I could dig up the roots of any likely taro plants to see if their roots conformed to the illustrations, though the book informed me that I dare not taste the root without cooking it as it was poison.

So I worked my way over the island, occasionally hacking at stalks or digging for roots, but I was largely distracted by the many unfamiliar and, to my eye, outlandish but beautiful plants and flowers I found— orange and purple and pink, red and white blossoms with waxy leaves and centers like spotted tongues projecting over their petals. They grew on vines and also from the mossy trunks of trees. Birds of white with plumy crests and others like the green and red parrot I had seen earlier

74

perched here and there and flew cawing from tree to tree, and once again I felt I was in a fairyland. I thought a bit ruefully of my plantings of English flowers and how modest they would be compared to these natives. I thought also of the boars, the ogres in this fairyland, but I was not molested by them, nor did I even see them, though I found some hoof prints in the mud along the small waterways I crossed.

In the late afternoon of the second day, I descended out of the forest and onto a beachy terrain like that I had first landed upon months ago. Roger had sprinted onto the beach in front of me and when I arrived I found him nosing what appeared to be an immense fat brown shield lying on the ground. It turned out to be the grandest tortoise I had ever seen. Its brown shell was reticulated so that it seemed to be constructed rather than grown. The fellow who wore this shield had entirely withdrawn into its shell and resisted Roger's many attempts to bring it forth. I thought that here might well be another source of meat for me and that the tortoise might also harbor eggs, though it would require some violence for me to access them.

The beach's surrounding presented another aspect of island landscape as there were several tall rocky structures standing out in the water upon which hundreds of white seabirds rested. Among the smaller rocks at their feet were pools in which stationary sea creatures in the shape of stars clung to the walls. There were also rounded hollow tubes, their openings fringed with small waving fronds, their insides a soft purple. I spent a long time gazing in wonder at these strange creatures that I did not know whether to call plants or animals.

At last, some distance up from the beach in a little palm grove, I made a fire and lay down to sleep, passing across my mind the phantasmagoria of marvels I had seen on my hike and yearning to share the experience with another person. As it turned out, a kind of sharing awaited me, but it was a horrible one.

Chapter 6 — Awl Is Not Well But A Stout Fabric Is Made

The next day I began my return trip along the coast as I had planned. I made no assault upon the tortoise as I was already quite burdened and would have had to transport his carcass. Also, I liked him and didn't want to kill him, or her. How does one determine the sex of a tortoise?

I traveled some distance up from the beach rather than at the water line as the walking was more secure and there was more shade from the merciless sun. It was easy going for the most part, though from time to time the beach gradually became more rock-strewn until my progress required climbing more than walking, and though this was arduous, among these rocks were more of the creatures I had seen in the pools the previous day, so I felt myself repaid for my effort by the sight of their astonishing forms and glowing colors.

At the end of the day, I was so exhausted that I made no fire, ate yellow fruit and coconut and laid down on the lee side of a sandy hill about thirty yards from the beach. Earlier that day Roger had gone off on one of his field trips and had not returned, despite my frequent calls, so I was in some anxiety about him.

Just as the sun was sinking, I heard a series of slapping sounds coming from the water. When I stood up to see what it was, I was utterly astonished to view three canoes, each carrying five or so men approaching the beach. My immediate impulse was to rush down to the water and hail them as the first human beings I had seen in many months, but caution overcame this impulse because I could not know if they would be friendly or not. They were nearly naked except for loincloths covering their sex and shell jewelry around their necks and in their ears. They were short, very brown and had jet black hair which they wore long and tied at the backs of their necks.

They jumped from the canoes and pulled the craft up on the beach. Then they dragged two bound captives from the bottom of one boat and flung them up higher onto the sand. I had foolishly stood in plain view all this time, but they had not yet noticed me, and at this point I decided I ought to make myself as inconspicuous as possible as their attitudes were warlike, so I silently slipped to the ground, though I was still able to peek through the scrub grass to observe them.

They built a large fire and drank a good deal of something they had brought in gourd containers. Their beverage must have been alcoholic because little by little they became louder, eventually working themselves into a sort of frenzy of singing and dancing. At last, they dragged the two captives into their circle, and each man stood above them and shouted imprecations which they punctuated by waving spears above their heads. Then the oldest one among them rose and all grew silent. I took him to be their chief since the others attended to him in a very respectful manner, and also his shell necklace was larger than that of the others and embellished with bright green feathers.

He delivered a speech whose tempo and volume increased as he went on and which culminated in his pointing accusingly at the two captives.

Then he turned and began walking back to the canoes while the others fell upon the captives and stabbed them repeatedly with their spears. The victims cried out from pain as their bright blood spurted onto the sand, but did not plead for mercy. When the two were clearly dead, their executioners returned to the canoes where the chief awaited them. They cleaned their spears in the water, climbed back into their craft and paddled away.

I was enormously dumbfounded by a combination of astonishment and fear. I had no way to interpret what I had observed, though it appeared to have been some sort of ritual of punishment. It certainly had not occurred to me to intervene; in fact, I had endeavored to stay absolutely undiscovered, and I was very grateful that Roger had not been here as he most certainly would have set up a great clamor of barking and running about.

I was very agitated and did not sleep for the rest of the night, only venturing down to view the victims' bodies more closely when morning came and it seemed that the canoes had gone for good. The bodies were those of young men, very smooth-skinned, wearing no shell jewelry and now very grievously rent. I assumed they had been left as carrion, but with my hatchet and hands I dug a hole and dragged them by turn into it, all the while looking often about me in fear that the murderers would return. I hoped that the dead would not mind sharing a grave as they had shared their deaths.

When I had covered them up, I stood above them, thinking I ought to say something elegiac, but I was still very agitated and could think of nothing more than "Rest in Peace." At this moment Roger bounded out from the wall of palms bordering the beach and I was tremendously glad to see him. He seemed perfectly all right, though his coat was burr-encrusted and his paws muddy. "Where have you been, Roger?" I asked.

"Thank heavens, you missed what happened here last night!" Roger jumped up on me repeatedly, and I held him to me and lavished pets upon him, partially as assurance to myself. He sniffed around the graves and the blood-soaked sand where the men had been stabbed, just curious and sharing none of my fright.

As we wended our way back towards our side of the island, my mind was much taken up with considering the implications of what I had seen, mainly that there must be an inhabited place within rowable distance of the island, though I, of course, had nothing to row, nor did I have the seacraft to row it. I also considered of my own danger from these men. I had no way to know how they would treat me if they were to find me, so I resolved to be prudent and try to avoid them. I also had no way to know how often they visited the island or if they came only to the side opposite my own.

I wondered as well what crime the young men had committed that had brought them such a severe punishment. The violence of the killing was ever before me and I felt guilty that I had not been able to stop it. I considered myself lucky to have escaped detection and wondered if I ought to plan my daily doings and my habitat with more view to defending myself. I thought about this continuously and from many directions. I did, after all, have guns, which might at the least frighten any who attacked me, and, if my aim improved, I might slay them. I would have to fortify my dwelling and my fields and be more systematic in guarding them. I felt very nervous and every noise made me look around anxiously. In the two and a half days it took me to walk back along the coast I could not arrive at any firm opinion or plan of action and was exhausted by my tense state.

It is not entirely accurate to say that I walked along the coast, as on a number of occasions I cut inland to follow waterways, and one of these trips provided a useful diversion from my worry. Despite the disquiet of my mind and its concentration on the horror I had witnessed, as I walked along I spied what for all the world looked to be the sugar cane leaf pictured in my book. It was indeed like a blade, dark green and about two inches wide and quite tall, at least five feet. I knew that the leaves were merely harbingers of sugar cane, that the sweetness lay in the stalks, so with my knife I cut a stalk and began to chew hopefully on its end. How the sweet juice flowed into my mouth, nicer than any candy because of its freshness! My book told me that new cane would grow from the segments of the old, so I took a number of stalks to plant in my own garden. I also set up a stone marker on the beach where the stream came down so that I could find this place again should my sweet tooth demand satisfaction before my own crop came up.

When Roger and I finally reached home, Miss Higgins and the goats were delighted to see us, especially the doe who was in some discomfort owing to her distended udders. I was pleased to see that no further damage had been done in the garden and that the plants had grown apace in the days I had been gone, sprouting little stalks and inviting weeds that I would have to pull out soon. I wanted very much to pull up a carrot sprout to see how big its root was beneath its lacy umbrella top, but I restrained myself so that the root could grow larger. I had no seed to spare to satisfy my curiosity, especially after the boar's incursion.

That evening I again took up what had grown to be my custom on the island: I prepared my dinner and ate it while I watched the sunset. This had become one of my main pleasures because the sunsets were so spectacular and at the same time peaceful—their luminous oranges, reds and purples passing gently from shade to shade until they disappeared into gray. As I watched I felt a momentous resolution forming out of the many thoughts and feelings that flowed from my having witnessed the killings by what I took to be natives of this part of the world. I decided that I did not want to spend my energy and spirit in creating a fortress to defend myself, nor would I attempt to deploy what weapons I had in anticipation of an attack. I would be prudent and practice concealment as I very much wanted to stay alive, but even if I were eventually to be killed by invaders, I wanted to make my time upon this island peaceful and productive, not pervaded by the enervating fear that had so dominated my return trek.

I had no control over being alone on this island, but I did have some control over my state of mind, and I did not want it to be one of constant terror or anticipation of danger. This resolution gave me much relief and, in fact, I felt somehow enlarged by it. The next day I set myself to weeding and planted the sugar cane segments, and though I continued to turn over the awful scene I had witnessed, wondering always what the young men had been killed for and if the natives would come back, I did so with less anxiety.

For the next months my days passed in tending the growing garden, milking the goats and making cheeses, gathering coconuts and yellow fruit, and playing with Roger and Miss Higgins. In the late afternoon I went bathing in the falls pool and then applied myself to one or another of my books before the sun went down. The incessant moralizing of Piers and Pilgrim, as I came to call them, was tiresome, and the Bible had been for me a great field of contradiction ever since I had stood by the fire as a young girl listening to my father and his friend Simon Petrie argue about religion, or rather, Simon argued and my father occasionally nodded yes or no. "But why did God command the Israelites to destroy *all* the Amalekites?" Simon would say. "What kind of mercy is that?" Simon was known in the neighborhood as a dangerous crank, but his questioning gave me a model for my own, and so the Bible often troubled me. Each time I came upon the passage in which God tries to kill Moses for no reason at all, I wondered how little attention was paid to this anomaly. Nonetheless I loved the language of the Bible and its frequent wisdom as well.

I also occupied my mind with questions related to the future produce of my garden—how much I could eat and how much I ought to allow to go to seed so as to have another larger crop next time. I considered how I might store the seeds and fruits and began again to weave reeds and grasses into baskets, the first of which were quite crude, though later I gained facility and even began to weave with an eye to decoration, so that eventually, I had a stack of unusual but useful baskets.

Of course, I realized that a basket alone would not stave off infestation by insects, vermin or water and that I needed something impermeable to line my baskets. What I needed was pottery, and I had only the vaguest notions of how pottery was made: I knew it required clay worked into a serviceable shape and then baked to become watertight. I figured I could try to perform this process and went in search of clay.

I dug into the earth on both sides of the stream that flowed down to the sea with no result other than to make myself very grubby. Then I poked about around the pool where I bathed and at last found a strata of clay, which I regarded as another instance of something being in front of my eyes, but not really seen. I dug out a goodly quantity of it and began to work it on a flat rock nearby; I kneaded it as I had many times kneaded bread, which made me think longingly of the brown loaves of good bread that I had so often made and eaten of. I had not kneaded bread dough for many years, though, and this is a process requiring forceful arm thrusts, so that in the evening my arms were heavy and very sore the next morning.

At last I had made several largish malleable wads of clay and set about molding them into bowl shapes. I also made a cup so that I could drink more conveniently than from the coconut shell halves I had been using since the tin cup I'd taken off the ship had rusted through. These clay pieces I let dry naturally and then made a fire into which I placed my pots. I left them in the ashes until the next morning. I eagerly lifted out the first one, but it broke to bits in my hand, as indeed did all the others. I had no great expectations of success, but I was nonetheless disappointed and looked with dismay at the mud chips that lay about me. I figured the temperature of the fire and the length of exposure to it were the elements I would have to get right in order to succeed, and so set about a series of experiments. Instead of making a whole new set of pots for each experiment, I decided instead to make small clay samples to test, and so over several months I made innumerable variations on my process, changing the fire's heat through different kinds of wood, and placing the dried clay into the fire at different times. In this way I created quite a large pile of clay fragments because none of my experiments worked, and I did finally get discouraged and resolved to use the sun-baked clay as liners for my baskets, which would bar insects and vermin though not moisture.

However, as I was clearing what I had decided would be the last pottery fire, I noticed a shard resting atop one of the stones with which I had marked off the fireplace. It had a sheen to it unlike that of the other fragments and when I picked it up I found it enormously hard, in fact, unbreakable in my hand! Huzzah! This minor success propelled me on to more attempts in which I made the pots of the thickness of my successful shard and also placed them on rocks that had been heated in the fire rather than putting the pots directly into the fire. At last I produced some watertight pots. They were very ugly globular things, but they were serviceable, and they reinspired me to continue my pottery experiments now that I had a basic method.

During my attempts to make pottery, I was also thinking about how I might process whatever flax would result from my garden, which was growing apace. To someone who had not grown up around the making of linen, the journey from flax to fabric would, I imagine, seem a very complicated one, though for me it was routine. I had done it many times, but the process as I had known it required tools that I did not have, such as the brake to first break down the plants and free the fibers from the unwanted part we called the boon, an odd name, as in other contexts a boon was a good thing. Nor did I have the wooden knife to beat the stalks to scutch them. I thought I might easily make some form of brake and scutching knife, but I was hard put to come up with a substitute for the metal heckling combs that remove the last bit of boon and the shorter fibers. Leora's horn comb was too delicate for the task.

Then, when I finally had my fibers in hand, I would have to make a distaff to keep the fibers from tangling and some sort of spinning wheel. Ah, again, I needed the wheel! It seemed that a good deal of human progress depended upon it, and I resolved to have one.

At last I began slowly harvesting my garden, saving most for seed, but eating some of its fruits. The lettuce had come first and how I had loved its taste! Then the green beans came on and what a feast of home they were, followed by the carrots, which seemed sweeter than any I remembered, and of which I could eat my fill as the seed was not contained in them but in their flowers. These vegetables added much flavor to my clam or goat stews. The marigolds made a pretty orange border, and I plucked some to adorn my bower and even stuck one behind my ear, though there was no one to see it and soon its strong odor overpowered me and I threw it away. I forced myself to get used to it, however, because if I pulverized the flowers and rubbed them on my body, insects were less inclined to make a meal of me. and from this time my appearance was less scabrous. I stored most of my crop in basket-enclosed pots at the back of my cave and thought to plant again as soon as I had worked the soil to give it strength.

When the seeds darkened and the leaves yellowed I knew the flax was ready to harvest as well, so I pulled up the stalks and spread them in the field to dry. At home we would have stored this year's crop in the shed to age until next year and begun to process last year's crop, but I did not have that luxury, so when my bundles were dried I drew them through the coarse wooden combs I had made out of ship's lumber and so performed the rippling stage. I was enormously pleased because I had spent many evenings making the combs. A picture would have shown me with the firelight flickering on my face as I carved and whittled away on small timbers from the ship, punctuating the night sounds with my own cries as I frequently cut myself, especially before I learned the simple truth that the sharper the knife the easier the carving and dragged my whetstone near the fire so as to frequently ply my knife upon it.

To ret the fibers I submerged them in the stream, anchoring them to its rocky outcroppings with some of the fine embroidery fibers from Leora's trunk. It struck me as another irony of my life on this island that I would use such expensive threads to nurture what would be very coarse linen ones. I was very glad I had a stream so as to avoid the indelible stink of retting flax that arose from our trough at home.

When the straw came away easily from the fibers I drew the bundles from the water, untied them and laid them out on the ground for a few days, turning them so they dried on both sides. When they were dry and crackly I stacked them up to age for a few more weeks, which gave me the time to figure out how to do the next stage, freeing the fiber from the unwanted parts of the plant. I easily made a scutching knife, which is little more than a flat piece of wood, and lustily set about beating the flax with it, which discombobulated Roger who set up a great barking as if to reinforce my assault upon the flax. I mused upon what an odd word "scutch" was and found myself repeating it over and over until it became utter nonsense. Then I varied it with rhyming—"scotch, much, fuch, hutch" and so on. Being so alone, my mind ran on with such games a great deal.

At home the next step required metal combs, and I was quite stumped about how I could make some. I had taken a good deal of metal off the ship, but none of it was configured to act as a comb and I had not the skills to work it. I thought a clam shell might be broken to make a sharp edge and I had a large pile of them, which I set about breaking into pieces. These I pressed closely together into a damp clay surface, which, when dried, anchored them fairly securely. Then I drew my fibers over them and found that the boon did stick to the shells, and left me with a bundle of light grey fibers as fine as human hair. This stage is called heckling at home and it gave me a grim smile to think of it when I inspected the damage to my hands. They were extremely chafed and cut from my whittling work, and I resolved once again to try to construct some gloves. In England the gentlewomen were at pains to protect their hands as their smoothness was one way the ladies could be distinguished from the peasants like me. However, I had always liked my big rough hands because they were capable, and I quite disliked the smooth, lineless hands of Lady Evelyn and Leora which seemed oddly dead, especially as they were always held in ladylike poses.

I invested great effort in the flax process because I considered that making more cloth out of the flax was imperative if my garden were to thrive. The awnings I'd made from the fabric in Leora's trunk were already much weakened by the sun and weather, but they were essential to preserving my seedlings, so I looked to their replacement before they wore out.   I had to leave the flax fibers to age for several weeks so I turned to considering the tools I would need to make cloth of it.

The condition of my hands also continued to nag me.   They had accreted some goodly calluses, but they were also painfully cracked. One day as I was munching on coconut its texture struck me as perhaps willing to yield oil, so I chopped a good deal of it very finely, added a bit of water and set it to simmer at the fire.   I tended it most of the day, keeping the fire low and at last had a buttery residue that indeed soothed my hands.   Later I wondered if I might shorten the process by shredding the coconut and somehow pressing or mashing it.   I returned to my primitive rock tools and pounded out a batch of fine coconut mash that was also quite soothing.   I resolved to try later to see if I might make an oil that would fuel a lamp to light my evenings, as I had long before burned down the candles from the ship, except for one, which I kept in reserve for a reason I could not explain.   I guess it was a symbol that my light could not be entirely put out.   My diet of heavily allegorical reading was casting my own thought towards the symbolic, so from time to time I said to myself, "Metaphors make us blind," a line from the opening poem of *Pilgrim's Progress*.

My need to make things kept me well-anchored in the practical, however.   I remembered looking with Leora at engravings of ancient Greek ladies who were spinning with an implement that seemed quite simple compared to our flax wheels, but since I had not enough memory to create or use one of those, I had to try to reproduce the complicated version.   I first drew a picture to remind myself of all the parts—the wheel, the treadle, the distaff, and the rods that connected them all.

Everything was easy but the wheel itself. For that I first made arced pieces from ship's lumber using the saw, the adze and the plane.

The big problem was how to hold the arcs of the wheel together as I had no glue and I feared splitting the wood if I were to nail it. I decided I would have to bind it together. I had made a crude groove on the outside of each piece, and here it was I ran acropper.

I was sitting on the ground, posing the adze against the wood at an angle, and as I hammered, it slipped off and drove straight into my calf, puncturing a deep gash that bled copiously and made me scream in pain. I limped into the cave to retrieve the spirits I'd taken off the boat, poured them onto my wound to cleanse it, and again cried out in pain. I bound the wound with clean cloth, which quickly bled through and had to be replaced. I spilt so much bright red blood that I grew very frightened. Eventually, the bleeding stopped, but I spent the rest of the day lying down, afraid that if I moved around I would restart the bleeding. Roger and Miss Higgins sensed some dire condition and stayed close by me. In this state my loneliness pained me more than usual. It seemed a vortex pulling me down. I could not bear my full weight on my leg for many days and so I crawled about to gather what I needed to make a crutch and hopped on that for a week. I limped for many more weeks afterwards. My spirits limped as well. I resolved to be more careful in my carpentry and I had a nasty two-inch red scar on my calf to remind me to do so. About my loneliness I could do nothing but accept it.

Despite my incapacity, after a few days rest, I continued to construct my flax wheel, using utmost care in pointing the adze as I completed the groove on the outer edges of the rounded pieces that I had been working on when I stabbed myself. I then cut off a narrow strip from the oilcloth MacIntosh I'd found in the trunk and bound it round the wheel parts, pulling it as deep into the outside groove as I could and tying it off in a knot that I knew would make a bulge, but which I hoped the continual wear of the yarn over it would soften.

At last, my spinning wheel was complete, and what a rickety contraption it was! I attached a bunch of flax fibers to the distaff, pulled them out and began running the treadle with my foot, which turned the wheel, over which the fibers ran in a lumpy but satisfactory enough way, and so I began to make thread over the course of many hours and days. When I finished the thread I then stretched and boiled it to set the twist and lay it out on the beach to bleach.

This was tedious work, and I often passed the time in singing. At other times the work was hypnotic and soothing and I enjoyed it. Many memories ran over the wheel as well. I often thought of the music my brother Richard coaxed from the violin and how expressive it was compared to that of the harpsichord over which Lady Evelyn forced Leora to labor.

The boiling part of the process was especially tedious as it cried out for a much larger pot than my relatively small one, so I had to sit by the fire through many batches. During this enforced sitting I planned my loom and continued to sing all the songs and hymns I remembered. I also thought of the stories about witches gathered around steaming cauldrons. Mrs. Laughton, the basket maker, was believed to be one despite her harping upon salvation.

It would have taken me a very long time to reproduce a loom like that we used at home, as large and complicated as it was. Instead I constructed a rectangular frame about six by four feet, at the bottom and top of which I put a series of nails, my idea being that I would attach fibers to these nails at both ends to form a warp. I affixed this rectangular frame to the frames I had previously built as the entrance to my cave, and extended the overhang to protect it from the rain. It was ready when the fibers were at last prepared.

I had also planed two long flat pieces of wood to slide in among alternate warp threads, which I might turn on their sides to lift half the warp at a time so I could slip the weft thread among them. As my beater I used Leora's comb.

I was both excited and apprehensive when I began to weave through my first thread, and then the second and third. Hallelujah! It worked! I was making cloth. It was not nearly as fine as even common English linen, but it was stout and would be very serviceable to me.

My first flax crop yielded three panels somewhat smaller than my rectangular frame. I was very pleased with them and immediately thought how I might improve my process. Eventually, I even thought to beautify my fabric by weaving in some of the embroidery threads from Leora's trunk. I also soaked marigolds in water as a bath to dye my fabric a pretty gold. Later on I was able to have purple as well after I read in my book on tropical vegetation about the shellfish from which I could derive this color. Over the course of the years I spent on the island, I several times replaced my garden awnings with my own woven cloth and was able to provide myself with other useful items as well; I especially appreciated the rough towels that I stored by the pool and wrapped myself in when I emerged from bathing. I also made hotpads by sewing a layer of tow between two linen pieces and thereby saved my hands from many cooking burns. I was well-provisioned in every way except for the company of other people.

Chapter Seven—The Fortunate Cave

Five years passed for me on the island according to the tree calendar upon which I had made a mark for each day. These days had been prosperous and lucky, particularly in that, though I wounded myself quite grievously on several occasions, not ever again so badly as the stab of the adze, and though my fever reoccurred and laid me low from time to time, my health was generally quite good. Though often marked with insect bites my skin was much browned and my hands and feet hardened since my coming, of course, and some would have considered these substantial injuries. I could imagine Lady Evelyn's dismay if she were to see me so, but I plied myself with coconut oil and rather liked my golden hue. I had lots of food and a comfortable house, and since I had no looking glass but the water, I had no accurate image with which to reproach myself. The weather was usually a continual caress; the air was warm and fragrant, and when it was very hot I had my own cool pool in which to swim. Roger and Miss Higgins and the goats made me laugh and warmed my heart. I was very grateful for my life and often enjoyed it.

Yet I was profoundly lonely. Each new discovery and achievement was shadowed by the lack of anyone with whom to reflect upon it. I knew now that the isolation I had created for myself in England was, in fact, a very partial one, always leavened by the presence of other people with whom to talk, trade news and opinions or even a slight glance that, I now realized, could convey enormous interchange. First I had sought quiet from the din of five brothers and then from the fatuity and frequent insult of life at Lady Evelyn's, but now there was a different sort of quietness at the core of my life that was less respite than muteness. My affection for my brother Richard had always warmed me, but as I could no longer follow his growth, it seemed frozen in time. The books helped a little, but since I mostly argued with their religious viewpoints, I found no sympathy nor any correspondence, so that even though I breathed air of which I could imagine none sweeter, I sometimes felt suffocated for lack of intelligent response and tasted of despair.

The only way to end my isolation would be to leave the island on my own by sea or to be brought off by others. I had seen no other humans landing on the island since my first year, and after much pondering how to take myself over the sea, I finally concluded that I had not the force to do what would be required to build a boat, which in my mind demanded the hollowing of a tree. I thought I might be able to fell a tree big enough to do this and that I might even be able to hollow it out, but I would not be able to move the tree from wherever I had felled and hollowed it to the sea itself. I simply did not have the strength nor the tools. For a time I thought over how I might harness the goats to pull my potential canoe to the water, but finally gave it up as asking an unfeasible organization be imposed upon the goats, a project that seemed no less absurd that harnessing Miss Higgins as a beast of burden.

Again and again I returned to the resolution I had made at the beginning of my island exile—to stay alive and hope I would sometime be rescued, and, in the meantime to continue to cultivate the island. I also resolved to press my exploration further. I had taken many short journeys, but never again one as extensive as that I had made when I observed the two murders; no doubt witnessing them formed part of my reluctance to venture far from my home base. In fact, I had been only halfway around the whole island on the coast, and though I imagined both sides were much the same, once I had given it thought, I felt silly not to have seen the whole.

My first foray, however, was underground. I had lived in my cave for five years, but had never seen just how far back into the earth it went, mostly because for a long time I had nothing with which to light my way. During the past year though, I had finally been able to produce a decent coconut oil and a wick to dip into it out of my linen tow, so I had a lamp for the evenings, though it was an awkward one, a mere dish with a wick. To crawl back into a cave carrying such a fragile lamp seemed too perilous and so I had not done so, but when I succeeded in making a shield out of a short tube of fired clay, I decided to make the attempt. I made pads to bind on my knees to protect them should I have to crawl a good ways, and filled my knapsack with a few tools and a bottle of oil to replenish the lamp. I had to displace my storage arrangements, bringing forward all the goods I had stored at the back of the cave and ultimately removing the cloth hanging over the far end's opening. At last I set out into the darkness.

I was immediately on my hands and knees, the rock a narrow dun tunnel about me. I put the lamp as far ahead of me as I could and then crawled to it inch by inch. The air grew cooler and staler as I proceeded, and my lamp sputtered, leading me to believe that soon the tunnel would narrow into an end, and I would simply crawl back, now apprised that my cave had nothing more to show, but I kept on to see how far the end would be. Very luckily, I pressed on, because after making a gradual curve to the left, the tunnel began to widen a bit. I reckoned I had crawled some forty yards, and it seemed my lamp burned more brightly, so I kept dragging myself forward, now with even more curiosity, and with much discomfort as well, as I did not like the enclosure of this rock passage which seemed to press upon me malevolently.

At last the tunnel widened as it had at my end of the cave and I crawled into what looked like my cave's opposite twin; I could even perceive a faint light in the distance that augured an exit into the day, but before I could find my way to it, my eye was waylaid by a horrifying sight that froze me in my crawl: There against the far wall lay a human skeleton, shreds of clothing still clinging to its desiccated bones, its shadow flickering large against the wall from the light of my lamp as if the creature were moving. I drew near and stared into the empty sockets of its eyes, at the ghastly wreck of a man's life, and I wondered at his end. Among the bones lay tarnished brass buttons, a belt buckle whose leather had been gnawed away and a narrow gold ring. To the side of the skeleton lay a small wooden chest. I slowly opened it. Resting inside were a heap of gold coins bearing what I took to be Spanish markings as well as many gems of green and red, some lumps of quartz, and some ornate jewelry-- a necklace of gold set with red stones and a broach set with amber ones.

My imagination put this evidence together to form a story of someone who had either been abandoned or had stolen away from a ship. He might have been shipwrecked as I had been, though his hidden state and the presence of the chest argued some kind of theft. It also argued that there was another entrance to my cave ahead, as I had a strong sense that this skeletal inhabitant had not crawled the same path I had, but had instead come in from the opposite direction.

Spurred on by my desire to escape this macabre scene, I left the eerie skeleton, his treasure and further contemplation of their meaning until later and went forward, now wholly upright and holding my lamp before me. Within a few minutes I found the exit, which led into a copse quite like the one that had hidden the cave's other entrance when I first found it. I struggled out through its brambles and tried to determine my location.

The position of the sun told me where the ocean would be; I went in that direction and soon sighted it, so I knew that I was a good distance below my cave in the direction I had explored much less than the region above it. I thought it must be about 100 yards below the grapelands, so I hiked in the direction I imagined they were to be found and soon ran into them. Over the years I had trimmed and cultivated the vines so that they would produce more and be easier to tend and had constructed a small roofed pavilion in which to rest and shelter from the sun, and I had provided it with a bench on which I now dropped down.

I was most amazed by the human remains I had found. It seemed obvious that the man had been hiding, but why had he never come out after his pursuers had left when he could have taken advantage of the island's natural abundance? I could not imagine that the fellow had crawled into the cave and simply sat there until he starved, so I concluded that he must have had an injury or sickness that prevented him from leaving the cave. The bones were disarranged, probably by predators, and so I could form no map to the cause of their possessor's demise.

He had certainly been able to hold on to his treasure. I wondered if he had turned over the coins before he died. Did he enjoy their golden glow or was he overcome at their uselessness and the price he would pay for them? I thought then of how many times in England I had heard people fantasize about finding a hidden treasure and what they would do with it. Then I dryly laughed to think that I had found one but how useless this treasure was to me. The gold was too soft a material out of which to make something useful, and the gems were pretty to look at but equally useless. I might wear the jewelry for a bit of fun, but that's all. It struck me quite forcefully, however, that if I were ever to get off the island, this chest might serve me well as it definitely had a high value in the human society I had left.

I was in doubt as to whether I ought to bury the man's bones but decided I would, though I determined to let the chest remain hidden. I went back to my own end of the cave the long way round as I did not relish the return trip through the oppression of the narrow rock tunnel. I fetched back my spade and one of the clay-lined baskets. I dug a hole large enough to accommodate it, and then girded myself to go back into the cave to retrieve the bones. It was a curious experience, combining ordinary gathering with the morbidity that came with consideration of what was being gathered. I tried to be respectful with the bones as I placed each of them in the basket. As I was gathering the last of them, I found on the ground a small iron ball, creased over its body with small nicks. I figured it must have been the cause of the man's death, a fatal gunshot the reason he never emerged from the cave.

I dragged the basket out of the cave and over to the hole I had dug for it. I pushed it into the hole and covered it with dirt. I stood over it for a few minutes and finally said "Rest in Peace" as I had over the graves of the two murdered natives. I also set up a stack of rocks to mark the place.

Burials are by their nature melancholy affairs, though usually one knows the person whose burial one attends. Because I did not know the man I was burying I was led to consider my own death more than I might have if I had had memories of him or sentiments of his loss to occupy me. Instead I wondered if there would be anyone to bury me. I considered if I might build my own coffin and lie down in it when I thought my time had come. I had once heard Lady Evelyn say that Dr. Donne had practiced his death by lying in his coffin, and I wondered if I might do that in lieu of being attended by others. I did not pursue this idea and soon stopped thinking about it, not deliberately, but naturally, as I was young and vitally inclined to the world around me.

Death certainly played a part in my world, as it always had. When my little flock of goats grew too big for me to milk them properly, from time to time, I had to slay one. I cut its throat with my knife, hung it from a tree branch to drain the blood, then skinned it. I scraped the hides as best I could and treated them using my own urine, and they proved very useful to me for making footgear, storage bags and many other things. The meat was most delightful and strengthening. Roger was especially keen on it, showing no sympathy for his fellow quadripeds. I tried boiling up the hooves in hopes of concocting some kind of glue, but succeeded only in creating an awful stink. I was somewhat more successful in achieving tallow, though because goats are little given to fat, my supplies were small. From what I got I was able to make a small store of a relatively effective soap by cooking the tallow with ashes.

The sea also often flung up its dead upon the beach. Usually, I buried these rotting sea creatures as soon as I could because of their odors, though occasionally, if their deaths seemed recent and there was evidence that they had died of wounds rather than disease, I cooked and ate them with gusto as they were often very tasty.

The most fortunate of these beach deaths were a great number of large sea birds that looked quite like the white ducks of England. Several times as I inspected the beach in the morning as many as twenty of them lay dead there, strewn about in awkward attitudes, wings akimbo. I wondered what had led to their mass death. I did not eat them, but I plucked off their feathers and made for myself a featherbed and several pillows that much softened my sitting arrangements.

I often sat upon these cushions thinking about the dead man who had lain in the far end of my cave for the whole five years I had been there and I completely unaware of him. When I thought of the chest of riches, at first I just chuckled and shook my head, but eventually I began to wonder if I should do anything to secure some of the fortune in the little chest. If I were ever to be rescued, it would be a most wondrous benefit in whatever my future life would be. I had often heard how the Cavalier ladies sewed their jewels into their clothes in order to foil the expropriation by the Roundhead government, so I hit upon the idea of sewing some of the stones into the seams of my old blue dress and stays that I had carefully laid away as relics of my former life.

Rather than crawling through the cave, this time I went the far way round to the opposite entry. When I again opened the chest and played my lamp's light upon it, I paid more attention to exactly what it held. Besides the stacks of gold coins, there were some thirty largish stones and more than a hundred smaller, more polished ones that I took to be rubies and emeralds. I took half the worked stones and several of the unworked ones, even a lump of the quartz I knew to be less valuable, but which somehow appealed to me. I went out the far end of the cave and hiked back around to my side and immediately began the task of secreting the jewels in the dress. I had made the dress in the French manner, which results in a narrow tube on the inside at all the seams. I opened up this cloth tube at several locations and slipped jewels into it, then sewed it back up. I stowed this wearable bank in my trunk as if to put away the thoughts of death that came with the jewels' discovery.

I had also brought back the necklace, the broach and the gold ring, and, when I was finished sewing, I took them down to the pond to model them. I swam about wearing only the necklace and fancied myself a mermaid. I thought I looked both grand and absurd, soon took off the necklace and never put it on again. I felt the unhealthiness of dwelling on this treasure, and so put it out of my mind.

Little by little my thoughts shifted forward, and some weeks after my cave exploration and the burial of its occupant, I prepared to investigate the side of the island I had not yet seen. Since the goats had recently borne their newest babies and were adequately milked without my assistance, I prepared to make a longer trip of about a week. I amused myself by thinking it might be something in the nature of a holiday. I had many times accompanied Lady Evelyn and Leora when they went to the seaside and even to Bath, and though these trips were never holidays for me because I had to attend as usual to Leora and her mother, I always enjoyed the change of scenery and seeing people from other locales. Now I would take my own holiday, though it would be shadowed by constant solitude.

In this spirit I packed my knapsack with the best of my foods and attached a small cushion to the bedroll I had fastened to my back. As usual I wore canvas sailor pants to the knee, sandals of goat hide, and a shirt belted round me. From my having worn it so continually, the straw hat I had taken off the ship had at last fallen apart, so using it as my template, I made a new one out of narrow reeds and grass. It was not as fine as the original, but quite serviceable, and I wore it as I set off. Besides the food in my pack, I carried the pistol, the hammer, my larger knife, a stout walking stick, and a handful of the black berries from the ship that I now habitually sucked. I should say that I had hauled a huge sackful off the ship, but nonetheless dreaded the day my supply would run out.

Because I was approaching my exploration as a holiday, I resolved to proceed slowly, to swim and rest often to refresh myself, and this I did as I picked my way along the coast downside from my cave. Roger absorbed my mood and ran eagerly before me. As in the opposite direction, rock formations demanded a good deal of climbing, which was more fun for Roger than for me; he often went ahead, then returned and looked at me as if to say, "What's taking you so long?" "I have only two feet to your four, Roger, and my two are not as agile as yours," I reminded him. I frequently talked to Roger and Miss Higgins and even to the goats, and though I knew they could not interpret most of the words, like all people fond of animals, I felt they did understand me in their own way. They certainly responded as if they did.

Roger was as interested as I was in the sea creatures I again found in the pools among the rocks. Seeking to dislodge them, perhaps to taste them, he put his paw as far into the pool as he could and snagged one of the fat purple tubes with waving fringe, dragged it out and nosed it about, but it was not to his liking and he left it to wither on the rock.

On the morning of my third day out I ran into a vast stream flowing into the ocean from the interior. I waded into it, but retreated when the water had reached my waist as I did not want to wet my gear. I went back to put my kit down and then waded back into the stream, carrying my walking stick to brace myself against the current. At its middle the stream seemed about four and a half feet deep and ran quite strongly. I pressed on and was able to gain the other side. However, my gear remained on the opposite shore. The tide was at low ebb, and the stream would swell as it came in, so if I were going to cross it, I should do so soon. I doubted, however, that I could cross this torrent without wetting my gear, and I weighed going on without it. That which would be damaged was mostly food and bedding. I figured I could eat yellow fruit and coconuts as I had done when I arrived and that I could bind my bedroll to the top of my head, with the pistol rolled inside it, and I could bob across the stream with my head above water and my walking stick steadying me. Roger had no trouble with the stream and went back and forth over it several times as I considered what to do.

I found a sheltered spot to stow the gear I could not carry, and in leaving my cushion behind, I realized that I was going to have a different holiday than the one I had imagined. With my bedroll tied to my head, I must have looked quite ridiculous, perhaps as if protecting myself from a falling meteorite, but I was able to splash through the vigorous stream to the other side to go on with my trek.

In light of what happened just a short time later, in retrospect I regarded the stream in the light of a warning and as a hurdle, so much was my future determined by my decision to cross the stream, though I did not know at the time that this was my Rubicon.

Chapter Eight—I Am Utterly Astonished

I passed the next day walking onward, tacking gently back and forth from the beach up to the inland in my explorations. I came upon another huge tortoise and found a plant I thought might be taro. I had not brought my botany book, so I put some of the leaves in my pack to identify them later and set up a marker at the spot where I found them.

Towards the late afternoon, my favorite time of day, when the sun sheds a rich golden light, I came upon a piece of ground that rose quite precipitously above the beach and thought it would afford me a most spectacular view of the sunset, so I put down my small bundle and made a little nest by a coconut palm that was also kind enough to provide me with my supper. I often remembered how my brother Tom had told me that heaven was furnished with many painters who had led good lives, and each evening God chose one of them to create the sunset. Whoever had the task this evening was making a splendid show of scarlet and orange-feathered stripes.

As I sat in admiration I saw upon the ocean some dark moving objects, which, of course, riveted my attention. With great excitement, I watched as they drew closer and grew larger. I saw that they were canoes of the same style I had seen five years ago, and their approach filled me with apprehension. I did not so much fear for my own safety as I dreaded witnessing more murders. I quickly turned over what I ought to do. I could retreat to the interior and would most certainly avoid these people and the carnage they might perform before me. However, my curiosity won over my caution and I stayed where I was. Luckily, in the intervening years I had schooled Roger to be silent when I bid him to be, and so he obeyed my command now and lay quite still beside me as I stretched stomach-first on the ground that overlooked the beach. I unwrapped my pistol and readied it and the powder and balls I would need to reload it, hoping strongly that I would have no occasion to use it. Roger made a low growl. "Hush!" I said and he obeyed.

By this time one of the canoes, of which there were two, had reached the shallow water and their crew had jumped into it to drag the craft to shore. I could see one captive bound in the bottom of the canoe, and he was pulled roughly from it onto the beach and then ignored as the others, nine altogether, dragged driftwood into a heap and built a fire. As the fire blazed up, they consumed a beverage they had brought in gourds. Again there was an older fellow who seemed to be the chief, wearing elaborate adornments of feathers and shells.

The men gradually grew more heated in their conversation and at last dragged their captive into their circle. The whole group grew quieter then, and each man in turn rose to address the captive, which they did in very reasonable tones. To me it seemed that they were in some way apologizing to him, so gently did they address him. He was himself quite calm and seemed to accept their apologies. At one point he said something that made them all laugh, and his expression made me think that he had purposely made a joke, as if he were at pains to make the others easier about murdering him.

As I watched this scene I was increasingly uncomfortable with the role of observer I had assigned myself, as I was very much struck with the noble bearing of the intended victim and how he conducted himself with such grace. I wondered what sort of crime he could have committed to warrant his execution.

Suddenly, one of the men who had hung back while the others expressed their apologies came forward and harshly yelled at the victim, then spit on the ground, at which point the others reluctantly raised their spears. I realized the murder was about to begin and also that I did not want it to. Something about this man had laid hold of me, and I wanted to save him. In an instant I grabbed up my pistol and fired it into the air. All the men looked around them in stricken fright and yelled mightily. I reloaded as quickly as I could, and while they yelled at each other and rushed about trying to determine what was happening, I fired again, and this time I aimed so that the ball struck one of them in the leg.

The sight of their screaming compatriot bleeding on the ground sent the rest of them flying towards the canoes, though one paused to drag his wounded fellow into the boat as well. Their intended victim had meanwhile taken the opportunity to run off down the beach as fast as he could. I loaded my pistol again and shot it once more to encourage the frenzied rowing that was rapidly taking the canoes away from the beach. I had one more ball that I quickly loaded. I put in my powder, but did not shoot again.

In a short time the canoes had disappeared from view; the beach was as quiet as it had been just an hour ago, and the last vestiges of the sun were disappearing above the horizon. A great deal had changed for me, however. For the first time in five years, I knew another human being was with me on the island. Though I did not know exactly where he was nor if our potential meeting would be amicable, and despite my extreme nervousness, I was determined that I would try to find him and show him that I was willing to befriend him.

With this aim in mind, I decided to make a show of myself on the beach so that he might easily see me before I could see him. So I called Roger and we went down to the fire the natives had made and rekindled it into a blaze. I sat down by it and waited, keeping watch into the darkness around me. I sat there all night, but the man did not show himself, and if he had kept running he could have been very far away by now.

In the morning I went back up the bluff in search of a coconut for my breakfast, still vigilant in observation. I split two coconuts and ate from one of them. The other I took back down to the beach and left on a rock; then I continued walking onward away from my camp. I hoped that if the man were observing me he would know that I had purposely left the coconut for him. I even yelled in what I hoped was a friendly voice, "Here's some food for you. Please come out. I will not hurt you." I figured he would interpret the tone of my language if not its exact content.

Then I began a leisurely walk down the beach in the direction I had been pursuing the previous days and in which I had seen the escapee running the evening before. I was demonstrating an attitude of nonchalance that was quite far from what I really felt as I carefully scanned the surroundings. I hoped my intuition about him was correct and that he was not a terrible felon.

In the afternoon I came to another small stream and followed it up a short ways to a shaded grotto in which there was a small waterfall similar to the one close by my camp. There was a series of lovely flat rocks invitingly surrounding it as if they had been divans. I chose the one that gave me the broadest view of the surroundings and sat down to rest upon it. I had taken off my hat, unbound my hair and was running my fingers through it in a vain effort to straighten it when I saw the man emerge from the woods at the far edge of the little grotto about forty feet away. Roger set up a great racket of barking. "Hush, Roger," I said, and like the excellent dog he was, he did, though he remained very alert throughout the coming exchange. "Hello!" I said loudly towards the man, but as mildly as I could, though I put my hand on the loaded pistol in my belt as well.

The man stood upright and said something that, of course, I did not understand, but he said it in a tone much like that I had used towards him. So I waved for him to come closer and said, "It was me that fired the pistol last night. I'm sorry it was so startling, but it seemed that you needed saving." As he drew nearer I was again struck with the man's easy gravity, his relaxed but alert bearing. He had high cheekbones in a large face with a slightly hooked narrow nose. His whole body was a dark golden brown clad only in a loincloth. He was, I thought, exceedingly handsome in a very foreign way.

At last he was close enough that we could look into each other's eyes, which we both did with enormous intensity, trying to read as much as we could about the other and our own relative safety. His eyes were sharp and black. I wondered if he had ever seen such as my green ones and what he thought of them. I smiled at him and gave a short bow. He did the same, and we both relaxed a bit. I laid one of the yellow tube fruits down on the rock at a distance as far from me as I could reach and motioned an offer of it to him. He smiled again and came over to the rock. He sat down, picked it up, peeled and quickly ate it in a most polite way. I just kept smiling.

"My name is Roberta," I said. I pointed at myself and said, "Roberta," wondering if he would know that I was indicating my name. I thought he might think I was saying my nationality or even my sex. He repeated it as something that sounded to me like "Woberra." I pointed at him with a question in my eyes, so he pointed to himself and said something that sounded to me like "Freeman," but when I repeated this back to him, he chuckled a bit, so I figured that I must have mushed or mangled his name as he had mine.

Then he said something that I heard as a question, but could understand nothing else of it. He looked pensive, then began acting out his query. He mimed a person asleep who awakens suddenly; then he filled his cheeks with air and rapidly expelled it very noisily while waving his arms, which I took to be his representation of an explosion and divined that he was asking me if I had let off the shots the previous night. I nodded yes. He raised his eyebrows and nodded too. Then he raised his hand to his chest and moved it outward, palm down and said something that I took to be "Thank you." I smiled and nodded again.

After another pause he placed another query. He pointed to the sun, then drew a circle on the ground, then mimed sleeping and waking a number of times in rapid succession. I took him to be asking how long I had been on the island, so I ran my finger around the circle he had made on the ground five times. He nodded and looked at me hard as though lots of thoughts were cantering through his mind.

I drew a crude picture of a ship in the sand. Then I assaulted the ship with sandy waves and made the noises of a storm. I pointed to myself and then to the ship and made as if my finger where a passenger on it representing me and I flung myself overboard. I then acted myself floating in the water and thrown up on the beach. As I made my

116

theatrical narration I kept glancing at him to see if he were following, and he seemed not only to be doing so, but to be enjoying it.

Then I pointed at him and motioned around to indicate the island and looked quizzically at him to ask why he was here. He put his head back, sighed and looked up at the sky as if to say, "That's a long story." I could see him weighing how to relate it. Finally, he poked his finger in the ground a number of times, making a series of marks very close together. Then he made one such poke much further away and pointed to himself. I took him to be portraying himself as at odds with his tribe. I already knew this. What I wanted to know was why they were at odds, but our limited form of communication apparently could not convey it.

We were quiet for some time. I wondered whether I should take him back to my camp or whether I should further plumb his trustworthiness before I did so. Just then he jumped up and gave me a sign that said "Please wait." He went over to the pool by the waterfall and slipped into it as easily if he were himself part water creature. He positioned himself where the pool ran into a stream that itself eventually rippled down to the sea. He stood there entirely still, gazing down into the water for quite some time, making me very curious if he had perhaps fallen into a trance. Suddenly he thrust downward with his arms and brought up from the water a medium-sized fish, flapping and wriggling. He turned to me with a look of glee, grasping the struggling fish. I clapped and made appreciative noises and was truly quite astonished as I had never seen anyone catch a fish barehanded before. In fact, I had had very little success doing so with a line and pole.

He knocked the fish out with a quick rap against a rock and then began gathering wood, which I took as a sign that he meant to cook the fish, so I helped. When he began to twirl one stick upon another against some dry grass, I took my flint and steel out of my knapsack and struck some sparks to light the fire. It was Freeman's turn to be amazed. He didn't act as if he had never seen this before, but as though such a thing were not a common sight for him.

When our little fire had died away to coals, Freeman thrust a stick into the fish's mouth and through its body, which he then held over the fire to roast. When it was done, he carefully unskewered the fish upon a large leaf, broke it open and deftly stripped out the bones all in one piece. He motioned for me to eat, which I did with relish.

As we ate, we occasionally looked up at each other, conducting further assessments. I wondered how he saw me. Did he recognize me as someone from the old world? Did that have meaning for him? Did he even recognize me as a woman? What were the women he knew like? I wondered what he thought his future was.

I wanted very badly to communicate with him and decided during our first meal together that I would try to learn his language and try to teach him mine if he were willing. So I drew another picture of the sun in the sand, pointed at it and said "Sun." He looked a bit puzzled, so I again pointed and said the name "Sun." Then he got it and himself said, "Sun." Then he said something that sounded like "Talu," so I repeated that, and he looked pleased. Then I pointed to the space around the sun in the drawing and at the actual sky and said its name. He said, "Sky" and then told me the name in his language. "Ornay" In this way over the afternoon we learned a number of words together and were able to speak of some of life's most important features in our first conversation—the sun, the sky, the moon and the ocean.

I still felt wary but I did not feel afraid. I also felt warmed by the presence of another person in a way that the golden sunlight of the island had never warmed me. Even in England I had never before so much enjoyed the company of another person, even though Freeman and I shared only tiny fragments of language. I suppose this was because I had been so long deprived of company that I appreciated it more than I ever had before.

I was very tired as the day drew to a close, as I had not slept the night before, but I was still wary enough to wonder if I could safely sleep with Freeman by me. I suppose he wondered the same thing. I further wondered if in his assessments of me he had decided whether or not he was stronger than I and if he would be able to overpower me. I wondered the same thing. We were roughly the same size as he was shorter than most Englishmen. I had grown quite strong as a result of my exertions upon the island, but I had little training in actual fighting, most of it consisting of fending off the horseplay of my brothers, though that was often quite rough.

At last Freeman mimed to me that he would sleep and he gathered and mounded up two heaps of brush and leaves about twenty feet apart. He tramped about in his in a very purposeful way and cupped his hand at his ear, meaning, I thought, to show me that if he were to move in his heap, he would make lots of noise. I was sensible of his tact in showing me that I would have warning were he to leave his heap and approach me, though I thought he might easily avoid making so much noise if he chose to. I also felt well guarded by Roger's presence. He had not yet bestowed his trust on Freeman and stayed close by my side. Freeman finally walked a ways into the woods to relieve himself, I assumed, and I did the same. We then settled into what for me was an uneasy, but expectant sleep.

Chapter 9 — What a Mess!

I awoke with a start at first light and quickly looked over to see Freeman still sleeping, resting on his side with his back to me. He had been very amiable the previous day and had made no attempt to molest me during the night, but one day's acquaintance with someone so utterly unknown to me was not enough to gain my trust, despite the winning openness of his looks, so I remained watchful and cautious and kept my pistol always by me.

As I washed myself by the pond, Freeman awoke and sat up to face me with a sleepy countenance. He stretched hugely and said what I took to be a greeting. We ate some more yellow fruit together, and then I motioned that I was going to continue on down the beach and waved for him to join me, hoping he would see that I was asking for his company, not commanding him to accompany me. He readily assented and we went forward, and so, for the first time on the island, I had a companion. Freeman seemed amused by all the gear I had strapped to me, and, indeed, compared to his virtual nakedness, I was quite swathed. I wanted to explain that my fair skin could not withstand the sun, but this notion was too complex for our rudimentary mutual language. However, we continued to ameliorate this deficiency as we had the day before by exchanging words for the things we pointed out to or drew for each other. Most of all, however, there seemed a mutuality of understanding brought about by our emotional responses to our surroundings—we shared through facial expressions and tones of voice our delight in Roger's capering and nosing into giant seaweed strewn about the beach. Freeman seemed to enjoy the beauty of our surroundings as much as I did, and I felt a keen pleasure and relief in sharing this.

When we came upon more tide pools wherein the mysterious star-like creatures and the fat tubes lay, Freeman gestured for my attention and with a stick gently poked one of the fringed tubes, at which it instantly closed up. Freeman looked up expectantly to see my reaction, and I obliged him by grinning, though I had created this same effect myself on an earlier occasion. He seemed very glad to have given me pleasure.

After a morning of trekking along the beach we rested in a palm grove. Freeman went off and was gone some time. When he came back he carried a most beautiful white flower. He handed it to me and again made the hand gesture I took to be one of gratitude that he had made the previous evening. I presumed he was again thanking me for saving his life and I bowed. Freeman then pointed at the flower and then at me, as if to say that I was like the flower. I do not think I have ever in my life blushed as I did then. I was so flustered I could only shake my head nervously and murmur "Thank you." I got up and again began walking, not looking at Freeman.

In England I would know what it meant if a man gave me a flower and told me I was like it, but for all I knew, in Freeman's country this might be a gesture one makes to one's mother. I could not tell exactly how old Freeman was, but he seemed to be of somewhat the same age as myself, but then again, I could not know how he would perceive my own age. As we walked along, I marveled at my line of thought, that I would be concerned about whether or not a naked savage was courting me. This was the first time I had thought of him as a savage, but that was certainly what everyone I knew would have called the almost naked man beside me. Perhaps I had been too friendly because of my loneliness.

Freeman sensed my withdrawal, but did not seem troubled by it and little by little I regained my composure, and we again began to exchange names and words and to practice them, though I resolved to keep a close rein on my urge to create a friendship with this deeply unknown human being. At the same time I decided to take him back to my campsite, which perhaps belied my previous resolution.

When we stopped for the evening, I tried to explain that we were going round the island and would eventually come to my home, though this latter notion was hard to convey. What sign would mean home to Freeman? At last I settled on representing a ring with a flame leaping up in it as my sign. Freeman nodded eagerly and his face showed that he had considered if I had a permanent place or if I wandered along the beach all the time. It was arresting that he had not made an effort to ask me where we were going, and he certainly acted as if it did not matter to him. As yet I could not know if this were an habitual attitude or if his escape from death had put him on a permanent holiday.

By the time we had gone all the way around the island, Freeman and I had established an ease with one another, and I began to look forward to showing him my homestead, which we gained on the sixth day after I had left it. As we approached, I saw that Freeman slowed his gait, noting, I imagined, that the environs showed the marks of human hands, and he looked very curiously at the pots and baskets I had left lying here and there. As we left the beach and went towards my cave, we passed my midden, which seemed greatly to interest him, perhaps as it gave evidence of how long I had been here. He would have paused many times as we went towards the cave, but I thought to take him straight home and later try to explain the things he saw.

Soon Miss Higgins bobbed down the path to meet us and rubbed her cloudy grey self against my legs in greeting. Freeman's eyes grew wide to see her, his look of wonder making me think that cats were not common amongst his people. He reached out his hand to touch her, and she obliged him by arching her back and beginning to purr, at which he laughed with delight.

I led him through the little maze of trees I had let stand before my cave and into the clearing directly in front of it, which for some time I had been paving with smooth stones and shells so that the daily rains would not make a muddy slough of my front door. I drew back the canvas I had fastened across the entrance and made a sweeping gesture that I hope said, "Welcome to my home!" I am sure it had a great deal of pride of ownership in it; compared to the dwellings of England mine was humble indeed, but to me it represented an enormous amount of work and its comfortable reward.

Given Freeman's reaction I might well have been showing him a house on the moon, so amazed was he and full of admiration. He pointed all around to this and that, which I took to be his asking if I had made all this, to which I nodded yes. He examined my table and chair and looked with wonder at the feather bed. I plumped it with my hand, sat on it and motioned to him to do so as well. He sat down, bounced a bit and grinned. As he fingered the red and yellow damask that I had hung against the wall, I thought that it would not have gotten any more admiring attention had it ended up draping Leora's windows as it was meant to. It did cross my mind that Freeman had seen how proud I was of my home and was perhaps exaggerating the part of the admiring guest so as to please me. Whatever the source of his reaction, it did please me and spurred me to show him all I had done.

He would have spent a long time examining my tools, and later he did so, but now I waved for him to follow me out of the cave and led him up to my garden. Not much was in season as I had harvested most of its produce before I left on my exploratory holiday, but the fence around it was impressive, and Freeman chattered a great deal in his language as he went round it, though he began with a long "Ah!" that was an unmistakable sign of approval.

At last he cupped his hands together and acted as though he were drinking from them, then looked at me in question, so I led him up to the pond and waterfall above the field, passing one of the goat pens on the way. Later, when we could talk with each other more easily, Freeman told me that when he first saw my encampment, he had thought that I had wealth beyond that of a great chief among his people, though I also came to learn that they moved around a good deal through their forest and so did not tend to accumulate goods. Also, I had the advantage of the metal tools I had taken off the ship, without which I could have done much less. When I showed Freeman my scissors and how they were used, it made me reflect on their profound assistance and of the countless times they had aided me in making things. Because I'd had so much time for reflection, I'd also thought many times of the people whose labor had made this tool—those who toiled in mines and foundries. When I contrasted their lives with those of Freeman's tribe who wandered in the forest, it seemed that the savage tribe had a freer life. Many would have said that they were nonetheless doomed by their ignorance of God's word and at least the foundry toilers would reap a heavenly reward, but this seemed to me an argument designed to stem the discontent of the foundry workers, though I never did share this opinion with anyone.

When we had seen the whole extent of my island estate, we went back to the cave, where I made a meal out of things I had grown and which I thought Freeman might never have tasted. He liked the carrots and beans very much and ate heartily of dried goat meat. The cheese he regarded with some suspicion, and I thought its texture might be unfamiliar to him. Our dessert was grapes with which he seemed wholly familiar.

As we ate, I wondered where I ought to lodge him, for I certainly did not intend to share my bed with him, though thinking of this threw me into a confusion I could not explain. I wondered if Freeman expected to sleep with me, or even if he thought of it at all. When we finished our meal, the light was dimming, so I took some canvas, a coverlet, and a cushion over to the lean-to I had made to house my loom and there made a bed, as Freeman watched me curiously. I waved him to his bed. "Good night," I said, bowed and went back into my cave. He readily understood me and lay down, though I saw that he did not use the cushion.

I could not go to sleep for a long time as I was awash with feeling. I was both excited and frightened beyond what seemed reasonable in the circumstance. At last I fell asleep and into a most unseemly dream of Freeman and I embracing, and I awoke in a great shame that further perplexed me so that for a while I did not behave naturally towards Freeman as I had in the previous days. I set myself to regain my former peace of mind through taking up my life of work. Freeman accompanied me, and if there were something heavy to lift, he would help me, but mostly he acted as an observer and as a guest, though all the while we continued our mutual language lessons. While in the very beginning of our tutelage we had been as infants, only naming things, we soon needed words for actions, and so our expression progressed. Hardest of all were words for notions that had no physical counterpart, so our discourse was in the main practical in its initial stages.

One day when I arose Freeman was gone and so was Roger, which disquieted me a bit though I went on with my own routine. In the early afternoon, as I was working in the garden, they returned with two rabbits hanging from a pole over Freeman's shoulder. "You are a hunter!" I said enthusiastically. Freeman stood taller and offered me the game, which I accepted with much gratitude. I set about cleaning them, but Freeman motioned that he would do it, and he did, so quickly and skillfully that I wondered if he had stopped me because he was offended by my graceless efforts. For Roger this outing had cemented his acceptance of Freeman. Miss Higgins had already been easily won by his willingness to pet her endlessly.

Gradually, a routine developed in which Freeman would spend his mornings away from me, usually returning with some kind of game or fish that he had caught. He never offered to assist me with my farming or goat herding, though he would help if I asked for his assistance with something more easily done with more strength than my own. This made me wonder if among his people, labor was apportioned so that women attended to agriculture and men to hunting. Eventually, I was able to ask this and found that it was indeed that way. In fact, I learned that Freeman was going over the line established among his people in helping me at all, though as our time together stretched out, he helped more often, especially after the cataclysm I will soon relate.

I was very interested in how he hunted, and though he seemed a bit surprised at my interest, he showed me a series of clever snares and traps and eventually he made a bow and arrows and used them to hunt. His fishing depended more upon the agility he demonstrated the day we met, and I knew I could never match it.

In the afternoons, Freeman did not work much, though he often went off on treks and urged me to go with him. At first it seemed to me that I ought to be working, but over time, I realized that I did not need to work as hard as I had been and that perhaps I had done so previously to offset my loneliness, so I began to take on more of the rhythm Freeman showed and became more as a "lily of the field." It struck me as ironic that I had criticized so much in Bunyan and Piers Plowman, but never their admonitions to work hard all the time.

One day we were taking our ease in the shade of the pavilion up at the grapelands, sitting together on the bench, when Freeman eyed me curiously, then reached over and put his hand into my shirt, grasping my breast firmly. I was most shocked and roughly pushed his hand away, at which he smiled and chuckled. I got off the bench with the intention to hurry back to the cave, but he grabbed me from behind and tackled me down onto the grassy ground. I squirmed and fought him, but he held me down and worked his hand into my pants and went to my sex. I violently wrenched myself away from him, scrambled to my feet and fled with all my speed to the cave, where I grabbed up the pistol from its hiding place with the intention to shoot him if he should he arrive.

My intense alertness wilted eventually, as he did not come back for the rest of that day nor the next, during which I tumbled through an array of outrage and hurt. How could Freeman attack me that way when we had become such good friends? Did he think I would welcome such an overture? Had I acted lewdly? It occurred to me that the way he had chuckled after he'd grasped my breast had about it something like satisfaction, as if I were behaving in the expected way. I had lost all my fear of him, but now he had revived it.

On the third day, as I was breakfasting, I saw him coming back. As he approached, I saw him register the pistol that lay beside me. We did not greet each other, and he sat down ten feet away from me. His face was dark with confusion, and, I thought, with grievance. I offered him some goat meat, which he somberly accepted. When he had finished, he went off again, and I thought he meant to take up his usual morning hunting. I went up to the field where I was busy spreading goat manure and seaweed that I had hauled up from the beach.

Sometime after noon Freeman appeared at the edge of the field and waved for me to come over to him. It was a rather peremptory wave and I thought twice about hearkening to it, but did so nonetheless. When we stood face to face, Freeman dropped a rabbit at my feet, barking what sounded like a command. Most startling, he also tore off his loincloth and dropped it at my feet with another command, and then he strode off, completely naked.

I had looked away when he'd denuded himself but could not help seeing his penis, dark brown with a pinkish cast to it. My brothers had made me no stranger to the looks of a penis, and I found them very interesting, though the manner of this one's revelation was shocking.

I picked up the rabbit and went to clean it. Despite the commanding tone, I would not waste food in a display of pique. However, I left the loincloth where it lay, not knowing what Freeman wanted me to do with it anyway. As I walked back to the cave, it occurred to me that perhaps he wanted me to wash it. Had he asked me in a nice way, I would no doubt have done it, but I felt no obligation to do so. Again, I wondered at the arrangements between men and women in Freeman's country.

When I got back to the cave, Freeman was not there. I rooted about among the clothing I had taken off the ship, found the captain's buff trousers and a shirt and took them with me, hoping to meet Freeman and offer him the garments. I went towards the beach and found him sitting on a rock overlooking the ocean, his broad brown face a scowl. I held out the clothing to him. He looked at it confusedly, but took the shirt, which he tore into a length he then wrapped about himself to form a new loincloth. I was a bit chagrined at the destruction of a good shirt, but did not feel I needed to impose a wardrobe on one who was native to these environs.

I suppose my Christian duty was to make Freeman aware of his nakedness, but I was already so poor a Christian that I reckoned this lapse would weigh little in the ultimate scale. Anyway, I could not wrestle Freeman into any clothes and our language had not yet advanced enough for me to make an argument with him. He still seemed very offended and disagreeable, which puzzled me as I believed myself to be the aggrieved party after his attack on me, and yet I had softened and brought him these clothes.

Then I made a mistake that made the whole thing worse. Meaning to put us together again, I gestured that I was shoveling in the field and asked him to come help me, at which he burst out with a loud oration, whose particulars I could not understand, but whose substance seemed to be anguish and confusion at my continued impositions on him. I shrugged and went back to the field in much confusion myself. As I shoveled I marveled at how we had come to this pass, as it seemed we had been getting on so well and enjoying each other's company greatly, though I experienced waves of feelings towards him that confused me. I wanted to draw him closer to me and push him away at the same time. It occurred to me that perhaps Freeman felt this way as well.

Over the next few days, we kept our distance, though I found that I was no longer angry about the attack and became convinced that Freeman felt himself to be misunderstood. To this time I had never seen the hesitations and furrowed brow that now characterized him and which reminded me of when I had seen people wrestling with some conundrum. It was not at all clear to me what conundrum Freeman was wrestling with, though it obviously involved me and our relation to each other.

Whatever it was that was bothering Freeman went very deep as one morning I found him lying in his bed, looking very ill and feverish. I set about boiling some of the willow bark into a tea. He descended further until he was barely conscious, and I was very worried; I fed him as much tea as he would take. I fetched more bedding from the cave and covered him to still his shivering. For three days I tended him as he alternately raved and trembled or lay as still as death. He yelled a good deal and seemed to be in a heated argument. I was sorely afraid he might die and found myself greatly troubled by the prospect of losing him despite our recent estrangement. I wanted desperately to keep him alive, but had little to offer him but my constant presence and a rotation of cool cloths upon his brow. "Please don't die, Freeman," I begged. I held his hand and talked to him as much as I could.

At last his fever broke and he slept, though whatever had ravaged him would require some time to repair. When he again awoke in his right mind, he looked at me at first with wonder and then with a great tenderness that grew over the days I fed him and sat by him as he regained his strength.

I had to absent myself from his bedside from time to time to attend to our food and to the goats, and one day as I was up in the grapelands to gather some fruit, I came across a plant bearing white flowers like the one Freeman had given me on our second day together. I plucked one and took it back to our camp, where Freeman was propped up against some cushions. He smiled as I approached. I proffered the flower to him, then pointed at it and at him as he had done when he gave the flower to me, saying in my gesture that he was like the flower, just as he had said to me. How I wish I could have recorded all the expressions that passed over his face when I did this! Some reprised those he had worn in the stormy days before his illness; others I had never seen on him before, but I liked them as they seemed reflections of some sort of new wisdom of a kind I could not fathom.

Freeman thanked me, looked thoughtful, and then drew on the ground the group of marks we had come to agree represented his tribe. But this time he then drew a line down the middle, pointed to one half and then at himself and drew a stick figure with a large appendage at its middle. I understood this was a penis and flushed scarlet. Then he drew breasts upon a figure on the other side, and I knew he was dividing the tribe into men and women. I nodded. He pointed at the women's side of his drawing and then at me and shook his head. I took him to mean that I was not like them. I imagine I looked a little downcast at this because I did not know if this were a good thing or a bad one in his eyes. I just nodded.

Then I made a similar drawing representing my own tribe and denoted the division of the sexes with the penis and breasts as he had done. I pointed at him and at the men of my tribe and made as if to say that they were the same in being strong, but also not the same in other ways. I think Freeman understood me because he pointed to the women's side of his own tribe and then at me and made a some caressing gestures with his hands and he pointed and looked with admiration at the flower, which reassured me that he thought I shared some of the characteristics of the women he was used to. For the first time it occurred to me to wonder if Freeman were married. He was certainly of an age to be, and I was aghast that I had not before considered such an important datum, but had thought of him only in relation to myself.

I took his hand and interlaced my fingers with his at which he chuckled, a sound that had something in it of the chuckle he had made when he attacked me. I was then emboldened to ask a question that involved making a gesture I had never before made in my life and which would have made Lady Evelyn drop dead on the spot. I made a circle with my thumb and forefinger and pointed at both women's sides in our drawings. Then I pointed at the men's sides and poked the index finger of my other hand into the circle and moved it back and forth. Freeman smiled very broadly and seemed a bit embarrassed himself, as I most certainly was, though I persisted. I pointed again at his tribe and moved my hands up and down, back and forth to indicate a certain violence. I also had one hand run towards the other and tackle it, as Freeman had tackled me. I meant to ask if sexual relations in his tribe featured this kind of activity. A great light went on for him then and he nodded vigorously. He pointed at my tribe and asked if it were the same for us.

This was a hard question for me since I had not actually had sexual relations, but I knew the chasing down part was not generally approved of, and I knew I would much prefer a gentler approach, so I said no. This set Freeman to nodding as though this fact explained a good deal to him. "Ah. . . ," he breathed, then paused and seemed to sink into himself. After a bit, he looked me full on and bowed his head, then raised it and lightly rapped himself on the face, and said a string of things I took to mean, "I'm so sorry. I was so stupid!" I bowed as well to say I accepted his apology, and I pointed to his tribe and made a gesture that tried to say that I didn't know their customs, at which he bowed.

That evening he was strong enough that we sat over the beach to watch the sunset. I spoke to him in the basic language we had learned of each other as I drew in the sand what I meant to be the ocean and the sky, a mere line of the horizon, a bird to say sky and a shell to say land. Then I drew a short arc over the horizon and pointed downward to mean the setting sun. Then I pointed behind me. Freeman nodded. Then I again pointed at the sun and this time pointed upwards to mean sunrise. He nodded and himself pointed ahead to say the future. We both nodded.

Then Freeman gestured again at the sun drawing and pointed up; then he pointed at both of us, and I hoped he was saying we were new, like the rising sun.

Chapter 10 — We Join and Plan a Hunt

While Freeman regained his strength, he stayed close to me and helped me as much as he could. Once, as I was teaching him how to milk a goat, I asked him if they had goats among his people. He told me no, but drew a fair representation of a pig as if to say they had them instead of goats. I then related to him the tale of the attack of the boar upon my garden. This interested him a great deal and seemed to plant an idea in him, though it worried me to think of his going after a boar. Already I could not bear to think of losing him.

As he helped me with various chores, I often wondered if men of his tribe did whatever task we were doing. Because we so often wanted to know about the customs or doings of the other's people, we had established a permanent representation of our tribes beside where we usually ate, consisting of small sticks stuck in the ground, instead of the finger pokes in the sand we had started with. When I asked him if the men of his tribe did particular activities, sometimes he answered that they did, but more often that they did not, which led me to believe that his men were either quite lazy or very privileged to be waited upon by their women. But then I reflected on my five brothers' reliance upon my work and my life of constant attendance upon Lady Evelyn and Leora and had to laugh at my judgment of Freeman's tribe. Freeman himself never struck me as lazy, though he was generally relaxed and easy-going. There was one thing he absolutely refused to do, however—his own laundry, but since it consisted of a loincloth only, I took it on with no feeling of resentment. I decided not to regard it as symbolic and not to care whether he did or not.

Freeman was very curious about all the things I'd brought off the ship, many of which he had obviously never seen before. The few books I had were especially curious to him. He first examined them as objects, turning over the red-bound Bunyan, holding it open, then hefting the *Piers Plowman* and riffling its pages with delight. The gold-tinted edges of the Bible drew his admiration as well. The books' contents, the endless lines of black marks upon each page made him shake his head. I began to read to him from the page, and he quickly understood that the marks on the page corresponded to words. "My tribe has no pictures of our language," he said, which astonished me, as I had never thought of language without writing. Freeman wanted to learn to read, and so I began to teach him. He regarded it as a fine game and laughed often when we were about it.

Over the course of a few months, we learned a great deal of each other's languages and were increasingly able to talk in our unique patois, which further eroded the loneliness that had been my lot for five years. There was a great deal of mutual enlightenment in this learning process, I think. I learned that having a name for something makes one perceive it. For example, Freeman's language had many terms for the dream states, such as the vivid dream one feels indelibly, but which quickly fades upon awakening.

Our language learning was also humorous. Freeman made many mistakes in his English, but I was sure my use of his language was also filled with errors. As I write here I am not representing these errors of his because to do so would make him seem silly and immature, when, in fact, he was neither. In fact, he was a very curious man who enjoyed learning.

Freeman asked many questions about England and my life there. I answered as best I could, but eventually brought out the embroideries I had made of scenes of the farm I grew up on and of Lady Evelyn's manor where I had spent nine years of my life. These scenes, as crudely as they were represented in thread, nonetheless quite fascinated Freeman, who posed many questions based on them. He pointed at the barn pictured in one scene and asked, "What is in it?" I told him of the animals and the hay to feed them. He knew of horses and cattle, but his tribe did not have any of them.

Of course, he asked me if I had been married and was much surprised and troubled when I said I had not been. Later I found out that an unmarried woman was completely unknown in his tribe, where each woman belonged to some man who was obligated to care for her. So that no woman would be alone, some men had more than one wife. This seemed like a reasonable practice to me as long as the woman was not forced to affiliate with a man if she did not want to. When I asked about this, Freeman looked quite shocked and told me that such a case had never arisen in his tribe. In mine, I said, it was not common, but neither was it unusual, as in my own case. He listened very carefully to my explanation of why I had not married.

Of course, the first thing I asked Freeman at the point when I thought he could fully answer me was why his tribe had wanted to kill him. It turned out that this custom of taking on unwanted women was at the root of it. As was the practice among his tribe, he had been married early, as soon as he was old enough to participate in a boar hunt. "She died in childbirth," he told me, apparently being not much more than a child herself. He said this in a way that told me he missed her still and I was touched with his sorrow. After her death, the chief demanded that Freeman take as his wife the chief's daughter, an ugly woman who compounded her lack of physical charm with a bitter and venomous character. She had already been married twice within the tribe, but had refused to stay with either husband. Freeman's refusal of the chief's order was the cause of his death sentence, and the other men's sympathy with his refusal to take her accounted for their reluctance to carry out the sentence.

Since our misunderstanding about Freeman's first sexual approach to me, he had not touched me again in that way. Again and again I went back over how he had put his hand on my breast and I began to wish that I hadn't pushed it away. Then I felt confused and wondered what was happening to me. I would now and again hear the echo of Lady Evelyn, who I had made to represent the voice of civilized society, saying "Roberta, he is an uneducated savage! How could you stoop so low?" I argued with this voice: "He may not be civilized in an English sense, but he is intelligent and sensitive, and he warms my heart. I'm all alone and I like him!"

When I had at last shut up Lady Evelyn's disapproving voice, I was left with much musing on how I could let Freeman know that I wanted him to touch me, but not in the way that he had at first. I didn't even know if they exchanged kisses among his people. Nor as my thoughts grew bolder did I shy away from considering the possible child that could result from a sexual union between us.

Though I had pored over this a great deal, I had come up with no strategy, but eventually my body spoke for me. One night as we rested by the fire, I simply asked him if the men and women of his tribe put their mouths together. He smiled broadly and his eyes lit up as he slowly nodded yes. I told him that we called this "kissing" and that among my people a woman would never ask a man to kiss her, but that the man might ask a woman and she might agree. He digested this, then looked at me and said, "I want to kiss with you." "Yes, I want it too," I answered, whereupon he moved very close and put his soft lips against mine very gently. I put my hand around his neck, caressed him, and kissed him back as gently, though with increasing pressure and desire. He responded in kind, though at every step I could feel his reticence at possibly offending me. "You show me," he said.

I got up from the fire and led him into my cave where I gestured for him to lie down on the bed, which he did with the leisurely grace I had come to admire so much and that excited me. He lay on his side with his head on his arm and watched as I undressed. I had never done this before, so I was nervous but I felt no shame. I knew my body was strong and I hoped it showed the rosy pleasure I was feeling. I took off my shirt and showed him my rounded breasts, my nipples large and dark. "Ahh. . . " he breathed. He took in my hips and my sex as I took off my pants, and because I enjoyed him watching me, I did it slowly. The feelings rolling over my body terrified and delighted me. I felt myself an explorer in all respects.

I lay down beside him on the bed and we again began to kiss. I placed his hand on my breast and rolled his finger across my nipple, a lesson he immediately applied to the other. Then with no prompting from me he kissed my breast and took one nipple in his mouth while he rolled the other with his fingers. My sex began to throb, so I took his hand and put it between my legs, rolling his finger softly over me as I had done to myself so many times. How utterly delightful it was!

I saw that Freeman's loincloth rose at an odd angle. As he fingered me, making slow forays further down into me, I pulled his loincloth away and saw his penis, brown and dark pink and full. When I took hold of it, he groaned, so I withdrew my hand, thinking I might have hurt him. But he took my hand and put it back on his member. I rubbed the shaft up and down, amazed at its simultaneous smoothness and hardness. I felt for his testicles and he groaned again, but this time I did not withdraw but went on feeling their novel and delicious texture.

At last I so craved him to enter me that I rolled onto my back and drew him forward. He put the tip of his penis at the edge of my vagina and pushed forward with a gentle but sure pressure, but could not penetrate me. "It's my first time, " I said, at which he looked utterly amazed and then very pleased. "I don't want to hurt you," he said. "But you must," I said. "Every woman must hurt her first time." And so Freeman pushed into me, but I was like an underground spring and eased his way so that I forgot the pain and felt him within me with the greatest pleasure. Thus we began the ride of love, the dance of love, the journey of love, the array of physical sensations for which even the greatest poet can find no good metaphor.

When we were spent, we lay together for a long time not speaking. At last Freeman said, "Why have you been a virgin for so long?" I explained that I had not wanted to have a baby and so had avoided intercourse and that, at least in polite society, it was considered wrong to do it before marriage. "Among my people it is common to see if the woman can conceive before marrying her," he said. "Some people do it that way among the English as well," I replied.

From that point on my misgivings withdrew behind the strength of my pleasure and though from time to time Lady Evelyn's face would float before me wearing an expression of utter disapproval and I would feel a hot shame, this faded as well. Freeman and I now always slept together in my bed and made love countless times. Sometimes we did it by the waterfall after bathing; sometimes in the arbor up at the grapelands. I grew to know every inch of his smooth brown body and to love him more than I can express. I think he felt the same way about me. He marveled at my breasts, which, he told me, were much bigger than those of his countrywomen. He frequently kissed my rear end, kneaded it in his hands and then slipped his fingers forward into me, which he knew I particularly liked. Even my speech about our sex grew easier and more explicit. When I asked him if our sex was like that among his people, he thought for a moment, then said that it was basically the same, though they did not put so much thought into it or treasure it so much as we did. As can be imagined, to me this was a wonderful answer.

I think I became pregnant several times, but each time I purged myself with a course of pennyroyal and cohash, which had, curiously enough, come in the packet of herbs from Leora's trunk. This was a very rough process that first sent waves of nausea over me for several days and then great cramps accompanied by a bloody flux. There came a time, however, when I resolved if I should conceive again, I would not want to go through that process another time, not only because of the pain and the copious bleeding, but for another deeper reason that required some sustained thinking.

Did I intend to give up all hope of rescue from this island? I had early on asked Freeman if he could build a canoe like those of his tribe that had brought him here. He said he certainly could, but then asked, "Where would we go? I cannot return to my people, as once condemned,

I am always condemned." "Are there neighboring tribes who would help us?" I asked. Freeman nodded sadly. "No, they are more likely to kill us than my own people." He did not know which direction we would go in to encounter Europeans. In short, leaving the island would be a great gamble for us. The chance that I might regain my own country seemed slight indeed and, I realized, much outweighed by the pleasure of life with Freeman on the island. Once again, all my thinking on leaving the island at last came to rest on the fact that if I were to get off, someone would have to arrive to take me off.

Having a child with Freeman would certainly complicate that possibility. Myself and the babe would both be viewed as strange cases. I imagined how Lady Evelyn would assume that I had been raped, as how else could a civilized white woman have had intercourse with a savage? I could not bear to think of Freeman cast in this role, nor could I think of him in England. He might be quite ready to journey there because he was such a curious person, but I could not encourage him to do so as I knew from what heights of superiority he would be regarded by most Englishmen.

I confronted the thought that I would never again see my native land nor any of the people I loved there. This saddened me, but also clearly limned the satisfactions that I had found in my life on the island, especially with such a fine companion as Freeman had become. But if we were to have a child, or even several, what would their futures be? As half-breeds they would everywhere be suspect except on this island with their family, but how could they then marry and make families of their own?

One day I found Freeman sitting above the ocean where we usually observed the sunset. He was looking pensive and at first would not tell me why. I asked him if he missed having other people around. He said,

"I miss having children around," and went on, "I wonder why I have not planted a child in you. Do you not want our child?" he added sadly. I could not bear to tell him that I had purged myself of his seed, but his question unleashed an honest torrent of my own thinking on the subject. After hearing me out, he said, "You are thinking too much of the future. You might trust our children to figure out their own destinies when they arrive."

I heard the wisdom in this, but found his desire to please himself in the present hard to accept. Much of my life had been founded on denying my own desires, so I was unaccustomed to consulting them in depth. Now, as we sat together on the bluff, I put myself the question: If there were no considerations as to the future, would I want to have a child with Freeman?

The answer came over me as a vast wave of joyous assent so overwhelming that I began to cry and was soon sobbing in great jagged bursts. Freeman was very distressed and drew me close, trying to comfort me. I realized that I had always held having a babe of my own as a privilege I could not aspire to, that I could only participate in this joy second-hand through Leora or my brother's families. But this was not true now, though there was indeed risk involved. But there is always risk in having children, I thought—it is risky in every way imaginable.

I think Freeman was under the impression that my sadness came from not being able to have children, so he was a bit surprised when I said, "I want to have a child with you, dear Freeman, but I have been afraid to." He said, "Yes, many die in childbirth," a melancholy reference to his wife. "I'm not afraid of that part," I said, an answer that confused him. I did not think it would be useful for me to further describe my own inner landscape on this matter even if I were able to, so I simply repeated, "I want to have a child with you," adding with conviction, "no matter how dangerous." Then I kissed him, and he understood that I wanted to begin the process right then. We made long, lingering love there above the beach against the backdrop of a scarlet and lavender sunset.

In the coming days Freeman applied himself to hunting and fishing with greater vigor, so that we were always supplied with very solid food. He once pried open a giant clam that we fed upon for many days as if it were a ham. I also found him building small rock and shell cairns by the water both at the beach and by the pond, which he explained to me with some embarrassment were to insure my fertility. The embarrassment, it seems, came from the fact that it was the women of his tribe who performed these rites, but since I did not know how, he wanted to do it, even though it was an intrusion into my sphere. I told him this was superstition, which I did a poor job of explaining because he simply shrugged and went about his business. I regretted my explanation as the cairns could not harm my fertility, and if they gave comfort to Freeman, I was for them. At this time I began to wear the gold ring I had found in the chest because I had married Freeman in my heart. He reacted to this much as I had reacted to his cairns.

Freeman also set about preparing to hunt the island's boar, and though he denied it, I think he believed that vanquishing a boar would establish his own male dominance on the island and make his seed more powerful within me. He prepared a number of special spears out of very hard wood, to which he attached arrowheads chipped from stone. I suggested he lash one of our knives to a spear. He was reluctant to do so, as, I imagined, he thought this would give him an unfair advantage over the boar, but eventually he agreed to do it as an experiment.

Freeman's tribe generally hunted boar as a group and doing so alone presented additional difficulties. I very much wanted to help, not only to add to Freeman's safety, but because it seemed an exciting thing to do.

Freeman solemnly told me that among his people women do not hunt, and I replied that we were not among his people. He eventually accepted my taking part in the hunt both because he needed me and because he liked to gratify me. However, he decreed, "You will not directly confront the boar."

We packed for a trek into the interior of the island where we had seen brief glimpses of the beasts. Freeman explained that the plan was to locate some sort of natural cul-de-sac into which we could drive the boar and there kill him. If we could not find such a place, we would build one. We could also construct a sort of natural obstacle course that would lead the boar into our trap. I suggested that we could dig a pit in the cul-de-sac into which the boar would tumble as we drove him forward. Freeman said that was a good idea, but was not how the boar hunt was done. Here again I understood the hunt's symbolic value trumped practical innovation. The idea was not just to kill the boar, but to kill it in a particular way. I withheld any further suggestions and henceforth acted entirely as Freeman's assistant.

We were unable to find a spot that was ideally suited to our purposes, though we did find a small vale with steep walls on two sides that formed a right angle. Freeman thought we could build a barricade out of branches to form a third side, and we set to it. We cut a great number of saplings, sharpened their points, laid them in a row on the ground and nailed cross pieces over them to form a fence, nails being an unorthodox novelty in the process that Freeman did not reject. This fence we set upright and drove each sapling as far into the soft earth as we could. More saplings were applied as braces from the opposite side. Freeman hauled a number of rocks to stand at the foot of the braces to anchor them.

Very early the next morning, Freeman woke me and told me we must get started. He drew from the bag he had so mysteriously packed some red earth to which he added some water and mixed it in his palm. He then painted stripes diagonally across his cheeks. When he finished, he paused and looked at me, gesturing to ask if I wanted to wear paint as well. I hesitated for a moment about what this would mean, but decided I would fully participate and nodded yes. He put the red paint on my cheeks just as he had on his. Then he drew forth some chalky white earth and mixed it in the same way, applying it in circles around his eyes and mouth. He looked askance at me and I nodded, so he painted me as well.

Lady Evelyn's voice was positively screaming inside me by now. "You've become a savage yourself, Roberta! How could you enter into such a pagan ritual? Your immortal soul is in danger!" I replied that I did not believe painting my face for a hunt had anything whatever to do with my soul, such as it was. In fact, though, I did feel transformed by the paint. I felt mysteriously more warlike, more ready for combat.

Freeman said we could not eat before the hunt, that our hunger would sharpen our desire and our senses, but we should drink a good deal of water. We did so, then set out towards the wallow where we had most often seen evidence of boar. Freeman's simple plan was to station me above the wallow where I would wait until a boar approached. I was then to create a ruckus that would frighten the creature and propel it in the opposite direction, where Freeman would be waiting to beat it towards the cul-de-sac we had built. I would then travel as quickly as I could on a path above Freeman's, making further movement and noise to discourage the boar from taking off in that direction. "What if it comes after me?" I asked. "It won't," Freeman replied. "They want to avoid us and will only attack when they are cornered." "So it will attack you when we have driven it into the cul-de-sac?" I asked. "Yes, and then I will kill him," he replied evenly.

Then he said we must now be as still as we could until the moment came to begin the chase. In fifteen minutes we reached the environs of the wallow. Freeman pointed out my station, which had to be far enough away so that the boar could not catch my scent. He told me to rest there, quietly alert. I wondered then if he found me a noisy person, but, of course, did not pursue the notion.

I sat at my post for what seemed like a very long time, and my attention at times flagged as I grew interested in the surroundings, which were lushly green and studded with the brilliant purple flowers I had come to love.

At last I heard a splashing and snorting beneath me, saw a grey-brown bearded boar, and knew I must begin to play my role. The boar was much bigger that I had imagined it would be, like a small cow, its belly bulging. Its yellowed tusks were a good foot long. I screamed as loud as I could and threw the stones that Freeman had piled beside me. The boar seemed a slow fellow, but at last he looked up in alarm, his black eyes beady, then began an awkward amble away from the wallow and towards Freeman's position. I began to run as fast as I could through the terrain towards my next post. In a few minutes I heard Freeman yell and heard the boar crashing back towards my direction. It was then that I tripped and fell head first into something very hard and everything became black.

Chapter 11--Multiplication

When I swam again into consciousness, I felt a heavy weight across my body. I was face down and had to squirm forward before I could tell that it was Freeman who lay upon me, breathing very hard. He rolled off when I moved. "Freeman, dear, are you hurt? What has happened?" I cried before I had had a chance to see what was around us. I very quickly found out, for a great animal odor assaulted me, and I saw not ten feet away from us the grey-brown body of the boar, two spears stuck in him, one in his neck, the other in his chest, dark blood running from both wounds, and his yellowed tusks dripping with it. Through a haze of pain in my head and in my left arm, where I found a deep throbbing gash, I struggled to understand what had happened. Freeman was conscious but lay quite exhausted and speechless, a great bloody wound in his thigh.

I struggled out of my knapsack and took from it the bottle of spirits I had brought along. I took off my shirt and tore it into strips; they were none too clean, but were all I had for bandages. Steeling myself, I poured spirits into my wound and cried out at the great burning. Freeman murmured, "Roberta, Roberta." "Your turn is coming," I said, as I awkwardly bound my arm, knotting the cloth at the end and pulling it taut with my teeth.

I lifted the bottle to Freeman's lips so that he could drink a bit and thereby deaden the sting of what was to come. He winced as I poured on the spirits, but was quiet. After I had bound his wound, and made him prop his leg up on a tree, I cradled his head in my lap and kissed his forehead.

I surmised that when I had fallen and had not called out to drive the boar back towards Freeman, it had continued on in my direction and finding me, had begun to dispatch me, hence the gash in my arm. Not hearing my cries, Freeman must have run towards me and arrived just in time to attack the boar and prevent its killing me, though the boar had put up a fight good enough to wound Freeman as well.

When he recovered enough to speak, Freeman confirmed my theory, adding that when he came upon us, the boar was trying to turn me over, that I must have been a curious catch, so he was trying to examine what he was about to tear apart and eat. "I ran at him as fast as I could and rammed a spear into his neck," he said. "He turned and flew at me, landing this blow on my leg." Luckily, my own spear lay on the ground beside me, so Freeman grabbed it up and when the boar had turned and come back at him, Freeman crouched down, let him get very close and held the spear up as a pike on which the boar impaled himself, squealing madly in terror and ire.

I kissed Freeman again and again and told him how brave he was and thanked him for saving my life. "I owed it to you, as you have twice saved my life," he said softly.

We were much weakened by our loss of blood and our exertion, but I thought we should try to hike home as soon as possible so that I could sew up our wounds and put clean bandages on them. We also needed to eat as we had fasted before our hunt. However, to my astonishment,

Freeman refused to leave until we had butchered the boar. "We have gotten honorable wounds," he said, "and must not dishonor the boar by not eating his meat." So, after a rest, and quite slowly, with our own ravaged bodies we cut away at the boar's body, taking the choicest parts, wrapping them in leaves and stowing them in our knapsacks. Freeman had originally planned to haul the whole carcass back to camp, as he knew uses for every part of it, but he was willing to modify his plan in view of our infirmities. He seemed quite unconcerned with the possibility of infection, but I was dominated by it and as we limped homeward I planned further treatment with spirits and the application of the remains of the linen intended for Leora's bridal bed.

I had never been so glad to see our camp. I felt that we had been through a hellacious experience, but Freeman was very cheerful and light-hearted as though we had won a great triumph. This strongly reminded me of my brothers who would return from wrestling matches at the fair all bloody and unable to work for a week, but in the highest possible spirits if they had won. This always made their attitude towards me more commanding, but, luckily, Freeman showed none of that. It's a good thing too, as I would not have stood it. As soon as I had this thought, I reflected that Freeman had given me little reason to suspect him of wishing to dominate me after our initial set-to, so I wondered why I bristled so at the possibility.

The one thing about the boar hunt that was as impressive to me as it was to Freeman was boar meat. It was deliciously juicy and flavorful, and I felt much feasted and fortified by it over many days and it was a good thing too. For several weeks we were both weakened by the encounter with the animal. We did only the necessary work and rested a good deal. Gradually, though, we recovered completely from our wounds. Freeman had insisted on packing them with spider webs, which were plentiful at the back of the cave. I thought this most horrible, but they were indeed quite effective; our wounds healed well, though they left us with scars that reminded us ever after of the hunt. Freeman wore his like a medal.

We had been back several days when it occurred to me that in all the chaos of the hunt and its aftermath, I had not taken sufficient note of the fact that I had not bled this month, that I might be pregnant, though I did not tell Freeman yet. One day about six weeks later he came up behind me as I was plying the spade in the garden, separating the onion sets, which, since the first solitary ones, had multiplied so that I was now able to ring the whole garden with them and discourage many a pest. The marigold border also throve, and Freeman was quite taken with their orange blooms as he had never seen them before. He had plucked one, and when he came up behind me, he reached around as if to present me with a piece of living gold. He stuck it behind my ear and then put his arms around my middle. Suddenly, he grew still, then turned me around gently to face him, an expectant look on his face. "Is there a baby growing in you?" he asked. I nodded yes. Freeman's lovely face took on the softest cast and a white light seemed to bathe it, so much did his happiness at this news pervade him. He held me very close. "I guess we should thank the boar," I said, meaning it as a jest, but he said quite seriously, "Yes, he was very helpful." And, really, how was I to know?

As I waxed large with our child, my pace of work slowed down. This worried me and made me feel that the baby would compromise my ability to survive. It would also mean that I would be dependent on Freeman in a way I had not been before, a fact I had not considered when I asked myself if I wanted to have a baby with him. Now, however, I accepted that my decision entailed entirely throwing in my lot with him and that in this task of having a child, we could not be equal.

It did occur to me to inquire of him what mothers and fathers did among his people, a question that greatly surprised and confused him, as the answer seemed so self-evident and obvious to him. "Mothers feed the babies, and fathers bring the mother's food," he said. When the children were old enough, the fathers showed them how to hunt. Fathers also taught the children about the tribe's history and its customs. "Fathers must also play with the children," Freeman said, shooting me a sly glance. "Ah," I said, "That is an important duty." In fact, his account sounded a good deal like what mothers and fathers did in England, though what constituted hunting was different, and, I thought, mothers were often the ones to pass along our tribes' customs, especially those applying to girls and which were invariably restrictive.

As I grew big with our child, Freeman made special efforts to bring me things to eat. One day he went off with the spade and came back with some dirt-crusted roots that he boiled and mashed. It was a bland food but fortifying. In my much water-damaged book on tropical vegetation I was able to find a barely legible entry that told me it was called manioc. Since I had never found any taro, I wondered if the book's authors had mixed up taro and manioc as the latter was indeed plentiful here.

When I got so big that walking to and from the beach was a waddling chore, my mind began to dwell on the birth itself and the fact that I would have no midwife to assist me as my mother and all the rest of our neighborhood had had Mrs. Sweet to assist them. She was adept and comforting though often both mother and baby died, so Mrs. Sweet was wont to remark that her job was equal parts joy and sorrow.

I asked Freeman how the native women gave birth and who helped them. He said they usually did it alone sitting up in a small tent a short distance from the camp and that the men had no part in it at all. "Oh,

Freeman, I don't think I can do it all alone. I hope you will stay by me."
"Of course, I will," he said, adding a bit wistfully, "I am no longer a part
of my tribe." "I am now your tribe, and you are mine," I said, "and we
are making our own customs." Freeman smiled at this, meaning to
indulge me. Over our time together I had identified a fatalistic element
in his character and now thought he might have believed the notion of
our making our own tribe was absurd, tribes being natural formations not
created by individuals.

I had been present when my last brother was born, though only twelve
at the time, but childbirth was continually talked of among the women I
knew, always with emphasis on its great pain, so I was frightened. I
knew that I would have to bear the pain for a long while and then push as
hard as I could until the baby came out, at which point I would be lucky
not to bleed to death as my mother finally had. I kept telling myself that
I had survived a shipwreck and made my way on an uninhabited island
for five years, so surely I could give birth. The baby's growth and
increasing movement within me aroused my love for it long before I saw
it, and I longed to get through the pain so I could hold my living child.

One morning as I milked the goats, a torrent of bloody water rushed
out from between my legs, telling me the time was at hand. The goat
whose teats I was pulling bleated forcefully as if to proclaim our
sisterhood, which struck me as funny, and so I started my labor with a bit
of humor.

I certainly needed it. I went back to the cave and lay down upon the
bed, hoping Freeman would soon return from his morning hunt. I was
assaulted with successive waves of tearing pain, growing more frequent
as the hours passed. At last Freeman returned and saw at once that the
birth was afoot. He brought me water and sat beside me, holding my
hand and speaking encouragement through the hours that slowly passed

in my labor. There came a point, however, when he seemed miles away and I could no longer hear him; I was seized with such pain that I thought death would be a gentler alternative. Shortly after that, I felt the great urge to push that women speak of so often, and I did indeed push, Freeman cheering me on. "Yes, yes, my dear one," he said over and over. Then there came a great expulsion and the tiny bloody body of our baby slipped into the world into Freeman's arms. Freeman shoved the knife at me, insisting that I cut the cord, which I was able to do despite my profound exhaustion. "It's a boy," he said, radiantly pleased. He gently wiped off the blood and handed our baby to me.

I cannot find new words to express the ineffable happiness of looking on his tiny face, his hands and feet, how filled with love I was, and how I vowed to cherish him and care for him always. For several days I lay in bed with our son often at my breast. When I did get up again and begin to work, I was buoyed by the continuous happiness of his presence and delighted with his every movement or sound. Freeman was just as besotted as I was. He showed me how to make a sling to carry the baby as the women of his tribe did, and to spare me toil, he even deigned to work in the garden as he had never done before.

I asked Freeman what his father's name was, thinking that we could name our baby after our two fathers, but Freeman told me that he did not want our boy named after his father, but gave no reason why, so I did not press him. "Is Tom all right with you? Can he be Tom Freeman?" I asked. Freeman considered it, then smiled broadly—"Tom is a good name," he said. "It means mountain in my language." I thought that was splendid in all respects.

So Tom Mountain Freeman came into the world. It was an odd world, but he didn't know it as each day he lived under the tender attention of his doting parents. He certainly looked like a combination of us; his facial features were mine, his nose and mouth and green eyes, but his hair was thick and black and his skin a golden brown a tad lighter than Freeman's. He grew into a sturdy little boy who could speak two languages, but he was not yet old enough to ask why or to know that not all little boys had a mother who spoke one language and a father who spoke another, a fair mother and a dark father who told wistful stories of very different faraway places.

Watching our darling Tom sprout into a sturdy little boy was to Freeman and me a constant entertainment, occasionally punctuated by the fear aroused by childhood illness or injury. Our dog Roger was the first thing outside my breast that Tom showed awareness of. Even as a babe he loved to stroke Roger's silky flanks, and as a toddler Tom staggered all over in chase of Roger. Often his momentum was more than his legs could accommodate, and he would trip and scrape himself upon a rock or shell, letting out a great wail.

It was not long though before he was energetically jumping, climbing, and paddling about the waterfall pool. Freeman took him on frequent treks, carrying the little fellow on his shoulders until he could make his own way and directing Tom's attention to the infinite variety of our surroundings. Always he was full of questions: Where do the birds sleep? Why do the flowers open and close? He had a fine imagination that allowed him to amuse himself on his own as well. After we told him that the trees had roots that went deep into the earth and that, if we could see them, would look like another whole tree upside down, he began to play that he was a denizen of that underground world, that he ventured up only to be with us, but had to return there where he had many friends. I had to teach him his numbers and letters on the run, but the idea that he could write down the stories of his underground world gave him great motivation to learn.

He was a very active, brave little boy, but at night as we sat by the fire he would always climb into my lap and rest there silently with great contentment. Freeman and I frequently looked at each other with a mutual understanding that our union had produced this dear treasure of a boy and we were grateful. Sometimes my happiness was shadowed by the loss of my family in England, yet I thought they could not understand my current family, who I would not trade for anything. We had everything we needed and took great delight in each other. In fact, I felt that I was a resident of paradise, that Adam and Eve before the fall were not as happy as we, and we had the advantage over them of knowing how happy we were. Such bliss ought to have been a harbinger of change, as that state cannot long last in earthly life. It seems we now and again pass through happy states on our life journey, but we are never allowed to settle in them for long.

Chapter 12—They Come Too Late

When our son was almost five our life altered drastically. One early morning as we all three came down to the beach to dig clams, to our utter astonishment we saw floating towards us a long boat like the one that Leora and I had boarded to get away from our sinking ship so many years ago. When it drew close enough we eagerly swam out to it. In the bottom were three men, all unconscious, all much burnt by the sun and all dressed and looking like they had come from the Old World. To me they looked English.

We pulled their boat onto the beach and dragged them out of it onto the sand. They were alive, but badly in need of water, so I ran up to our camp to fetch some. When I returned I held the bottle to their cracked lips and poured the water into their mouths. "We must get them out of the sun," Freeman said, so one at a time, he heaved them over his shoulder and carried them up to where I made pallets for them in the loom lean-to where Freeman had slept when first he came to the island.

I bathed their faces and arms with water, rubbed them with coconut salve, and prepared a broth so that when they were able to they might eat immediately. I tended them as I wish someone had tended me when I arrived. The looks of them struck at my heart; two of them were young and reminded me so strongly of my brothers, and the other could have been any of a dozen older men from our village.

At last one of the young ones opened his eyes and looked around with great amazement. "Where am I?" he said, in English. "You are on an island in the Atlantic. Your boat washed up a few hours ago," I said. "Aye, I thought I might be in heaven, as you look like an angel to me," he said. "Don't tire yourself, sir," I said, though none too harshly, "There will be time to talk when you are recovered. Take some of this broth." I lifted his head and spooned some broth into his mouth, after which he lay back down and slipped into sleep. Thus it was with the other two as well, though neither favored me with the angelic compliment.

As they slept, Freeman, Tom and I watched them. Tom was excited beyond measure, full of questions about where these men were from and what they were doing here. He was suspicious to hear they were from England, and I then realized with a start that he must have thought my England was imaginary, like his underground tree world. He crept close to the men and tried to touch the buttons on their jackets, but I shooed him away, and as they showed no animation, he soon calmed down a bit and went about his play, running back now and again to see if the men had awakened. However, Freeman stayed, watching me as much as the newcomers. "Do you think we need to fear them?" he said, a question I had not considered until that moment, such fellow feeling had they unleashed in my breast, a dangerously naïve posture given the wealth of unknowns about these men.

Now it occurred to me that they outnumbered us. "They are weak and have no weapons and will be no threat for a time," I said. "I think we should not let them know of our muskets and the pistol, and we should keep our knives about us." We agreed that we would offer our full hospitality to these men, but keep very alert until we knew them better.

Towards evening they all awoke. The two younger ones introduced themselves as Jack Martin, and Monk Singletary, the elder as Herbert Crent, all seamen on the Langland, sailing from Bristol, the port from which Leora and I had set out ten years ago. "We were sent out to hunt up some game as we lay by an island, but a storm blew up," Monk said, his statement taken up by Jack, "and we couldn't get back to the ship. We tried, but we were blown out of sight of her." "So, here we are, ma'am," Jack said politely, "where we never expected to find a fellow countrywoman to rescue us." "Praise be to God," said the dark older man, Herbert Crent, and fell to praying, "Thank you, merciful Lord, for sending us to your handmaiden to preserve us from the deep. Amen." The other two said amen as well. I was much astounded and must have shown it as Herbert asked, "Are you a Christian, ma'am? Are you indeed an English woman?" I said I was and to their immediate inquiries about my presence on the island, I related the tale of my own shipwreck.

Freeman was close by during this exchange, and when I got to his entrance into the story, I took his hand and said simply that he had arrived, that we had married and that Tom was our son. "You are welcome to our land," Freeman said in clear but accented English. The three sailors were surprised and gaped at him. "You say you are married?" Herbert said to me, ignoring the gracious statement Freeman had directed to him. Hearkening to a shade of menace in his tone, I said, "Yes, we are, though since we have no clergy here, we have pledged ourselves on our own, doing what God would want us to in the absence of his minister." Though it had never occurred to me to be concerned about how my union with Freeman was formalized, it seemed useful to present ourselves as normally as possible to these men so that they would remain friendly guests.

"You've made a lovely bower here, heaven-like," young Jack said, as if to palliate Herbert's rudeness. But Herbert would have none of it, "There cannot be a heaven where there is no God," he said, and now I recognized him as the kind of religious man who imposes himself on others as arbiter of their lives, a type I have always loathed.

"God is everywhere, is he not, sir?" I said, more in statement than in question. "Let us have a meal that his bounty has made available to us here." We ate goat and beans and carrots, coconut and manioc pudding, for which Monk and Jack were loud in their praise, and Herbert was enough taken up in eating that he stopped inflicting his notion of God on us. Jack asked Freeman if there was any hunting on the island, and Freeman told him of the rabbits and boar. Herbert never looked directly at Freeman and Monk seemed unresponsive as well. I was angry on Freeman's behalf though he himself appeared unconcerned. The meal sent the three sailors into a torpor and Tom had as usual fallen asleep in my arms, so we bid them goodnight and went into our cave from where we could soon hear them snoring.

"Now do you think they are a danger to us?" Freeman asked, his tone telling me that he had not formed an opinion. "I have concluded that Herbert is unpleasant, but as yet they don't seem dangerous. What would we do if we thought they were a peril to us?" I asked. "Kill them," he said. I must say I was shocked, but as I considered further, I saw that Freeman had simply arrived sooner at the conclusion I eventually arrived at. We lived a peaceful life here. If their intentions were honest and honorable we would share it with them; if they threatened us, we would put an end to their threat. We could not imprison them or send them away, so our only choice would be to kill them.

In the next days, we showed the men over the island, and they much admired what we had built. Herbert inquired where our chapel was, and I told him that we considered the whole island a chapel and a testament to God's glory. I felt like a prig saying this, but it was my actual opinion.

Young Jack quickly entered into the work of the place and Monk went off to hunt with Freeman of a morning. Herbert Crent exhausted himself with expressing his opinions and calling them God's, and did little work, but was not troublesome other than as an annoying beadle. He constantly plied me with rudely intrusive questions: Did I mind that Freeman was a savage? Was I not worried that my soul was imperiled by mating with a heathen? He said "mating" as if Freeman and I were cattle. When Jack or Monk asked an innocuous question such as, "Did I much miss my family?" Herbert often answered it for me: "Of course, she misses her family and her native worship too," at which he would look pointedly at me.

Finally, I had had enough and took him aside to speak privately. "Mr. Crent, I beg you to allow me to answer for myself whatever questions are posed to me. Also, please refrain from imposing your opinions upon me and mine. We do not need your interference, and, in fact, you are our guests; we saved your lives and are feeding and housing you. Please amend your manners."

He was momentarily silenced, but my declaration had evidently breached the dam of his restraint. "What I say is for your own good!" he exploded. "You are living in sin with a savage and will burn in hell for it." "Even if it were true, it is none of your affair. School yourself to that fact or we will put you in your boat and set you adrift," I said, going further than I meant to. "How dare you?!" he sputtered. "You are a woman, a sinful vessel, and must be instructed by men. You are wearing pants, usurping the place of men. No wonder you mate with a savage over whom you can dominate." I shot back, "You heard what I said and I meant it. We have guns here, and we will use them if you harry us too far," then added, softening my tone, "Look here, Herbert, you're on an island with five other people. Use Christian charity and forbearance. Practice love." He snorted, "Practice love as you have practiced it? Ha!" At that I walked away.

Crent did not agree to what I said, but in the following days he did moderate his stream of disapproval somewhat, though I noticed him trying to cozen Freeman, and especially Tom, into telling him where the guns were. Freeman, of course, would not and played on Crent's assumption of his stupidity to hold him off. Tom did not know where they were and so could not tell.

My dealings with Jack and Monk were an entirely pleasant contrast. When they had recovered from their ocean ordeal, their boyish enthusiasms and teasing made me miss my brothers very much, especially Richard, opening up a vein of feeling that had hitherto lain unexposed. I told them about my bothers, and they agreed that they would like to join that band as "there could be no more excellent sister than I, a brave woman who had settled an island." This praise was more than I ever got from my actual brothers, and whether or not it was meant to flatter me or was a sincere expression, I took it as the latter and was proud. I began to wonder what, in fact, my brothers would think of my adventure.

At the same time, thinking of them brought into greater relief my relation to Freeman, who had allowed me to be my own person and also his beloved, and my respect for him grew. I did not think any of my brothers capable of the change that Freeman had gone through.

Tom was entirely delighted with the Englishmen and trailed them everywhere, alternately telling them what we did on the island and plying them with questions about England. He listened eagerly to their tales of seafaring but most wanted to hear about the English cities where thousands of people lived all together and where there were great buildings taller than any tree on our island. "I want to see them," he cried time and again.

One day about a week after the men had washed up here, as Jack and I gathered grapes and laid them out to dry so that there would later be raisins, he asked, "When we are rescued, will Freeman go back to England with you?" Tom burst out, "Oh yes, Mama, can't we go to England. I long to see the great buildings and the men in red coats!" "Tom, dear," I said, "please go fetch us some more baskets." "But Mama. . .!" he cried. "Go now, dear," I said firmly.

I was quite discombobulated by Jack's question and by Tom's response to it. I had accepted that I would never be rescued, that my future would always be here with Freeman. I finally answered Jack: "I don't mean to alarm or disappoint you, but in the ten years I have been here, you men are the only people from the Old World to arrive. It's unlikely that any others will." Jack was undaunted by my pessimism. "Oh, no, I'm sure our ship is searching for us. You might as well begin packing!" "I don't think I can go back, Jack," I said. "My family is here now." He was shocked. "How can you say that! They are only two people, while at home you have scores of relatives and a native country!" "I just don't feel as you do about it," I said, as he continued to look at me with incomprehension. "You could take Freeman and Tom with you, or at least Tom. He wants to go," he said. "He's a small boy and has no notion of English society. I don't think Freeman would be comfortable in England," I said in great understatement, "and I would never take Tom from him, nor take myself away, for that matter," I added.

That evening as we sat at dinner, Jack said to the others, "Roberta thinks it unlikely that we will be rescued. And if we are, she does not intend to go with us." There was no hostility in what he said; he seemed to be making an announcement. "Not be rescued! Not going with us! Why you're insane, woman. You'd rather be a barbarian than make your way back to civilization?" screeched Herbert. "Perhaps a civilized person takes civilization wherever he or she goes," I said, thinking that Herbert Crent was one of the most uncivil persons I had ever met. He looked at me darkly, "You imperil your salvation, Roberta, and your son's. You imperil all of us with your sin." I knew he sincerely believed this rot, so I was restrained in my reply, though nonetheless acidic. "It's impossible that my conduct could sully someone as virtuous as yourself, Mr. Crent." Everyone laughed, which greatly annoyed Crent, though I had come to see him as the sort of person who preferred others to be sinful so he could feel superior and reproach them. Meanwhile, Tom was in his customary place in my lap at the end of the day. He had been looking back and forth at us through this dialogue and at last sleepily put in, "Oh please, let us go, Mama. It would be so jolly."

"I hope you are wrong about our not being rescued," Monk offered wistfully, "as I long to see my sweetheart and my old mother." "Oh, Monk," I said, "I hope so for your sake as well." He had made me imagine what it would be like to be reunited with my own relations, to see Richard and Tom. It was indeed a sacrifice, but not one I thought within my reach anyway.

In the event their expectations were justified and my prediction wrong as several days later Tom dashed up to the camp wild with the news that there was giant boat coming towards us. I ran down to the beach and saw there the billowing canvas of a great sailing ship, whose enormous size left me open-mouthed. Here was a representative of civilization indeed. The three sailors were vigorously yelling and gesturing, though it seemed to me that the ship was already aware of them. "It's the Langland! It's our ship!" Jack shouted. "Mistress, you must fire your gun, so that they will know we are here," Herbert demanded. I wanted to refuse him, but it was a reasonable request, so I fetched the pistol and let off a round, which was quickly answered from the ship. Moments later a boat was lowered into the water and came towards us.

What a welter of thoughts and sensations ran through me as the boat approached! How deeply I had longed for this very thing to happen, and yet now I was filled with dread as well as excitement. At first I was taken up in welcoming the new arrivals, who were the first officer of the Langland and four seamen who embraced their three lost shipmates with gusto. The two young ones were ebullient and even Herbert smiled broadly, momentarily relieved of his burden of censure.

After their initial greetings, Jack led the officer to me and introduced us. "Lt. Morgan, this is Roberta Crousseau, the brave woman who saved us. She has been on this island since she was shipwrecked ten years ago." "How do you do, sir," I said, watching with amusement as the officer scanned me from head to foot. I was clad in my usual pants and belted shirt and must have been a great contrast to any woman he had ever seen before. He was gallant, "It is a great pleasure to meet you, ma'am. I thank you for rescuing our mates. It will be our privilege to assist you back to England."

"Oh, she doesn't want to go back," Jack broke out, but I hushed him, "We can talk about that later," I said. "Let me introduce the Lieutenant to my husband Freeman and my son Tom." The young officer was much astonished but proved himself a gentleman by extending a hand to Freeman, who to him must have been but a naked brown man. Freeman hesitated at first, shaking hands not being a custom among his people, but he was, as usual, a quick learner and extended his own after the slightest pause. "You are very welcome to our island," he said. "Please go with us to our camp." "He has good English," the Lieutenant said, looking at me and making his comment as if Freeman were a specimen. "Yes," I said, my initial regard for the man lessening. "Let us go to our camp where we can offer you refreshment." "Thank you, Madame, but if you are amenable, I would like to return to my ship to advise the captain that we have found our men, and to bring him back here with me." I readily agreed to this plan, and so the Lieutenant and his men rowed off again, taking Herbert Crent with them, but leaving Jack and Monk who, assured their removal was immanent, said they preferred to spend the remaining time with us.

I went back up to prepare a meal and also to change my clothes as Lieutenant Morgan's reaction had stung me a bit. I dragged out of the chest the blue merino dress in which I had arrived here ten years ago and into which I had sewn the jewels. I wondered if the dress would fit me. I laced myself into the odious stays, vowing that if for no other reason, I would stay on the island to avoid being trussed up like this for the rest of my life. As it turned out the dress was a bit too large for me; even though I had had a baby, the work and the diet of the island had made me lean and muscular. Of course, both my stays and the dress were heavier for the stones I had sewed into them, another reason to treasure my more relaxed garb. Later I would be profoundly grateful for that weight.

I brushed my hair and hoped I looked presentable as, having no looking glass, I could not know. It occurred to me that I had never missed having one, that the waters of the pond reflected as much of me as I needed to see and that my reflection in the eyes of Freeman and Tom made be feel quite pretty. I made a meal much like that I had given Jack, Monk and Herbert when they arrived. I had no idea how many men would come, so I made a great deal of everything. I arranged my homemade crockery on the table and felt the want of cutlery very much. It seems that in welcoming the ship's captain, I was presenting myself before English society. I even wondered if he might know Lady Evelyn and the fate of her daughter Leora.

Within the hour the captain, a Mr. Ellis, appeared. He was a short cheerful man, with a red, weather-beaten face, rather large ears and a flowery way of speaking. "My dear woman, lost daughter of Albion," he greeted me, "I am so proud to make the acquaintance of such a tropical survivor." He greeted Freeman very kindly and kneeled to look Tom in the eye, "What a fine young man you are," he said kindly, disposing me to like him.

I invited the company to dine, excusing the rough conditions, but the captain allayed my apprehension; putting his nose to the air he said, "My dear, it smells divine and I am a lover of food!" He ate heartily and praised everything, continuing his praise when after our meal we showed him what we had built on the island. "What ingenuity! What industry! My dear, you are a marvel!" He spoke to Freeman in much the same way he did to me and showed great interest in Freeman's descriptions of his tribe. I liked him and began to think that if there were many more like him in England then it might be possible for Freeman and Tom to go there with me.

After our tour, the Captain offered us brandy he had brought from his ship. He had not previously asked about the circumstances of my own shipwreck, which struck me as odd, but now he did. "I wanted to give my whole attention to your story, and I was hungry when I arrived," he explained, chuckling, "that's why I waited to ask you." So I told him what had happened, though I did not mention the names of my English mistresses, waiting until the end to do so, perhaps because I feared hearing that they were dead.

"My mistress was Lady Evelyn Hordsley. Her daughter Leora was going to the New World to marry Sir Thomas Overby. Are you acquainted with them, sir?" I finally asked. Captain Ellis's eyes grew very large, "Why bless my soul, I certainly am. I have met Lady Evelyn on several occasions in Bristol and have heard of her daughter from her own mouth." "Do they both live?" I asked. "They do!" he replied. "Leora Hordsley was rescued and taken on to Virginia where she now resides with her husband and children—three I believe. And Lady Evelyn is herself quite in the pink of health." "I'm so glad to hear it," I said, rejoicing. "Leora was just a girl when we went out, so sweet and full of hope. It was hard to think of her being lost so young. And to contemplate the sorrow of her mother at her loss was very sad also." "I believe that in telling me this story," the Captain said with wonder, "she mentioned you, though, of course, I did not know at the time it was you. She said that a very fine woman, her servant, had been lost at sea and not recovered and that she grieved for her still." It wrung my heart to hear this, and I was gratified to think that Lady Evelyn had valued me and cared about me.

I thanked the captain for this news and invited him to stay as long as he liked on the island, the fruits of which we would put at his disposal. "Ah, how lovely that would be," he said, "but we must sail tomorrow. We are long past due in England. Mr. Crent told me that you will not sail with us, and he urged me to change your mind." I shook my head. "That would be a waste of time," I said. "My life is here now. I have a family." "Yes, but they could come to England too. You will be most welcome. I'm sure Lady Evelyn would most eagerly take you back into her service and employ your husband as well."

Then was cast before my eyes the picture of me again waiting on Lady Evelyn, listening to her litany of ladylikeness, while Freeman dug shrubs on the grounds. It was a ludicrous picture and had never entered my thoughts as part of my life should I return to England, not only because I now had access to wealth, but because I could no longer think or act except as an independent being. I did not know if the captain would understand this, but I did not feel compelled to explain it to him, saying instead, "My mind is made up. I would like my brothers to know my fate and that I think of them. I will also write to Lady Evelyn, but I will stay here." The captain nodded. "That is my loss as well," he said, "as I would have enjoyed your company on the voyage. I think your son will be disappointed too." I grimaced to think of this because Tom's youth would prevent me from fully explaining my reasoning to him. Shortly Captain Ellis and his men went back to the ship. We agreed that he would send another boat to take on some supplies. "Good luck to you, my dear," he said in parting, "your tale will be told in England."

Chapter 13 — Grief at Sea

The next morning I worked on my letters. I contrived with Freeman to persuade Tom to go into the forest where Freeman was teaching him the rudiments of hunting and forest craft. Though he was too little to practice much of it, he longed for the time when he would be able to hunt and liked to play at it, a practice Freeman indulged, as indeed, we indulged Tom in most things. I wanted to occupy Tom during the ship's departure, but I would not deprive him of a farewell to Jack and Monk. Freeman worried that he might miss the sailors when they came for provisions, but I doubted they would arrive so early. "You won't stay away long and will certainly be back in time to say good-bye."

So I was much surprised to see another small boat arriving from the ship very shortly after Freeman and Tom went off. It carried Herbert Crent, Monk Singletary and two other men I had not met. I greeted them and directed them to the stores I had amassed for them—several large bags of vegetables and grapes, coconuts and yellow fruit and a basket ofdried goat meat. "This is very generous of you," Monk said in a shamefaced way that puzzled me. "Have you not changed your mind about going with us and regaining your home and your faith?" Herbert Crent said. "No, Mr. Crent," I said, "I'm resolved to make this island my home and resting place." "Then I am sorry for you," he said, seizing me around my shoulders while one of the other men looped a rope tightly around me. Much surprised, I screamed as loud as I could and struggled against them, but they shoved a rag in my mouth and bound my feet, so that I was suddenly immobilized, able only to writhe tortuously like one of the beached sea creatures I had often eaten of. "You'll thank us for this later, Mistress Roberta," Crent said. "It's for your own good, so rest easy." When they put me in a large bag they had brought, and it became clear that they intended to take me off the island by force, a swirling stew of rage and panic overwhelmed me. I gasped for breath but continued to struggle until one of them landed a great blow on my head and all went dark.

When I awoke, my head pounding, I was still in the bag, but no longer on the beach. From the rolling under me, the creaking sounds and the musty smell, I knew I was on board the ship, though with no sense of how long I had been there. A raging anger possessed me and I thrashed wildly around in my prison sack, but I could neither free myself nor make myself heard enough to attract attention. A welter of thoughts threaded my rage: I wondered if the ship had already set sail; something about the rolling filled me with fear that it had. I wondered if the captain knew of Crent's kidnapping plan and surmised that he did not as even if he had agreed to the plot, I thought him too kind to keep me thus tied up and sequestered. More likely, Crent was waiting to make my presence known to the captain until the ship had gone too far to turn around and take me back. So assured of his righteousness was this blackguard that he risked great punishment to carry out his will, though he called it God's will.

At last I ceased to struggle. My limbs were very sore; I was both thirsty and needed to relieve myself, but my physical misery was small compared to my heartsickness. I thought of Freeman and Tom's distress upon returning home to find me gone. Freeman would know that I had not gone of my own free will, and so he would worry that violence had been wreaked upon me. Tom would miss me immeasurably, and since my loss would be the first sorrow of his life, it would be quite indelible. To spare him that I wished we had killed all three sailors when they first arrived at our beach. I could easily have sunk a knife into Herbert Crent's chest and twisted it too. My powerlessness had made me bloody.

My mind was a welter of rapid surmise and calculation. I quickly realized that the stones I'd sewn in my clothing were the wherewithal to bring me back again to the island, no matter how long it took. I blessed my extraordinary luck and prescience in putting the stones in this hiding place and in wearing the dress to greet the sailors. My mind ran far ahead: I did not think I could be held in England against my will, and with the stones I could purchase my way back to Freeman and Tom.

After what felt like many agonizing hours, I heard someone approach. The bag was untied and I looked into the eyes of the only person on earth who I hated--Herbert Crent. "There, there," he said, with a strange gentleness, "Will you promise to be quiet so that I can give you water?" he asked. I nodded, as my thirst was extreme. He pulled the rag from my mouth and handed me a flagon from which I took a good long draft. "I wonder, Mr. Crent, how God appointed you to judge on his behalf? Did an angel appear? A flaming sword, perhaps?" I knew Crent was far beyond reason and so I broached no reason with him. "God's work is plain for all to read," he said, "but you have forgotten it in that sink of heathen iniquity, and so I have rescued you. I look forward to the day when you will show me your gratitude." "Shouldn't I rather show my gratitude to God," I said, "or are you God himself?" At this he slapped me. "You must be schooled, Mistress," he said, thrusting the rag back in my mouth and padding off.

I lay in the sack for a good while longer, immobilized by ropes that cut increasingly into my flesh, my body a field of pain, my mind ceaselessly running through the possibilities of my situation. I drifted in and out of anguished sleep until I heard the sound of many feet coming towards me and the light hit me from the sack's opening. I gazed up into the kind face of Captain Ellis, Jack Martin and Lieutenant Morgan beside him. "Untie her and be gentle about it, Mr. Morgan," Captain Ellis ordered. "My dear Mistress Roberta," the captain said, looking at me with profound concern. "I am so sorry. I had no idea what Crent was up to. Can you speak?" The rag had so dried my mouth and throat that I could barely croak, "I think I am all right. Please take me back," I gasped, creaking to a sitting position. At this the captain looked very sad. "We must see to your comfort and then we will discuss what course of action to take."

I was able to stand and, with the Captain's assistance, make my way up to the deck where the fresh air struck me as a blanket of relief. "Please take me back right away." I pleaded, "My family will be so worried." "Dear lady, you must rest and take refreshment and then we will discuss it." "Rest! I cannot rest," I sputtered while the captain held my arm as if I were an invalid. "There, there, my dear," he soothed, leading me to what I later learned was the first officer's cabin. There I was provided with a basin in which to wash, bread and meat to eat, and some of the very fruit I had given the ship from off our island. "After you have rested, and when you are ready, come forward to my cabin," the captain advised.

I washed myself and ate a bit, but rested very little, so eager was I to arrange my return. My apparel was not improved by my sojourn in the sack, but I smoothed its blue folds as best I could, adjusted the kerchief over my bosom and went up onto the deck and forwards to the captain's cabin on the foredeck. In my passage I saw down through a grill into a hold wherein Herbert Crent was bound to a wall, looking very abject. I was again suffused with rage. "So, Mr. Crent," I said, "your captain did not approve your kidnapping." "My captain in heaven will reward me," he said sullenly. "Ah, your delusion is quite monumental," I said and spat upon him. "You are damned!" he screeched after me. "That would gall me the less were I not sure that hell would contain you." I shot back.

I must have looked a red-faced lunatic as the Captain ensconced me in his cabin and treated me with much solicitation. "I am so sorry that you have been the victim of Crent's zeal, my dear. I had heard his ranting disapproval of your residence and relations with the native, but Mr. Crent makes a career of disapproval and threat and so I did not take him seriously. If he were not a first-rate seaman I would have dismissed him long ago."

"It would have been a boon for me if you had, Captain. I appreciate your apology, but all I really desire is to be returned to my home as soon as possible," I said firmly. At this the captain looked quite downcast. "Oh, my dear, if only it were so simple. You will remember my haste in departure. It had to do not only with our lateness in turning back towards England, but also with the season and the directions of the winds. Though we have been gone from your island for only a few days, it could take us weeks to get back, and by then the winter storms would be so far advanced that we could not turn again for many more months. I'm afraid that you must go with us to England where I will do everything in my power to aid you in whatever you wish to do."

I was very much angered and frustrated by this address and my feelings must have contorted my face. I struggled against crying.

"Again, I am so sorry. I assure you that Crent will be severely punished," the captain said. "How so?" I asked. "He will be flogged," the captain replied. While this prospect satisfied my desire for vengeance, that desire was much dwarfed by my sorrow and loss, which loomed larger with each passing moment as I realized how very long it would be until I could be reunited with Freeman and Tom and how many things might happen to prevent it in the meantime. I said, "Could you not pound molten nails into Crent's hands, or tear his skin off his body in tiny strips?" The Captain looked askance for a moment, then smiled, "Ah, Mistress Crousseau, through exaggeration you mean to convey that there is no punishment commensurate with the crime that Crent has done you. And you are right, but I must flog him nonetheless. Naval justice demands it." I shrugged, utterly uninterested in naval justice, so angered that I thought my rage alone might be enough to reduce Crent to a pile of cinders.

"We will try to make you as comfortable as possible upon the ship," the Captain said. "It so happens that when we were berthed in Cuba, my cousin, the wife of one of the planters there, was very angry her husband, whom she accused of beating her, and she appealed to me for asylum upon the ship, which I granted her. The man came every day with all sorts of gifts trying to make it up to her and they were soon reconciled." The captain must have seen me struggling to understand why he was telling me this story in the midst of my ire and despair as he hastened to say, "I tell you this because in the speed of her departure, the woman left a number of garments on board, which might be useful to you now." I fought a small childish battle within myself about whether acceding to this offer would constitute too much acquiescence to my imprisoned state, but the thought of wearing the same clothes for many months struck me as a further punishment to myself, so I nodded to the captain. "Yes, perhaps some clothing would be useful."

At this he loaded me down with a great heap of garments that made me wonder at the veracity of his story of how they had come onto his ship. Later, when I saw the size and nature of the gowns and petticoats, which were made for one stouter and shorter than I and which were of a rather ornate character, I wondered if the captain had had a mistress aboard or if he himself enjoyed wearing the women's clothing, as I had heard some men do.

I returned to my cabin and sat upon its bunk. I sank down amidst the slew of linen, cotton and silk the captain had given me, utterly sick at heart and dispirited. I finally gave way to my grief and cried so that the whole ship must have heard me, but I did not care; my sorrow demanded a witness. After a long time, when I was entirely dry of tears, my face a swollen cloud, I calmed myself and remembered a very similar time when I was first upon the island and had then to gird myself to survive. I was again at such a point and accompanying it was an awareness of the irony in my situation. On the island I cried because I could not get off it. Now I cried to get back on it. The knowledge that conditions can so alter saddened me further because it made me wonder if subsequent changes might make me loathe to go back to what I now wanted with all my heart. I made a conscious decision to abandon this thought and to commit myself again to survival, not just to my bodily survival, but to the survival of the life I had found on the island with Freeman and Tom. I vowed that nothing could prevent me from returning. With this resolve, I sat up and began to root among the clothing to see what I could make of it and soon went to beg of the captain needle and thread so that I might set about altering both my clothes and my circumstances.

By lowering the hem, taking in the waistline, and removing some redundant cascades of lacy flounces, I soon had a serviceable dress of dark red satin with a white petticoat beneath. This garment would have been above my station as a lady's maid, but then I was no longer in that station, and, I hoped, my hidden treasure would prevent me from being so again. It was further dispiriting to dwell again in the sticky realms of "station." So gradually had this complicated web of expectation and restriction receded from my life on the island that I had never felt the relief from it so greatly until forced to contend within it once again.

As I sewed, my thoughts feverishly alternated between concern for the life that was receding from me and that which approached. Freeman and Tom would be so worried and sad, and I could do nothing to comfort them. I cried to myself as I stabbed the needle in and pulled it through the layers of cloth. I also realized I would need some sort of plan to execute upon my arrival in England. That would not occur for several months, however, so I had time to consider it well.

When I could bear the closed cabin no more, I went up on the deck clad in my new estate. I stood in the stern, gazing back in the distance where I conceived Freeman and Tom to be, missing them with all my heart when Jack Martin approached me with a gentle address. "Mistress Roberta," he said, "If I had known what Crent planned I would have told the Captain right away. It was only after he had you in the hold that Singletary hinted at some great doing in which he had aided Crent, who I noticed sucking on his pipe with great contentment. Perhaps it was Crent's good humor that most made me suspect his crime," Jack said, which at last brought a smile to my face.

Jack related that he had gone to the hold to test his suspicion, found a life-sized sack and gone to tell the captain, who had then come and freed me. Jack was a very good fellow and I did not want to punish him with coldness. I shook his hand and thanked him for rescuing me and let him know that any failure of my attention had to do with my sorrow and concern for Tom and Freeman. "They are lucky fellows," Jack said. His open demeanor again reminded me of Richard, and for the first time I felt a tiny flame of anticipation at reaching England and seeing him again.

Amidst my sorrow, anger and the tiny seedling of my hope, my life on board the Langland very soon devolved into a routine in which in the mornings I busied myself with handwork, further altering the secondhand assemblage the Captain had given me so that by the time we reached England I had an elegant wardrobe consisting of the red satin dress, a green watered silk one, and one of very good wool, a dark blue but more bright than navy. I enjoyed the feel of these fabrics very much, but it was hard to school myself again to the encumbrance and restriction of such garments after years of loose pants and shirts, but I had no choice but to do so.

In the afternoon I walked upon the deck, noting the changing face of the sea and the sky. When I first began my deck promenade the Captain had rushed down to present me with a parasol. "I'd forgotten this most necessary lady's companion," he joked, though he reflected a true sentiment among English ladies, who did not like the sun to touch their bodies so as to preserve the whiteness of their skin. Of course, I was not a lady and had come to enjoy as much of the sun as my body would stand, but I took the parasol and counted it as a token of the country of manners I was reentering.

In the evenings I dined with the captain and his officers in his cabin where we had many an interesting conversation. The captain always treated me very well, as if I were the daughter of a friend or even his own niece, which set the standard that governed how the others treated me as well, though their knowledge that I was the daughter of a common farmer and had worked as a ladies maid before my shipwreck put them in some confusion as to how to regard me. Always my relations with Freeman lay as the shocking unbroached topic between us. As I imagined it, they could not regard me as a respectable woman, but then neither was I a whore. Their inability to place me made our relations stilted, though over the months of the voyage, they became more natural, and several of them later gave me a good deal of help when it was clear to them that I was as fond of Freeman and as dedicated to him as any good wife would be to her husband. I tried to conceal my assumption of island ways as I thought this "going native" offended their decorum more deeply than my sexual apostasy; I carried the parasol in recognition of this.

Often the captain invited me to converse with him after dinner when the other officers went about their duties. He never tired of hearing of about how I had made my way on the island, and he suggested that I ought to write it down as many other people would be equally interested. He provided me with paper and that which you now read was there begun. Captain Ellis may have wanted to help ease my distress by filling my time, and for that I'm grateful to him. Indeed, he calmed me. I'm also grateful for the many hours of conversation we had together as our back and forth helped me to clarify and order my thoughts as my single scrutiny of them had never done.

He was particularly interested that I had had books with me and that I had read them. "Ah, Captain, when I was entirely solitary, I came to crave human speech, and the books were the closest to it I could get." Captain Ellis was quite familiar with the Bible, of course, and he also knew both *Piers Ploughman* and *Pilgrim's Progress*. "Is it not an interesting coincidence that you are now riding on the Langland?" he quipped, alluding to William Langland's authorship of *Piers Ploughman*.

"Ought we not to call it Unlooked for Coincidence with a capitol "u" and "c" and think of it as a living, talking being who will lecture us about his nature?" I replied, referring to the relentlessly allegorical character of Langland's book. "Ah," the captain mused, "*Piers Plowman* does have a hectoring quality about it, does it not?" "Indeed it does. One is forever in a schoolroom enduring reproof for one's many shortcomings. Sometimes it made me tired; sometimes I was moved to contend against it, simply to beat back its constant disapproval."

"Did Bunyan please you better?" he asked. "Yes, much better," I replied, " for though salvation is equally his only topic, the figures he uses in his story are more human-like and less mere signs of sinful or holy attributes." "He tells a better story, doesn't he," said the captain. "I wished for more story and less teaching," I said, immediately wondering if I had been injudicious. The captain chuckled, however, and showed no disapproval as he was no prig. "You must have liked the Bible best of all then," he said, "as it is filled with many stories." "Yes, you're right," I replied, inwardly halting any indulgence of my less laudatory and entirely outlandish views of the Bible, though I could tell that the captain would have liked to engage me in further discussion of it. My own close reading of the Bible, combined with my early exposure to the unorthodox views of Simon Petrie, had reinforced my resistance to regarding it as the word of God. I wondered very much what made me so different from others who found so much comfort and wisdom in the text, but it was simply too risky a subject to speak about.

The days passed as pleasantly for me as was possible given my grief over the loss of Freeman and Tom, a grief that grew rather than ebbed as we made our way back to the old world, so that I ached with the pain of it. On the morning appointed for Herbert Crent's flogging I kept to my cabin. I heard his agonized cries, but they gave me no comfort. I reckoned he took pleasure in his martyrdom.

As we drew closer to England, the captain asked me what I wanted to do upon our arrival and how he could help me. I told him that I would like first to ascertain a return passage and then I would travel to visit my family and friends before departing. He assured me that he would pay my passage and also provide me with some other monies. Carefully, he added, "When you see your family again, it is not impossible that your resolve to return to the new world will alter." "I will be truly glad to see my family and nothing is impossible, but I cannot conceive of that anything could keep me from returning to my husband and son." "I only mention it so that you might know that should you decide to stay in England I would be most glad to help you establish yourself." I was very grateful for his kindly attitude towards me and so did not tell him that I likely carried with me enough wealth to do what I wished.

In the middle of June, 1719, I once again viewed my native land of England as we sailed into Bristol harbor.

Chapter 14 — I Come Home

It was a typical grey English day. The hills lay dark on the sides of our passage, and the brick buildings at the wharf rose up black red. Though the weather and my constant sense of loss arrested my enthusiasm, I nonetheless quickened at the sight of my native land. For so many years I had yearned for this moment and I felt sharply this pent-up longing. I was eager to be off the ship and onto the land. Captain Ellis provided me with a trunk in which to carry my new wardrobe and a portmanteau for sundries.

We went directly from the ship to the office of its owner, where he was warmly greeted and I was introduced. The owner, Mr. Grafton, a lean, bald man of the captain's age was much amazed at the tale the captain related of me. "I greet you with a hearty welcome back to England, Mistress. It must be a great happiness to you." So began a conversation I was to have many times in the days ahead and the first of the myriad astonished faces that turned my way when I said, "I will be very glad to see my people here, sir, but I intend to return to the island where I have married and established a family. I wish to book a passage back on the earliest ship." The man spluttered a bit and looked at Captain Ellis as if to ascertain my sanity.

"It is true," he said, "Mistress Roberta is an enormously resourceful woman. She has created a prosperous and happy estate in the tropics and only the crime of one of my crew, who took her off her island against her will, has deprived her of it." I wondered if Mr. Grafton saw an image of a large manor in a well-tended garden when the captain spoke of my "estate." How much further would my sanity be in doubt if he knew I yearned to return to a cave and a man in a loincloth against whose image I increasingly compared each man I saw and found them all wanting!

"I will look up the soonest departure," Mr. Grafton said. "Though now is not the season to make towards that part of the world," he warned as he leafed through various papers that I took to be schedules. "Here it is: The Northhampton, sailing in September." Three months until I could leave again and two or three more months en route! It seemed an eternity. "Don't fret, my dear," the captain comforted me when he saw my crestfallen face, "you will have enough time to see all your friends and to fully weigh your future course. Should your resolve to return continue, you will have the opportunity to provision yourself with those things that you lacked upon the island." Though he questioned my resolve, I took his speech as a kindly one anyway. It had not occurred to me that I could take necessaries back with me, and right then I could think of nothing I wanted beyond more seeds and books for Tom's education. Later I would think of many other things.

"You speak wisely, Captain Ellis," I said and then turned to Mr. Grafton, and said, as if in contradiction, "Please book me for the Northhampton, Mr. Grafton." He wrote up my ticket and I put it immediately in my portmanteau as a surety that I would again see my beloved Freeman and Tom.   After we consulted the coach schedule so that I might travel to Somerset, Captain Ellis escorted me to an inn where I was cordially greeted by a woman of his acquaintance who showed me to a room. He had introduced me as a lady just returned from the new world and did not elaborate, for which I was grateful. "I would take you to my own home, my dear, but a young woman staying there with me, a bachelor, would quickly be the gossip of the town. I shall return to share dinner with you," he concluded. I thanked him for all his kindness and he took his leave.

I took off my stays so that I might take a deep breath and lay down upon the bed in the green silk dressing gown I had sewn upon the Langland. The room was warmed by a small fire and was quite cozy. I felt in it a deep stillness and solidity after the constant rocking of the ship. It seemed in my body I was still rolling with the waves, and it took several days for this sensation to pass. Somewhat later I ventured out into the high street and was delighted by the banter of daily English life, but also appalled by the filth and muck of the street. I had not realized how clean my life upon the island was, and I'm sure these Englishmen would not have believed that those in savage climes lived in cleaner surroundings than they did.

I went into several shops, where I found myself very happy simply to see and speak with other women, as I had not known I missed them so much. I asked to see things merely to hear their voices and to look into their eyes. Since I was dressed quite well I was taken for someone of quality and great courtesy was extended to me, so that I felt as though I were in a disguise, and, in fact, I was. Not only was I dressed above my class, but I had been a denizen of another world that these women did not know. As I felt the fabrics the clerks put under my hand, I saw myself in my sailor's pants and belted shirt and smiled to imagine how differently they would have treated me in that attire. I doubt I would have been admitted to the shop. I do not mean to blame them for this; it merely struck me as a fact.

That evening my decade-long yearning for roast beef was satisfied at dinner with the captain. Over our meal I told him of my visit to the high street and of the thoughts it engendered. "I should imagine your thoughts will be a most interesting realm over the next months," he said. "You now have something against which to compare civilized life, which hardly anyone else does." "Ah, perhaps I lack confidence that only European life is civilized," I said. At this the captain looked at me sternly. "You must remember, Roberta, that you took your civilization with you, that you were able to make your way as well as you did because you had the benefit of the many tools and materials you brought off the ship. Also, you really know only one native, so your experience of other peoples is, in fact, quite small. I say this not to rebuke you, but to remind you of important facts." He said he did not mean to rebuke me, but I felt his words as such, and justly so as there was truth in them. I did not have to judge all aspects of my life on the island superior to that of Englishmen in order to justify returning to it, but my experience with Freeman had also shown me that civility was not the exclusive possession of the old world.

The next day, dressed in my new blue dress, I boarded a coach for my journey down into Somerset. "Best of luck to you, my dear Roberta," Captain Ellis said as he handed me in. "I shall see you again in a few months," I said, adding, "Please know how grateful I am for your excellent treatment of me. I shall always count it as a great blessing even though it was occasioned by such violence and sorrow." "Yes, such is the changing face of life, but let me not detain you with philosophy," he said and soon his kindly figure receded as the coach rattled off.

During the many hours of my rumbling homeward journey, a more brutal form of rolling than that of the ship, I devoured the countryside with my eyes. I was struck with the difference in the light of England, somehow more opaque than that of the island, both darker and gentler. The palette of greens in the land was more subdued and the shapes of the vegetation were rounder while the buildings filled the scene with right angles. Most of all England seemed a crowded place, though it had never struck me so when I lived there.

When I turned my mind to what lay before me though, analysis flew away and my heart quickened. I had imagined broadly that my older brothers would all be much as I had left them, good-natured men working hard on the land. I assumed they would all be married and that there would be many nieces and nephews I had not met. I wondered most though about Richard, who I had not seen since he was 12 and who would now be a grown man. Would he have followed the path of all the others?   Would our communion be preserved?

I wondered if any of those who had known me would recognize me; perhaps my being turned out so like a gentlewoman would disguise me more than any changes wrought by life on a tropical island. I looked forward to aiding them all with the wealth I had brought back, and I wondered if I should have first gone up to London to convert the jewels into money before going home. That would have allowed me to send word of my arrival, which now would take them by surprise if not with shock. However, I was on my way and found my desire to see them so strong that I wanted no long detour to London.

I was let down from the coach in Somerton, a village I had visited countless times in my early life. The sleepy, mossy character of its few shops and public house, its little grey church and parsonage were quite unchanged and I felt a resurgent fondness for it. In the small grain shop I happily recognized a taciturn old man who had served there all the years I had lived in the region, but he did not recognize me, and I was loathe to identify myself as that would entail so much narrative, so I remained incognito. When I asked him if I might hire a wagon to take me to the Crousseau farm, he looked me up and down curiously, and I could sense a thread of gossip would soon spin its way through the whole village. "I have some business there," I said to forestall his inquisition.

He summoned a slight young fellow, told him my wishes, and we were soon upon the road in a wagon behind a roan mare. The young fellow's questions I could not hold off. "Are you part of the Crousseaus?" he asked. "Yes, but I have not seen them in many years." I answered, then put my own eager question: "How do they fare?" "Oh, quite well, all in all, though one was killed last year when he fell out of the barn. And one of their wives has lost several babes and young Willie was very ill and now walks lame. George's daughter Eliza is very beautiful. . . " he went on, though his speech drifted past me as I was arrested with dismay at learning that one of my brothers had died. Which one? This fact of death cut me very much and put a shadow on my anticipation.

Soon my birthplace came into view, a stone house sprawled low against the ground, the thatched eaves overhanging it. I felt that I should hail it, almost as if it were a being, so well had I known it. It was not, however, a sentimental feeling because enfolded in it was the relief I had felt when I had left this place; there had been many satisfactions, but I had been put to much hard toil and sorrow there.

As we pulled into the yard around dinner time, I saw a tow-headed child contending with a squawking hen. She looked eagerly towards us as to a novelty and ran to meet us. "I am Loretta," the lovely sprite said to me. I climbed down from the wagon and said softly, "I am your Aunt Roberta. Are your father and mother within?" "My Aunt Roberta died at sea," Loretta said, wide-eyed. "No, she did not, for I am she," I said, which made the child stare at me open-mouthed and then sent her shooting towards the house shouting, "Pa! Pa! Aunt Roberta has come home!"

Soon there emerged from the house a tall sandy-haired man I knew indubitably to be my brother Tom. So it was not he who had died! Behind him was a woman I did not recognize. As they drew closer he looked at me with a mix of recognition and disbelief. "Roberta?!" Tom said. "Is that you?" "Yes," I said as he gathered me into his arms and crushed me to him. When he released me he held me at arm's length and searched my face with tender interrogation. "For these many years we have thought you were drowned and lost to us forever. But here you are," he said, again embracing me. "How can it be?" "I was not drowned, but cast up upon a island where I lived for many years until an English ship took me off and brought me back just recently," I said. "Praise be to God!" Tom said.

The stout, blonde woman who had been standing by attentively introduced herself. "Welcome home, Roberta. I am Susan, Tom's wife," she said warmly. When I had left Tom had been married to May, a tiny brunette. He saw my confusion. "May and our youngest children all died of the small pox the year after you were lost," he said sadly. "But Rachel and Roland were spared," he said gesturing toward a gangly blond boy and a tallish, bright-eyed but pock-marked girl of about fifteen who had followed them out of the house. "Susan here took us into her care two years later and we have three babes together." "I am one of them," cried the sprite Loretta, slipping her hand into mine. "Come in now and let us make you comfortable," Susan said. "Later we can tell of sad things." "I must send Roland off to tell the others," said my eldest brother, who now, I gathered, was called Old Tom. "Scoot off, my boy," he urged and his son sprinted off across the meadow. The boy had not been able to speak to me, but his dispatch signaled his regard.

Tom and I sat at the table while Susan and Rachel prepared tea. I could not take my eyes off him, so happy was I to see his broad genial face, though it bore the effects of the time and care that had passed since I last saw him. I tried to delay telling my whole story until more brothers had arrived, as I would be in for a world of repetition if I did not, and, indeed, I was more interested in finding out about what had happened to them.

"I heard that one of our brothers was killed," I said, filled with apprehension. Tom and Susan nodded sadly, "Yes, it was Arthur, a year ago last October. Leaving a wife and three young ones," Tom said. "But Anne, that was his wife, will remarry soon, and we don't begrudge her as it will be a boon for the children." "And what of the others?" I asked, at once sorrowing for Arthur, but relieved that Richard lived. "Oh, we are all carrying on pretty well," he said. "George has the farm at the bottom of ours, rented from Mr. Barclay, and his sons help him work it. William, you know, he has a head for figures; he's a clerk for Watts' drapery." "He's the only man patient enough to bear with the monster Watts," Rachel said. "Now, Rachel," Tom said, "you mustn't speak ill of your elders." "Why not, if they deserve it?" his daughter said. "I wouldn't say it to his face, of course," she added and looked at me as if to assure me that she knew common courtesy. I liked her immediately; she seemed to be asking out loud the sort of questions I had always held inside. Her scarred face made her a visible exception, and she seemed to have taken her marking as excusing her from some restrictions.

"And what of Richard?" I finally said, asking after my youngest brother and trying to deflect her parents' unease about Rachel's forward character. Tom grinned, "Ah, yes, young Richard was always your favorite, Roberta," he said, falling into familiarity as if I had never been away. "He lives here with us and will be home soon. He's a good fellow but rather at loose ends." "How so?" I asked. "Restless, impatient," he began to explain, when Richard himself burst through the door, a much larger, more expansive version of the blond boy I had left behind. He filled the room with vitality. What a joy it was to see him!

"Is it a miracle in truth?" he called excitedly and when his eyes found mine, he rushed towards me, pulled me up and lifted me off my feet in a bear-like embrace. "Oh Roberta, how we missed you! Where have you been?" He looked me up and down. "Wherever it was, you've prospered. You're a handsome woman, though a little on the brown side," he teased and immediately our old easy relations were reestablished. "And have I come back to be made fun of? So it always was," I said and held Richard in my own close embrace. I saw a little war in Rachel's face as she watched Richard and me. I reckoned she had become his favorite and would not like being displaced. I resolved to reassure her somehow, though I could not disguise my pleasure in Richard.

Little by little all my brothers, their wives and children arrived to greet and embrace their prodigal sister and we had our own Crousseau holiday. Food was brought out and cordials were drunk and many children were introduced to me. Those who I had known as babes were now strapping lads and pretty lasses, though there were many I had never met. "You are doing a good job of populating Somerset," I said. "We are trying!" George said and saluted his wife, who blushed. William, the thinnest of my brothers, introduced me to his pretty wife Tabitha, who disconcerted me a bit by curtsying. How it warmed my heart to see them all; looking like so many copies of their fair selves, broad faces and green eyes.

When the pandemonium had subsided somewhat, I began to tell my story and all except the very youngest listened most attentively. Little Loretta sat beside me and again put her hand in mine. With a pang she reminded me of my own little Tom. I told them of the storm at sea, my landing on the island and later finding the ship, of what I ate, what I planted, of my goats, how I made pots and wove linen.

"Ah, what an adventure you have had!" exclaimed Richard with great admiration. "But so alone," William said, to which I replied, "Yes, it was so for many years, but then another came to the island, a native of the mainland. We grew to love each other. We married and we have a son ourselves. His name is Tom," I said with a glance at my oldest brother who beamed. At this there was a general murmur of approval and smiling faces. My brother Tom asked, "But where are they? Why are they not with you?"

Then I explained how I had been kidnapped. "The blackguard!" Richard said after hearing of Herbert Crent. "But at least you are home," he added and all the others cheered in agreement. I thought it best to make my plans known immediately. "I intend to go back," I said gently, "for I can not live without my husband and son." Richard looked quite stricken. "No, no, you shan't leave us again. They can come here," Tom exclaimed to general agreement. "Of course, she must be with her husband and son," Rachel interposed, becoming my champion. I gave her a smile of thanks, and said, "Let us speak of it later. Now I want to hear about your doings."

I wanted to deflect this discussion, and I indeed wanted to hear their stories. Since people usually like to talk about themselves, our party went on for many hours until I was exhausted from so much human company, and Susan led me to a cupboard where I could lie down. "Roberta, I am so deeply glad to see you," Richard said, bidding me good-night. I saw then that there was in him a sort of disquiet at war with his geniality, and I resolved to ask him about it on the morrow.

When at last the house was quiet, and I thought all had gone home or were abed, I heard a low call. "Aunt Roberta?" There was Rachel, holding in her hands a batch of papers. "What is it, dear?" I asked gently as she came forward. "I wanted to show you these," she said and laid the sheets before me. They were drawings of the farm and all the people on it. She had captured the look of everything most perfectly, and yet all was pervaded by a personal spirit. "My word, Rachel. These are truly wonderful. It's as though you've drawn not just the scene but the eye that saw it." She beamed at my praise. "You are an artist, my dear," I said with great admiration for I had never been able to draw with anything like the similitude much less the vision that she had, as my embroidered pictures showed all too well, and I held in awe the skill of those who could in the same way I admired those who could make music. "I'm so glad you like them," Rachel said. "Doesn't everyone?" I asked. "By no means," she said. "They want the picture to look exactly like the thing as they see it," she said a bit sadly. "Well, then, they must draw their own pictures. As for me, I like seeing through your eyes. It's hard enough to know how others think and feel, but you give us a way with your pictures." "Do you really think so?" she said. "I do indeed, and I hope you will make some drawings for me." "Of course, I will," she said eagerly. "I'll start tomorrow." "Then you'd better get some sleep tonight," I said. She gave me big kiss. "I'm so glad you've come back, Aunt Roberta," she said.

I lay awake, conflicting feelings churning through me. How sweet was the society of this talented young woman! How comfortable I felt amidst my family! How like me they were! Even after ten years apart we easily caught each other's meanings and references. Their familiarity acted as a powerful tide pulling me towards them. How painful it was to be gone from Freeman and Tom, to sense their presence ebbing as my family's waxed. Worry ate at me and kept me from slumber for anxious hours.

The next day I sent a note to Lady Evelyn, informing her of my presence and telling her of my intention to visit in a few days. I wanted very much to see her and to hear of Leora. For several days thereafter I was made much of in my brothers' houses, which I visited each in turn, accompanied by my nieces Rachel and

Loretta when their mother could spare them from the work of the house and farm.

I imagine my fine wardrobe had as much to do with the sometimes exaggerated politeness with which I was treated as did my ten-year sojourn on the island. Many neighbors came to visit as well, most eager to hear my story. "And how was it that you fought off the savage tribe?" one fellow asked. "I did no such thing," I said. "What made you think so?" "I heard it of George's wife's niece," he answered, and so began the legend of Roberta, filled with all sorts of nonsense and daring-do.

It interested me that my brothers were more interested in my stories than were their wives whose treatment of me had in it the edge of coolness I remembered from before I went away and which had played a part in my going into service. In fact, it took only days for them to begin bidding me do various tasks. They could place me only as a maiden aunt, someone who had had an adventure and somehow gotten nicer clothes, but who was, fundamentally, superfluous, and should make herself as useful as possible to them. William's wife Tabitha was especially hard to be around, alternately fawning and mutely accusatory, as if I had offended her in some way. Only Rachel took seriously my intention to return to the island. She saw me as a woman who had traveled the world, a being such as she had never known. The way she asked questions reminded me of how Tom had quizzed Jack and Monk as if he could not drink in their tales fast enough.

Lady Evelyn had sent me a return note in her spidery filigree, telling me of her great joy at my arrival and that she would send a coach for me within the week. I smiled to think that she also fell into treating me without consultation about my own convenience. I felt no resentment about this, only amusement. After all, I was the one who had changed, not those I left behind. Even this was not entirely true, however, as I found my brothers and their offspring had subtly and, occasionally, forcefully altered in their opinions, especially my brother Richard. Tom had described him as restless and impatient, but to me he seemed fired with an ambition that had no outlet, questioning how and why he was unable to go forward with some enterprise of merit. "What is it that draws you?" I asked him. "That's it, sis. I don't know what I want, just what I don't. I don't want the old round. I want something different, something new." It gave me great pleasure to think that I would be able to help him towards that something, though I did not want to speak of it until I had a more exact notion of my wherewithal. When at last he broached his desires, I was surprised I had not thought of it myself, but that is matter for later in my story.

Amidst their changes, one thing had remained very much the same among my family: I found them all still arguing about religion, though there was no longer anyone playing the role of Sylvester Petrie, from whom I had absorbed my own questioning attitude. Was there too much silver plate in the church? Ought there to be more or less hymn singing? More or fewer sermons? That people were so exercised over these questions amazed me.

On the evening before I left I took Tom aside from one of these discussions to tell him that I had found a few jewels on the island

and of my plan to sell them in London. "For goodness sake, Roberta," he said. "That is a fine thing. Perhaps you might bring back some candy for the little ones then?" I smiled, knowing that I might be able to bring back a good bit more than that. It was a fine secret to rest upon.

On a bright Thursday morning, Lady Evelyn's coach rumbled into the yard and the stocky green-coated coachman, who was vaguely familiar to me, asked for Mistress Roberta and invited me to mount. I took my trunk with me as I had it in mind to go up to London from Lady Evelyn's in order to sell my jewels. Rachel hugged me and said, "You will come back, won't you?" "Of course, I will," I assured her. I kissed Tom and Susan and the other children goodbye and went off. It was a drive of no more than an hour and a half. The day was fine and the coach window framed a succession of lovely views of the countryside. How pretty green England was in the sunlight, how soft and gracious! At last through the trees I caught sight of the white stone seat of the Hordleys set amidst an emerald chase. It was an elegant building of two broad stories with a marble staircase leading to its broad wooden door.

Lady Evelyn must have been awaiting our approach as she quickly appeared on the doorstep and came down to meet me, immediately hugging me to her bony torso and kissing me several times. She wore a large powdered wig and a bright yellow brocade dress. "Roberta, you can not know how very happy I am to see you and to receive you back into our bosom," she said. I was very happy to see her too, and she immediately amused me as she always had. After embracing me she held me at arm's length to inspect me, just as my brother had done, but with an eye attuned to different standards. "Roberta, you have not been taking as good care of your skin as you ought. We must begin a regimen of cucumber salve right away," she said and led me into the house.

"I am very happy to see you too, Lady Evelyn. I was relieved beyond measure when I heard that Leora had been rescued and lives a good life in Virginia," I said, as we settled into the blue brocaded drawing room. "Ah yes," Lady Evelyn said fondly, "She has three little ones. Last year she came for six months and we had a most happy time together. She will be so very glad to learn that you also survived. She often reminisced about how you had carried her on to the deck of the ship and held her in the lifeboat." Lady Evelyn handed me a cup of tea and added, "You really ought to have had a sailor assist you. That is what men are for." Here I smiled, feeling myself cast again into Lady Evelyn's milieu, which now appeared to me more bizarre than ever.

It quickly became apparent that Lady Evelyn had little interest in my life after the shipwreck, that she took it for granted that it was a most horrible interlude. "I'm sure you don't wish to be reminded of it all the time," she said. "On the contrary," I said, "While I was for many years very lonely, I nonetheless enjoyed myself quite well. The surroundings were very beautiful and the weather so gentle that one felt constantly in a sort of caress." I surprised myself with this lyricism and I shocked Lady Evelyn, who was quite at a loss for words and gave me a wide-eyed look as though I had said something lewd. "Yes, well, that's over now, dear, and you're back in the 'caress' of your own people."

I did not want to upset Lady Evelyn, who seemed to have a plan for my future, but I thought it wise to make known my own plans as soon as possible. "Lady Evelyn. I am married now to a man native to the southern climes, and we have a son named Tom. He is almost five-years-old. I love them both very much and will return to them as soon as I can. You see, I was taken off the island by a deluded zealot who thought he was saving my soul."

I knew Lady Evelyn's mind very well and saw that when I mentioned my marriage she glanced at my clothes. I imagined that she must think that my improved wardrobe meant I had married a man of some means, and her next question proved me right. "I had no idea you were married," she said with a slight tinge of annoyance. "Is your husband a planter then?" "Yes, on a very simple scale. We are both planters and raise all we need on our estate." "Of what nation is your husband," she next asked. "He is of the tropics," I said. "How were you married?" Lady Evelyn pressed on. Here I could no longer accommodate her ideas. "We had no clergy, isolated as we were, so we pledged ourselves to each other on our own," I said. Her sharp intake of breath told me of her shock. "Then you are not legally married?" she said. "Not by English law," I answered. "Or any other law?" she asked. "By the laws of our affection," I said. "My dear Roberta," she said with a relief that puzzled me. "In fact, you are not married at all. You are only saying you are married because you have had a child. I can understand you perfectly. You were alone on an island, entirely at the mercy of this man. What could you do? But now you are back among us and all can go on as before. I have even prepared a separate room for you," she ended quite pleased with herself.

Lady Evelyn was essentially a kind woman who helped those in need in her neighborhood, but she also lived in a world the urgency of whose rules had never pressed upon me as they did upon her, though I had had to abide by and pretend obeisance to them. Now I no longer had to pretend, though I did not want to punish her and said as gently as I could, "I feel entirely married, Lady Evelyn, and will return to my husband as soon as I can. I have already booked passage for September. I have come into some money and will be able to make my own way."

Poor Lady Evelyn was quite crushed and seemed to shrink into her chair. "Oh Roberta, I was so hoping we could again live as we did before you left." Now I understood that to her I represented a time before she had lost her daughter and that she was herself lonely. I put my hand on hers. "I will be very happy to be here with you for a while so that we can recollect those times together," I said. She brightened a little, "Perhaps after spending time here, you will realize that this is where you belong." "I doubt of that, Lady Evelyn, but I want you to know that I thought of you and missed you many times during the years I have been gone, and I will think of you and miss you when I again go away." She smiled and looked pleased though her pleasure had about it some suspicion that I was condescending to her and that condescension had previously been hers to dispense. "You've always been a good girl, Roberta, though a bit careless of your appearance. Now that you are a woman of some means, you ought to devote more time to it. I will be glad to help you." "Yes," I said, "I would be most grateful."

Indeed Lady Evelyn was supremely competent in the narrow domain she had taken as her own, and I knew I would benefit from whatever ministrations she visited upon my appearance. She had been a great beauty as a girl and made a marriage somewhat above her own station to an impecunious nobleman who ate into her fortune and would have devoured it all had he not fallen from his horse and been killed. It was Lady Evelyn's earnest desire that her daughter marry upwards into wealth that had led her to part with Leora, whose marriage to Thomas Overby brought her into one of England's best families.

Chapter 15—I Am Waylaid Yet Fortunate

ady Evelyn and I spent the evening together engaged in recalling Leora's exploits as a child, and I was given a very detailed account of her offspring, two boys and a girl, all of whom, according to Lady Evelyn, were superior in every way to all other children. Since I believed that this position was occupied by my own boy, we contended a bit over their various excellences and agreed that they might share the honor.

Lady Evelyn sent for her maid and told her to take my belongings into the creekside bedroom. "But you told me to ready the staircase room," the young woman protested. Lady Evelyn gave her a sharp glance. "Yes, but now you will prepare the creekside chamber." This was a much better room, as I knew because I was utterly familiar with how the rooms in the house were ranked and realized I had been promoted in Lady Evelyn's mind, no doubt as a result of my improved wardrobe.

I liked the room very much and recognized its pretty lace counterpane and Turkey carpet before the fire as items I had long ago cleaned. "You will, of course, take your meals in the dining room with me," Lady Evelyn said as she bid me goodnight, further confirming my improved social position. All was comfort and elegance, and I slept well enough after my usual visitation with the sorrow of being gone from Freeman and Tom.

The next morning as I entered the breakfast room I saw there an unfamiliar man who rose to meet me. "Roberta, I'd like to present my manager, Mr. Benjamin Miller, who I have invited to join us." He was a tall man of about forty, fair, well-made and lively-looking with clear blue eyes. "I'm very happy to meet you, Mistress Crousseau. I have heard much of you over the years. I hope to hear more of your recent adventures, if you are not already tired of repeating them," he said very nicely. "I would be most happy to tell you of them," I answered. "I have not had a chance to wander about the grounds yet, but from what I saw on my way in, you have made them flourish, Mr. Miller." "Oh, yes," said Lady Evelyn. "He's a marvel of efficiency and application, quite perfect, in fact, except that he lacks a wife," she said pointedly. Mr. Miller caught her implication as well as I did and treated it very lightly, so as to diminish our mutual embarrassment. "It's good to have a wife," I said, "at least I hope my husband thinks so." Lady Evelyn looked annoyed and Mr. Miller looked a bit surprised. "Ah, somehow I had thought you were all alone in your island exile. I'm glad to know that you were not."

As we ate our sausage and eggs and drank tea, I recounted some of my life, and I also listened as Lady Evelyn and Mr. Miller spoke of matters pertaining to her estate. He spoke with such good sense and good-humored management of her idiosyncrasies that by the end of the meal I had gained respect for him. He invited me to tour the estate and I agreed to do so in the afternoon.

For the rest of the morning I submitted to Lady Evelyn's ministrations regarding my appearance, which consisted of being plastered with various oily applications followed by astringents daubed on at her direction by her current maid, Nelly, the girl I'd met the day before. This girl had constantly to restrain her native exuberance to conform to Lady Evelyn's more sedate character. "Now calm down, Nelly," her mistress would say, "You'll rub Roberta's flesh right off the bone and she has none to lose!" I must say I enjoyed this process. While we were about it, I asked Lady Evelyn to assist me in finding a reputable jeweler in London, which occasioned much probing as to why I needed one, though she assured me she knew several, and would send notes telling them to expect me, but she added, "You must not leave too quickly, Roberta. I have just got you back and will not give you up so easily." I had planned to go within a few days, but she was so sincere in her appeal that I decided to prolong my stay. I could not leave England for several months longer and while I was here I might as well gratify this woman who had been good to me, especially given the novelty of her so attentively tending to my well-being.

In the afternoon, Mr. Miller arrived to show me around the estate. Lady Evelyn's husband had been ready to sell the land out from under her, but his untimely death prevented it, so hundreds of acres and a number of rented farms in the area still belonged to her, and to her credit, she wanted to improve them. It was a pleasure to walk over the grounds accompanied by a man who truly loved them and devoted himself to carrying out this improvement. My own experience made me able to enter sympathetically and knowledgeably into a discussion of agriculture and building with Mr. Miller, so we spent several hours so engaged. Mr. Miller asked frequent questions about my own practices upon the island and made some useful suggestions. I had described to him how we fetched our water and he suggested a simple installation of clay pipes to ease our labor, a scheme I resolved to implement upon my return.

Our easy discourse and mutuality of interest were a pleasure to me, and, apparently, to him as well. "Madame Crousseau, I cannot tell you how long it has been since I have been able to talk to someone so profitably. I'm going to take your advice about using more sand with the carrots." I laughed, "Yes, I've had much more experience with sand than the average Englishwoman." "You are far beyond the average Englishwoman in every way," he said, then hurriedly took his leave as if he had exceeded what he felt appropriate to say. I was myself a bit discomfited, especially as I found myself wondering how he would look in a loincloth.

In the afternoon one of Lady Evelyn's dearest friends came to call; it was the grey-haired Miss Higgins after whom I had named my cat. As we sat at tea I smiled often, realizing how well-chosen kitty's name was as Miss Higgins was herself quite feline, not only in her looks but in her attempts at sly indirection in questioning me. "I suppose your husband misses his connections in Europe a great deal," she said, angling to find out from whence he came, as she assumed he had gone out to the new world in the same way I had. "I imagine he misses me very much," I said, "I am his only connection in Europe." "Oh, his family is among the older settlers then," she said. "Oh yes, the very oldest," I said, at which she smiled in calculation that this meant he must be very rich. "Is his estate very large, then?" "It consists of an entire island that takes the better part of a week to go round," I answered honestly.

Though I knew I was misleading Miss Higgins and was enjoying the game a bit, my deeper motive was to prevent the dismay that both she and Lady Evelyn would feel if I gave a more accurate picture of Freeman that did not rely on their preconceptions; I simply did not want to contend with them. As I reflected later on this encounter I realized I would have liked to give a truer picture, that my oblique approach to description landed me once again in the loneliness that had been my lot in England before I left. How I wished there were someone with whom I could speak freely! Now that I knew what intimacy was, I felt the lack of it most keenly!

Over the weeks I spent with Lady Evelyn, our lives assumed a routine: The mornings I had to myself. I often walked about the grounds, musing upon an agenda consisting of what I would do for my brothers and what I would take back with me to the island, interspersed with fervent imaginings of what my own boys were doings and hope that they continued well and secure in the knowledge that I would come back to them as soon as I was able.

Little by little Lady Evelyn began to ask me to do things for her. "You were always a marvel with a needle, Roberta. Do mend my nightcap as Nelly is all thumbs." I was happy to do these small things, but soon the requests became more like orders: "I will need my pelisse this evening, Roberta. Will you see that it is well pressed?" At last I said I had something else to do and would not be able to accomplish the task she had assigned me. At this her face reddened and I felt her displeasure at being balked. "What can possibly occupy you, Roberta?" she demanded. "A collection of small things," I said, further denying her authority either to order me about or to interrogate me. She swept away in a huff, and the orders abated for a bit, but she could not help trying to reassert her dominance over me, so when she did I simply went outdoors to avoid her.

On my walks I often saw Mr. Miller at work. Not only had he improved the look of the estate enormously, but he was also engaged in making it more productive by planting fruit orchards, recovering arable land that had fallen into disuse and draining swampland to stem disease.

He often hailed me and explained what he was about, which I always enjoyed.

Once I said, "How lucky it was that Lady Evelyn was able to engage your services, Mr. Miller, as your talents seem fitted to a wider prospect." Miller blushed and looked very uncomfortable at this, so I surmised that, like me, he had his own secrets. He said, "I sought a remote employment as I like the quiet and country scope of things here." I felt that I had blundered and caused him pain and was very sorry. "Oh yes," I said banally, "the beauty of one's surroundings has everything to do with one's state of mind." We walked on in silence until he said, "I like you very much Madame Crousseau and do not want to put dishonesty between us. I met with some trouble in my previous employment, and I could not get a good character of my employer. I was lucky that Lady Evelyn was willing to take me on without one." "No, it was she who was lucky, Mr. Miller," I said. Of course I wondered what sort of trouble he spoke of, but I did not ask as he had gone quite far in telling as much as he had, and I was not yet prepared to be equally honest with him. I liked him but did not trust that I could say to him, "My husband wears a loincloth and hunts with a bow," and that he would receive such a declaration with equanimity. I was further disturbed that this way of putting my relation to Freeman made me feel ashamed. My discomfort was always practically symbolized by the pinch of the corset I was obliged to wear. Its ever-presence grew ever more odious.

In the afternoons I sat with Lady Evelyn in the drawing room, talking and sewing, a time when she seemed to enjoy my company for itself and forgot our social relation. I told her of the embroidered pictures I'd made on the island, so she set me to work one, suggesting that I sew a scene of the island. As we sewed we usually talked about Leora and her family, which I knew was for Lady Evelyn a way to feel her daughter was with her and not thousands of miles away over an immense ocean. And, even though she made some efforts not to treat me as a servant, our previous relation had not habituated her to discussing my feelings or memories and that attitude continued. I would have been glad to speak more than superficially of what I had experienced after the shipwreck, but I quickly grew tired of the many times I had to relate the main story to the neighbors who called upon Lady Evelyn, often with the express purpose of viewing me.

On one such occasion, attended by Miss Higgins and another lady of the neighborhood, a dark, stout lady named Miss Pitcaithley, who was swathed in such enormous amounts of lace that she appeared a gargantuan cake, Lady Evelyn invited Mr. Miller to join us as Miss Pitcaithley was much interested in flowers and wanted to discuss her hydrangeas with him. At a lull in the conversation Mr. Miller inquired if he might look at my embroidery, which I had held closely. When I showed it to him, his eyes grew quite wide and he exclaimed, "My word, Madame Crousseau, what a striking scene! Can it be such colors are truly to be found in that region?"

I had depicted an island sunset bordered by a palm tree and the purple, pink and yellow flowers found so plentifully throughout. "Yes and no," I replied, "In fact, I have not the array of colors I would need to depict it accurately, nor can one perceive the golden quality of the light nor the fragrance of the air that surrounds one." So heartfelt was my answer in conveying how I missed the island that Mr. Miller looked at me quite tenderly. The ladies were carefully attending my speech as well, and I saw that I had even penetrated Lady Evelyn's resolve to ignore my experience of the last ten years. She understood that I was not ignoring it and even a little that I was indulging her in not putting it before her. "My dear," she said, inspecting my piece, "that is quite beautiful. We must have it framed and if you will let me, I will hang it here in the drawing room." I readily agreed. Thereafter, though she still tried to persuade me that I ought not to leave England, she showed more cognizance that an attractive alternative was ever in my mind.

When the time came for me to go up to London, she insisted that Mr. Miller accompany me, and for this I was very glad. I was not frightened of the big city, but I knew a male companion would be a great help. She directed Nellie to brush my dark blue dress as she thought it best for traveling.

The journey took four days during which Mr. Miller and I were left to our own conversation, punctuated by various new passengers from time to time. It was most agreeable to see the English countryside, but there were also on the road many wanderers, including women and children, all of whom looked ragged and poorly fed and walked with downcast faces. "What accounts for these people upon the road?" I asked Mr. Miller. "They are probably going up to the city in hopes of finding work. They used to weave at home, but are more and more displaced by the factory, and their little garden plots have been enclosed and can no longer support them." "That is very sad," I said. "Is there no way to help them?" "It is widely believed that they will naturally find their way into a new life and that it would be wrong to interfere in that process." "What could be wrong about helping those who are suffering?" I asked. Mr. Miller shrugged, "It is the new thinking from those who study economy." "It does not seem to conform to Christian charity," I said. "I think those who espouse such economic beliefs think it would eventually go worse with people if they were helped," he replied. "How can it go worse than to die of hunger?" I said. "I daresay the dons with these ideas have never been hungry themselves." "I daresay you are right," Mr. Miller replied. "I have tried to do what I can to keep Lady Evelyn's tenants from ending up on the road," he said quietly and sadly. "I meant no reproof to you in my observation," I hurried to say. "No, I did not take it so, but it is a sorry subject about which one can do so little," he said, and we broke off talking, each sinking into our own thoughts as the coach rolled over England, most of which I had never seen before and whose customs presented themselves as a vast field for my imagination.

This imaginative journey ended abruptly on our third day of travel. About an hour after we had taken lunch at an inn, four men on horses overtook us and we felt the coach roll to a sudden stop. I looked out the window and was startled to see one of the mounted men pointing a heavy pistol at the driver. He saw me and said, "My mate is on the other side with another of these, so do nothing to annoy us." I was more surprised than afraid. It seemed the stuff of a romance story, though indeed it was happening.

This slight, youngish fellow, the lower half of whose face was covered with a green silk scarf, instructed us to climb down. "We won't hurt you if you are nice to us," he said jocularly but with an edge of menace. Mr. Miller put his arm around me in protection, a redundant gesture as the bandit had made no move towards me. "I have no designs on your lady, sir. I have designs upon her valuables," he said rather gaily and jumped off his horse. "So give them to me, and we'll be on our way." He took Mr. Miller's wallet and grabbed my reticule. "Hold out your hands, Madame," he instructed. "A nice ring," he said, pointing at the gold band I'd found in the cave and worn in token of my union with Freeman. "Hand it over." "But it is my wedding ring!" I exclaimed. "I'm sure your husband will hurry to buy you a new one," he said, grinning at Mr. Miller and then demanding his watch. "But oughtn't a lady dressed as you are have more jewelry about her?" he asked. "Perhaps it is in your trunk?" he suggested and directed one of his henchmen, all of whom seemed very young and who said nary a word, to take our bags off the top of the coach. He demanded the keys and proceeded to ransack each one, throwing the garments helter-skelter on the ground.

I watched him toss my old blue wool dress aside as unimportant, as I was pretty sure he would. I felt little anxiety as to the brigand's discovering my hidden jewels in it. Had he been a careful observer, he might have wondered at the contrasting quality of the dress I wore and the one I carried in my trunk, but he struck me as almost exclusively focused on his own display. "It seems you have no jewels, milady," he said. "Are you on the decline? Going up to London to get a loan, perhaps?" "My business is none of yours, sir," I said. "You are a lively woman," he said, "perhaps you would like to return to my camp with me?" "No, indeed, Mr. Brigand," I answered. "No? Too bad." At this, he mounted his horse, waved to his minions and they began to ride off.

Suddenly, the young leader reined in his horse, turned and trotted slowly back towards our group, none of whom had emerged from astonishment at what had befallen us. The brigand pulled up in front of me. "You amuse me," he said, "I think I'll take you with us for a bit." At this Benjamin thrust himself between me and the young man's horse. "You shall not take her," he said gallantly. The young man drew his sword and thrust it down close to Benjamin's throat. "I'm sure she would rather come with me than see her husband spitted like a capon before her," he said, adding as if to an audience of superiors who were not there to hear him, "I shan't keep her long. I easily tire of things." I stepped forward. "Of course, I shall be glad to go with you. I may also be amused," I said, as though agreeing to accompany an acquaintance to a bazaar. I do not mean to say that I was not frightened, but at the same time, I perceived a note of falsity in the young man's menace, and his companions increasingly struck me as puppies in the train of a dog only somewhat more mature than they. I saw in their eyes that their leader's intent to abduct me had alarmed them. "Reassemble the lady's trunk," he called to one of them. "Her sojourn with us will not interfere with her toilette."

Benjamin was still poised at the end of the sword point, his face drained. "Don't worry, Benjamin. I believe the man. He will treat me well." "Roberta. . . " he began, but the brigand pushed against the sword to quiet him as around us his minions threw my clothes into the trunk, including, I saw, the blue dress. Then he reached down, grabbed my arm and dragged me up onto his horse, a painful maneuver that pulled my shoulder unnaturally and made me cry out. "I'm so sorry, madame," he said as he turned his horse, dug his spurs into the animal's sides and galloped us off, holding me tightly around the middle. I was much unnerved as, besides the unpleasant novelty of being abducted, neither had I much experience upon a horse, and under the spur of its master, this one threw us wildly up and down as it cantered through forest paths and hedgerows. Despite the violent thumping of my bottom I was still able to wonder just how far this fellow's playacting would extend, what distance he would travel in his assault of me.

We had ridden for what seemed over an hour when he signaled his troop to slow. He drew from his pocket the scarf he had worn when robbing the coach and tied it around my head. "You must not know where you are, Madame," he said. "Have no fear. I have no idea," I assured him. We traveled a good deal longer, me in a blinded state, until at last we slowed and he pulled off my blindfold. Before us stood a stone cottage such as commonly formed an outbuilding to some grander place.

The young men dismounted. "I must go now," one of them said in an adolescent croak and turned his horse. "I will be missed." "I as well," said another and hurried away. Soon I was left with the chief and only one of his followers. "They are such spoil sports," he opined, as he dismounted. "Come down, Madame," he said, holding up his arms that I might ease my way to the ground through them. Face to face with him, I saw that he was handsome, his face angular, his hair a light brown, but a furtive air about him reminded me of a small rodent. Looking to the door of the cottage, he said, "Do come into my cozy lair and I shall give you some refreshment."

I went forward into the place and found it richly furnished with satinwood tables, settles and damask-covered cushions, far above what would be expected in such a place, though there was a sort of incongruity to the décor as though it had been assembled from different households. "Is this your clubhouse then?" I said, perhaps too acidly, for the brigand replied as if I had violated the rules of our game, "Do not mock me. I do not like it." "You have abducted me, sir." "I said I would not harm you," he said petulantly. "However, you greatly inconvenience me and worry my companions," I said. "And why should I believe you won't harm me?" "Because I am a gentleman," "In what code of gentlemanly behavior do robbery and abduction figure?" I asked. "I give the money to the poor," he said, motioning me to a seat upon the settle before the fireplace in which his sole companion was kindling a blaze. "Ah, you are Robin Hood then," I said. "You have a sharp tongue upon you," he said. "You look softer than you are. I prefer a soft woman." There was enough menace in this to quiet me. "Ah, you take instruction well. Now you must amuse me." At this the other man went out of the cottage as if upon a signal. Now I was worried.

"Who are you?" I asked, quite sincerely. He searched my eyes. "I will tell you. I am the scapegrace son of a great man. I am insufferably confined by his greatness and must get my pleasure as I will. At this moment you are my pleasure." "How sad for you to be reduced to me for your amusement," I said. "Nothing can improve my situation," he said, his words backed by a vast reservoir of self-pity, "but you shall do for the nonce." "Who are you?" he then asked me. I thought quickly, inventing the most innocuous identity I could on short notice. "I am the companion to an elderly woman. I travel to London at her bidding to visit her ailing sister. My husband manages her estate." He sighed in a way that told me I was indeed a disappointment, then looked up. "You have more spirit than those circumstances would warrant," he said. "Are you not yourself bored?" he asked. "Not at all. I am very satisfied and grateful for my life." "Very satisfied and grateful," he said in a wheedling imitation. He had drunk off several glasses of wine by now.

"Well, I must do the best I can with you. I will give you a little adventure. Take off your dress." "What?" I said. "I spoke in plain English. Take off your dress." "You said you would not harm me." "But I did not say I would not harm your sensibilities. Take it off at once. I will help you." With this he pushed me around so my back faced him and he began to unlace my dress. "Stand up," he said. When I did so, he pulled my dress off my shoulders, took one sleeve and then the other and pulled them off too, so I stood half-uncovered in my stays and shift, my breasts quivering above them. "Go on, take it off," he ordered. I pulled it over my head. He surveyed me. "So much fabric below the dress," he said, pulling at my outer petticoat until he had loosed its strings. "Step out of it," he said. Then I stood with only my underpetticoat covering my nether regions which formed a dark patch through the white cambric of the petticoat. He stared intently at me. I wondered if he intended to rape me. "Now take the rest off," he commanded. "Why do you find pleasure in humiliating me?" I asked. "I'm not sure," he said, "mostly I just want to look at your body. You women go around so swathed, we men long to look at you." "But most men don't force us in this way." "Didn't I tell you to take off the rest?" I slowly unlaced my stays and took them off; I let drop the petticoat, then slipped the shift over my head and stood naked. "Hmmm. . ." he sighed. "One of your breasts is larger than the other. Did you know?" he said, surveying me and taking a swig at his wine. "And you are rather used in the belly, no?" "I have had a baby," I said. "How unfortunate for your belly!" he said as if making a quip. I saw now what sort of humiliation he favored.

"Now I want you to piss," he said, an order somewhere deep within which I heard a strain of shame. "I fear I cannot do so upon command," I mustered as my first response to this very odd request. "Then you must drink until you cannot help yourself," he said and thrust a glass of wine at me. I had not before been truly angry, but now I found myself utterly enraged at the juvenility of this show, but I fought to control myself as I wasn't sure exactly what my part required and feared to push the villain. "Where am I to do this elimination?" I asked. "There in front of the fire," he pointed. "And into what receptacle?" He looked around. "Into this bucket," he said and fetched an oaken one from the scullery. "You are aware that women do this in a different manner than do men," I said. "Naturally," he said.

There seemed no way out. I squatted over the bucket, but I had been serious when I told him I could not pee upon command and found I could not emit a drop. "It must be an uncomfortable posture for you," he said, "so you had better do it." "Your concern for my comfort is quite touching," I said. I set myself to think of all forms of water and to try to forget the brigand's presence. I thought of the ocean off the beach of the island and of the riverine rills running down to the sea, and these thoughts brought Freeman to mind. What would he think of this perverse circumstance? Luckily, entertaining his image relaxed me enough that I was able to let go a small stream of urine into the bucket. I could feel it splash against my bottom. "Very good, Madame, I knew you could do it," the young man said with genuine pleasure. He tossed me a napkin to wipe myself and I did so.

"It's rather cold," I said. "Oh, I'm so sorry," he replied. "Let's see what's in your trunk then," and I sensed that this strange ritual might be nearing its end. His henchmen had brought in the trunk and it now sat near the wine table. He tried to open it but could not. "Locked again? I don't suppose you have the key?" "No, it was in my bag, which was taken by your men." At this he raised his boot and viciously kicked against the lock until it yielded to him. One by one he drew out the garments--the red satin I had altered upon the ship and several undergarments. Then he pulled out the blue wool dress in which I had been shipwrecked and in which was sown my hope of getting back to Freeman, Tom and our island. "This does not seem the sort of garment a lady of your station would wear," he said, curious. "No, it is the dress of my maid, Nellie. Your men must have mixed our clothes together," I said with disdain, having only the instant before decided upon a gamble. I most certainly wanted to leave this place with the dress and it seemed possible that it might allow him an opportunity to further degrade me. He paused for a time. "Let's see how it looks on you," he said, throwing the dress at me. "Let's see the lady in the maid's garb." He had taken my bait!

How disgusting he was, thinking to further humiliate me, but I did not feel humiliated, just relieved that he'd done as I'd hoped and forced me to wear the blue dress. I felt as if I were at a rite of Freeman's tribal chief, though it would not, apparently, end in my death. I started to put on my undergarments, but he stopped me. "No, just the dress. You will feel the full force of the coarse fabric that way," he said, as if administering me a lesson in social caste. I pulled on the dress, glad to button it over my breasts. "It fits you very well, you know," he said, "not entirely unbecoming, though utterly without style, of course."

"Now I shall return you to the road. You may have some trouble regaining your husband, but I'm sure whatever difficulty is entailed will ennoble your character," he said as if from a well of wit. I thought nobility must be quite a foreign subject to him and so did not inflame him with the natural reply that it was a realm in which he had never traveled.

When he had mounted his horse and pulled me up in front of him, he again fastened the scarf round my head, and we rode off, myself blinded to whatever sights we passed. This time the ride seemed shorter. He pulled up and I felt him turn the horse around several times. "You are but a short distance from a major route," he said and more or less pushed me off the horse, not as if he wanted to hurt me, but rather that he did not want to unblind me. "Count to fifty before you remove the scarf," he said, "and take care." He had spoken for all the world as if we were friends. It was another astonishment to add to the list I had accumulated that day.

Naturally, I did no counting. I pulled the scarf off soon enough to see the young man's back and the chestnut flanks of his horse cantering away into the more wooded fork of what I saw was a crossroads with the nearest villages conveniently marked on a post. It seemed the young villain had little care for my knowing that he dwelt on a great estate somewhere in this vicinity. It ought not to be too hard to find out who he was; how could he be so blatant? The sun declining to the left of me and London being to the east, I took the road that led to the right and began my hike towards Kelchester, according to the sign. I was cold and felt the want of my underwear.

Chapter 16—A Matter of My Purse

I was also hungry. I had no idea how far Kelchester was, but I walked as rapidly as I could for the warmth of it. I smiled a bit at the relief of at least being free of the hateful stays, but as I walked further I reflected briefly on the strange character of the young man who had abducted me. He was like no one I had ever before encountered. Soon, however, graver thoughts much like those I had had in my early days upon the island forced themselves upon me: Survival was uppermost in my mind.

I had no money, and, although I carried what I believed to be a valuable collection of jewels, I could not reveal it in my present circumstance. My maid's attire did not justify my having jewels, so I would be thought a thief. Nor could I trust that whoever I attempted to trade with would think I might have more jewels and set upon me to find out if this were so. I decided to let this problem simmer in my mind until I reached Kelchester and found out exactly how far from London I was.

Then there was the matter of Benjamin. What had he been doing in my absence? I was sure he had reported my abduction to a constable as quickly as he could, but how quickly would that have been and where would he be now? If it had been me, I would have waited in the neighborhood of the robbery, but I was not even sure where we had been at the time. I thought somewhere about fifty miles from London.

I was so caught up in my calculations that I was surprised by the sight of fellow travelers ahead of me on the road. As I drew closer I saw they were some of the tattered poor that I had noted in the previous days from my seat in the coach. Their group was a woman in a dun shawl and a greasy grey dress and two children, a girl of twelve or so and a younger boy. None of them had shoes.

When I drew abreast, I said, "Hello. Can you tell me how far it is to the village?" They looked at me indifferently, though there was some curiosity in the boy's eyes. "It's but a quarter mile to the village," said the woman. This address told me that even in my maid's costume, I seemed of much greater degree than they. "What are ye doing upon this road alone, ma'am, with no coat nor nothing?" asked the boy. "Hush, Jem. Mind your business!" scolded his mother. "I don't mind. I am lost," I said. "I was parted from my people some ways to the west and am trying to find them." "We are all lost," the woman said sadly. "Have you no destination this evening then?" I asked. "We're going to my aunt in Kelchester," the boy piped up. "For what good it will do us," the girl said, speaking as if she thought it were a waste of her breath. "No, Margaret, Auntie Louisa may know of some work," her mother said wearily.

By now there were more of us upon the road, a cart pulled by a worn horse and several men with sacks upon their backs. In the distance I could see chimneys. Soon the buildings to which they belonged came into view, a line of plastered cottages, a field of grass before them, a stone church at the end of the road. My companions halted before one of the cottages, a small but brilliantly white-washed one. "This is where we stop," the woman said, adding shyly, "perhaps my sister would make some tea for you." I smiled my ready agreement as she rapped upon the door, which soon opened to reveal a woman who looked almost exactly like her. "Ah, it is you, Caroline," she said with what I thought was a sort of affection mixed with resignation. "Can you take us in for a bit, sister," my companion asked. "Yes, yes, come in," she answered, looking at me askance. Her sister explained, "This woman has been separated from her people and is lost upon the road. Might we offer her some tea." "Certainly, come in. I am Louisa Southwood," she said as she led the way into a small room furnished only with a rough table, two benches, a bed and a cupboard.

"You are very kind," I said. "My name is Roberta Crousseau. I am trying to find my way to London as that is where my party is going." Both women looked at me as if they wanted to ask me just how I had become "separated" from my people but were too polite to do so. "We are not so far from London," said the sister, who was busying herself preparing tea, "though I have never been there myself." "Perhaps the vicar could help you," she said, then sighed and shook her head. "When you have finished your tea, I will take you to him."

Twenty minutes later, Louisa and I walked the length of the village and knocked upon the door of the vicarage, a cottage much grander than Louisa Southwood's, though still modest. An aproned woman answered the door. Louisa announced the purpose of our visit. The aproned woman nodded and led me inside. I looked around to see Louisa retreating. "You're not coming?" I asked. She nodded no. "I'm not needed," she said simply.

I was led to a small, comfortable sitting room, where an elderly, bewhiskered, potbellied gentleman in spectacles sat before a fire. He looked up at me with curiosity. "She's lost," said the woman who must have been his housekeeper as I could not imagine a wife would have addressed him so indifferently. "Lost is she? Ah, well, we are all lost without the lamb, aren't we?" he said in what I took to be an instructive sort of jest, though he was the second person who had said the like today, a day that had been very long. I was suddenly struck with a great weariness and could take no more falsehood.

"Yes, sir. Traveling to London on the coach today I was robbed and then abducted by the robber, who took my clothes and gave me my maid's garment to wear. If you can assist me, sir, my relations will be most grateful and reward your beneficence," I said.

"Robbed, is it? Abducted, is it?" he said, examining me with an extraordinarily minute gaze. I felt again that I were being undressed, but in a much more kindly way. Perhaps the Vicar of Kelchester thought I was mad. "I assure you my tale is true. If you would bc so good as to address a note to Lady Evelyn Hordsley in Somerset, she will confirm who I am, and she will certainly send me the means to rejoin my party."

"Lady Evelyn Hordsley, is it? Young woman, I am quite certain that you labor under a severe delusion," he said in an oddly satisfied way and folded his hands over his little belly. "I have studied every sort of delusion," he said, gesturing to a well-filled bookcase, "and yours is not an uncommon sort. You think you are of a higher station than you are. You speak well enough and think to convince me thereby, but I am not convinced. You cannot fool me."

I drew myself up. "Sir, I assure you I am not in the least deluded. I am only unfortunate. I pray you to help me establish the truth of what I say. I must get to London." "Oh, I will quite willingly help you," he replied. "Though by no means do I believe you, I find your story most interesting and would like you to describe more of it to me. An adventurous delusion indeed!"

He rose and called to his housekeeper. "Rose, please lay a place at table for this young woman and make up a bed for her in the west room." He glanced at me. "In the morning I will give you a bit of money. You might even go to London with it," he said with a merry laugh as if we shared a capital joke. I thought this might be as well as I could do. "I am most grateful, sir, and will accept your help, though when I am able I will repay you and you will see that I am truthful." "Yes, yes, they all say that," he said, ushering me to the dining room where cold roast pork, bread and butter and beer were spread out. I was ravenous and the vigor with which I ate could only have supported the vicar's conviction of my station.

When I had finished and his housekeeper had taken away the dishes, he brought out a worn red account book, opened it in the middle and sat with his pen poised. "Now," he said, "tell me the whole story." "Do you collect stories, sir?" I asked, thinking that if I were to tell him my whole story he would surely take me for a mad woman. "Not just any stories," he answered. "I make a study of delusion or mania. There is such variety in it." "Is it not sometimes dangerous?" I asked. He looked surprised. "Why no, not so far. Everyone in this village and those for several miles around have given me their stories and no danger has come of it." "Everyone?" I asked. "Do you mean that everyone in these parts suffers delusion or mania?" "Yes, indeed. Every single one. And just like you they all avow that they are telling nothing but the truth," he laughed at the childlike absurdity of everyone around him. Now I understood Louisa Southwood's reluctance to come into the vicarage with me and the housekeeper's indifference. They must have tired of the vicar's assurance of their delusion. "And what of you, sir? Are you the only one in this region who is not deluded?" "Why that is a very clever question, my dear. I think there is hope for you. Now tell me your story. I am most interested."

I then did tell him my whole story by which he was most amazed, making interjections from time to time. "An island in the Atlantic, is it! My word!" "And then you married the native in your heart. How novel! It's a wonder you've been able to get any work done with your sort of imagination!" Finally, I stopped asserting my truthfulness and gave the story to the old man as a gift. At last he sat back with an entirely satisfied sigh. "Why don't you get some rest. Perhaps tomorrow we can talk again if you find you've left anything out of your story," he said, giving me a look suggesting I might spend the night making up some further exploits. He closed his account book as though he had accomplished a very great task.

The housekeeper led me to a room at the back of the house where on a small table was a water ewer and a bowl. She pointed out the towel on the made-up iron bed. "Thank you," I said. "You're welcome," she said matter-of-factly, leading me to think that I was one in a long line of "deluded" people who had spent the night here. Whatever the reason, I was most grateful. I took off my dress and lay down at once, slipping into sleep after only a few moments considering the two varieties of strange people I had met today and thinking about Freeman and Tom and how they would marvel at my adventure, though I would certainly censor it for Tom.

The next morning I was treated to a fine bowl of oatmeal and given ten shillings. "And I thank you, my dear woman, for giving me one of the richest examples of delusion I have ever encountered. Truly remarkable." "You are welcome, sir. Thank you for your generosity." I wonder now if he has ever read this account and found his own portrait in it.

"Where is the nearest location that I might find a London coach?" "I will ask the ostler to take you to Lime House Station," the vicar replied. "You might enjoy each other's tales on your way. He thinks he's the son of the lord in the next county!" he harrumphed, though I was inclined to believe the ostler must indeed be the lords's son. The vicar fetched his hat and led me through the Kelchester high street. Spying a modest maroon cape in a small market stall, I asked the vicar to wait while I bargained for it with the stall's proprietress. "You'd best be careful there. She thinks money carries disease. Have you ever heard the like?" "Why yes I have. Does not the Bible identify money as the root of all evil." "Why, yes, but Mrs. Trent here doesn't mean it in a metaphoric way." I could have argued on, but instead went inside and found Mrs. Trent a very mild lady willing to let me have the cape for three shillings.

As the vicar spoke to the ostler, a beefy, red-headed young man, I noticed that all his parishioners treated the vicar in much the same way, with a sort of exasperated weariness. I said good-bye to the old man and took a place beside the young man on the cart. When we had gone a distance the young man said, "I'll wager the priest took your story and said you was unhinged, as he does everybody." "That is exactly what he did," I answered. "Yes, and he's the only real madman for miles around," he said. "Why is he tolerated?" "What's the harm in him? It ain't a crime to have a delusion. That's what he always says." I laughed and found I had arrived at Lime Station in no time.

The coach was not expected for several hours, so I went into the public house and tried to make myself inconspicuous by sitting in a small nook near the door. From there I saw an official-looking fellow nailing a notice to the board outside. My small glimpse of this paper made me jump up and propelled me outside where I saw a poster reading "Reward for the safe delivery of Madame Roberta Crousseau, abducted Tues. upon the London Rd." There followed a very flattering description of me, Benjamin Miller's name and the address of the London Inn at which we had arranged to stay. I was impressed and touched by the dispatch with which he had set about trying to recover me and felt confirmed in my belief that proceeding to London was the right thing to do. I tore down the notice and followed the man I had observed posting it.

"Sir," I said. "I am Roberta Crousseau. My abductor freed me yesterday. " The man looked me up and down, perhaps wondering why one so modestly attired as I would be sought so emphatically. Into his silence I said, "I intend to take the London coach and rejoin Mr. Miller in London. Will you let the authorities know that I am safe and no efforts need be made to recover me?" "Oh don't worry about that," he answered blithely. "Why what do you mean?" I asked. He grew embarrassed and stammered out his reply. "It's just that we know who did it, and we knew no harm would come to you." "You know who did it? Please tell me," I said with some heat. "'Twas Sutton Norman, the Earl's son. He's a blackguard and a mischief-maker that causes his father as much grief as ten bad sons might." "Why is he not arrested and imprisoned then? Surely, a noble birth does not permit one to commit robbery and abduction with impunity," I said with a sense of my own grievance. Again the man hesitated, searching for a way to tell me what I later realized were to him the facts of life. "Earl Norman owns the land for miles hereabout. He's the chief magistrate. He tries to control his son as best he can and always makes it up to the devil's victims. And we like the Earl. He's a good old man, very kind to his tenants." "I see. Then why bother to post the notices?" "Because Mr. Miller paid for it." "Did you tell him what you've told me?" "Something like it," the man said sheepishly. "Very well then. I hope he has not worried unduly about me." "No, ma'am." When the coach finally came, I paid my fare and took a seat. During the afternoon's journey into London I turned over in my mind how an entire county had been made a playpen for a strange, rotten child.

At last we reached the outskirts of London, which had appeared for some time as a dark cloud upon the horizon. The further into the city we went, the darker and noisier it got as the streets narrowed into lanes crowded with dirty brick houses of several stories. "It's as though a permanent twilight prevails here," I said to no one in particular. The only other passenger in the coach was an elderly gentleman who surely thought I was talking to him for he replied, "It is the smoke of many thousands of fires that screens the sun." "It is a sad way to live and cannot be very healthy," I said, thinking of the pristine brilliance of the light on the island. "It's not always like this," the old man said. "Often it is quite lovely and many people feel that the company to be met here and the diversity of both improving pursuits and amusements is worth enduring some foul air." His way of saying this made me think he must be one such person. The filth upon the streets made a wretched stench; I thought I would have to be very amused to endure it for long.

The coachman was kind enough to let me down close to the rooming house where I hoped to find Benjamin Miller. I had only to thread my way through a few very dirty streets asking here and there for further direction before I found it and rang the bell. In a short while a very lean, gaunt woman opened the door and admitted me. Her initial appearance reinforced my impression of London as an unhealthy place, but when she found out who I was Mrs. Stanley was most jolly and accommodating.

"Roberta!" sang Benjamin Miller, who I turned to see jumping out of a chair in the sitting room adjoining the hallway. I was so glad to see him! He came rapidly towards me, enfolded me in his arms, then drew back. "Forgive my enthusiasm," he said. "I'm so relieved to see you!"

"And I you," I said. "Are you all right?" he asked. "Yes, I'm completely unharmed, except a bit in my dignity," I said. "Come in, sit and tell me what happened," he urged. "I will bring some tea," Mrs. Stanley sang out. "Yes, that would be lovely," I said, newly conscious of what a friend I had found in Benjamin Miller. He continued looking at me quizzically. "I was afraid that the goal of our trip to London had been defeated," he said. "But you do not seem disturbed." He feared I had lost what I had meant to sell in London, so I reassured him. "No, my goods are not apparent and continue safe," I said, at which he smiled. "My dear Roberta, your goods are all too apparent." It was a forward speech, but it made me laugh, and I liked it that he was calling me by my first name.

As we sat he suddenly said with puzzlement, "What has happened to your dress?" "The most fortunate thing you can imagine," I said and then told him all that had befallen me, except that I did not tell him about undressing nor about being forced to piss while the young man observed me, which, of course, was the strangest bit of the whole business. "He did not molest you, did he?" Benjamin asked as if to make sure, as the way I was conveying the story had not entailed the terror that would have attended such an event. "No, he is an awful fellow, but not really dangerous," I said. "He sought only to humiliate me." "That is what the constable told me as well," Benjamin said. "Is it not extraordinary that such a predatory young man is allowed to feed upon a whole community because he is bored?" I asked rhetorically. "Unfortunately, it is not so rare as it ought to be," he said. "But, Roberta, I understood that you were to make some financial transactions. How is it still possible?" I smiled broadly. "Partially because of the viper's very need to humiliate me. He made me wear this dress." Benjamin looked at me very curiously. "Whatever do you mean?" "I must postpone telling you until I get some new clothes," I said. "I hope you will forgive me for being enigmatic." "Certainly. I am so glad to see you again and to see you unharmed," he said, again taking my hand. "We shall inquire of Mrs. Stanley where we might find a dressmaker and we shall have a celebratory supper as well."

Benjamin told me that after the thieves had galloped off with me, the coach had gone on, but stopped at the earliest opportunity to inform a constable of our robbery. "It seems this band of young thieves has been harrowing the road for some time," Benjamin said, "but there has been no success in apprehending them. 'We thinks he's got friends in high places,' the man whispered to me conspiratorially. Then his companion said, 'For god's sake, we know who it is, Lord Norman's son, Sutton. He's a devil and a rake, but none can touch him because of Lord Norman's sway.'"

After tea Mrs. Stanley took me to my room, which was charmingly decorated with oaken chests and a flowered counterpane. I inquired after a dressmaker. "As you can see, I am in need of everything," I said. She gave me a look that said she was quite aware I had nothing on under my dress, a fact I had tried to conceal from Benjamin by keeping my cloak upon me, though I must not have been assiduous enough since he had commented upon my dress.

Mrs. Stanley looked as though she were considering a riddle. "It will be hard to acquire garments on such short notice. You might have a dress made in two days, but undergarments, and a dress to tide you over will be needed until suitable attire can be made." She paused. "It is possible. . ." she hesitated. "What is it, Mrs. Stanley?" "Lady Evelyn wouldn't like it." "I have no clothes, Mrs. Stanley. I cannot afford Lady Evelyn's preferences," I said with some resolution. At this Mrs. Stanley put on a conspiratorial smile. "Well then, there are certain shops where gentlewomen in what one could call distressed circumstances take clothes to be sold, all very clean and very fine. Such a shop might answer your need." "Yes, indeed," I said with thorough approval. "Would it be possible that you might be so good as to go to one of those shops and procure some undergarments and a dress for me?" "I'd be delighted. I enjoy these places very much, but one must have an occasion to go to them. That is, one must have some spending money." "Oh yes, you shall have that," I assured her, thinking to borrow from Benjamin and repay him after I had sold my jewels.

He was more than willing to assist in this enterprise. Then I remembered that he had lost his wallet. "True," he exclaimed happily, "but only a fool would keep his money in his wallet upon the road. I can offer you the loan of whatever sum is needed. I shall also accompany Mrs. Stanley and carry back whatever she acquires," he volunteered. Mrs. Stanley was already tying on her bonnet. "Please, bring me a bonnet too and a nightdress if you find one," I asked her. "Oh yes, I shall find you a complete outfit!" she assured me enthusiastically. "Something very subdued. Nothing too elegant or likely to inspire notice, please," I added. "Mr. Miller knows you. He shall be my guide to your taste," Mrs. Stanley said. "Let us go, Mr. Miller," she said, taking his arm and pressing forward as if setting off on a great adventure.

When they had gone I went to my room, whereupon I discovered a great exhaustion and sank upon the bed into a sleep in which Sutton Norman rode away from me again and again. When I awoke, I felt sad and nervous. I wondered if I was strong enough to endure what life had given me. I remembered feeling just this way periodically upon the island before Freeman had come. In the end, one just feels this way, then walks on. I suppose there is nothing to be done but bear what happens even if one is not strong enough, unless one decides to end one's life, and that prospect usually returns one to some other point of view.

Voices and movements below brought me out of my dark reverie, and shortly Mrs. Stanley came in, loaded down with parcels. "We've been most fortunate, Madame Crousseau, most fortunate," she enthused as she unloaded her trove upon the bed. Like a returning hunter, she was anxious to show me the prizes she had bagged. First she drew out a silk shift, edged with an inch of French lace, then two petticoats, an under and an outer sewn with the same lace. "Are they not lovely?" she said joyously. Evidently, such fine work much delighted her. It did me too, but not so much as her.

Next she gently unwrapped a large folded bundle that unfurled into a dark blue dress not unlike the one I had worn on the journey, except that this one was finer in every way. I had altered the original one to fit me, but had done nothing to adorn it; whereas, this one alternated tiers of fine soft wool with tiers of plush velvet, both on the skirt and bodice. "I hope it fits me," I said, and really meant it, for to wear such a garment would be to wear a work of art. "Of course it will fit you," Mrs. Stanley assured me. "We will adjust your stays so it must." With this she brought forth a set of the blasted stays. They were very lovely of their kind, but it would be hard to make a torture wrack seem attractive, for that is how I regarded the stays. "You must try it on," Mrs. Stanley urged and left me alone to take off the faded wool dress and put on the shift, the stays and the petticoats. I laced myself into the stays, trying not to care about their stifling restriction, and when I had pulled the dress over my head I called Mrs. Stanley back in to lace me up.

When she was finished she turned me towards the small mirror on the chest. "Ah, it is perfect," she said. "It could have been made for you. It needs nothing, not even a new hem." From what I could see, she seemed right. The dress felt very well. It was so fine it made me feel taller. "I have also got you the cloak to match and the bonnet," Mrs. Stanley said, unveiling a velvet bonnet the same hue as the tiers in the skirt. "Very charming. You must show Mr. Miller. It was really he who chose it. I might have gotten the green satin gown instead, but he said, 'No, Mistress Crusoe would like this one better. It is finer but asks less to be told so.' I'm sure he meant it as a very nice compliment to you," she said in a way that made me wonder if Lady Evelyn were match-making through Mrs. Stanley's offices.

"I shall wait until dinner to greet Mr. Miller in my new duds," I said, adding, "I wish my husband could see them too." Though she was slightly confused, Mrs. Stanley nodded. "Yes, of course. I shall go and see what cook is up to." "Thank you very much for making such successful purchases for me, Mrs. Stanley. I see no need to engage a dressmaker at all. I appreciate your efforts very much." "I'm happy to do it. After what you've been through you should have something nice." "I wonder who had to sell these things," I said. "Oh, they don't tell you that in the shop," she said, "though the madame did hint that it was someone very high up who sought to gain some money she could hide from her husband."

Early next morning, before prosecuting the reason for our journey, Mr. Miller and I inaugurated my fine apparel by going out to see the great sights of London. We hired a cab and drove to the Cathedral of St. Paul, to Parliament, and to Whitehall. I was awestruck at the grandeur of these buildings. "To think that we are walking where Good Queen Bess trod!" I exclaimed to Benjamin Miller. We drove on Bond St. and through regions of fine houses and saw Buckingham Palace, so I saw that the city's squalor was offset by its evidence of man's great creations. "Perhaps we should call on Queen Anne," I suggested. "I'm sure she would be most interested in your adventures, but we would have to wait months to be admitted, I fear," said Benjamin in a way that made me unsure if he knew I had jested.

As we drove about I pondered the many evidences of civilization I saw, the great buildings, the paintings and immense glass windows of St. Paul's, the houses of a complex government. Compared to them our island garden, goat herd and modified cave were immeasurably puny. Then I consoled myself with the sure knowledge that any aspirations I might have had to participate in the making of the grand buildings, paintings or government would have met no welcome here. Though our achievements on the island were modest, we were able to bring them about ourselves with no permission from anyone else, nor any prohibitions from doing them based on my sex. So far during my stay in England, there had been no occasion for me to wish to do something I could not do, other than rid myself of corsets, but I was certain such would occur if I were to spend much time here. It had already begun incipiently when Mr. Miller and I had discussed my water project before Lady Evelyn. "You'd best leave the building to your husband, Roberta," she'd said. I had become another person in my time away, and I could not resume the restrictive mantle I had outgrown upon the island. I had become a provider, a cultivator and a builder, albeit on a simple scale, and it had given me enormous satisfaction. Nonetheless, I was glad that I had seen some of these fine and magnificent things created by an elaborate society and looked forward to telling Freeman and Tom about them.

After dinner the previous evening I had occupied myself removing the stones from the seams of my old blue dress and stays. I picked at the threads until I had a small pile of red, green and opalescent gems before me. I had also included a few pieces of gold and one dirty grayish stone

I had not recognized. I had no idea what my pile was worth and was very curious to know.

At breakfast, I showed the trove to Benjamin. "I have no experience with such things," he said in amazement, "but it would seem to be a goodly quantity of jewels." Then he asked me where I had hidden them. I told him in the seams of the blue dress. "You are indeed a wonder, Roberta!" he said. "I was lucky," I said, "the brigand could so easily have sent me off without the dress." "The wise men say we make the conditions of our luck, and I can well imagine you did that. After all, you hunted a boar." He said this in a way that was not entirely free of irony.

The next day Mr. Miller escorted me to the jeweler Lady Evelyn had recommended in the Jewish section of London. In its narrow streets bearded men in long shiny black coats came and went from many shops. We entered in at one whose gold nameplate said Melchior Luna and Sons. We were met by a very polite young man, one of the sons, I thought. "I have some gems," I said. "I would like to know how much they are worth and perhaps to sell them." "Certainly, Madame," he said, courteously. "Please show them to me." I took out the cloth bag and emptied it on a piece of black velvet that lay across the glass counter. The young man's eyes grew quite wide. "I must get my father. Please excuse me," he said and disappeared behind a partition.

In a short time an older man, tall, bushily bearded and broad in the chest came out, his son behind him. "Good day, Madame and Sir. I am Melchior Luna," he said. "This is my son Solomon, who says you have some interesting gems." "I have little idea how interesting they are." I said. "I hope you will tell me." "Gladly," he said. He picked up each gem in turn and looked at it very carefully through a heavy lens he held to his eye, betraying nothing about his evaluation of the stones. He seemed especially interested in the dirty grey one that I had thought least promising.

"Where did you acquire these stones, if I may ask?" he said at last, as he scrutinized one of the gold pieces." "I was shipwrecked on an island in the Caribbean. I found these in a cave." Mr. Luna looked at me with wonder. "It is quite true, sir," Benjamin assured him. "She was presumed lost for ten years, and has just recently come back to England. "Ah, so you don't know where they originated," Melchior Luna said, looking at me with new appreciation. "I have no idea," I said.

"The gold is Portuguese," he said and showed me some very small marks upon it. "They were so marked by the king's treasury representative," he explained. "It's likely these gems come from South America. They are extremely good. Each of them can be cut into very valuable jewels. The gold is obviously valuable as well, but your prize is this stone," he said, holding up the dirty grey one. "It is a diamond of at least 8 carats. It alone would make you a very wealthy woman," he said and looked to me for my reaction. "Very good," I said, smiling just a bit. "I look forward to being wealthy. Are you willing to buy the gems?" I asked. Mr. Luna laughed. "Ah, would that I could buy them all! I suppose I could try to persuade you to accept what I could pay you, but that would be to cheat you. Have you shown these stones to anyone else?" he asked. "No," I said, "but I intend to," and told him two names. "Yes," he nodded, "they are excellent judges of stones and also honest men. Let me make you this proposition: I would like to assemble a small group of my compatriots to buy your stones. I will write down how much we will offer. You can compare my offer with what the others say the stones are worth and what they offer. Then I hope you will come back to me," he said and handed me a slip of paper. "You are very fair and generous, sir. I thank you," I said, gathering the gems and putting them back into the bag without even looking at the paper. "Madame, you are carrying a fortune. Allow me to send with you two of my assistants to guard you," Mr. Luna said. I agreed as we had, after all, been robbed and now my gems were not disguised.

While we waited for the guards to arrive, Mr. Luna served us tea. He was much interested in my shipwreck and asked many questions about it. "And now," he said, "you will be a very wealthy English lady. How will you live? Will you purchase a grand estate?" "No, indeed," I replied, "I intend to return to the tropics to rejoin my husband." At this Melchior Luna's eyes grew wider than when he had seen my gems. "I do not mean to be rude, Madame Crousseau, but is it not most primitive in those environs?" "Yes, but it is also very lovely and free," I said, at which Benjamin Miller looked at me curiously, as I had never used the word "freedom" with him in describing life on the island. "You have found paradise then," Mr. Luna said, somewhat wistfully. "Watch out someone doesn't take it away from you." "Ah, it has already happened," I said, though I turned over his warning in the days to come and it led to a crucial idea. It turned out, however, that I did not pay his warning nearly enough heed.

As we mounted the coach to go on to another jeweler, Benjamin said, "Aren't you going to look at the figure on the paper." "I had forgotten," I said. "You are quite astonishing, Roberta," Benjamin said as I unfolded the slip of paper I had crumpled in my fist. I gasped as I read the figure written on it. It said, "100,000 pounds." "I can't believe it," I exclaimed as I showed the slip to Benjamin. "I could never have imagined their being worth so much." "My word, Rebecca, you will be one of the wealthiest women in the kingdom," Benjamin said with both awe and a look indicating genuine happiness in my good fortune. "What will you do?" he asked. I was flustered. "I will go back to my husband," I said.

"Ah, yes," he replied. "I cannot imagine that money would alter your feelings, Roberta."

I hoped what he said was true, but almost immediately alternative futures were opened up to me. It gradually dawned upon me that with such wealth I could choose many different lives, lives that I had yet to imagine. At the end of the day, I had heard from two other jewelers who confirmed Melchior Luna's assessment of my gems and who had offered comparable sums to purchase them. I returned to Luna, however, and arranged the sale with him and within a few days I had an account at the Bank of England with 100,000 pounds in it.

Chapter 17—I Am Seen in New Lights

In the evening of my fortunate day, Benjamin Miller and I sat beside each other on the tartan settee before a fire in Mrs. Stanley's bright parlor. "It is as though you have become the heroine of a fairy tale," he said. "You have something like a magic carpet to take you anywhere you choose." "Yes, it is remarkable," I said, though a picture of my odd treatment by Sutton Norman flew across my eyes. He went on, "Perhaps before you go back to your island you might travel a bit in Europe. Have you not always longed to see the great cities—Paris and Rome?" "I have not." I said, staring a few moments into the fire. "Perhaps since I lacked the wherewithal to fulfill such longings, my imagination refused to engage with them."

"What did you long for, Roberta?" he asked. I had to think for a bit to give him an answer. "Truthfully, when I lived in England, I never longed for much of anything beyond some release from the foolishness that so often surrounded me. I suppose you could say I had a resigned character. Now it is less so because I have had another life." "Besides returning to your husband and son, what do you long for now?" he said. "I hope for more children," I said, surprising myself, as I had not been aware of such a desire before. " I also hope to solve the problem of living on an island inhabited only by my family, where there are no other children for mine to play with, nor to marry when the time comes." "So you want more people upon your island? Won't that necessarily entail the foolishness that you left in England?" I laughed. "Probably so, if foolishness is an inevitable accompaniment of human society. It is indeed a riddle. However, on the island, I can be assured that the foolishness will at least be of a different character." "You would be the ruler, the queen, so you can control all activities," Benjamin elaborated. "My goodness! I've never considered such a thing," I said. "Well, you ought to, for if you have people you must have government."

"And you, Benjamin, what do you long for?" I asked, turning the subject. At this question he looked inexpressibly sad. "Another world entirely," he said. "I would need an island of my own to bring it about." "Why is that? What could you want that would need another world for its realization?" I asked, thinking that his sex and station protected him from the indignities from which the island had allowed me to escape. "I couldn't explain if we had all day," he said. I divined that he did not want to go further in that direction, so I asked, "What is your second choice then?" He brightened a bit and said, "I would like land of my own, of course, and on it I would build a greenhouse where I might conduct some agricultural experiments." From his description I knew that this was something he had often pictured in his mind, and though I had known him only a short time and was not related to him, I resolved to help him get what he wanted. Therein I discovered the first delight of having a fortune. "I wonder what Lady Evelyn and your family will make of your new estate?" Benjamin mused. "I truly have no idea." I said.

At last we went up to bed and Benjamin kissed me on the cheek as if he were one of my brothers. I did not want him to make love to me, but he was an attractive man and I wondered why he did not. Of course he was too honorable to approach a married woman, or perhaps now he feared I might think him after my fortune.

During the next days in London I exercised my new bank account in buying presents for all my family, including several books of engravings and paper for Rachel, and for Lady Evelyn I bought a very beautiful cashmere paisley shawl from India. I also bought many things to take back with me to the island, including an array of clay pipes so that I might implement the water system Mr. Miller had helped me design. I purchased a large supply of willow bark at an apothecary, and I bought tools, nails and screws, lye and large pots of glue, the lack of which had hampered me in many projects. I bought wheels of several sizes, and I acquired a real loom and the proper gear for curing flax to replace my haphazard arrangements.

"Do you still intend to labor so hard?" Mr. Miller asked. "Women of wealth generally hire others to do much of their work, you know," he said as if to explain to me the ways of the world. I realized that it had never occurred to me to alter our way of life upon the island. "I like working," I said, perhaps too jauntily. "I like to use things I've made myself. And now that I have seen how the factory workmen live, I am even more glad to make my own things." "But what about those pipes and the nails," Benjamin said gently. "They were factory-made." "Yes, I guess I am a hypocrite," I sighed. "It is a hard question. I can only do a part." It was a feeble answer, but all I could manage, and to this day I have never solved this riddle.

In London I also sought a solicitor to administer my affairs in my absence. I chuckled to think that I was now a person of "affairs."

Benjamin introduced me to Mr. Felix Gorman with whom several of his acquaintance had profitably dealt. This gentleman's curly hair and lively grey eyes gave him an elfish appearance. I explained to him my situation and his intelligent questions and kindly manner made me trust him immediately and gave me leave to spring my great idea on him.

"I would like to know how I might buy the island upon which I was shipwrecked," I said. "Who owns it now?" Mr. Gorman asked and I told him I had no idea. "Most land in that part of the world is owned either by Spain or Portugal. I've never attempted a sale with a foreign government before, but it sounds very interesting and I will make inquiries. We must have a map of the exact location in order to begin any discussion, of course." I thought Captain Ellis of the Langland might be able to provide such a map, so I told Mr. Gorman that I would arrange to have one sent to him. I felt a small tug of anxiety towards the notion of a map, for if I knew exactly where my island lay, others could know too, but, apparently, this could not be helped.

At last, Benjamin and I set out for Somerset. At the beginning of the trip I had told Benjamin that I preferred that Lady Evelyn not know that we had been robbed and he had agreed that we would not tell her. I was sure it would provoke her to impose restrictions upon me.

As we left London the scenery became progressively greener and the air less smoky. I was relieved to be in the countryside again even though it was often gloomy, with rain and fog the backdrop for the many sad, ragged people we saw upon the road. When we stopped at an inn, I addressed two letters to Kelchester, one for Caroline Southwood and one for the vicar, and put money in both of them. Again, I saw how in contradiction to the old adage, money could indeed bring happiness, for I felt very glad to be able to ease the Southwood's poverty. After several days of bouncing about over bruising ruts, albeit in interesting conversation, we finally clattered again into Lady Evelyn's courtyard.

She herself bustled down the marble steps, very glad to see us. "Roberta, I have missed you excessively, my dear. Come in to tea immediately," she said, her white wig towering over her like a small permanent cloud. As we sat together, I told her that my stones had fetched a good price. When I gave her the paisley, she appeared to gain some idea that such a costly present must betoken a "good price" indeed. "I don't mean to be indelicate, my dear, but just how much money did you get? You have little experience with money and I might be able to help you."

She was sincere in her offer, but very unprepared for the huge sum I revealed to her; her mouth dropped quite open and she stammered, "Roberta, that is, that is. . . ." She could not decide what it was, so out of the natural order was this news. In a bit she seemed to have sorted it out in her mind and turned to me with a very stern face. "Roberta, you must realize that this fortune changes everything. You simply must stay here in England now. Wealth is not a gift; it is a responsibility. You can no longer answer to your own desires alone. I know you are going to say that you are married, but, in fact, you are not legally married. I know that you will think me too blunt, even indelicate, but I must tell you the truth."

I was astounded by her tone of admonishment, quite unlike any she had ever used with me before even in my days as her servant. "Lady Evelyn, I now have more money, but I am still the same person. I have the same desires and aims that I had before I went up to London. There is no use laboring at changing me. In fact, my new wealth confirms me in hewing even closer to my own desires." At this, as from a height, Lady Evelyn said, "That, Roberta, is why the lower orders are not to be trusted with wealth," and then swept from the room, leaving me quite flabbergasted. I found on going to my bedchamber that my wealth had promoted me; my things had been moved to a larger suite, one used for visiting grandees. Before I slept, I turned over Lady Evelyn's reaction in my mind and was alternately amused and angry. However, I found the large bed and the fine sheets very comfortable indeed.

The next morning at breakfast, she had softened. "I was rash in how I spoke to you, my dear," she said, putting her hand on mine. "But my substance was correct. Please promise me that you will think more on your plan and give greater consideration to what you might do with your wealth if you were to stay in England. You might make a fine marriage at the very least and take a respectable role in society. And there's so much good you could do. You think that I am utterly immired in the trivialities of life, that I have not heard or understood your comments about the lives of those such as you saw upon the road to London, but I have. And now you have the means to act on your own assessments. Is it right to run away to a tropical island? It is the lotus-eater's solution and it will not do." She patted my hand. "I'm so fond of you, Roberta. Please promise you'll think about it."

I had never heard her speak so seriously. To please her, I promised. I was going on to my brothers to distribute the gifts I had brought, and I thought that would be a good escape from Lady Evelyn's certitude about what my future ought to be, but I was sincere in my promise to her that I would reconsider my plan. I didn't want to hearken to her opinion but found myself doing it anyway; its very vehemence commanded my mental attention, even though, when I consulted it, my body yearned for Freeman and Tom.

As I rode the coach towards Somerton, I kept the promise. Since I had never had money, I had never wandered in considerations about what was appropriate to do with it. I had no desire whatever to make a great marriage or to cut a figure in society. For one thing, the little I knew of society told me emphatically that in it I would be no more than a novelty, an oddity. The shipwreck and my subsequent life had made me an oddity, but I had no attraction to making a profession of it. On the other hand, it would be possible to live a very quiet life and employ my money to many good ends. I thought of the ragged people I had seen upon the road to London and how I had none of the new-fangled economic beliefs that would hinder me from helping them. Now it seemed that from one point of view going back to the island meant abandoning other people. I had long ago concluded that I could not bring Freeman and Tom here, but I now reconsidered. Perhaps they could be happy in England after all if money could insulate them from indignity.

By the time I had arrived at my brother Tom's house, what I had regarded as my iron resolve to return to the island was at the least somewhat corroded. When I saw little Loretta and Rachel running to greet me, their faces so glad to see me, my resolution melted another degree. "Aunt Roberta! Aunt Roberta!" Loretta called, ran to me and slipped her hand into mine. "I have made everyone wait until you returned to pick up the new kittens, as I remembered you saying you had not seen any in ever so long," she said.

Tom and Susan were equally warm in welcoming me. "Can she see the kittens a little later?" he asked his daughter gently, "I have something else to show her." Loretta consented to go along, and hand in hand we followed Tom, Susan and Rachel across the yard to the edge of the orchard where an old shed had stood for many years. Now I saw that it had been much improved and made a cheery rustic picture with whitewashed walls and green shutters. "Look inside," Tom said proudly. I did so and found a small apartment containing a bed, an overstuffed chair, a bureau and a stove, a comfy nest indeed. On the wall was a lovely watercolor painting of a window through which one saw the trees that bordered the creek. "It's for you, Roberta. We wanted you to have quiet place of your own," Tom said. "I painted the picture," Rachel added proudly.

I was quite moved. "You are very considerate and have gone to much trouble and expense to make such a sweet retreat. I thank you," I said and kissed them. "It's not everyday that your sister you lost for ten years comes back," Tom said, his broad face flushed with feeling. "I know you want to return from where you came, but while you are with us, you shall be comfortable." My trunk was carried down to my new cottage as were the numerous parcels containing the presents I had brought. These were exciting great curiosity among the children, and so I handed round the boxes and invited the children to open them, which they did with much glee. Loretta looked at her new doll with wonder. "She is beautiful, and her dress is very fine," she said solemnly. "She will be my best friend." Rachel was much amazed and transported by the engravings and the fine paper. "You knew just what I would want, dear Aunt," she exclaimed.

The packets I gave Tom and Susan held a length of fine heavy blue wool that would make a coat for him, and there were brass buttons to go with it. For Susan there were three pieces of silk, one in soft green, one dark blue, and one of white with a length of lace for trimming. "Thank you very much, dear sister," Susan said, though both she and Tom looked worried. "Why are you so dour over your presents?" I asked. "Because you must have exhausted your funds with such fine things," Tom answered. "And there are so many things we need more," Susan said, quickly adding, "though I do not mean to seem ungrateful."

"Ah," I said. "You mustn't worry. I got a great deal more money for my jewels than I ever could have imagined. You shall have whatever you require and more." "But Roberta. . . " Tom said, looking very puzzled. "Yes, it's true, Tom. Your sister has become a very wealthy woman, and it is my intention to ease the hardship of my family and see that my nieces and nephews are well established." Susan stood there blinking, trying to assimilate this news. "Why that is splendid!" Tom burst out. "You have descended like a very angel!" "No, not at all," I said, embarrassed. It would be just as bad to have them all treat me as a genie as it had been to be treated as a maiden aunt.

Tom now looked around the little room he had created for me. "It's not much for a woman of wealth," he said in a crestfallen tone. "Oh Tom, it's extraordinary and made so by the thought for me that went into it. I shall enjoy it immensely." "But if you have such a fortune, won't you want to have a fine house?" Susan asked. "I might want a house if I were going to stay here, but I am returning to the island, as I told you before," I answered.

"But surely not now," Tom said. "And why not?" I said. "Well, because. . . because things are different. All has changed." "My sentiments have not changed," I said, with a surety that was under assault both without and within me. Susan and Tom looked as though they were conjuring new arguments, but I forestalled their presentation: "I'm a bit tired from the journey. I would like to take a rest in my new room if you will let me," I said. "Yes, yes, of course," they murmured. "Do you think the rest of the family might visit soon?" I asked, "As you see I have a great many presents to distribute." "We shall summon them at once," Susan said and right then I witnessed my wealth turn into a form of power. "I'll go," Rachel called. Lady Evelyn had told me that now I had responsibilities; Susan and Rachel interpreted my desires as commands.

Towards evening the rest of the family started arriving, bearing various dishes to make a feast. They had heard enough of my new wealth to make them expect a party. My brother poured out drams for the men, and even some of their wives had a glass.

"So, Roberta, you are become a woman of the world!" said my brother George. "Let us have a toast. To Roberta!" said Richard. "She has come into a fortune and she deserves it as she survived ten years on a desert island!" "To Roberta!" they shouted as one. I did not think I had done anything to deserve such cheers, but I suppose they were celebrating the good fortune they would have through me and I was glad of it. I gave them all presents and was pleased to see that I had not forgotten even one of them. Giving presents gave me a very nice feeling indeed.

When at last all had eaten, the children were occupied with their toys or had dropped off to sleep on one of Susan's quilts, my sisters-in-law sat down at the enormous table at which I had so often supped as a child. A short distance away, my brothers and I sat at the fire together, the firelight playing upon our faces. I saw Rachel looking confused, wanting to join both groups, settling for the position at the table that was closest to the hearth. Richard was playing a pretty tune upon the fiddle but stopped abruptly. "It is too bad Arthur is not here with us," he said. "Yes, his absence makes a gap in our felicity," George added. We toasted our absent brother and had a moment of silence to remember him.

Then I asked how my fortune might best help each of them. Tom said he would like to buy the adjoining land and to build a new barn. In his slow, deliberate way, George told how he wanted to own some land and "not be laboring always for someone else's benefit. Perhaps I could set up a mill." William said he wanted to buy the haberdashery where he worked. "Mr. Watts who owns it is old and ready to sit by the fire. He would be glad to sell to me." They wanted dowries for their daughters and the fees to send their sons to school or to buy costly apprenticeships.

"Because of you, Roberta, we are allowed to hope for better lives for our children," Tom exclaimed.

I wanted to forestall too much gratitude, so I broke in: "Richard, you have said nothing. What would you like to do, dear?" In fact, it was him I most wanted to help. Richard straightened to his full height, looked me in the eyes and astonished me to the core by saying, "I would like to go to your island with you, Roberta." The others gasped, and I was genuinely shocked, but soon suffused with pleasure at the possibility that rather than entirely leaving my English family, I could take some of it with me, and that it could be Richard! How I longed to have Freeman and Tom meet him, though such an eventuality fanned out many difficulties in my mind almost immediately.

"Richard, you do me a great honor to think of this. Having you near me would be a great comfort and joy, but one would need to think long and hard about such an undertaking," I said. "I can not adequately describe how different life is there, and I have no idea if it would be to your taste." "I have already thought long and hard on it," he said. "I want to have an adventure. I could come back if I didn't like it, couldn't I?"

Then we heard a voice from the rim of our group. It was my nephew Roland, Tom's son, a big boy of 14. "I would like to go as well," he said eagerly. "I have dreamed of nothing else since I first heard you describe the place, Aunt Roberta. I long with all my heart to see it." I saw that Rachel was about to speak when Roland's mother Susan burst out, "But you shall not go! You are only 14. She can not take you!" "Now, now, calm down, my dear," Tom said, "the boy was just saying what he wanted." Susan was not to be quieted, however. "Why must Roberta go back to a God-forsaken island anyway? If she has so much money, let her husband and son come here. It's improper for an Englishwoman to abandon her family to play at being an adventuress. She should stay here and be among her family to look after them and not take green boys into danger because of her whims." "Susan, you are speaking out of turn," Tom said. "Roberta has been most generous with us and you are repaying her in odd coin." "What kind of generosity is it to take my son onto the danger of the seas?" Susan said angrily. "But Roberta did not suggest it, Mother. Roland did," Rachel said, taking her hand, but she was not to be placated. "He would not have if she had not presented him with such temptation," she said, great distress upon her face.

I had sat through this outburst quietly. "I'm not sure it would be wise for anyone to accompany me back to the island," I said, thinking it would be expedient to end the evening as soon as I could. "But Roberta. . ." Richard began. "No. I must try to think it through. I'm going to go to the little house that Tom and Susan have provided me for some rest. I thank you all for this pleasant evening and I bid you all good-night." They protested my departure, but seeing I meant to go, they kissed me and thanked me.

"Don't mind Susan," George whispered. "It was only the thought of losing her son that made her so mean." "I know," I said. Rachel embraced me affectionately. "Dear Aunt," she said, "I think you are most wonderful." "Thank you, dear. You are wonderful as well," I said, hoping she knew I truly meant it.

I was tired, but I did not go directly to my apartment. There was a full moon in a clear sky, so I followed the little path down to the pond and stood gazing at the lovely scene made by the moon upon the water. The night air was cool and fresh and the sounds of insects and water animals surrounded me. I was not upset by what Susan had said about me. I felt I could have delivered a withering speech to her, but she did not deserve to be withered. She was reacting as a mother whose young were threatened.

I was engrossed with Richard's desire to go with me to the island. I wondered how life on the island and the relations between Freemen and me would be affected by the presence of my brother. Since I had not been forthcoming about Freeman, Richard had probably formed a very wrong idea of him. I would have to be more honest with him.

I wondered as strongly if it were my right to bring someone else to live with us without first consulting Freeman. Then again, having association with another Englishman besides me would give Freeman more information upon which to base a decision about whether or not he would like to visit Britain. I found that for myself, the notion of having my brother near me was wonderful indeed. He would fill our lives with music. But would his presence subtract from my intimacy with Freeman? That would be a grievous development. I could not know the answers to these questions, but I knew it was wise to preview as many of them as possible.

As I walked slowly back to the cottage Tom had made for me, I heard ahead of me the voices of two women whom I recognized as George's wife Emily and William's wife Tabitha. "She's one to be putting on airs," Tabitha was saying, "she as was no more than a lady's maid. And I daresay her 'husband' is a heathen darkie. Why else would she be so close-mouthed about him?" "How can you be so unkind when she is sharing her money with us?" Emily said. "Ah, but not fairly," Tabitha replied. "Tom is to get heaps of land, while William is to get a little shop." "But she asked each of them what he wanted," Emily rebutted. "She should have divided the money equally among them. That would have been fair." "But it's her money. She is not required to be fair." "She is outrageous. I don't want her around my girls as I don't want them absorbing her ways. You can already see how Rachel is smitten with her. She's like to give Susan no end of trouble now."

The two women continued past me and their voices faded away. I was hurt and angry to think there could be such opinions about me. One immediate effect of my eavesdropping was, however, the resurrection of my resolve to return to the island, which came as a jolt through my whole body. Not because these particular remarks were so wounding, but because my sister-in-law Tabitha's calumny was only a sample of what would surround me if I were to stay here. I did not like to think that my example could make Rachel's life harder and realized that I had egotistically thought I could only help her. I reminded myself that Emily had stood up for me, but I was more sensible of the scorch of Tabitha's denunciation, and it kept me awake for a long time.

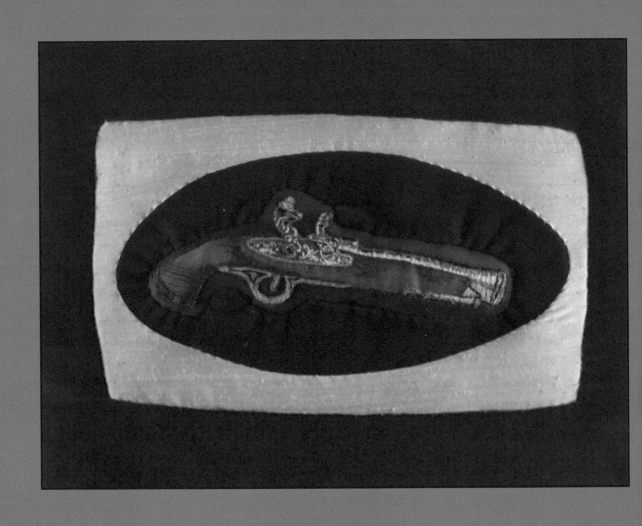

Chapter 18—I Dispense and Am Dispensed With

That Tabitha had rendered such a harsh judgment on me galled me more than I could have imagined. I recited to myself all the reasons it ought not to bother me—that she was jealous and small-minded and that I could effectively prove myself superior to her criticism by ignoring it. Nonetheless, I continued angry and aggrieved the way one does as a child when one is falsely accused and cries against the injustice of it. In the same childish way I envisioned slapping her face and calling her a hypocrite. At last I reduced my boil to a simmer by resolving to visit her the next morning, thinking that my mere presence would induce an apology and lead to a new amity.

Of course, that was another delusion. When I arrived on their doorstep, William and Tabitha were just finishing breakfast. "Ah, Roberta, I'm so sorry, but I'm just off to the shop," William said, gulping his tea and tearing his napkin from his neck. "That's quite all right. As it happens, I came to visit Tabitha," I answered, very mildly, though Tabitha betrayed some alarm, evidence, I imagined, of a guilty conscience. "That's delightful, isn't it, dear?" William said, pecked his wife on the cheek and, I later realized, literally ran out the door.

"Would you care for some tea, sister-in-law," Tabitha inquired of me, as if I were not a person but merely a position on the family tree. "Yes, thank you," I replied. She fetched a cup and saucer and set them before me. "What lovely china," I said. "Yes, it is much like that Mrs. Applewhite received for her wedding from her great-aunt Lady Whirlet." She said this as if I would understand what weighty significance this fact held, and right then I put her down for a fool. My dealings with Herbert Crent ought to have schooled me in the damaging potential of fools, but I went forward anyway, for reasons I reflected much upon afterwards.

"Tabitha," I began, "after I left Tom's house last night, I was standing by the lake to admire the moon when you and Emily passed. I could not help overhearing your conversation, and its condemnation of me. I admit I was stung and wondered much about how I could have given such offense to you in the short time I have been here, when, in fact, we have never even spoken together at any length. I would like to be friends with all my brothers' wives. That is why I've come this morning."

During my speech Tabitha's face had played through an array of expressions from surprise through mortification to petulance, at last freezing into a sort of cross between indulgence and dismissal, "Why, Roberta," she said slowly, "I wonder that a woman who has hunted down a boar and fought off all sorts of dangers unimaginable to women such as myself, accustomed only to the gentle domestic sphere, could be so disarranged by something I said." At this she sat up very straight, as if to exhibit her rectitude in contrast to my imputed "disarrangement." "You can't be serious," I said. "You make it sound as if I sought such adventure, rather than having it thrust upon me," I said. "Not at all, you had no choice and did well enough in your circumstances, I imagine. Your mistake is in presenting your adventure as something to aspire to, to fire the minds of the young so that they veer from the paths that keep them safe and respectable." "Tabitha, I did no such thing. In fact, I discouraged anyone from following my example," I answered hotly. "Perhaps you said so, but they saw something different. To Rachel and Roland, Loretta and the others, you are a romantic heroine who makes their mothers seem dull and old-fashioned."

I thought she spoke balderdash, but had to admire the way she built her case so as to leave me no defense. "In your construction, the only way I could have avoided the injury you impute to me would be not to have come back at all. But then I could not have shared the luck of my wealth with my family," I said, thinking I had played a trump, but I underestimated her. "You could easily have done so in absentia through an intermediary." "Your cruelty is most remarkable," I said. "You would deprive me of seeing my family, to which I am related by blood, not as you are, by marriage, and you seem to think there would be no deprivations for them in that course." "There would have been none for me," she said, "and if you had not come, how could anyone else have missed you?"

I rose to leave. "I came in hopes that perhaps I had misunderstood you, Tabitha, and I was right, but not in the way I had believed. I thought we might be friends, but you are a cold unloving snake. I pity my brother." She pretended a gay laugh. "A snake, is it? No, Roberta, I am simply a lady, a state you cannot understand." "You are not lady," I said, "You are a brittle bone," I said and went out the door. I wanted to strike her, proving, I suppose, that I am not a lady.

I hurried down the lane away from the house, more deeply upset than I had ever been upon the island. I realized that I had gone to George's house with the conviction that my approach was magnanimous and that I had hoped to enjoy Tabitha's embarrassment, and so I was ashamed. I was confronted with my own naiveté. I had been shown a sort of intransigence that struck me as inhuman, almost depraved, though certainly of a different brand than that of Sutton Norman. What torturous reasoning Tabitha employed to blame me for my fate and for my natural feelings!

It began to rain as I neared the cottage Tom had built me, and as I closed the door a deluge descended. I threw myself into the large chair, my head awash with Tabitha's denunciation. There was a partial justice in it, I was forced to conclude, in that I had given no thought whatsoever to my effect upon my brother's children. I had thought of myself in no light but a beneficent one.

Could encouraging Rachel's drawing unsuit her to the wifely realm that was her only possible future, if, indeed, her smallpox scars did not foreclose even that option? Was Roland now implanted with a yearning for the sea that would eventually take him away from his family? Turning these questions over and over, I came to no conclusion other than that I would do well to cultivate more awareness of my motives towards and effects upon others. Just because I had for so long judged myself as of little importance in the scheme of things did not make it true. Finally, I concluded that I would be glad to throw Tabitha into a lime pit, a fantasy I amended so that if I were to find her in a lime pit, I would be sore put to pull her out. I laughed at how I had changed my revenge so as to put myself in a better light.

My mind was still a maelstrom when Susan knocked upon my door. She had brought me a buttered scone and a mug of tea. She sat down on the bed and said, "I'm very sorry to have said what I did last night. I know that Roland is like any boy and wants an adventure. It is not at all your fault. Please forgive me." I had a feeling that Tom had made her say this, but I was sincere in my response. "Please don't trouble yourself about it," I said. "You just want to protect your boy. I understand that with all my heart." I must have put the force of lamentation into the latter statement as Susan looked at me with a dawning understanding. "Of course! You miss your own boy!" she said. "I'm sorry that I have not thought enough of what suffering that must be for you, Roberta." I felt at last that someone understood how I felt, so we embraced and were reconciled, and I thought if I were to stay in England I could in time have a friend in Susan if not in Tabitha.

I wanted to execute my brothers' desires as quickly as possible to conclude matters by the time my ship sailed, so later that afternoon, Tom and I called on the old squire who owned the land next to ours. His own estate looked seedy and much reduced, and he was quite glad to entertain a good offer for his field. We also went into the village to visit a carpenter who might give us some idea of what a barn such as my brother wanted would require. I left it to Tom to make the arrangements and wrote a bank draft for the required amount when we had returned home. I was very pleased by the way my brother's countenance seemed to relax and his posture straightened as these things were arranged.

William wrote me a note that he had asked the owner of his haberdashery to speak with me and he was willing to do so the next day. Richard agreed to drive me there and I welcomed the time to speak with him about the island. As we rattled along in the misty morning in Tom's trap, Richard tried to assure me that he had given the matter serious thought and that he strongly wanted to go with me. "There's no place for me here, Roberta. I don't fit into anything. And I so want to see a bit of the world!" he pleaded. "Dear Richard, I take your desire seriously, so I must open to you a fuller picture of what my life on the island has been. You cannot imagine how very isolated life is there. In my ten years only one ship from Europe arrived. Freeman, Tom and I are the only ones there."

Here I paused for a moment, then plunged in. "The truth is that I rescued Freeman when the men of his tribe brought him over from the mainland in order to kill him. It took us a long time to learn to communicate. In his outward appearance he is nothing like an Englishman, and any Englishman who saw him would take him for a savage and be much shocked at my liaison with him."

Richard listened wide-eyed as I spoke. "Despite this appearance, however, Freeman is a very amiable, kind, intelligent man, who I love with all my heart. I could not bear to subject him to any difficulties. I am not sure I have the right to bring anyone else on to the island without his consent." Richard nodded his head. "I had not viewed the matter in that light," he said. "I had been thinking only of my own desires. I am sorry," he said, "but what you have said does not alter my desire to go with you. I could only be respectful and friendly to this man you love, no matter what his origin or customs. Could I not simply go with you to visit? Perhaps I would not want to stay. Perhaps I could go out with some goods to trade on the mainland and set up there as a merchant. And now that you have money, could you not hire a ship to stop at the island now and again to alleviate its isolation?" "I suppose so, but its isolation is part of the island's beauty. You also underestimate the difficulties of travel," I said, "and the prevalence of danger, but what you suggest is not impossible. I will think more on it."

For the rest of the journey, I described in much greater detail our life upon the island, its subsistence character, how we gardened, raised goats, and hunted. "But we play a great deal too," I said, returning in my mind to the hours we spent running about on the beach or lying above it to watch the sunset. "You cannot imagine how beautiful it is, how warm and fragrant." "Oh Roberta! Don't torment me with such visions if you will not let me go with you. A place without cold gray days must be heaven itself," Richard said. Then I remembered that as a boy he had always chafed against the weather. On rainy days he would chase through the house trumpeting his desire for the sun to appear until one of the older boys demanded he be still; then he would lie morosely on the floor and stare at the fire. For the first time I thought that perhaps he would indeed be happier in a tropical climate. It was a momentous conversation and one whose every word I turn over in my mind to this very day.

Arriving in Thorington at the appointed hour, Richard left me at the neat little shop where William had labored for almost as long as I had been on the island. "You may come in if you like," I told Richard, but he firmly declined. When I met William's employer, Mr. Watts, I found out the reason for Richard's reluctance to join us. Watts was a bent old man who led us into his parlor where an equally bent old woman served us tea. He whined and fussed about the meal and gradually enlarged his complaint into a blanket condemnation of the state of everything. William humored him throughout, a strategy I imagined he had honed through many years as the old man's employee.

Finally, I said, "Mr. Watts, if you were inclined in the near future to retire from the many afflictions of business and if you would trust my brother to carry on your trade, we would like to make you an offer for the shop." Mr. Watts gummed his lips for a moment, then looked at me as if I were out to pull the wool over his eyes. "And just what would that offer be?" he asked. "What is your price, sir?" I said. "I have no experience of these matters, so you must guide me." Mr. Watts' face registered a succession of thoughts that read to me as a text on how he might cheat me instead of being cheated himself. He eventually came out with a figure as if to test the waters. My brother lightly gasped, so I said, "That's rather high, I believe." "I thought you said you didn't know anything about such matters," Watts whined. "Nor am I entirely ignorant," I said and named a counter-price. "I'll take it," he said as if to pounce upon a larger offer than he expected. Then he grew dark again. "How do I know you actually have the necessary funds?" he said. "Oh, you will know when the draft arrives from the Bank of England," I said. "If you are agreeable, I will have my solicitor draw up the documents. Or you may have your own solicitor do so, if you like." "Yes, my solicitor will do that," he said craftily, as though he were once again foiling my plot against him. "We shall await the papers then, and you shall have the money shortly thereafter. I wish you a very happy retirement, sir," I said and took my leave.

William followed me out. "You were magnificent, Roberta! The old boy didn't cow you a bit. How did you learn to deal so?" he said. "I never did," I said. "I simply pretended I was Lady Evelyn!" "Good show, dear Sis. How can I ever thank you?" "By being happy, William. That would be the best thing." Though how he could be happy with a woman like Tabitha stumped me. I imagined they had reached an accommodation I could not fathom.

Richard came towards us from the village inn and William told him of our successful visit. "Did Roberta keep her head above the water with the old fox?" he asked cheerfully. "Indeed, she did," William said and then turned to me as though animated by a great notion. "You really ought to stay here, Roberta. You have so much ability for a woman. We could start a trading concern. Tom and George and I would be the public face of it, but you could direct it. We could employ the whole family eventually. You could visit your island for holidays and bring your husband and son here," he exclaimed, ignorant of his insult and as though his own enthusiasm for such a future could act as a wave to sweep away any objections I might have. "No, William, you must be the family merchant. You will be a fine one." "But Roberta, I need you," he said with a bit of a whining tone he must have learned from Watts along with skills in haberdashery. I waved him away. "Richard and I must be getting back now," I said and climbed into the trap.

Arriving back at Tom's farm I was handed a letter by little Loretta. It came from my solicitor, Mr. Gorman. In it he told me that he had received the map I had asked Captain Ellis to send him. He was to meet with the Portuguese ambassador on the morrow to find out if his nation laid claim to our island and would let me know of the meeting's result as soon as possible. There was also a note from Lady Evelyn asking me to return to her as soon as I could.

I had now been in England for nine weeks and had three remaining. Though I was full of a restless energy that would have made me welcome the chores my sisters-in-law pushed upon me, since I had become rich they had stopped their efforts and instead waited for me to command them, a posture which they nonetheless resented. I would regret losing Rachel and Loretta's affectionate company, but I was willing to spend my remaining time at Lady Evelyn's, partially because there I could walk freely about the grounds and I craved the exercise. I also wanted further discussion with Mr. Miller about my projects at home, so I returned a note saying that I had still some business to attend to, but would rejoin Lady Evelyn soon and that I planned to leave for Bristol from her house. I knew she would not like to be reminded that I had not changed my mind about leaving, but I did not want to dramatize the situation by leaving her unaware of my plan.

Over the next few days I settled matters for George, who had for many years wanted to buy his wife's uncle's farm. He thought he could run it and continue as the manager at Holcomb, thus substantially increasing his income. "I shall send my boys to school now," he said.

"They are very bright and might win scholarships to Cambridge, and now they will have the preparation they need. I'm very grateful to you, Roberta."

When I told Tom of my timetable and that I would be leaving within the week, he looked much downcast. "I could cry for losing you again, my girl," he said, which scraped upon my heart. "I know you've heard enough of our begging you to stay, so I won't badger you more," he said, "but remember that we will welcome you and your husband and son wholeheartedly whenever you return."

Rachel looked at me with eyes shiny from tears, as though I were receding from her that very moment. If anything could have again made me question my course, it was Tom's frank manner and Rachel's yearning, though my exchange with Tabitha had put the linch pin in the certainty of my desire to return to Freeman and Tom. Everyday I ached with missing them, but the questions of whether or not they could like England, and the more pressing matter of whether I might take Richard back with me roiled back and forth in my mind.

At night in the little cottage on Tom's farm, I lay in bed thinking of these questions and also of all that I would be leaving behind—my growing connections with my brothers' children, especially Rachel, my ability to be on hand to help them and to relieve them when needed, my wider ability to help those in need who I did not know. My few months in England had also awakened my affection for the cool green lands of the English countryside. I would miss them, but when I thought of my approaching departure and how each day would take me nearer to Freeman, Tom and the island, my heart cracked open with yearning for them, and I was very impatient to be off. At last I concluded that it would be wrong to deny the immense magnetism of my former life. No one else here could understand it, so I must stand fast within my own recognition despite their doubts and importunings. In a way this resolve was like that I had taken upon the island to do all I could to survive, come what might. After an enormous struggle, I decided also that I would accept the risk of taking dear Richard back with me. I trusted that Freeman would accept him and do his best to like him.

I took Richard apart in the evening and told him of my decision. "Oh Roberta," he said, "you will never regret it! How happy you've made me." The others were much less happy to hear of this development as I was not the only one that loved Richard best. He was a very good-natured and helpful person who all liked to be around, but Tom expressed the general sentiment when he said, "You must go your own way, Dick. We will miss you awfully, but it's nice to know that Roberta will have one of her own people with her." "We must get you a kit together," Susan said, and I could see her planning how she would care for him from afar through the things she would send with him. This again made me aware that I liked her and that I would miss the company of women on the island.

On the evening before my return to Lady Evelyn's we all gathered for one last feast together. Several of the children gave me keepsakes. Little Loretta insisted that I take two of the kittens. Initially, I thought I could not do so, but more reflection produced a happy assent. After all, Miss Higgins had come to the island aboard a ship. She was very old now and might not welcome young kittens, but neither could I look forward to living without a cat around me. Rachel gave me a folder of drawings she had done of the farm. "So that you will not forget us, Aunt Roberta," she said. "As if I could ever forget you, dear Rachel," I said and held her to me.

As the evening drew to a close and William was leaving, I asked him if I might come by his shop on my way to Lady Evelyn's. "Of course," he said with some alarm, "though I don't think Mr. Watts has altered his decision." "It's not about that," I said. "I wish to make some purchases." William smiled, "Ah, you wish to take some clothes to your husband. You shall see what a fine salesman I am! I shall sell you half my stock."

My leave-taking from Tom and his family was a hard one. Tom held me to him very hard and I clung on with all my strength. "Take care of yourself, dearest sister. And come back to us whenever you can," Tom breathed into my ear. "I shall, Tom. Remember that you can always apply to Mr. Gorman if you are in any need. I will think of you very often and always remember your kindness." I kissed Susan and Roland and Loretta and hugged a sobbing Rachel to me, then got into the trap with Richard. "Someday I shall come out to your island," Roland said boldly in defiance of his mother. My trunk and other parcels were already packed into the rear and I held a box with the tabby kittens in it on my lap. As we rattled away I turned to wave goodbye. I wondered if I would ever see them again; their receding images were clouded by my tears.

"What's our business at William's shop?" Richard asked, putting his arm around me as if to shelter me from the pain of the departure. "I need some trousers," I said. "Ah, you will take clothes to Freeman and Tom." "Yes, I will do that, but I will also begin your introduction to the shocks of island life right now," I warned. "The trousers are for me. I wore them from the very beginning of my term there as they are more protective than skirts and one can work more efficiently in them." Richard eyed me as if to visualize me in pants and then he let out a mighty laugh. "You needn't look so severe, Roberta, as if you had committed a sin. I am not so easily shocked, and I can well imagine that trousers would suit you well. What does Freeman think?" I was relieved at Richard's reaction and thought it boded well for his sojourn among us. "In fact, there are those who believe it a sin for women to wear trousers," I said, adding enigmatically, "Freeman prefers neither skirts nor trousers," I said enigmatically, which made Richard laugh again.

When we reached William's shop I suggested that Richard would do well to supply himself with a number of lightweight white shirts. "It will be warm, but you are fair like me and will need to protect your skin from sunburn," I explained. "I shall get some later," he said. "For now I must allow Susan to make up my kit as it pleases her so." I thought him a fine fellow for this sentiment.

William greeted me warmly and welcomed me to the shop with the expanded character of a new proprietor, nattily dressed in a striped waistcoat and dark green coat. "How may I assist you, Madame?" he asked, gesturing towards a wall entirely taken up with row upon row of shelves laden with fabrics of all kinds. "Mr. Watts is not present and there is only your humble servant to attend you," he said. "I need some trousers, William," I said. "Of course, what size is the gentleman who will wear them?" he said. "I must have measurements." "The trousers are for me, William. Please do not be shocked. I thought to avoid your knowing, but I did not want to deprive you of the trade." As soon as I said this I knew how foolish it was. I must have wanted them all to know. But why? William was indeed flabbergasted. "Life is very strenuous upon the island," I explained. "Skirts and petticoats are cumbersome, even dangerous, and so for work I began to wear the sailor's pants I found upon the shipwreck. They never fit me well, however, and I have had to hold them up with a belt that is also too big. I long for some sturdy trousers that fit me," I said.

William looked stricken. "I am quite shocked, Roberta. Of course, I have never made any trousers for a woman. I do not know how to go about it. I do not think it is proper. I might even be taken before the magistrate if it were known." "Don't be ridiculous, William. No one will know as I will never wear them here." William looked at me in a very hard way. "I'm sorry, Roberta. I simply cannot do it. An accident of life has led you into unconventionality, but you ought not to cultivate it further, and I shall certainly not abet you in it."

I must say I was nonplussed and not above reminding him of my generosity towards him. "I've made it possible for you to own your shop and you will not do me a simple favor?" I said. "It is not a simple favor, Roberta. You ask me to violate respectability. I simply can not do it." Here William drew himself up to his full height, and I saw that he felt himself a courageous defender of principle. "Oh, William, if only you would take your stand on a more important matter," I said. "We have different ideas about what is important," he said. "Indeed, we do," I said, feeling a rambunctious anger gathering in my breast.

As it grew, the shop bell rang and two women entered, one of whose voices I recognized as that of Tabitha, William's wife, who shot me a haughty glance. "Hello, my dear," he said to her and to the other woman, both of whom were quite burdened with adornments of bows and laces. "And good morning to you, Mrs. Applewhite." "My husband requires a new cravat, Mr. Crousseau," Mrs. Applewhite said in a way that indicated that she was accustomed to condescending to tradesmen. "Yes, Mrs. Applewhite. We have a fine selection for you to peruse." "I would not wish to interrupt, sir," Mrs. Applewhite huffed and looked askance at me, as if in irritation that someone had been in the shop before her. "No, no, ma'am, this is my sister Roberta. She is soon leaving to go across the ocean. She wished to inquire about some trousers, for her husband, but does not know his size."

Mrs. Applewhite bestowed a glacial look on William as if to say, "Why do you bother me with that which is irrelevant?" "Hello, Tabitha," I sang out. I was intently scanned by the horse-faced woman who was Mrs. Applewhite. "You must be the famous Roberta of shipwreck fame," she said quite as if I had been announced upon a carnival bill. "I find that it is useful to know one's husband's measurements," she went on in a tone of reproof. "Ah yes," I said, "but I was forced to leave home with too little notice to attend to such vital things," I said. Tabitha stood there red-faced, but I did not know if this were on my behalf because of Mrs. Applewhite's rudeness or on her own behalf because of my very existence. Then I was seized by the imp of the perverse. "Tabitha," I said, "I've come to buy some trousers, but William won't fit me. Perhaps he would fit you instead. The neighborhood seems of the opinion that you wear the pants in the family." "Why whatever do you mean?" Tabitha sputtered. "Oh nothing really, just a whim," I replied and swept out of the shop.

William rushed out after me. "I see you bear a grudge about the trousers," he said. "Why did you even have to mention them? Tabitha wants very much to be active in Mrs. Applewhite's circle, and though this has no attraction for me, it would please her and so I assist in her efforts as best I can. In fact, your money has helped her project immensely," he said and looked shame-faced. "I apologize for Tabitha, but why did you throw it up to her?" "I can't eat everything, William," I said. At this he looked very perplexed and I softened. "It is all right, William. Good-bye, dear brother," I said and embraced him. "We will not forget your generosity to us, Roberta," he said. Richard pulled me up into the trap then, and we set out for Lady Evelyn's, while William went inside to pour oil on the troubled waters of his clientele. As we rolled along I was ashamed of the barb I'd thrown at Tabitha, which is not the same as wishing I hadn't done it. In fact, I wished I had said something more clever.

I was glad to see the stone pillars that announced Lady Evelyn's estate, and she was again very glad to see me. "You must forgive me if I cannot refrain from trying to change your mind about leaving, Roberta," she said as soon as we were settled in for tea in the blue drawing room where cook's best cakes were set out. I saw that Lady Evelyn had already hung my embroidery of the island and was touched. "I am an old woman and I like to get my way, but I love you, dear, and I want what is best for you." I was very affected by this speech. No one who has never been a servant could understand how against the current order of things it was for a noblewoman such as Lady Evelyn to say such a thing to me who she had so recently correctly identified as belonging to the "lower orders."

Apparently, it was easier for Lady Evelyn, a noblewoman, to bend than it was for my brother, an aspiring merchant. "I will always prize your affection and your opinion, Lady Evelyn, as I love you very much as well." She dabbed her eyes and turned away as this much sentiment quite overwhelmed her. "Oh yes, several letters have come for you, my dear," she said, handing them to me and sniffing into her handkerchief.

The first was from Solicitor Gorman. He had spoken with the Portuguese attaché in London and ascertained that Portugal indeed claimed all the islands off the coast of Brazil. He strongly suggested that I stop in Lisbon on my way home and petition for the sale of the island directly to the king. He had taken the liberty of sending to find out if the Northhampton were to land in Lisbon and had asked the captain to write directly to me about it. The second envelope contained the captain's answer. "Our course includes Lisbon. I look forward to meeting you and welcoming you aboard. Yours, etc., Capt. Humphrey Fitzhoward."

Lady Evelyn had watched curiously as I read. "Good news, Roberta?" she asked. "Yes, I think so. I am trying to purchase the island. My solicitor tells me I must apply to the King of Portugal for it, and I will be able to do so as the ship will stop there."

"Purchase the island! The King of Portugal!" Lady Evelyn exclaimed, her eyebrows raised almost to her hairline. "What will you wear?!" she said with the utmost heat. "We must begin at once to outfit you as we have so little time." "I doubt I will actually inquire of the king himself," I suggested. "Someone less august will probably address my petition." "Oh, yes, I suppose you're right," she said, crestfallen. "But you must nonetheless have a grand ensemble in which to appear before whoever it is. You will need to present an image of authority." "Why?" I asked. "Because the sort you will meet expect it. They will treat you according to your clothes. It is just the same there as it is here, only more so."

I wondered from where Lady Evelyn got her knowledge of the Portuguese court, but nothing animated Lady Evelyn as much as questions of wardrobe and since she seemed so energized by the need to accouter me, I was quite willing to go along with it. I remembered how she had outfitted Leora so many years ago, and it warmed me to think that she was treating me as she had her own daughter.

Benjamin Miller was also glad to see me, and we spent the sunny afternoon tromping over the grounds, our talk alternating between his projects and my proposed ones. When we reached his lodge, he invited me in. It was a relaxed, masculine abode in browns and greens with books lying about. "I have drawn some plans for your water system," he said and showed me a small album in which he had diagrammed how I ought to link the clay pipes together. He had also written down an explanation of the principles that governed the conveyance of water, for which I was particularly grateful. "I have also amused myself with a more fanciful plan," he said, handing me another sheet. It showed what I took to be a large overhead pipe that I recognized as an aqueduct. "The Romans mastered the art of providing plentiful water," he said. "Perhaps you might emulate them in miniature. From what you have described to me, I think you have all the materials you would need to build a modest aqueduct such as I have pictured." "It is magnificent," I said, looking eagerly at the drawing. "I am very obliged to you for your efforts on my behalf." "I have found a friend in you and will miss you," Benjamin said. Then without any reflection I burst out, "Why don't you come with me?! You said you would need a new world to make you happy, and that is just what I have. Come along and help build this aqueduct!"

Benjamin looked at me with a very happy but resigned face. "I appreciate your offer more than I can say and am much tempted by it, but I cannot go now. It would not work." "But why not?" I pressed. "For one thing, my mother is very old and I could not leave her." "Oh, I did not know you had family. I'm sorry."

"Perhaps someday I will see your island," he said more brightly. "I want to very much, though even it could not be the new world I long for." "Why not," I said. "It is almost completely unwritten upon by human beings."

Benjamin turned away, took up a lacquered wooden box that lay upon his desk and handed it to me. "This is a gift for you," he said. I smiled and opened the box to find therein a pistol with a silver and ivory handle. "It was my father's," Benjamin said. "I have no use for it and would like for you to have it in case you are set upon again by robbers." "It is a very fine present, Benjamin," I said, quite astonished. "I am honored that you would give me a family treasure."

Just then Nellie arrived to tell me Lady Evelyn wished me to come to her and so I did not get an answer to my question. As I departed I said to Benjamin, "One thing we lack that the Romans had is manpower. We would need that to build an aqueduct." Benjamin laughed and told me he would see me at dinner.

.

Chapter 19—I Am Teased Royally

My remaining time in England passed either by racing at a feverish pace or crawling along at a glacial creep. One minute Lady Evelyn was rushing me from the dressmaker to the milliner; the next I was endlessly watching rain roll down the window in the parlor, thinking of how Tom splashed in the pool by the waterfall or how dear Freeman kept the woodpile supplied without my ever seeing him do it. I so longed to touch his face.

I tried to occupy myself a good deal with lists of what I was taking back with me so that I would not omit anything I needed and could feel that I was taking care of Freeman and Tom. Lady Evelyn occasionally read out one of these lists. "Lamps and oil for them, knives and other cutlery, nails, clay pipes, glue, seedlings including raspberry, blackberry, apple, pear and peach, a loom, scissors, soap, an anvil, paint and paint brushes, varnish, linseed oil, blankets, dyes. 100 books including a geography, Euclid's Geometry, and all these works on how to do things, pottery-making and tanning. My goodness, you could equip a shop with what you are taking with you," she said, adding, "I'm going to write in some other things that are for the care of your hair and hands which you have forgotten." "Yes, please do," I said.

At Lady Evelyn's insistent urging, in record time the dressmaker completed the ensemble I thereafter referred to as my Portuguese outfit. It was an elaborate gown of pink satin with lace inserts in its skirt and a very low neckline ruched and braided to accentuate my bosom and requiring special stays to make my breasts appear to be rapidly ascending to the ceiling. Lady Evelyn insisted that this feature would aid my petition and I believed her, though I was a bit apprehensive that a breast would, in fact, escape.

Topping the Portuguese outfit was a hat so large, beribboned and befeathered it quite weighed upon my head and made me feel as if I belonged in a museum of buffoonery. "You don't take enough account of the effects of pageantry in getting what one wants," Lady Evelyn reproved me. I was sure my Portuguese outfit would take top marks in a contest of pageantry.

"Did you save any of your jewels for your own adornment," she asked, rolling her eyes and answering her own question. "Of course, you didn't. Here," she said, handing me a string of pearls interspersed with what I took to be sapphires. "Don't worry, my dear. They are paste and I shall miss them only a little. It quite delights me to think of you wearing them to a foreign court." I thanked her heartily for her care of me, though I thought it very likely that my business in Portugal would be conducted in a small dark office where the Portuguese outfit would quite overawe the presiding official if it did not make him fall down laughing.

I spent as much time with Benjamin as I could, consorting with him about our mutual projects. He was just then working at draining a marsh adjacent to one of Lady Evelyn's farms beside which lived a family whose members frequently sickened from fever. Benjamin thought the marsh implicated in this disease, and it was this reason as well as the increased acreage he would gain for planting that motivated him.

I was standing by one day when his three workers were installing a pump. They had brought the heavy engine to the site in three pieces, each of which was to rest atop the other, the whole engine setting on an iron frame. They were now fitting the pieces to each other. I thought to suggest that it would be better to assemble the pump in the water because of its weight, when the pump toppled off the frame and fell heavily into the marsh, pinning one of the workmen, Davy Squires, beneath it. The water was shallow so he would not drown, but it was essential to get the machine off him as soon as possible in order to assess his injury. He was not complaining, but his strained face indicated more pain than he was acknowledging.

Benjamin and I had been standing only ten feet away. We both waded immediately into the dark water and applied ourselves to lifting the pump off the fellow, a task that was complicated by the lack of sure footing in the slimy marsh bottom. The mud sucked us down. I waded over to retrieve a pole that Ben was able to shove under the pump. "Let's put our shoulders to it now," Ben said, and we bore down upon the pole, moving the pump enough to pull out poor Davy Squires. We dragged him up on the dry land where after a short time he assured us he was all right. "No injury done sir," he said, "the soft mud spared me bones."

In our relief we relaxed enough to inspect our utterly muddy and bedraggled selves. "We must get you back to the manor, or you will catch your death, Roberta," Ben said. "Lady Evelyn will have my head for this," he added in a way that told me he was serious. "But why? It was an accident," I said. "Yes, but I'm sure she will say that you ought not to have been involved in it," he said, ushering me up the path.

I tried to evade Lady Evelyn by going round to the kitchen door and asking cook to make me a bath in the servants quarters, but Nellie happened to be there; she looked me up and down and ran out of the room. Before I had even taken off my dress, Lady Evelyn had bustled into the kitchen. "Roberta, whatever has happened to you? Are you injured?" I assured her I was not and explained what had befallen the pump. As I related the event her countenance became ever more pursed in disapproval. "It need not even be said that you should not to have gone into the water. The further fact is that you ought not to have been there at all. What business of yours is drainage?" "But, Lady Evelyn, the man was in danger." "The other workmen would have aided him soon enough. They were, as you say, bounding o'er the hill, were they not?" "Yes, but my act was of an instinctive sort. I was needed." At this Lady Evelyn looked very arch. "A great part of civilization is the regulation of instinct, Roberta. Not only was it not your place to jump in the water, but you have disgraced those men by performing the sort of task by which they prove their manhood."

All of a sudden I was very tired and wanted desperately to shed my sopping gown. "I'm sorry to have distressed you, Lady Evelyn," I said. "May I take this dress off and have a hot bath?" "You many not take your dress off in the kitchen, Roberta. Please go to your chamber. Nellie will attend you there." At this she exited with many mutterings having to do with virtue and unseemliness.

When I had at last shed my dank, clammy dress and sunk into hot water, I reflected on what Lady Evelyn had said and could not arrive at agreement with her view. Why, for example, was I responsible for the manhood of the workmen? I wondered how much worse her censure would have been had I not merely been present at the building enterprise but wanted to be active in it as well. What a bore life could be here! Later, when I went to the drawing room, Lady Evelyn greeted me with a little sigh that provoked me. I said, "Lady Evelyn, again I'm sorry to have distressed you, but I think your judgment is wrong. One is a human before one is a woman and I behaved as a human." "I don't hold it against you, Roberta. You simply don't know better," she said. "It's in the blood, and I have come to the conclusion that you can't be taught." "I've come to the same conclusion about you," I said brightly, as if we had reached a happy agreement. Lady Evelyn huffed, but I thought I saw a thin smile.

At long last the day on which I would leave for the port of Bristol arrived. How different it felt from the day ten years ago when I had gone out with Leora. Then I had been an attendant. I had not minded going, but neither was I eager. My destination was mostly a blank in my mind, and I expected my life upon arrival to consist of the same round of chores that had been my lot in England.

Now I was excited beyond measure to be going and my destination was always before my eyes. How I longed to see Tom recognize me and come running across the sand to meet me! How I longed to hold him against me, kiss him and muss his hair. Even thinking about Freeman made me feel very warm, and I found myself creating scenarios of us enmeshed together in all our favorite haunts.

My fantasy and anticipation was leavened by fear that some sickness or accident would have befallen them since I had been gone, or that I would arrive and they would not be there at all. I tried to push these thoughts away as they were useless, but from time to time they would fly across my mind like evil crows.

Breakfast on the last day was extremely difficult on account of Lady Evelyn's grief and her effort to dissemble it. Despite her disapproval, she was much attached to me, confirming my opinion that disapproval and love are very often compounded in our relations to one another. Her aging face crumpled again and again, but each time she held back her tears. Seeing this I resolved to arrange that the island be visited more frequently by a ship so that I might write to her and I told her so, which brightened her a bit. She had been motherly to me and I felt the good of it. "Remember," she said, "You are always welcome here, and no reproaches shall greet you if you should return," she said in an oddly negative way. "It is not impossible that I will visit England in the future and that I will bring my husband and son," I said. "And they shall be welcome too," she said graciously. We stood upon the doorstep and tenderly embraced, both weeping and trying not to. Then I gently disengaged from her, climbed into the carriage and left through the stone pillars and the groves of lofty trees that in all likelihood I would never see again.

Benjamin Miller was accompanying me to Bristol and would then go on to pay a visit to his mother. Since Richard was to meet me at the port, we were alone for the journey. When I had recovered sufficiently from my leave-taking with Lady Eleanor to converse, I told him that I had been a trial to her, adding, "but it seems she likes me anyway." "She has been a trial to you too, Roberta," he said. I asked Benjamin to tell me about his family and upbringing. "It seems we have always talked of me, and I don't want to go without knowing you as well as I can," I explained, "as you have become a true friend."

He related a happy childhood in Hertfordshire, going to a public school and then to Cambridge, "Unlike you I had no brothers or sisters and as a child was much alone or with my mother, my father having died when I was nine." "I am sorry," I said. He went on, "It would have been good to have my father with us, of course, but my mother and I formed a very close connection, and I am still devoted to her." "Then why are you so far away from her now?" I blurted. Ben looked pained. "As I told you earlier, I had some trouble in my native neighborhood and was forced to go away."

He did not enlarge upon this "trouble", though I wanted to know very much what it was. I could not imagine he could have done anything so terrible that I could not accept it. "Why don't you bring your mother here then. I'm sure Lady Evelyn would be agreeable," I suggested. Ben brightened a bit. "In fact, I had never thought of it, though I doubt she would care to leave her home." "You might ask her," I said. "Benjamin, it is quite all right if you don't want to tell me what your trouble was, but I want you to know that my good opinion of you has been formed through my experience over these last months and could not be altered by something that happened in the past." "You are very kind," he said, "but it is not that sort of trouble. It has rather to do with my character." "What can you possibly mean, Ben? You are a kind, intelligent, gracious fellow. Everyone agrees." Ben looked at me as one might look at a child of whom one was fond. I said, "You're pitying me as if I have an obtuseness that cannot be penetrated." He laughed. "Even though you have traveled halfway across the world, your experience is still somewhat limited, Roberta," he said, and I felt chastened. "I suppose that could be said of anyone," I retorted. We both occupied ourselves with the view from the carriage windows for some time thereafter.

I was very troubled. I told Benjamin Miller that I had found in him a true friend, yet neither of us could trust the other with our secrets. I remembered how my loneliness upon the island had opened me to such rewarding communion with Freeman and the isolation of so often concealing my thoughts and feelings here in England. I at last decided to risk them with Benjamin. I turned to him. "Ben, I have felt that your regard for me has been partial because you have withheld your secret from me, even though I have no right to know it. The truth is, however, that I have also withheld secrets from you, and I wish to tell them to you now, not thereby to extort yours, but for my own relief."

Benjamin looked quite astonished and worried, but I charged on, relating how I had met Freeman and how he would appear to a European. "To you he would seem a savage and that is why I have never been honest about him and have even had moments of shame, and then felt shamed by my shame!" I exclaimed. Benjamin took my hand and looked at me tenderly. "Roberta, your silence about your husband spoke quite loudly, so your secret does not surprise me so very much."

"But there is more, Ben," I said. "Can I bear more?" he answered a bit facetiously. Again I charged on. "It's about religion. I don't believe in it. I believe in churches, if only they could go on without religion. It all seems so silly to me, and so many people have been killed for it. In short, I am an unbeliever and a blasphemer!" I concluded.

Through my oration Benjamin's eyes had gotten wider and wider, I had thought from shock, but at last he broke into a great full-throated laugh, which dismayed me, as one does not like to be laughed at after sharing a secret. Ben saw my chagrin and immediately apologized, putting his arm around me. "I laugh because you judge yourself so harshly, subjecting yourself to the verdict of a source you deplore," he said. I saw that this was true and began to laugh myself.

Then Benjamin grew thoughtful, finally saying, "But you have laid your soul bare, and I must do so too, or I could not be your equal." "Do not feel obliged if it is too painful for you," I said. "It is very painful and may cause the loss of our friendship for it is counted by the world as far worse than unbelief." Before I could demur, he went on. "In my home county of Sussex I was estate manager to the greatest landowner there, Sir Philip Henston. When his son Charles returned from Oxford, we became great friends." Here I saw in Ben's face a succession of feelings that charged me with pity. "We became more than friends. I loved him and he loved me. He foolishly declared this to his father, who then ran me off the estate and spread it about that I had debauched his son." Here Benjamin lightly rapped his hands against his knees. "In short, I am a Sodomite, Roberta."

I was a welter of emotions at this confession. It explained why Ben had not tried to make love to me as well as his attachment to a bachelor's life. I did not know what I thought of sodomy, having never considered it. I first felt a sort of revulsion, but this quickly faded as I looked beside me at my friend, so humbled by what the world had made of his desires.

"Dear Benjamin," I said, "how you have suffered. I am so sorry. You have honored me with your confidence and I value it immensely." He looked at me very searchingly and said, "You must conceal your love's reality from those around you, but at least you have your love. I can never have mine," he said sadly. "Surely, there are others who feel as you do," I said. "You would have to be discreet, of course." "That's just the problem," he said, "being discreet is such a drain upon one. But this is a sorrow I have long borne and it cannot be helped." "How I wish I could help it," I said vehemently. Again he took my hand, "I know you would help me if you could, Roberta, and I love you for it. You have given me a gift simply in not turning away. Thank you for that." "Benjamin, you may always count me as a true friend and again I extend to you the invitation to come to our island, where you could live as you like." "Your Freeman has no animus against sodomy then?" he asked wryly. "I don't know," I said. "But he is very understanding," I said and Benjamin laughed in a way that told me he could not believe it, and yet we looked at each other now without the scrim of our mutual withholding between us, and rode the rest of the way in clarity and peace.

When we finally exited the coach at Bristol's brick station, I was very tired, but the sea air at once reawakened my urgent longing to be gone and on my way home. We went immediately to see Mr. Grafton at his the shipping office and ascertained that the bulk of my freight, which I had sent ahead, was there. Mr. Grafton seemed to give Ben a particularly sharp look upon their introduction and now I imagined I knew why.

Ben installed me at the inn where I was to meet Richard, and then I accompanied him to the coach, which was going on within the hour. "I will ask my mother about coming to live with me," he said. "I'm grateful you suggested it. My regard for you is enormous and I will miss your friendship more than I can say." "I have also found much comfort and enjoyment in you, and I hope very much to see you again in this world," I said, putting my arms around him. "As our conversation has led me to think that you believe in no other world, my dear heretic, I shall also hope we meet again in this one," he said. With this, we again embraced, and Benjamin remounted the coach.

As I was still watching my dear friend depart, I saw Richard jauntily approaching on the other side of the street and so could not dwell on the loss of Benjamin. "Ah, Roberta! You are here!" Richard said, "and we shall soon be underway for the new world." I smiled to think that he was as excited as I was, though for different reasons. He looked very handsome, a healthy young man animated by the energy of an extraordinary new enterprise. I was very proud of him.

The ship would set sail on Thursday and it now being Tuesday, we had two more days of waiting. We occupied ourselves in strolling the streets of Bristol, reexamining the lists of goods I had made to see if anything vital had been omitted, and talking about the island.

As we promenaded among the seaside cottages of grey stone and whitewashed shutters, Richard was very curious and asked pertinent questions. "I wish I had more experience of boating," he opined, "as it would be useful for us to sail to and from the mainland, don't you think?" "I know almost nothing of it," I admitted, "though it might be that those who live there would not welcome us," I said and explained Freeman's condemnation by his tribe's chief. "But things change," Richard said, undaunted, "and if we went there fully armed, we could protect ourselves." "You envision an invasion, then?" I asked with some sarcasm that seemed to wound Richard. "You think me too weak?" he asked. "Not at all. I think you fully capable." I said. "It's that I'd rather not adopt such an aggressive posture towards the natives of the continent." "But they are primitive. They can only benefit from civilization," he asserted. "I have no faith in civilization at the point of a gun," I said and began to wonder if I had been right to bring Richard with me after all.

I had thought he had a pacific temperament, but it occurred to me that such a character might have been all that was available to him in his own native circumstances and that a different field might bring out a different character. "You exaggerate," he said. "I only meant that if we were to go to the mainland, we could protect ourselves from attack, not that we would go with the intention of making one." Richard seemed quite serious in this rejoinder, which eased my concern, though I harbored a doubt that I had not had before and which only future experience could dispel. I wondered how we would govern our island.

In our walk we passed a ship's chandlery. There I bought three pairs of sailor's pants already made-up, a simple transaction about which Richard asked nothing, assuming, I imagine, that the pants were for Freeman.

We had looked from the pier at the Northhampton, the ship upon which we would embark. At present sailors swarmed over her huge body, polishing her brass, scrubbing her decks, stowing supplies and tending to her great web of rigging. On Thursday morning when we did board her, the ship's officers greeted us.

The captain was a solid, weather-beaten man of fifty named Fitzhoward. Ensign Moore, a young man who coughed a good deal, showed us to the tiny cabins that would be our homes for the next few months. I remembered that ten years ago Leora had alternately enthused over or complained about these quaint miniaturized accommodations. When we had settled our belongings, we went back up to the main deck to observe the weighing of the anchor.

"We are in luck, Madame Crousseau," said Captain Fitzhoward, "we have a favorable wind to carry us out." Then he began the shouted string of orders and replies that sent lines and pulleys clattering and seamen running up rope ladders. The sails unfurled and I felt the ship begin to move over the water. Gazing at the low hills around the harbor, I said to myself, "Good bye England," knowing I might never see this land again and feeling the sadness of that knowledge, but I turned towards the ship's bow and thought, "I am coming Freeman. It won't be long now, my darling," and I felt the breeze in my hair as if in answer.

Our trip out to Portugal passed uneventfully except for Richard's extreme seasickness. For more than a week he kept to his cabin, retching and miserable. I felt very sorry for him and nursed him as well as I could. "Why are you exempt from this scouring?" he asked. "I don't know, a difference in our constitutions, I suppose," I answered. "Ugh!" he groaned and collapsed onto his bunk. At last he came around, and was then upon the deck asking all manner of questions of the officers and seamen. He always liked to hear a good story and they had many. He joined the resident fiddle player for duets and their music seemed to me sublime, especially under the stars.

Our converse with the captain was cordial, and he seemed at ease with Richard, but with me he remained oddly formal and there was not the avuncular warmth that had animated the relations between myself and Captain Ellis on the Langland. At meals we spoke only of general topics. The captain seemed uninterested in his passengers, asking few questions of us beyond how we liked the day's weather, but that did not prevent me from asking him questions. I was especially curious about what I might meet in Portugal. "It is a well-run government," the captain said. "Pedro II is called 'il Pacifico' because he ended the long war between Spain and Portugal and also because he is a temperate man—not hot like so many of the Latins." "Has he had his throne for a long time?" I asked. "Yes, for many years. He was regent for his brother, a poor paralyzed idiot, but eventually deposed him and took over in his own name. It is also because of Pedro that you must get his approval for your purchase rather than that of the Dutch, for Pedro reclaimed the Portuguese possessions by defeating the Dutch fleet." The captain's knowledge of the regime prompted me to ask him to accompany me to make inquires at the Lisbon office to which the Portuguese envoy had told my solicitor I should go. He graciously agreed.

Richard was looking forward with great anticipation to his first visit to foreign soil, and many of his questions to the crew concerned what he might expect there. Listening to the seamen's replies, the captain was moved to say, "Mr. Crousseau, if you craft your Portuguese itinerary according to these fellows' instructions, your grand tour will consist of a progress through grog shops. You had best come with your sister and I, and while she is conducting her business, we will take in the city sights." "That is very kind of you, sir," Richard said enthusiastically. "I am much obliged." I was also gratified and began to conceive that behind the captain's indifferent exterior was a kind but circumspect man. This suspicion was fortified by the Captain's solicitude for his young ensign Moore, whose coughing I had noted my first day on the ship. "I fear he is consumptive, and his case has gone too far," he told me at one point.

I had not been in any other country either, but my curiosity about it was secondary to my interest in acquiring legal title to the island. It struck me as absurd that a European country could claim for itself a part of the world so distant from it, but as long as it had an army to enforce its declarations of ownership, I would have to deal with it.

Despite its remoteness and the unlikelihood that someone would try to expel us from the island, I wanted to make our own claim as sure as possible. I knew Freemen would think the whole notion of ownership very strange indeed as his people regarded the land as belonging to everyone. They had only spears and bows to enforce their idea, however, and so it would take second place in any clash with Europeans carrying guns.

As we entered the harbor and drew closer to the main wharf, Lisbon revealed itself as a colorful city of narrow wooden houses plastered over in pinks and greens and blues and decorated with fanciful carvings and wrought-iron balconies. When at last we came off the ship, the captain engaged a small carriage to take us through the crooked streets to the palace of Pedro II, King of Portugal, which sat on a hill in the south of the city. I had arrayed myself in the Portuguese outfit, but had put over it a cloak both to cover my bosom and to offer myself a more modest exterior.

However, the weather was very warm and I could not stand the swelter under the cloak so I took it off in the carriage. Both Captain Fitzhoward and Richard gave me most admiring glances, and the captain's manner toward me immediately warmed. I saluted Lady Evelyn's wisdom!

We applied for information in a vast yellow courtyard at the center of which there was a most imposing fountain spilling water over its successively larger levels. My documents from the Portuguese ambassador in England gave us entry into a series of outbuildings, and we were gradually admitted to a further series of increasingly ornate anterooms in the interior of the palace, each an extravaganza of mosaics, gold-crusted furniture and religious paintings. I was very glad for Captain Fitzhoward's company as he was able to speak Portuguese to the array of personages whose increasing grandness matched the rooms they inhabited.

At last we were led through into an immense hall where a swarthy man wearing a snowy wig greeted us and invited us to sit down, assuring us that the minister would see us in a short while. We were soon summoned to the presence of a very august, rotund man whose dress was even more elaborate than my own. He gazed at me approvingly. Again I silently thanked Lady Evelyn.

"I am Joao de Balcanza do Peron y Maseta," he announced in heavily accented English, "Foreign minister to his royal highness King Pedro. And you are Señora Roberta Crousseau, Richard Crousseau and Captain Humphrey Fitzhoward," he continued, as if his naming us made us officially who we were, for him at least. "Yes, your excellency," I said, plucking this honorific from my little store of them, though with no idea if it were the right one. I thanked the minister for seeing us then went immediately to my request. I explained about the shipwreck and my labors upon the island, about the kidnapping and my sojourn in England. "In my time there I grew to love this island and I am now on my way back to it. I would like to secure my life there through purchase of the island, and so I have come to you," I finished.

"How very extraordinary," the minister said, looking at me with a combination of superciliousness and craft. "Excuse me for just one moment," he said and turned to murmur something to the secretary who had conducted us into his presence. "Countless islands make up our realm," he said. "Which one is it that you want?" At this I unrolled the map that Captain Ellis had provided me and pointed out the speck upon it that represented the island and also noted its longitude and latitude.

"Ah, it is a modest purchase you have in mind, Señora, no?" "Yes, it is not an extensive property, but I have grown to love it and want to tend and improve it." "Very noble sentiments." he said, "Who will be with you?" "My husband and son and my brother whom you have met here." "Where is your husband, if I may ask?" said the minister, looking askance from under heavy eyelids. "He remains upon the island. He does not know what happened to me. I pray that he and my son are safe, and I want to return to them as quickly as I can." "It seems then that you would like to carry out your transaction *tout de suite*," the minister said. "Yes, indeed, besides the pressure of my own sentiments, I cannot delay the captain's ship," I answered.

At this moment the secretary returned and whispered something in the minister's ear at which he smiled and murmured, "I thought so." He turned to me and said, "I have made your presence known to the King, and he wishes to meet you, that is, if you have no objections." Of course, there was no question of my having any objections. The minister rose and motioned for me to follow him. The captain stayed seated, but Richard rose to accompany me. "The king asked only for la Señora Crousseau," the minister said, "too many people tire him. I must ask you to await your sister here where refreshments will be provided for you." Richard reddened and muttered, "Of course," and I was led off through a gilded hall.

I wondered if kings spent their days sitting upon their thrones, but this notion was dispelled quickly as I was led into what seemed to be a drawing room, a very well-appointed one to be sure, but still a room with purple silk settees, a pianoforte and heavy rugs upon white marble floors. A frail elderly gentleman sat in a chair, spectacles upon his nose and a large book open upon his lap. My guide said, "Your Majesty, may I present Señora Roberta Crousseau of England." The elderly man looked up over his spectacles and smiled. "But she does not want to be of England. She wants to have her own country, doesn't she?"

I curtsied as low as I could, as Lady Evelyn had spent some time instructing me. "Yes, your highness, though it is a very small island and hardly qualifies as a province much less a country." He motioned me to come closer and continued to peer up at me over his spectacles, though in a very friendly way and I perceived that he was teasing me. "Ah, but still, you will rule your little island, will you not?" "Truthfully, your highness, we are too busy growing our food and raising our goats to do much ruling. There are no other people but my husband, son and I, and now there will be my brother who is going out with me." "Won't you sit down, Señora Crousseau," he said. "And we will have some tea in the English fashion." At this several ornately liveried servers wheeled a massive tea service up to us and I was presented with a porcelain cup so delicate it seemed made from a lark's eggshell.

"Has anyone tried to take this island from you, Señora?" the king asked. "No, sir, but I would like to forestall such a possibility as I have grown to love the place and have put much work into it." The king nodded as he sipped his tea. "How much are you willing to pay for this island?" he asked. "It is for you to set the price, your highness, and for me to see if I can meet it." "The price will be very high," he said. "Perhaps so," I said, "though I hope not." "It is unusual for a woman to act as you do," he said with no animus, as if merely stating a fact, but this statement scared me anyway; for one thing I did not know which part of my behavior he found unusual. I said, "I did not seek to be unusual, your highness, it was thrust upon me and now I am trying to make the best of it." "Well said," exclaimed the king. "I must say though that you do not appear to be a farmer," he said, scanning the Portuguese outfit and smiling. "Evidently, tillers of the soil can look quite ravishing in satin." "Thank you, your highness. You are too kind," I said though I thought my reply somewhat senseless.

"I would like you to pay us a visit here before you go on to your island, Señora Crousseau," said the king. This statement made me very uneasy, and I was at a loss how to answer as I did not want to delay the journey for any reason. "You highness does me a great honor," I said. "and I am most anxious to oblige him. Only a mother who was torn from her young son, who has not seen him for almost a year, and whose son in turn does not know if his mother lives or not—only the mother of this son would plead to be excused from extending her visit at this time." The king watched me steadily as I delivered this speech. "Very well," he said with only a slight bit of peevishness. "I shall not detain you for a long visit, but I must have you for the rest of the afternoon. I want to hear the whole story, and I am much interested in your observations of my Brazilian realm."

And so the peasant woman spent the afternoon with the King of Portugal, relating the story of the shipwreck and life upon the island. He asked many questions of me, especially as regards the customs of the natives "Were they cannibals?" he wanted to know. "Not to my knowledge," I answered. He inquired about what minerals or gemstones were to be found. I told him truthfully that I had found jewels and money, but had not found any ores, explaining that I had not been to the mainland and had not seen many natives. "From where did these jewels you found come from?" he asked. "I don't know, your highness," I said. "How do you know that they do not belong to me?" he said. "I cannot know, your highness," I said. "Don't worry, Señora Crousseau, I shall not strip you of your fortune. And now I will release you. You see that I am an old man and must rest more than I used to. I thank you very much for giving me your company for this afternoon and wish you a safe voyage." At this the small man got up from his chair for the first time and I saw that he moved with great difficulty.

The king had not told me what I most longed to know, however-- whether or not I could purchase the island, but I felt it unwise to importune him about it, but to inquire instead of his minister who I hoped would still be about. I was led out through the series of anterooms, but did not come upon the minister, though I caught an odd glimpse of an elaborately dressed fellow who looked very familiar to me, but I could not place him. At last, the major-domo led me down to the courtyard, telling me that a coach would take me back to the ship and that my brother and Captain Fitzhoward had already gone on.

It was early evening and the harbor was made golden in the light of the sunset when I reboarded the ship. Richard rushed to meet me. "So, Roberta, you have met a king! It is quite marvelous, is it not?" "It was interesting," I said. "But he did not say if he would let me buy the island." "I say! What do you make of that?" "I don't know what to make of it," I said. "Well, for now come to the Captain's cabin as we are about to dine," he said.

At table I was much questioned about the visit, about the king and the palace, and the men made much more of me that evening than they ever had before, no doubt because I was still arrayed in the Portuguese outfit. I was myself quite flummoxed, however. The ship was to leave the next morning before it would be possible to again visit the palace to get an answer. As I sat over my meal I thought I would simply have to accept the provisionality of our tenure on the island. No one had tried to take it away from us before and probably no one would in the future. And if they did, we would fight them.

When the men brought out their cigars, I excused myself and went to my cabin. I lay upon the bunk, thinking over the day. How unthinkable it would have been to me ten years ago that I would ever be in the presence of a king! Now, having had the experience, it seemed to me quite unexceptional and something I would remember as an oddity rather than as something intrinsically valuable. The king of Portugal seemed a pleasant man, but why did he play with me about the island? At this thought there came a knock on my cabin door. Opening it I found the ship's first officer, who said, "Madame Crousseau, a Portuguese messenger has come for you."

I went topside and found there a man in the purple livery of the king. "Madame Crousseau, this is for you," he said, bowing and handing me a square packet, "with the king's compliments." Before I had a chance to open it, he clicked his heels and departed. The ship's crew stood about waiting to see what I had received, and I saw no reason not to gratify their curiosity, so I took the cord off the packet and unwrapped it. In it there was a miniature portrait in oils of the king beneath which there was a rolled parchment and another piece of folded parchment. I unrolled the larger one to find it written all in Latin, but the note was in English. "I hope this title to your island is not too cheap a price for the pleasure of your company this afternoon," it read and was signed Pedro II, King of Portugal followed by a roster of ten other names and titles. I was astonished. "He has given me the island!" I said to Richard and smiled more broadly than I had since I'd left home.

Amongst the ship's officers there was enough Latin that we eventually read the rolled parchment, which said that the island designated by the following latitude and longitudes was given to Roberta Crousseau by the kingdom of Portugal for all time and that a copy of this document would reside in the Portuguese chancellery. A heavy red wax seal was affixed to the bottom where there was also an illegible but grandiose signature we took to be that of the king.

"You have made a conquest, Madame Crousseau," Captain Fitzhoward said, "Bravo!" There were bravos all around and I was very glad.

Chapter 20—Battle and Standstill

I arose the next morning much eased in my mind and went up to the deck with a light step. There I saw the seamen bringing aboard several richly-made trunks, which were soon followed by their owner, who turned out to be the very man I had seen at the palace the previous day and who had struck me as familiar. When he drew close enough that I could see his face, I stood stock still and stared in shock, for I recognized him as the horrible Sutton Norman who had robbed the coach, kidnapped and humiliated me. He looked equally surprised to see me and for a moment I saw the nakedness of his youth, but that door shut very quickly, and he made a tight-lipped smile. "You certainly cut a wide swathe, Madame," he said, making a bow ironic in its sweep. "Perhaps not as wide as yours, sir," I said, nodding my head slightly, very much astonished.

As we both masked our dumbfoundedness, Captain Fitzhoward approached. "Ah, there you are, Sir Sutton. I had begun to worry that we would have to leave without you. I see that you have met Madame Crousseau." At this the young man could not help himself from exclaiming, "This is Madame Crousseau?" as if he had known he would meet such a person but not what she would look like. The Captain raised his eyebrows. "Why, yes," he said. "Had you expected someone else, sir?" I asked. "I knew that a woman of that name traveled on this ship, but I have not had the pleasure of making her acquaintance," he said, recapturing his manners.

Then I fought a little war inside me. I felt the urge to blurt, "You have most certainly made my acquaintance when you abducted me, stripped off my dress and ordered me to pee into a bucket." I restrained myself and did not say this because at the same time I envisioned how awkward things would be after I said it, though I resolved to communicate at least some of my knowledge to the captain in private.

"Sir Sutton's father, Lord Norman, is one of my patrons," Captain Fitzhoward then offered. "I consented to take his son from Lisbon to South America and so you will have some company more lively than my own, Madame Crousseau." "I cannot imagine his company would be better than yours, sir," I said, a statement that did not arrive as I intended it to, as the captain grew embarrassed.

At this point Richard appeared and was introduced to young Norman, who shook hands with him warmly and plied him with friendly inquiry. "Have you been out to the southern climes before?" he asked, and when Richard told him no, he said, "Nor I. We can wonder together." Open-hearted Richard was gratified to be addressed in such a friendly way by a nobleman, and I could see how Sutton Norman was able to corral the allegiance of the young men who had helped him in robbery.

"Let us show you your cabin, Sutton," the captain said, "if Madame Crousseau will excuse us. You can return to her shortly." "Please do not hurry on my account," I said and shot a look to Sutton that said he would be wise to avoid me. I wondered if he felt any fear that I would tell the captain what I knew about him. Perhaps he relied upon my reticence to say exactly what he had done to me. Indeed, I resolved not to tell the worst of it.

When the occasion presented itself that I was alone with the captain, I found out that Sutton had no reason for fear. "Captain Fitzhoward," I said, "Do you know Sutton Norman well?" His usually resolute face grew clouded. "No, but I know of him. He has brought a great deal of trouble and sorrow to his father, a man who has done me much kindness in the past, so that when I got Sutton's note last night, I could not turn down the request. Perhaps the young man will make a new start. I want to help him for his father's sake. Why do you ask, Madame Crousseau?" "I fear to tell you as it is most unpleasant and shocking."

I then related the story of how Sutton Norman had played the highwayman and carried me off to his hideaway. As I told the story, the captain assumed it as a burden. At last he sighed and said, "I am not surprised to hear it, and I am very sorry that you had to endure such things. I don't know that there is anything to be done about it now, but I will try to protect you from contact with the young man." "Oh, Captain," I said, "I had no expectation that anything could be done about the past. I merely thought to warn you." Captain Fitzhoward smiled kindly at me. "That was good of you, Madame Crousseau. You will be glad to know that I am already on guard." "Perhaps the young man will make a new start," I said, mostly to cheer up the captain. "I would not begrudge him that." "Tell me, what did he take from you?" he asked. "Nothing except my wedding ring and that did not really belong to me as I found it in a cave on the island," I said with some merriment. "Indeed!" the captain laughingly exclaimed. "You are a most unusual person, Madame Crousseau."

In the many days upon the sea that followed, Sutton Norman and I avoided each other as much as possible and I returned to happy contemplation of owning the island, which animated the days that followed, many of which were tedious in their sameness, for after we passed the Azores and a few other islands there was nothing to be seen but the sea and the sky, though the weather was hotly pleasant. My conversation with Captain Fitzhoward warmed as we became further acquainted, and he was endlessly willing to tutor my observation of the sea so that over the many weeks I was able better to appreciate its subtly changing face.

I learned to recognize the many gradations in the water's colors between the obvious extremes of deep grey and crystalline blue and where I might expect the flying fish to leap through the air. I walked a good deal back and forth upon the deck, a distance of about thirty yards, and often came to rest in a tiny sheltered alcove near the prow. Discovering my habit, the captain had a canopy set up so that I might read or embroider protected from the broiling sun. Sometimes he would join me at my perch.

One day I asked him a general question about his naval career that resulted in a rather impassioned reply. "I wanted to serve in the British navy, but I could not buy a commission." "And yet you are now a ship's captain," I said. "Yes, a merchant captain, not a naval captain," he replied, "though I have had a good run of it," he said.

"Does one not need to purchase a commission as a merchantman?" I asked. "Yes, but the price is much less," he answered. "It is an odd way to run a navy," I said. The captain looked at me strangely. "How does one get the best men if only those with money are eligible?" I asked. "Because the propertied classes constitute the best people. The pool is identical," he said rather severely. "And yet you were excluded from it," I returned. "Yes, my grandfather and father were both impecunious and so their scion paid the penalty." "But I suppose Sutton Norman, a very ignoble man, could easily get a commission?" "Yes, quite easily," the Captain said. "That does not seem right. It is very impractical," I said. "You are not a leveler, are you, Madame Crousseau?" the captain asked. "I've never given it much thought," I said rather disingenuously, "but it seems to me that the current system is very wasteful of ability." "No, Madame, the current system ensures that there will be men of ability at all levels and that is a great benefit to us." "I am myself from the lower orders," I said, remembering how Lady Evelyn had so labeled me, "but money has allowed me a wider scope of action. I could, for example, buy my son a commission, could I not? Is this a harm to the social system?" "No, indeed," the captain replied coolly. "The system must always make way for new men ennobled by application, education or luck. Your son, however, would have to find a regiment that would take him, no matter how much money you spent, and regiments are controlled by those who have risen in the current system." "Yes, I see," I said. "but would you say that the issue would hinge on how great an amount of money were involved?" "Yes, probably so," the captain agreed. "And so the having of money confers enough virtue to offset one's origins?" "To a certain extent, yes, of course. So it has always been. But cases such as yours are anomalous," he said pointedly. "Surely you agree?" "Yes, money has always constituted a trump," I said. "But there are other more important values," the captain said rather priggishly. "That is exactly the principle that governed my comment at the beginning of our conversation," I said.

I enjoyed this sort of sparring with the captain as it enlivened the days a bit, but his view of society, as universally held as it was, disturbed me, and I hoped the future would be different. I felt the captain clung to his view as a way of consoling himself for his own disappointment.

Inevitably, at last Sutton Norman stopped by my canopy to inflict himself upon me. "Good-day to you, Madame Crousseau," he said, his tone implying that we were somehow complicit in hiding our previous acquaintance. I had been forced to dine in his company, but I had never addressed a word to him, nor he to me, from shame on his part, I had assumed. "I prefer not to converse with you or have anything whatsoever to do with you," I said now. "Yes, it must be hard to sit at table with someone who has seen you naked," he snickered.

Such an assumption destroyed any hope that he might not be as disgusting as I had thought or that he might be trying to make a new life for himself. I imagined that to most people he was amusing; he was superficially charming, sharp-featured and fine-skinned. I was unwilling to mar the social fabric to the extent of making a scene amongst the seaman who worked around us. Instead, I asked him the questions that had stood in my mind since our encounter. "Why did you play at robbery and abduction, Mr. Norman, when you had no need to goad you?" He gave a snorting little laugh. "You cannot know the poverty of a country gentleman." "Indeed, I cannot. Most terrible is it? I had heard your family is very rich, so to what sort of poverty do you refer? " "To that of scope and amusement. You cannot imagine the dreariness of country life where one is expected to walk exactly the same steps as did one's great-great grandfather. Nothing is ever new. One is always expected to act in the same old way." "You cannot be so barren of imagination as to choose thievery and abduction as the only alternative to boredom," I said. "I suppose I had read too many books," he replied. "I like to cut a figure." "Do you call your treatment of me cutting a figure? Perhaps you should have been an actor." "I should have liked that, but my station precluded it," he answered.

It seemed he had thoroughly rationalized his conduct. "Besides, you are not guiltless. You lied to me about who you are," Norman said. "I lied to protect myself." "I'm sure all liars say that," he returned. What an exasperating fellow! "It will surprise you to know that most of what came from the robberies I deposited in the poor box," he said with a feint at humility. "Ah, you are Robin Hood, then. All is forgiven," I said and turned my gaze again to the sea. "You are most free in your ridicule when you yourself were able to escape your assigned station," he said as if scoring a coup. "I did so through accident," I said. "And luck," he added. While this was true, I wondered what he particularly referred to. Seeing the question in my face, he went on, "Finding a treasure in a cave —now there's a story to rival Robin Hood. And foiling the erstwhile highwayman by sewing it into a plain dress—the very dress I gave back to you--what a heroine!" "How do you know these things?" I asked. "Oh, you are all the talk of Lisbon, Madame Crousseau. No sooner had you told your story than the minions of rumor spread it everywhere. I was close by so I heard it early."

Now it dropped as a hammer upon me that Norman was the man I had glimpsed as I left the palace. "Everyone at the Portuguese court knows you're a serving woman who found a fortune in an island cave, but that you are insane because you want to return to it." "Is that what is said?" I asked. "No, it is what I think," he replied. "What were you doing at the Portuguese court?" I asked. "Paying my father's compliments to the king." "Ah, I suspect your father sent you away to be rid of the trouble you cause him," I said. The young man sighed. "Yes, you are correct. I am an exile, expected to turn a new leaf. And there will be a new leaf for you as well? Owner of your own kingdom? Tell me, is there any more treasure upon your island, another cave that I might crawl into and emerge wealthy in my own right?" Norman said this in a mocking way, but I trusted him so little that I was immediately suspicious. "Any wealth that you would understand has been entirely exhausted," I said. "I return only to my family." "Ah, yes, the savage with whom you consort," he said, and seeing my face harden, added, "You cannot insult me with the implication that I am sensitive only to money and not expect to be insulted in return. You see, unlike most men, I do regard you as my equal, Madame Crousseau." With this he bowed and went away, leaving me alone to ponder.

Some days later, when I was again at my roost, the sailor on watch shouted that he had seen a vessel off our port side. I emerged from my alcove and quickly joined the captain, who had taken up his glass to spy what sort of ship it was. "It shows the flag of Portugal," he said, "and it bears down upon us. Perhaps the king has learned of your leveling tendencies, Madame Crousseau and has decided to reclaim his portrait," the captain joked, though he quickly turned to readying the ship for a confrontation. "But the Portuguese are friendly to us," I said. "Oh, but anyone can fly any kind of flag. It is a common pirates' ploy to enable them to draw near their prey and seize it." My first thought was that this would be a cruel impediment to my return home though I knew it was a selfish impulse.

The captain had called his men to arms and had unveiled the guns that had lain asleep behind the steep walls of the ship. However, as the other ship sailed closer to us, we saw upon the deck several men who appeared from their dress and demeanor to be the counterparts of our own captain and his officers. One of them hailed us, first in Portuguese and then in rough but very affable English. "Are you come from Lisbon?" shouted the man I took to be their captain, since he wore the most elaborate dress. Our own captain shouted back that we were. "Will you come aboard us for some brandy so that we might hear news of home?" the Portuguese inquired. "Or may we come over to you?"

Captain Fitzhoward quickly weighed this request. "Yes, come over to us," he said. "But I must ask you to leave your arms at home." Suddenly, a sliding door on the hull of the other ship shot back, revealing the black mouth of a cannon. "This one is too heavy to take with us!" its captain exclaimed right before an enormous blast sounded and a ball tore across our ship rending a hole in its side, splintering all in its path and putting a great fright upon me.

At this I saw our captain's face light up as I had never before seen it. "Aha!" he shouted, "They are pirates, just as I suspected." He ordered his guns to fire upon the pirate ship, and his men sprang into the drills to ready them, so I soon saw balls from the Northhampton fly across the interval to wreak reciprocal havoc. Torn as it was though, the other ship came closer and closer to us until it drew near enough that I could see the roguish faces of the pirates who lined the gunwales, brandishing sabers and pistols in anticipation of boarding us. "Go below, Madame Crousseau," the Captain shouted as he grabbed his own sword from his orderly.

I did indeed go below, but only to grab up the pistol that Benjamin Miller had given me. I was filled with rage at these pirates who were intent on hindering our voyage, and I meant to help defend the ship. I loaded the pistol and was leaving my cabin when I caught sight of my determined face in the small looking glass. I quickly tore out the linen kerchief that I wore over my bosom and covered the pistol with it.

I peeked up out of the hatch to see a battle at close range. The air had grown gray and thick with the smoke from pistols and another hot odor arose from the men who were slain upon the deck. Everywhere men strove against each other in hard combat with swords or wrestled hand to

hand. From where I was I could not tell which side had the upper hand.
Sutton Norman had joined the fight, wielding a bloody sword with much
bravado. I also saw my brother flailing about with a length of plank,
knocking pirates off their feet and then knocking them in the head. He
took down several of the antagonists this way, and one of them,
determined to deal the same to him, had just finished reloading his pistol
and was pointing it at him. I raised my own pistol and shot the man in
the chest. Richard looked around to identify his savior and had just
enough time to register his surprise that it was me before another of the
brigands attacked him with a sword, the thrust of which Richard blocked
with his plank, tearing the sword from the man's hand.

The enormous fact that I had killed someone had to yield consideration
to the further demands of the moment. I reloaded my pistol and from my
little bunker let off shots as quickly as I could, though in the chaos it was
increasingly difficult to tell friend from foe or to aim accurately.

After what to me was an epoch, the pirates reversed course and tried
to make their way back to their own ship. It must have been that our
crew had put up a stiffer fight than they were willing to linger amidst.
They mounted their sails so as to move off from us, at which I heard our
captain order the gunners to hit them repeatedly. They quickly turned
their ship so as to present to us its less broad aft portion, though one of
our balls plowed through it, and as it limped away we could see the
pirate crew hopping around their shattered gunwale, trying to contain the
damage.

As the smoke cleared, I saw Sutton Norman standing with his sword
poised on the throat of one of the pirates. The pose was so rakish it
seemed he had preserved it so that we might observe him. "That will do,
Norman," the captain ordered, and it was plain the young man was
disappointed he had not been able to run the man through.

There were a number of other men, our own and some of the pirates, fallen upon the deck. Two of our sailors hoisted their bleeding comrade from the deck and carried him below. The captain quickly assessed the damage to his ship and assigned the remaining crew to begin emergency repairs. "Lieutenant Morgan, attend to the rigging and bring forward some timber to patch that hole," he ordered, pointing to the first wound the pirates had visited upon us. Among those fallen, I saw, was the pirate chief who had apparently been stunned and was now picking himself up and letting loose a long string of curses quite original in their blasphemous obscenity.

By this time I had climbed out of the hatch hole from which I had played the sniper and was standing mutely in a sort of shock. The captain rushed over to me. "Madame Crousseau," he said, scanning my smoke-blackened face, "are you injured?" "No, sir," I said, though in fact my hands were burned and the report of the pistol had so thoroughly shaken me that I was a field of aching flesh. "You are quite dirty, Madame, which you might have avoided if you had gone below as I instructed you to do," he said, offering me his handkerchief. "But Captain," Richard burst out, "She saved my life and that of several of your crew as well. She fired from the hatchway," he said, pointing to my battle post. "Yes, she dropped a few of those shiteheads," said one of the sailors. "Watch your language, sir," warned the captain. He looked at me with much consternation, "It seems that you are an apt candidate for the navy, Madame," he said. "And I have the money to buy a commission!" I said and tried to laugh more than the joke warranted, probably as a way to release some of the tension of the previous hour.

Our wounded sailors were taken below where their injuries were bandaged. We were lucky in that though two were killed none of the others had severe wounds. Four of the pirates lay dead upon our deck and three more wounded ones remained as well. These were put into a large cage that constituted the ship's brig, though it had until recently held a pig that had been brought along to help feed us, and the pen still showed evidence of its former occupant.

After some converse with the pirate captain, our captain locked him into one of the passenger cabins. When I inquired why he got better treatment than the others, I was told that he was a nobleman. "How noble can it be to commit piracy upon the seas?" I exclaimed. "Oh, he shall hang," the captain assured me, "and probably quite brutally in a man-shaped cage at the entrance to some harbor, but until then he shall be treated according to his station." I suppose there was consistency in the captain's odious thinking. Those who had fallen in the battle were wrapped in canvas and all the ambulatory crewmen gathered around while the captain said some solemn words. Then the newly dead were dumped into the sea.

When I went to my cabin and dropped down upon the bunk, the fact of my having killed a human being presented its weighty self to my mind. I was not sorry I had done it; I was sorry I'd had to do it. I did not feel heroic; I felt grim, marked in a way that could never be expunged. Because of me a fellow creature had ceased to live, and I would have to hold this knowledge ever after. I began to bear then one of the heavy burdens I bear to this day.

I was much surprised in the evening when I went to Captain Fitzhoward's table to find that the pirate captain, the author of his crew members' demise, was to dine with us. When I appeared, he gave me a very deep bow and during the meal he spoke to me in an ingratiating way, as if we had just met at tea. He introduced himself as Guillermo do Placidia. He was a man in his thirties; his features were pleasing but showed the scars of life at sea and the roughness of his profession.

"How is it you came to pirating, sir?" I asked. "Ah, it was my misfortune to be born the youngest son," he said. "I had not the calling to the church, nor to scholarship nor law, so at eighteen I set off for Brazil to attach myself to the estate of a relative there. On the way our ship was captured by pirates, the chief of whom adopted me and bequeathed me his trade. I had a knack for it," he said with a fillip. "Evidently not," I said, "for here you are a captive." "Ah, but I have lasted longer than most. I am an old veteran." "Do you have a family, sir?" I asked. "Several," he said, a glint in his eye. "As I move around a great deal, I am welcomed as Papa in a number of ports." At this Captain Fitzhoward's narrow face hardened. "You ought not to broadcast your immorality, sir," he said. Guillermo do Placidia shrugged. "Everyone concerned is quite happy with the arrangement," he said. Sutton Norman took this in as great fun.

After dinner we all went up from the Captain's stuffy mess to take the milder air on the deck where a full moon was making a resplendent silver show once in the sky and then again in reflection upon the water. Norman tried to engage the pirate in discussion, but the man ended up by my side.

"If a scoundrel such as myself may ask you a question, Señora," the pirate said to me, "what is the purpose of your voyage?" "I am returning to my home on an island off the coast of Brazil." "Your home?" he said contemplatively. "I wonder if I have ever been there. How large is the settlement?" "Very small," I said. "It must be very prosperous," he said, at which I looked at him with raised eyebrows. "Only prosperity could nurture such beauty, Señora. Please do not be offended by my familiarity. Have you been absent long from this island?" "About a year," I answered. "Oh, that is hard," he said, adding plaintively, "I know what it is to be lonely." At this I burst out laughing. He looked injured and said,

335

"Why do you make fun of me?" "Because I suspect you of seeking to add another port to your familial itinerary," I said. He looked at me with his soft brown eyes, "I would not mind as you are very lovely. Your eyes are an extraordinary green, and I long to touch your hair. Do you call its color copper?" He lowered his eyes. "I call its color brown," I said. "I am too familiar, but what I said is true," he went on. "I am often lonely." "Please stop, sir." I replied, "I refuse to feel sorry for you. Only a few hours ago, you killed several of this ship's men, and you would have killed us all if you had been able to." "Not at all," he protested. "I prefer to kill no one, but force must be used in my profession." "Your profession is crime, sir." He gave his charming shrug. "I am what my life has made me," he said. "It has made me very appreciative of women," he went on. "Good night. I hope your loneliness does not impede your sleep," I said and turned away. "It will," he said sorrowfully. "I don't understand why humans are so cruel to each other when it lies in their power to minister to suffering."

It was somewhat difficult to leave this conversation as I felt I was in the presence of a professional seducer and, such arts having never been practiced upon me before, I was curious. He was very attractive and persuasive and I felt his remarks about my eyes and hair as a sort of balm. I was disgusted to realize that had I not been so fully invested in my own honest tie to Freeman, I might have been willing to share his bed, especially as I would have been glad not to be alone with my thoughts this night.

In the event, I was indeed alone with my thoughts, but they were not morbid. I was struck with the many strange discoveries sea voyages had brought me and the great luck that had been mine and I was grateful. I think the limitless expanse of the sea led me to ponder such things.

Until we put him off on a British navy ship a few days later, the pirate plied me with his charm. Before he was led away, he kissed my hand and said, "If only we had met at another time and place. . . ." "You ought to have been a diplomat, sir," I said. "No, I had not the application and one deals so much with men," he replied, bowed and went away. In spite of myself I liked his absurd perseverance. "My, what a conquest you have made," said Sutton Norman, and even Richard laughed as I blushed. The captain looked at me in a most odd way, as if he wanted to say something, but he did not.

Despite the pirate's diverting presence, each passing day increased the strength of my longing for home and my eagerness to reach it. The captain insisted on following the most rational route for his own purposes which entailed a circuitous progress through a number of lively, dirty ports for the delivery of goods and the taking on of various native produce including many kegs of molasses and sacks of coffee berries. The captain discouraged me from going alone into the towns, but would accompany me on brief walks. I enjoyed these occasional experiences of solid ground beneath my feet.

The ports' inhabitants were a motley lot of humanity as various in hue as the sea itself, some gaily dressed, but most wearing grey-brown rags. I was saddened to see the bowed heads of the black slaves who did the labor and was most startled when the captain suggested I might buy several of them to help me build an estate upon my island. "That would allow you to be much more ambitious in your creation." "I am not so ambitious," I said. Sutton Norman, who I could not prevent from strolling with us, said, "Africans live in savage darkness. They know no civilization. Their place in the scheme of things is to learn from more advanced peoples and contribute their labor to the designs of their superiors," he said. "That is a fine set speech," I returned. "It is so self-serving that I feel sure no Africans were consulted about it." "The Africans themselves offer their fellows for sale," the captain rejoined. "So some Africans show themselves as venal as some Europeans. That is a point of equality between us then," I said. Captain Fitzhoward was clearly exasperated with me. "You enjoy setting yourself against the common wisdom, Madame Crousseau," he said. "Not at all, but there will be no slavery on our island." "As you will," he said, ending the conversation. I believed the captain was tiring of my company, and I don't think even my donning the Portuguese outfit would have mitigated what he saw as my waywardness, though in this I turned out to be quite mistaken.

We were increasingly concerned about Ensign Moore, whose consumption had taken a sudden turn for the worse and whose aspect looked more wasted with each passing day. One morning the captain made my heart race by informing me that we were about a week from my island. He said, "I wish to ask you a very great favor, Madame Crousseau. You cannot but have noticed Ensign Moore's decline. I fear that he will not be long for this world, and I would like for him to be able to die at home with his family." "Yes, of course," I said. "It may already be too late," he went on, "but if we were able to make for the nearest harbor where we might find a ship set to sail for England, we might put him on it and get him home before he expires." Now I saw where this was tending. "Doing this would mean delaying your own arrival home by as much as several weeks," he said, "and that is why I am speaking with you about it."

Indeed it was a blow. I felt I had taken myself to the edge of my endurance over the long months away from Freeman and Tom, and now I was asked to steel myself anew. I knew I had no choice, but I could not completely conceal my disappointment when I said sadly, "Certainly, it must be done as you suggest." "Thank you, Madame Crousseau. I know this is a sacrifice for you." I asked myself how a few weeks more of separation could be much of a sacrifice and knew in my reason that it was not, but my heart was much stricken and when I went below I sobbed into my pillow.

Later that day, I visited Ensign Moore who lay in his bunk. He struggled to sit up when he saw me. "I must thank you, Madame Crousseau," he said. "The captain told me of your generosity. I hope to see my old mother once more before I am extinguished, and I know she would want me to thank you as well." Later I realized that whenever I did see Freeman and Tom again, the time would be sweeter because I had honored the principle of love in my dealings with Ensign Moore. This was a good lesson from a personage I wryly named Wider Love in the allegorical mode of Pilgrim's Progress; although I dislike the pedantic way of thinking that makes everything in life emblematic of something else, ten years of having nothing but this method as my reading matter had taken its toll.

Thus it was that in a week, instead of landing upon the dear shores of my island, we sailed instead into the port of Trinidad, a rollicking place that made the crew quite elated, so well-known was it for all forms of pleasurable iniquity. Here at last Richard got his "progress through grog shops." After a night from which he arose very sick and dejected, he whined, "Why did you let me do it, Roberta? You should have prevented me." "I am in no way your parent, and if I tried to act so, you would let me know it very forcefully, I'm sure," I replied. "Please don't shout at me, Roberta!" he pleaded, though I had been speaking in a normal voice. "You must drink a lot of water," I said, "then you will feel better."

Chapter 21 — It Cannot Be

Ensign Moore was quickly transferred to a ship that, as luck would have it, was to depart for England on the morrow, and I was very touched by the tender way Captain Fitzhoward cared for him and bid him farewell. When the young man had been carried away, the captain turned to me and said, "Now, Madame Crousseau, I am completely at your disposal." At that very instant an immense blast sounded, and we were both knocked off our feet and pounded heavily onto the deck. When I opened my eyes, I saw men hurrying to and fro with buckets amidst much smoke and felt myself half lifted and half dragged out onto the pier. I had been struck deaf, so the scenes of chaos seemed to be happening in a dream.

The captain was leaning over me, mouthing my name. My look of recognition relieved him. He pointed to my ears. I nodded "no" to signify that I could not hear, and he pointed to his own ears to indicate that neither could he. As I lifted my head, the worst sight of my life arose before me: Richard lay still upon the pier, a great gash in his head. I struggled to my feet and staggered over to him. "Richard! Richard!" I shouted, though I could not hear my own cries. The captain knelt beside me and put his hand to Richard's throat. After a few moments, he looked at me gravely and shook his head. Very slowly he said words whose meaning I could see upon his lips, "He is gone." "No, no," I cried, put my arms around the dead body of my brother and clutched him to me. "It can't be. It can't be," I keened, rocking his body back and forth.

Everyone knows what it is to lose someone dear and so will understand when I say I felt myself sucked into the dark maw of a grief so great I did not think I could myself continue to live. At last the captain gently lifted me up and hoisted me into his arms, but I hardly noticed as I had then begun my tenure in an alien realm where nothing lived and nothing mattered. The captain carried me across the pier to an inn where I was laid upon a sofa and my face was bathed by a plump woman I took to be the proprietress. She gave me some brandy and sat beside me as I slowly recovered my senses, if not my sanity. The captain mouthed to me that he would return and then went speedily out. A heavy hammer pounded a refrain in my mind, "Richard is dead. Richard is dead," and this refrain went on and on, informing every moment; even when I was speaking to someone, it rang behind my words.

When the captain returned, I was again able to hear. I asked what had happened. "Apparently the arsenal of the ship next to ours exploded," he said. "Was anyone else injured?" I asked. "No one else on our ship, but several on board the other were killed," he said. "I cannot tell you how sorry I am about your brother. It was a freakish thing, had he been standing half a foot in either direction, he would have been spared." "But he was not," I said flatly. The captain's face told me how anguished he was on my behalf, but I could not summon the energy to comfort him.

"I am much loathe to burden you further, Madame Crousseau, but I must tell you that our ship has been seriously damaged. A spar struck the main mast and cracked it." "How soon can it be repaired?" I asked, suddenly thinking that the only thing that could anchor me again in the world would be the sight of Freeman and Tom. "The mast will have to be replaced; how long it will take depends on how quickly we can locate a suitable timber. Setting it in place could take a week or more." "Can the ship sail with a cracked mast?" I asked, seeing those I loved recede ever further from me. "It would be very foolhardy to do so. I am so sorry, Madame Crousseau. I feel the responsibility of persuading you towards a course that has caused you so much horror and grief. I am so very sorry, my dear."

If it were possible to increase an already full cup, mine of grief expanded then, and I was overwhelmed with a thought I had never had before—that I might not get back to Freeman and Tom. I was unable to restrain the sobs that shook my whole body. The captain seemed to divine my thoughts. "Do not despair, my dear. You will get back to them. You have met a great trial, but from what I have seen, you have the strength to meet it." His encouragement did not really comfort me, but it did recall me to at least a sliver of desire not to impose myself too heavily upon him. "I would not have put this hurt and disappointment on you for anything," he said.

Eventually, I gave a sigh and straightened myself, at least I did so on the outside as if I were an actress. "It is not your fault, Captain. Please forgive my demonstration." "It's quite justified in the circumstance. I want to cry myself," he said with genuine sorrow. "I must go back to the pier now to see to the ship. I will procure a burial for Richard as well. I will return this evening," he said, took up his hat and left.

I felt utterly bereft. Now that I was alone, my mind spawned new verses to the dirge that began "Richard is dead." Had it not been for me, he would be alive in England, perhaps discontented and restless, but alive to be prized by a family who dearly loved him. They had entrusted him to me, and in my care he had met his death. Tabitha had been right. I was a bad example. It would have been better if I had not returned. My guilt felt like a cloak of lead.

The next day Richard was buried in a tiny churchyard overlooked by palm trees. At least he would rest in a warm climate. For a week thereafter I kept to my room at the inn and for some time did not speak with anyone, even the Captain, my only company the band of buzzards that were my thoughts. I could not eat and my sleep was a meager garment imprinted with dark images. I did nothing at all with the painful exception of writing a letter to my brother Tom to tell him of Richard's death and to beg his forgiveness. From time to time, the innkeeper, Mrs. Lewis, would tell me someone had come to call; all the officers from the ship, even Sutton Norman came, but I could not face anyone.

At last there came an insistent pounding on the door and the voice of the captain. "Madame Crousseau, I am coming in," he said and did so, finding me in my usual place sitting on the side of my bed. "I am sorry to break in upon you, but I must," he said. "Put your bonnet on. We are going for a walk." "No thank you," I said dully. "But you must. Please don't make me suffer so much on your account." That I was paining him roused me from my gloom enough to put on my bonnet and go out with him. He gently led me down the street. I saw with my mind that it was a lively and colorful place, but its music could not penetrate my heart's numbness. The Captain did not force conversation, though from time to time he pointed out sites of interest—the Custom's House, the market, the sailor's shrine to their patron Saint Elmo. As we walked along the concourse by the ocean the sun shone upon the water, making it a sheet of gold and silver, and the air was mild as a caress. I tried to appreciate it all, but I could summon no joy or cheer. We might as well have been strolling a frozen wasteland. Indeed, that is where I now lived.

Six weeks crawled by in this way—no appropriate timber was found and I found no peace in my mind. I was hourly assaulted by my responsibility for Richard's death and by a chorus of reproaches based upon my presumption. I accused myself of pride, of selfishness and stupidity. I lay all sins at my own door and could open it to no light. Finally, on one of our walks, the Captain reproved me. "It is not like you, Madame Crousseau, to linger so long in the shadows. You must come out. I surmise that you blame yourself for your brother's death, but you must reconsider that in doing so you deny your brother his own will. He chose to accompany you. Indeed, he told me you had lifted him out of his situation as from a pit." "Only to consign him to another," I said bitterly. "You take too much on yourself. It is egotistical." I protested that I was only thinking of Richard and what we had lost in him. "You are also thinking your family will blame you. Perhaps they will, but that will not make their judgment correct." I felt something inside me crack open, and I told the captain, "My sister-in-law said I had done all the children a disservice by setting before them an example of a life outside the conventional." "Your sister-in-law is an ass!" he exclaimed, and thereby produced the first laugh I had made since Richard died. It was a weak one, but encouraged the captain. "What would your brother think of your behavior? He would be disappointed, I'm sure. You were his idea of a heroine, not merely surviving, but making a success of yourself shipwrecked upon an island. But here you are defeated by that which harries us all. Buck up, my dear. I can no longer bear to see you like this, so small and wilted."

I listened to his speech quietly, and said little, but later, in my chamber, I turned it over a great deal. I concluded that, indeed, I was not approaching this problem as I had others; I was simply letting fate work on me, rather than taking a hand in determining the shape of my fate, and

I resolved to take myself in hand and try to change my direction. The Captain was right that Richard should be allowed his own agency. He had not been a child. I felt the sphere of my culpability contract the slightest bit, and this seemed to open the floodgates of my longing for Freeman and Tom. If I had not killed Richard, then perhaps I deserved to return to them. I would do anything to get back, stained though I was with guilt and sorrow.

On my next promenade with the Captain I asked, "Is there any progress on rebuilding the mast?" I asked the captain. "Not yet," he said and sighed. "It's certainly not your fault," I said, adding, "Thank you for being so patient and kind to me, Captain Fitzhoward, and wise as well. I will work to reform myself." At this he huffed a bit, unused to compliments. "Not reform, my dear. I didn't mean that."

On our way back we were hailed by Sutton Norman. "Madame Crousseau," he exclaimed, "I see you have emerged. I hope you will sometime allow me to walk with you as I'm damnably bored." "I'm sorry to have been remiss in facilitating your amusement," I said. "Ah, you prick me with selfishness, but I most assuredly intend my intercourse with others to be mutually amusing, Madame," he said softly. I supposed he meant it. "Very well, I will walk with you," I said wearily. "Excellent! Excellent! Good day then." I looked askance at the captain who said, "Young Norman can be quite charming. He had a good education. Perhaps had his mother lived, she would have better schooled his heart." "When did he lose her?" I asked. "As a babe, when she bore him." Then I felt some sympathy for Sutton Norman, who had never known a mother.

That evening as I lay in bed, my mind worked as it had not for the past six weeks. The example of looking at Sutton Norman from another viewpoint impressed me, and it finally occurred to me that the

Northhampton was not the only ship around, that there were other vessels, that I had money and I might hire one of them to take me home. I wondered why I had not realized this fact much sooner and recognized it as not only the result of my torpid grief, but also as an artifact of my life before the island, in which I had had little power but to accept my fate. Then I did not love someone and yearn for him, so I had not been melancholy; I had merely been ironic.

When I arose the next morning, I went looking for Captain Fitzhoward who was lodged in the same inn and found him at breakfast. As I approached the table, he noted the transformation in my attitude as he rose and said, "Why, Madame Crousseau, you are looking much improved. I am glad." "Thank you, sir," I said and immediately broached my subject. "I can wait no longer to return home. Will you help me find another vessel to convey me?" The captain looked at once surprised, perplexed and dismayed. "That will be difficult," he said. "Ships stop briefly in Trinidad. Those that stay are like us, here for repairs." "Surely there must be some way," I urged. "A smaller craft, perhaps," I suggested. "Perhaps something local." "The smaller the ship the more dangerous the passage," he said. "I don't seek danger," I replied, "but I must get home. I cannot wait any longer." The captain inspected my face closely and at last his own showed resignation. "I'll put myself to see what can be done," he said, shaking his head a bit. "Thank you," I said, adding. "I could assist in this quest perhaps." "Perhaps," he said, "but it would be best first to allow me to make inquiries. The ports of the Caribbean are renowned for their thievery and skullduggery, so we must be careful." I agreed to this course, and the captain rose to execute it directly after his meal.

Meanwhile, I strolled upon the quay in a lighter mood and with greater appreciation of my surroundings than I had done since my blighted arrival. I finally appreciated the lilting speech of the inhabitants and their easy manners with each other as I strolled among the little stalls at the market where wizened old women with young children at their feet hawked fish, onions, and the fiery vegetables called chiles. I saw that there was brilliant color and pattern all around me, but that my extreme grief had drained them to gray. I bought some crimson flowers and went to the churchyard to put them on Richard's grave. "Please forgive me, dear brother," I whispered. There was, of course, no answer, but I did hear fiddle music wafting from the market as if Richard played there.

That evening Captain Fitzhoward came to tell me that so far he had not found a suitable craft but that he had received information about one that he would explore the next day. The following morning Sutton Norman called to invite me for a walk and I consented. As we walked, Norman conversed pleasantly, asking me many questions about the island and my life there. "And you were there alone for so long and later with only your husband and son. Were you not ravaged by loneliness?" I looked at him squarely, wondering how much I wanted to share with him. Finally, I said, "When I was alone, I was indeed lonely, but with my husband and son I was most content." "When you found your treasure you must have been jubilant." "On the contrary, it meant little to me as it had no value in the circumstance." "But it must be a great comfort to know you are sitting on a fortune. That at any time you might wander back into your cave and inspect it." "You mistake me for a miser in a play," I said. "Perhaps you will find more treasure," he said playfully, and I began to find the conversation peculiar. "I think I told you before that there was no more." "Indeed, you did, and that is just what I would say in your place." "But it is true!" I said with some exasperation. "Of course," he said. "Forgive me for trying your patience. Fortunes fascinate me. Would you care to take some lemonade?"

I did not enjoy Norman's conversation as it seemed devious, and I had good reason not to trust him, but I could not imagine he could do me any more harm. Even if he were to disembark on the island with me, he would not want to be stranded there, and so would leave when the ship departed. Meanwhile he could rifle the cave to his heart's content.

I did not see the captain again until the morning two days later. "I'm sorry I did not come to you last night," he said, "but I got in so late that I could not disturb you." "Did you find a vessel?" I asked. "Perhaps," he said gravely. "A Spanish captain retired from his ship here some years ago. I was told that he kept the pinnace from his ship for his own use. He lives a good distance from here and has the pinnace moored there." "What is a pinnace?" I asked. "It's a bit larger than a lifeboat and can be propelled with both a sail and oars." "And did you find this pinnace?" "I did and it is in good repair. I also met its owner, Don Reynaldo de Cassis." "Is he willing to let me hire the boat?" I asked. "He is, though it will cost a great deal." "If that is why you are looking so grave, do not concern yourself," I assured him. "No, I am quite aware of your resources, Madame Crousseau. You need not remind me of them." I was taken aback as I had not realized I had thrust my wealth upon his notice, but I suppose I had. In a softer tone, I asked, "What then is the cause of your gravity, Captain?"

"A craft is as good as the man who sails it. You will need at least two men. They will need to be very good sailors and to know the region well. Otherwise, such a voyage would be too foolhardy." Here the captain stared hard at me. "You could easily die en route. Would it not be better to be patient and insure that you will return home at last?" "I am very grateful for your counsel, Captain," I said, "but my own experience is proof that a larger ship is no guarantee of a safe voyage." "Of course not," he said, "but the odds of success are much greater."

I was very appreciative of his concern for me, especially in light of how much he disapproved of my opinions. I suppose this was Wider Love at work. "I cannot imagine how we can be sure that whatever sailors might take on this job would have the skill to take you safely home." "Could we not rely upon the recommendation of the Spanish captain who owns the pinnace?" I asked. "I inquired this of him already. He stays close to home and has little contact with the city. He suggested I acquaint the harbormaster with my need and allow him to make suggestions." "Why, yes, why not do so?" I asked. The captain shook his head. "The harbormaster of Trinidad is notoriously deceitful and a paragon of stupidity. Any recommendation from him would guarantee the idiocy of the proposed sailors. That the Spanish captain would suggest consulting him affirms his own assessment that he has lost touch with the city." "Surely there must be something we can do?" I said.

At this the captain looked at me very severely, "Sometimes one must simply bow to the situation, Roberta," he said, calling me by my given name for the first time. "Your will cannot overcome all circumstances." "I think, sir, that you have a wrong impression of me," I replied. "The better part of my life has been a school in that truth, the most recent events but an instance of it. Though I was able to gain some other kinds of education, I was a servant, my fate always to be subservient to the will of my masters. Then I was shipwrecked and for five years no person told me what to do, but I was subject to the much greater demands of mere survival. When my husband came to me, I discovered for the first time the felicity of merging my will with someone else's, of being neither servant nor master. That is what I am so eager to return to; it is the best life has given me, not a willful whim as you seem to think."

"I am sorry," the captain said immediately. "I did not mean to paint you as a childish brat. You are more decided in your opinions than most women are, but that is not why I am severe. It is because I care for you. I do not want you to risk your life, and I fear you go to an extreme." When he said this he took my hand, and his hawklike, honest face showed a tenderness that was a revelation. I said, "Thank you, Captain Fitzhoward. You have given me a great gift in saying so. Let us think more on this situation. Perhaps there is a way to find some sailors who you would trust." "Yes, very well," he said wearily, letting go of my hand. "I must go." He took his hat and left me without again meeting my eyes.

I sat in wonder. Had Captain Fitzhoward made me a declaration of love? And if so, how could he since he so thoroughly disapproved of me? I did not think that he meant to do it; it was rather forced out of him.

The oddness of the world had once again been painted before me. As I thought of this occurrence and interspersed it with the problem of finding some sailors, I could not help but try out in my mind the alternate life that the captain's declaration suggested. I was not attracted to his body, though it was solid and strong, but his honesty, his steadfastness, his skill, his kind treatment of me and of his men, all made me respect him, but it was the tenderness that endeared him to me. Then I wondered if the torment his declaration seemed to cause him might have its root as much in the difference in our social positions as it did in my being married, since he approved of the current scheme of social divisions and my origins were so much lower down on that ladder than his own.

I soon felt these thoughts as a kind of fetter, that, in fact, a life with Captain Fitzhoward would be one filled with a wide variety of fetters such as I had already rejected. I had always thought that I called Freeman by that name because when he told me his name in his language, it sounded to me like Freeman, but now I realized that this was to me his essence as well. I must get back to him. I did not want to cause pain to Captain Fitzhoward, but life with Freeman was what I truly wanted, as had been shown to me again and again.

The Losers Win My Favor

uring the night I thrashed about, sifting how reliable sailors might be obtained to take me to the island. At last I hit upon a promising scheme and was eager for morning so I might broach it to the captain. I was already at table when he came down to breakfast. He greeted me in the coolly courteous way he always had, as if nothing revelatory had occurred the day before. "Captain," I said, "I have an idea for identifying good sailors." He looked up curiously. "Could we not stage a competition? It would be a game of sorts. You would design a test course through which the competitors would show their skills. I would offer prizes and you would be the judge."

Captain Fitzhoward evinced no reaction at first, then he said, "You show your usual innovation, Roberta." I noted that he continued to use my first name, which I liked. "Such a thing is unusual, but could fit under the rubric of a regatta." I thought that for the Captain to approve of the idea it must be regulated through a known category. "However, such a thing would take some time to bring about. My ship might very well be ready to sail by the time this competition took place and you would have spent money to no purpose."

I was loathe to tell him once again that the money was of no concern to me. "It cannot take so long to put it about that a competition will be held," I answered. "Would it be very difficult to design the course?" Captain Fitzhoward thought for a moment. "No, not for calm weather, but the flaw in your scheme attaches to rough weather. It is rough weather that tests the seaman, and there is no way we can ape rough weather." This seemed so true that I was downcast and silenced. "But I could try to ascertain from the way a sailor solved certain problems what he would do should foul weather beset him," the captain said in an obvious attempt to alleviate my disappointment. "Why yes," I said appreciatively, "if you think it possible." "At the very least, such a competition would be diverting," he said, which surprised me as Captain Fitzhoward did not seem the sort of man for whom diversion was a legitimate goal. "Indeed, it might enliven Sutton Norman's life a bit," I said, then realized that the captain probably meant the competition would be diverting for me.

With his help I composed a handbill and went to seek a printer directly. The printer whom I engaged consented not only to print the bill but to take on its posting as well. By the end of the day I saw notices everywhere announcing "A SAILING CONTEST FOR ALL SEAMEN! PRIZES OFFERED!" In smaller type it said, "First, second and third prize to those who sail over the appointed course showing the best skill in seamanship. 20 pounds, 15 pounds, 10 pounds. December 15, 10 a.m. Main pier, Trinidad." I had wanted the competition to be sooner than the six days hence announced in the bill, but heeded the captain's counsel, "Most sailors cannot read. You will need time for this notice to go by word of mouth from the few who do to the many who do not." In view of this fact, we also hired a crier to go among the taverns to shout out the news of the competition.

"What if no one wants to compete?" I later worried aloud. "You are offering twice what a man can earn for a whole voyage," the captain assured me. "You will have no shortage of competitors." He had now entered wholeheartedly into the project and had sent his lieutenant hurrying hither and yon to make various observations. Sutton Norman was eager to participate as well. "You will see that I can be useful, Madame," he said with a short bow.

For the whole day the Captain strode about the island's shore. In the evening he explained to me that the course he had plotted would require the sailors to pass over several reefs, to maneuver through tricky currents and to negotiate a rocky coast. I could tell that he was trying to explain these things to me in layman's language without using the language of sea navigation he would have used with a fellow sailor.

I had appended to the bottom of the handbill a statement that inquiries could be made at our inn, and it wasn't very long before the interesting array of humanity represented by sailors started to arrive. The first was an ancient bearded fellow who seemed a miniature version of the god Neptune, though I could not think a god would express himself so slowly. "A sailing contest for all seamen with prizes," he read out to us, pausing lengthily between each word. "Yes," I said, "just so." The old tar continued to read out the whole bill, at the end of which he looked up and said, "I have been at sea since I was fourteen," he said. "but I do not see as well as I once did, so I will not enter this contest." "Then why did you come here?" I asked. The old man answered in the same measured way he had read. "To let you know why I would not be answering your call," he said. "Thank you, sir. We appreciate your effort," I said. The old man bowed slightly and creaked slowly out of the room.

A steady stream of sailors followed him, mostly younger, though many of them were intent on repeating to us exactly what was written on the handbill. I asked the captain why they did so. "They want to be sure it is not a hoax. They do not have great faith in print," he said, adding, "They look a good lot for the most part." I thought so too as there were many men who looked fit and intelligent, though the captain cautioned me that the look of a man was no indication of his seacraft. "Is that true in your own case, sir?" I teased. Consternation momentarily stiffened his features, but quickly passed. "I do not know if I look a good sailor or not," he said. "though I have tried to cultivate a sober exterior as a good influence upon my crew." He ended this speech with a pointed look at me suggesting that I ought to do the same.

Sutton Norman reported to us that all of the town was talking of the competition and had seized upon it as a social occasion. "I heard one lady in the street say that she must get to her dressmaker as quickly as possible if her gown were to be ready in time. We are very *au courant*," he said. A furrow grew upon the captain's brow.

As the week progressed, we saw vendors setting up to sell eatables on the pier, including a man assembling a small stand for which he planned to charge for a seat to view the competition. Captain Fitzhoward suggested that I have the prize money on display to the competitors before the contest as they would be encouraged by this literal show, so when the appointed day arrived I had ready three bags of coins before me on the raised table from which the captain would address the sailors and explain the course to them. I had dressed carefully for my ceremonial role in a red satin dress and had bought a white flower for my hair. As the men assembled, one of them shouted, "Ah, you would be a plumper prize than any of them bags, milady. You're a well-formed one!" This brought on a blush in me and a chorus of laughs from the other men, which set a good holiday tone for the affair.

The Captain called for order and began to explain the course. We had the use of several pinnaces from ships anchored in the harbor, including that from the captain's own. The men would work in pairs, each pair to be provided with a map of the course. Captain Fitzhoward had prepared a chart on which were listed a series of maneuvers: Sail NNE one league to Point Este, land the boat and retrieve the marker you will find on the beach. Regain the boat, sail back out to sea SSW three leagues to Point Alba keeping a distance of one-quarter league from the shore. There the current flows off the point. Sail to the point and complete a triangular path to the shore as indicated on the map. (The Captain had told me that this maneuver would require the sailors to navigate cross-currents.) From there, row back to Point Este. Raise sail and come home.

As the captain read through the chart the men interjected comments: "If we have to work in pairs, how will you know who is the real sailor, sir?" "Oh, that Point Alba is a tough one. That will show the real seaman!" Several men looked very downcast. "I can't read the map," one said, "but I can read the water better than anyone." "Then you must be in a pair with a man who can read the map," the captain cautioned. "How will you judge us?" To this question the captain replied. "I shall be upon the hill behind the town with my glass. Captain Hostettler of the Raven will be at Point Alba and my Lieutenant Smyth will be at Point Este. It is from him you will retrieve the marker that you must fetch back. I shall leave it to you to form up your pairs and then we shall begin," he concluded.

There was a vast buzz among the men and a few raised voices as the sailors began to separate off in twos. "But I cannot find a mate!" one man yelled. "You're a good fellow, but you can's see four feet in front of your face, Ned," someone else shouted to the first man's chagrin. Some of those left single found mates amongst themselves. There turned out to be twenty-seven pairs. "More than I had expected," Captain Fitzhoward said to me. "This will take most of the day."

A glorious day it was too; after a brief morning shower the air had freshened and the sky was now a brilliant, cloudless blue. As soon as the pairs had formed, bystanders began to evaluate them and make bets upon their favorites. "The red bandanna pair—they will win for sure. That's Bill Spradlin and Abel Mullins off the Raven. There are no better seamen." "No, no, they cannot best Hatcher and Diaz. They are part fish." "But those fish will be caught by that pair with the old man and the young one—the Moseby's, father and son. Steady wins the day."

Before the first boat shoved off, Captain Fitzhoward again addressed the group. "Remember, men, this is not a race. It is a test of skill. Don't dawdle, but don't rush. Just get through the course efficiently and safely. Each boat is loaded with the same weight of cargo; carrying it is part of the test. Good luck to all!"

The first pair entered their boat and rowed out a bit, then raised their sail. In ten minutes another boat followed. When the third boat was set to launch one of its sailors fell into the water while trying to enter it, setting off a laugh amongst the crowd, which by now was dotted with the parasols of the island's women fending off the sun, some fashionable, others plying their trade in the holiday atmosphere. They stood in loose poses against the whitewashed buildings, their yellow and scarlet skirts hiked above their knees. I noticed Sutton Norman nodding to several of them as if he had already made their acquaintance.

I went with the Captain up the hill behind the town where he provided me with a spyglass so that I might see the action. Sutton went with Lieutenant Smyth to assist in handing out the markers to the sailors who arrived at Point Este. One of the captain's ensigns stayed at the pier to direct each pair to set off.

I confess that for the most part I could tell little difference between the boats' maneuvers upon the water. The Captain, however, perhaps for my benefit, made frequent comments upon the action before us. "Ah, that was clever of Wells," or "That fellow made a clumsy run." I could make only one definitive judgment about the seacraft I observed—that the pair who capsized their boat were not my men. When I said this the captain retorted, "But even the best sailor will tip his boat sometimes!" "Then how are we to judge of them?" I said with some exasperation. "One must observe the steadiness and the finesse," he said and pointed out to me how one pair trimmed their boat very close to the current and easily crossed from one to another while another crew sailed far off and ended up sitting still for a good while. "On your voyage, you'll want to keep moving, so your sailors need to know how to find a wind and a current."

By the time the last pairs launched out, I had been schooled enough to appreciate them. They were the father and son, Colin and Harry Moseby, sandy-haired Englishmen, and the larger pair, Hatcher and Diaz, a sturdy bald man from Suffolk and a dark-bearded Spaniard. "It seems these men work very well in concert. The smoothness of their movement in the boat produces a fine flow across the water," I said. The captain looked pleased. "Yes, it is a pleasure to watch their surety, is it not?"

The Mosebys and the Hatcher-Diaz pair had apparently held themselves off until last so that their skill might constitute a climax to the competition, and they were also ignoring the captain's instruction that they were not to make a race of it as they had deliberately set off at the same time. "They can not help it," the captain said when I noted this fact. "Speed is generally of value in sailing, and besides, competitiveness is part of their mettle."

The two pairs ran very evenly all the way to Point Este, but there the superior agility of the young Moseby, who leapt from his boat and tore up the beach to retrieve the marker and then tore back again, gave his boat the edge as they turned for Point Alba. "Ah, this should be capital," the Captain said, "Now the Mosebys may frustrate Hatcher and Diaz by riding athwart their entering path and then turning at the last moment. But would you look at that, they are not doing it! And Hatcher and Diaz are trying a very clever thwarting maneuver of their own. Aha! the Mosebys slipped out of the trap rather nicely."

I watched with fascination as the two boats ran upon the water, alternating their oars and sails so as to bring them through the cross currents and to the exact points designated upon the coast. They glided into the pier one after the other, just as they had gone out. As the captain and I hurried down the hill back towards the pier, I said, "How will you choose? They seem quite equal." "I am thinking on it now," he said. "I must confer with the other judges."

While the captain and his cohort huddled together to determine the prize winners, the competitors engaged in a round of epic boasting, almost every pair claiming victory, though I noticed the two pairs most likely to win, the Mosebys and Hatcher and Diaz were the quietest and also the most relaxed. Hatcher held a mug of beer out to the younger Moseby, "Here, lad, drink up," he said, thrusting the mug with such force that it spilled all down the young man's shirt. "Not so quick after all, eh, lad," Hatcher joked, bringing on a laugh at the young man's expense. Moseby made as if to challenge Hatcher, but his father held him back. "Not worth your while, son," he said.

Soon Captain Fitzhoward and the other judges mounted the small dais and the captain called for the sailors' attention. "We have made our decision," he said. "Madame Crousseau, are you ready to award the prizes?" "I am, sir," I said, taking my place above the bags of guineas. "Third place to Lavecque and Pereira of the Santa Teresa." These two men looked surprised, hugged each other and accepted claps upon their backs from their fellows. "Merci, Madame," the one I took to be Levecque said to me as I handed him his prize.

"Second place to Colin and Harry Moseby," the Captain read out. The young man looked disappointed, but his father gave a deep bow as he accepted the prize. "Thank you very much, milady, we are much obliged."

"First place to Hatcher and Diaz," said the Captain. "I knew it would be us," exulted Hatcher. The bright sun glinted off his bald head as he and Diaz came forward to claim their prize. "Good work, men," the captain said.

I was disappointed that the Mosebys had not won because I liked them, though I could not really judge their skills. "A round for everyone at the Calvado!" Captain Fitzhoward shouted, indicating the tavern across from the pier. As the men went off in a noisy pack, the Captain joined me.

"So, you have had your competition, Roberta. Do you still want to sail off in such a small vessel?" "Yes, indeed," I answered. "I think I will be quite safe with Hatcher and Diaz." The captain looked at me askance. "Why would you go with them when you prefer the Mosebys?" he asked. I was somewhat astonished. "If the Mosebys are the better sailors, why did you not choose them to win?" "There is no difference to speak of in the seamanship of the two teams," he said, "but there is some difference between the men, I think." "Yes, I quite agree," I said happily. "It had not occurred to me that I was not obliged to hire the winners." "You are free to do as you like, is that not so, Roberta?" the Captain said with the teasing edge that was becoming habitual in his converse with me. "Why yes, Humphrey," I said, for the first time using the captain's first name. He gave me a long look. "Indeed," he said dryly. "Shall I have someone request that the Moseby's attend you at our inn this evening?" "Yes, please do," I answered.

Sutton Norman appeared from among the crowd. "Most diverting, Madame Crousseau. Thank you very much. I am most amused." He wore such an elated expression that one might have thought he himself had won the contest.

At seven when Colin Moseby and his son Harry arrived and stood before me, hats in hand, I thought either might model for Steadfast were they to appear in *Pilgrim's Progress*. They were moderate in all aspects, but their bearing softly broadcast competence, one of a graying middle-age and the other of a young man approaching his prime. After the Captain introduced them and I asked them to sit, I laid out the map whereon my island was depicted in relation to Trinidad and explained. "I would like to sail to this island in a pinnace such as the one you used today. I would like you two to be my crew and to take me there." The two men looked at each other and then at me.

"It is not a hard trip, Madame," the elder said, "but it is not an easy one neither." I smiled to think how differently Hatcher would no doubt have greeted my request. "We have confidence in your abilities, sir," said the captain. "You proved yourselves today. Madame Crousseau will pay you 100 pounds for the trip, half in advance, half to be paid by me when you return." The Moseby's looked incredulous. "That is a great deal of money, sir," the young man said. "Yes, it is. Madame Crousseau wants very badly to go to join her husband who lives upon this island." "Ah, I see," the elder Moseby nodded. "I think we could do it, Harry. What do you think?" he asked his son mildly. "Why yes, I think so too," the young man said, a broad smile across his face. "When will you be

366

wanting to leave?" he asked. "As soon as we can provision the pinnace according to your design, with the assistance of the captain, of course." I answered. "You can be ready the day after tomorrow," the captain said. There followed a long conversation about what supplies would be required and what the best route would be. We agreed to meet again on the morrow to gather what was required and to stow it in the boat in the afternoon.

As the Mosebys were leaving, I saw the older man take the captain aside and speak to him in low tones, two solid competent men looking each other in the eye. When the captain returned I could not help but ask what they had been talking about. "He asked if I had not chosen them as the contest winners in order to deflect the wrath of Hatcher from his son with whom he had previously had a fight," the captain replied. "And did you?" I asked, very interested that such a drama might have been afoot and I completely unaware of it. "Perhaps," the captain said and walked on.

Early the next day, we began to accomplish the provisioning of the small vessel with water and food. At the captain's urging we mounted a small canvas awning somewhat above midships to shelter me from the sun. At the end of the day Colin Moseby pronounced the little vessel "shipshape." "We'll see you in the morning, then," the older man said. "Yes," I said. "I am very grateful to you for taking on this voyage." "Why it is a great pleasure to us, Madame, and the pay that comes from it will be more useful to us than you can imagine," he said, his eyes filled with a story I hoped to hear in the coming days.

That evening the Captain and I dined together for the last time. I felt very sorry to lose his company, as beneath our disagreements we had forged a bond, but I was awkward in telling him how I valued it. "I am in your debt, Humphrey," I told him. "I will always treasure your friendship." "Do not sound so elegiac, Roberta. I will see you again as soon as my ship is repaired and I can sail to deliver you your goods." "Yes, I know, but tomorrow ends an interlude and I wanted to mark its importance," I said. "Ah, you believe in some ritual then," he said, though he seemed to be resorting to the tenor of our former badinage in order to hold his own feeling at bay. "Of course, I do," I said. "You cast me as a scoffer at tradition, but I am not. One is not obliged to embrace the whole of tradition, nor to reject it wholly either." "But if you pick and choose what you like and what you don't, how can there be order and continuity?" he chided. "One needs either an island of one's own in one's mind or in reality," I said, at which he smiled. "I will never forget you, Roberta," he said. "You are an original." "I would take that as a compliment, but I know that you hold originality in suspicion." "Perhaps," he said. "You think you know me very well, but there are things in all of us that pass beyond the knowledge of even the best observer." "In fact, if things were different. . . ." Here he seemed at a loss. "What I mean is. . . ." "I think I know what you mean," I said, "and I thank you for it from the bottom of my heart." The captain took my hand, kissed it very gently, and excused himself.

Chapter 23 — We Are Made Whole

I rose very early the next morning, elated by the expectation that I would soon be be at home, that I would soon be in the arms of Freeman and Tom. I had decided to dress in the sailor's pants I had acquired in Bristol because this would be a much more convenient attire for the circumstances of a boat, and also this is how Tom and Freeman knew me best. However, I covered myself with my cloak, and since the day had not yet become the sweltering oven it would be later on, I did not look too ridiculous.

Captain Fitzhoward rose from his breakfast, looking me up and down as I came towards him. "You wrap yourself closely," he observed. "I am wearing trousers, and I do not want to shock anyone," I said. "Trousers?" he said as though these were an extreme oddity and not a constant part of his own attire. "Yes, I always wear them upon the island as they are better suited to the climate and to the labor. They will suit the boat better as well, don't you think?" The captain harrumphed. "Perhaps," he finally said. "May I see them?" he asked, an inquiry that probably cost him something. "If you like," I said, pulling aside my cloak. He looked me up and down. "Very remarkable," he said, rather stunned. "I have never before seen a woman in trousers. I am astounded." "Will you survive it?" I said, drawing the cloak about me once more. "I'm not sure the world will survive it," he said.

I had little appetite and soon gathered my things and anxiously made my way down to the pier. I had brought only a small bag containing a comb, several handkerchiefs and a vial containing an emollient I had promised Lady Evelyn I would wear faithfully. My straw hat hung by its cord upon my back. "You are a picture of eccentricity, Roberta," the captain said jovially, having once again recovered his bearings. "I am not striving for that, sir," I returned. "Madame Crousseau, Roberta, I know that. I have the utmost respect for your integrity and, indeed, for everything about you," he said in a low tone so as not to be heard by others. "You have educated me a great deal," "And you have educated me very much as well. Thank you, Humphrey," and in saying it I knew it to be true.

At the pier the Mosebys were already busy upon the boat. It seemed the son was checking items as his father read them off a list. "They are a fine pair," the captain said. "I cannot be sure of your welfare upon the sea because the sea is fickle, but these fellows are not, and they will do the best they can for you. Good-bye, Roberta," he said and handed me into the boat. "May God bless and keep you." "And you as well, Humphrey," I replied. "I look forward to your arrival at my home."

As I said this I thought for the first time of a meeting between Captain Fitzhoward and Freeman and wondered how it would be for two such different men to be in each other's company. The captain's reaction, I imagined, would be something akin to seeing me in pants only more so. I smiled to think how kindly Freeman would treat a man who had been kind to me, hospitality being one of the great values of his people.

I seated myself on the bench in the middle of the boat. "Are you ready to cast off, Madame Crousseau?" the elder Moseby asked. "Yes, Mr. Moseby," I said. "Let us be on our way." He untied the line mooring us to the pier and took his place at the oars with his son. "We won't raise sail until we're clear of these large ships," he said. The Moseby's set to plying the oars and we began to draw away from the dock. I waved to Captain Fitzhoward, who waved back and shouted, "God speed!" He watched us until we rounded the point and I could no longer see him.

When Harry Moseby raised the sail, and I felt the wind lift us forward to slide upon the water, I was filled with a novel feeling compounded of glee, relief and fervent hope. I hoped I was not taking a foolish chance; I hoped we would arrive safely; I hoped with all my heart that Freeman and Tom were all right. My yearning for them vied with anticipation of again seeing their dear faces. Released from my former preoccupations, I could think of almost nothing but them, though from time to time the taste of grief rose to my throat, and the bright scene darkened in my mind. How Richard would have loved this adventure!

Colin Moseby interrupted my reverie to point out a large creature leaping upon the sea. "A dolphin, I think. It is perhaps a harbinger." "It might be," said Harry Moseby from his place at the side of the boat. "They are wondrous smart and happy too," he said.

We were mostly quiet that morning of our first day out; I was occupied with my own thoughts and the Mosebys with getting a feel for the craft they were manning. They took their jobs as guardians of our safety very seriously for which I was grateful, because the further we sailed from Trinidad onto the open sea, the smaller the boat seemed and the more willful my determination to get to the island without the delay of waiting for the larger vessel to take me. It was too late now to reconsider, of course, so I set myself to assist the Mosebys in whatever way might be needed and to maintain an observant posture so that I might do so.

"We are lucky in our weather," said Colin Moseby, perhaps sensing the sober plane on which my spirits had landed. "Yes," I answered. "Tell me, Mr. Moseby, have you always been a sailor?" "Yes, ma'am, though not always upon a merchant vessel. My father and grandfather before him, all the Mosebys that I know of have been fishermen, but five years ago Harry and I lost our boat in a great storm off the Cornish coast and had to go to sea to earn our living then." "I am very sorry to hear it," I commiserated. "It's a very different life on board a sailing ship than it is upon one's own vessel, no matter how small it is," he went on. "I can well imagine," I said. "I was a servant myself for many years, but escaped into mastery of myself through my shipwreck." "I had heard of your great good fortune," he said. "And this voyage will help my son and I become our own masters again, for with the pay you give us, we shall buy another boat of our own." I smiled to hear this and was less critical of myself for insisting upon the venture.

The sea was calm for all of our first day. In the evening we made for the coast and found a beach whereon we built a fire and cooked a meal of fish that Harry Moseby had caught us. "How nice to escape the dried mutton that was our lot upon the Northhampton," Harry Moseby said. "Why do sailors not eat more fish upon their voyages, since it is so plentiful around them?" I asked. "It is a strong feeling they have against fish," the elder Moseby said. "Harry and I don't have it, having been fishermen ourselves, but most sailors would rather chew on hardtack as tough as rocks than eat a tender, tasty fish."

The Mosebys slipped into sleep very quickly, having done all the physical work that day. I was pleasantly tired from the constant assault of the breeze, warm as it was, but my apprehensions for the next two days and my anticipation of home kept me up for some time.

We awoke to a lovely tropical morning and were shortly underway upon the sea again. The Mosebys had conferred together over the map for some time on the previous evening because today we would have to cross a treacherous patch of reef played upon by conflicting currents. We could sail very far out to sea to avoid their peril, but doing so presented other problems and would add a day to the voyage, perhaps more were we to be caught in a storm. The Mosebys had so advised me, and I had chosen to take the route closer to the shore despite its dangers.

There was a stiffer breeze today and the sun fell upon us with its full force as the elder Moseby had counseled the dismantling of the canopy so it would not compete with the sail and contribute to something going awry.

As I was folding the canopy I was brought up short by a most startling sight. I saw upon the sea to my left another small craft similar to ours plying the waters fifty yards away from our own. I gasped and the Mosebys looked up and saw it too. "Blow me down! We've got company," said Colin. Had I not been in great wonderment about this other craft, I would have marveled at his expression. Apparently, seamen do say "Blow me down!"

As the craft drew nearer one of its occupants stood up and called to us. "Yoohoo! Madame Crousseau! I just couldn't bear to lose your company so I'm coming with you." It was Sutton Norman. "Looks to be Hatcher and Diaz manning the boat," said Richard Mosby. "What the devil!"

I was nonplussed. What mischief did this demon have in mind now? "I reckon he thinks there's more treasure to be had upon your island, Madame Crousseau, and so he's followed us to make sure of the location," said Colin. Then flowed in upon me the memories of how Norman had spoken of the island; the questions he asked now arranged themselves in a pattern of meaning. He must have heard about my treasure in Lisbon and come aboard the Northhampton on purpose to follow me. "Oh blast the man!" I exclaimed, clenching my fist and using an oath for the second time in my life.

"What would you like us to do, Madame Crousseau," Colin asked. "I have no idea," I said, steaming. "What courses do you think available?" "There is no more treasure," I lied, "but I don't want this man upon my island if I can avoid it," I said. "We can't outrow them, so we'll have to put up with them for a while," Colin said. Neither he nor Harry seemed nearly as alarmed as I was.

Meanwhile, the other boat had drawn nearer. "I say, Madame Crousseau, you're not being very welcoming. I just want to see this fabulous island that has the power to lure a rich woman away from the pleasures of civilization," Norman said in his ironic tone. He was dressed as a young nobleman out for a sporting sail, white duck trousers and a blue satin waistcoat. I said, "You, sir, are a rogue who thinks to enrich himself, but you are, in fact, an idiot. There is no more treasure upon the island. I told you that on several occasions." "You did indeed, and maybe you're not lying, though I suspect you are. Nonetheless, there must be many caves upon your island that you have not explored, but I mean to do so." "How dare you impose yourself upon us!" I said angrily. "You are merely a servant who has grown wealthy," he said haughtily."You cannot be imposed upon." His gall was most monstrous. "And you are a nobleman who has dragged his father's name into a sty. Almost any man upon the street is your superior in every way," I said. "And you men," I went on, turning my gaze to Hatcher and Diaz who had been quietly rowing as Norman discoursed, "are you aware of this scapegrace's plan? He's a criminal. He used to play at robbery on England's highways. Now, it seems, he plays thievery at a distance." Hatcher and Diaz kept rowing. "Well, answer me. Just a few days ago I handed you a hundred pounds. Is this how you repay me?" "We won the hundred, mum," Hatcher growled. "And we're poor seaman. This fellow is paying us a great sum to take him," Diaz added sheepishly. "I hope he paid you in advance, as it's unlikely he will pay you when he finds no treasure," I said. "There's nothing you can do about me, Madame Crousseau," Norman put in, "so you'd best school your anger and put on a more fetching demeanor. Women look so ill when they are unpleasant."

"Can you row us away from them," I said to Colin and Harry. "Yes, ma'am," Colin said, putting more force into his oar, and sending us of on another tack. "Fine enough, if that's how you wish to play it. We shall just follow you at a companionable distance," Norman shouted as we drew away from his craft.

I sat with my head in my hands. How it pained me to think of Sutton Norman playing any part in my homecoming! How awful to impose him upon Freeman and Tom! "Madame Crousseau, do not fret so," Harry said gently. I looked up. Again I noted the Moseby's lack of alarm. For a moment I wondered if they were in league with Hatcher and Diaz, but immediately rejected the notion as incompatible with all that I had observed in them. "Do you know something I don't?" I asked. "Is there a way we can evade them?"

"They will have to encounter the rocks here," Harry said and pointed to the location upon the map. "As will we," I said. "Yes," said Colin, "and it may be that none of us will make it." "But we stand the better chance," said Harry. "Why is that?" I asked. "Because we are indeed the better seamen," he answered. My face must have registered doubt based upon their equivalent performances in the contest, for Colin said, "Yes, they did win, but it was a contest and not the real thing. And they have with them a scurrilous fellow who besides adding weight to their vessel cannot but be a hindrance," he said. "Why so? His character is rotten, but he's a strong young man who can help the seamen more than I can help you," I said. "We'll see," said Colin. "We'll see."

For many hours we wended our way upon the water, shadowed at a distance by Norman's boat. From time to time he would call out inanities to taunt us. "Having a lovely boat trip, aren't we? Jolly good lark upon the sea." We ignored him as best we could.

In the early afternoon, a series of tall escarpments grew upon the shore, formations of rocks frozen in cascades beneath them. "Are these the rocks you spoke of," I asked, as they looked cruelly dangerous. "Yes, we want not to end up on those killer stones," said the elder Moseby, "and the currents will try to throw us there. It was as practice for them that your captain planned his course to Point Alba." "And it's for keeping you off them that you're paying us," Harry Moseby added gaily.

As we approached the hazardous area Harry pointed out to me how one could read the waters over it. There did seem to be a peculiar churning, but it was very subtle and I would not have noted it if he had not showed it to me. However, as we drew closer to it I felt its pull beneath us and the pinnace began to slide into it. The elder Moseby took the helm and ran the sail while Harry took the oars. "Can't I help with an oar?" I called over the increasing din of the water. Harry thought for a moment before replying, "Another arm would help, but can you do exactly as I say?" "Certainly, you must command me," I answered.

Behind us I could make out Hatcher and Diaz slowing their oars, while Norman seemed to be urging them on. "They'll wait to see how we do it," Harry said. "Let's attend to our own business, son. We're almost upon it. All right, now, row!" the father called out as I felt the boat slipping into the current's strong stream. "Pull now, Madame Crousseau," Harry said. "Follow my rhythm." Our combined rowing seemed to be only enough to produce the impression that we were standing still, but that impression lasted for a mere moment as the current began to master us. "I'm going to bring the sail round," Colin shouted, "reverse the oars and keep your heads down." "He means we must row the other way," Harry said. Colin shouted out his action. I ducked and the boom swung over my head, as we continued to pull with all our might. The boat leapt over the current, but it was swinging shoreward in a wide arc that seemed destined to send us crashing fatally up onto the rocks.

I was very afraid. Our destruction seemed certain and rushing at us so rapidly that in my mind I said, "Good-bye dear Freeman and Tom." I wished I believed in a God who would watch over them or even save us. Colin Moseby called another command, and so I was distracted from my doom by the need to duck as the sail swung to a new position. Suddenly, miraculously, we careened away from the rocks. We repeated this maneuver several times, each as hair-raising as the last. I shuddered, thinking I should have paid more attention to the captain when he described the danger of the voyage.

Finally, after one more tack that seemed most certain to ram us against the rocks, we slid into a narrow cove. "Are we through?" I asked. The Mosebys exchanged looks. "No," Colin said. "We have one patch to ride over. But you might look out how here we are hidden from the other boat." I saw that this was indeed true, and that we could not be seen by their crew until they came right by us on their tack. The Mosebys kept their two stout gazes on me and at last I grasped the prospect they were refraining from making explicit. "Yes!" I shouted. "I would indeed like to take advantage of this opportunity." I grabbed my oar and extended it in front of me while still maintaining a firm hold upon it.

Just then the other boat burst out of the eddy into sight only a few feet from us. Sutton Norman turned his head, saw me, and stood up, his look shouting the triumph of catching up to us. I slammed the oar around and struck him full force in the stomach, knocking him out of the boat and into the sea with a great splash. "Row, men," I shouted to my own crew and reapplied my oar once more. In the distance I saw Norman rise sputtering to the surface. Diaz held out an oar to him while Hatcher controlled their craft, but it would not be easy to haul Norman into it.

I had no time to gloat as our boat was entering the last stretch of dangerous water, though I'm sure my pleasure at dealing Norman a blow lent strength to my arm and helped us over the current that reached to drag us on the rocks. At last we coasted out into a calm patch from where we soon regained a good cruising speed through quiet waters. The Mosebys were smiling broadly. "You pounded the puppy. Good for you," Harry cheered. I returned his grin. "No shame, eh, lassie. He deserved it," Colin added. Of course I felt no shame; if the Mosebys only knew how Norman had used me. "Did you think we wouldn't make it at first?" Harry then asked me. "I confess, I thought we were to become shark bait," I said. "Ah, a sailor's expression. We shall make a tar of you at last," he said. "Were you not worried?" I asked him. "Not much," he said. "It was a rough situation, but we have seen many such."

"Hatcher and Diaz will recover Norman, won't they? He won't be drowned or be killed against the rocks," I asked. The fellow was a devil, but I didn't want to kill him. "No, they will fish him out, but they'll no doubt be stranded for some time," said Colin. "And by then, you will be safe on your island, and they will not find you," said Harry, beginning again to row.

"That is most excellent!" I exclaimed, very relieved, though almost against my will, I found myself concerned about the welfare of the other seamen. "Do you think Hatcher and Diaz can recover their craft?" I asked. "Oh yes, ma'am. They'll have to scuttle their voyage is all," Harry said lustily.

They seemed so much more sanguine about this experience than I did. Is it that men enjoy physical danger in a way that women do not? I had wondered if this were part of hunting's allure for Freeman, and I remembered the lively illumination of Captain Fitzhowards's face when he realized we were in for a battle with the pirates. I suppose it is an age-old question involving, perhaps, the sexes' relative strength. I felt myself to be quite strong, yet I was heavily averse to putting myself in dangerous situations as a form of recreation. I was quite happy to ride upon the calm waters hour after hour secure from Sutton Norman when, it seemed to me, the men would have been glad of another bit of peril.

Another one seemed on the horizon where grey clouds gave way to a black sky that closed down around us, at first spitting upon us and finally becoming a steady stream of rain. There was, however, no wind, so we moved very little as the Mosebys decided to wait out the storm rather than to expend energy in rowing that might be urgently needed later. And so we sat for several hours in the rain.

The canopy had been remounted for me. It was more fit to deflect sun than water, however, and I was dodging dripping streams that made me as wet as the men. My hair and clothing were soon plastered against my body and my breasts stood out clearly against the wet cloth, causing me some embarrassment. The Mosebys tried not to look, but their occasional smiles told me that they had not succeeded. At least I was a distraction from our drenching; luckily, the water was not too cold or the misery would have been less supportable. "Should we perhaps row for the shore to take refuge?" I asked. "We would have to cross over the reef again," Harry said, "and it would be harder in the rain."

"How about a draft of brandy," Colin Moseby called, so I drew out the flask and handed it around, taking a sip myself at last. "That warms a bit, does it not?" Colin said. "A bit," I said. "Can you estimate how long such a wet doldrum could go on?" I asked. "Oh, it could be days, ma'am," said Harry. "Now, Harry, don't go scaring the woman," said his father. "But it's true!" Harry said. "Though not likely," the more temperate older man said. "Perhaps we should row in hopes of coming out of the storm," I said. "Very well, we shall if you like," Harry said, and he and Colin set to it.

They rowed for more than an hour, but we did not emerge from the downpour. "We'd better set ourselves to bailing," Colin advised. Indeed, so heavy was the rain that the water had collected to several inches in the bottom of the boat. "I can help," I said and took up a bucket, glad of some employment. Bailing was hampered by the waterlogged state of our clothing, which acted as a weight upon us, but the exercise gave me the illusion of making progress.

The rain did not go on for many days, as Harry had said it could, but it did go on for two, which at the end felt like two weeks so sodden and dejected was I. The Mosebys, however, seemed little affected, and I thought that a life at sea must persuade one towards a stoic attitude.

At last we felt a light breeze, so Harry hauled up the sail, and we were soon making headway towards a faintly brighter strip that appeared between the clouds and the sea. As we approached it, the clouds gradually withdrew, and we found ourselves in the golden light of a late afternoon like those I had grown to treasure on the island. "Ah, how lovely. This is how the island is almost every afternoon," I said, smiling. Colin Moseby said. "I reckon we will reach your island within the next few hours." "I had not thought it could be so soon," I said with astonishment, for we had set out only four days earlier. "Aye, and I did not want to tell you so until I could be sure," he said, pointing to the shore at a peak with a leveled off top, "but that has got to be La Mesa you see pictured here," he said, pointing to the map, "and here is your island." "So close!" I said, and my heart pounded.

I began to scan the horizon in earnest, looking ever more eagerly for something recognizable as the boat cut through the water between me and my dear ones. When I thought how I must look after sitting in rain for two days, I could only shrug. I made a futile attempt to comb my hair, but its tangles resisted, and it occurred to me that I would arrive at the island for the second time almost as disheveled as I had been the first.

Then I saw it! I could not say exactly how I knew that this particular far beach was the one I yearned for; there were so many that seemed identical to it, but I knew indubitably this particular disposition of palms against the sky, the angle of the land against the hillside behind it, and the small spit beyond it where the ship had eventually wrecked upon the rocks belonged to my island. "We are here, " I said eagerly. The Mosebys scanned the coast as eagerly as I.

The closer we got the more familiar it was, and I could soon make out the flagpole we had erected on our sunset hillock to amuse Tom. We were several hundred yards from shore when I saw a slight figure running upon the beach. It had to be Tom! As we came closer, he stopped and began wildly to wave his arms, having sighted us. "That is my son," I said with utmost happiness. "That is Tom and he has seen us!" "We must take you through the surf before you can embrace him, my dear," Colin Mosby said affectionately. "Yes, please make it a swift passage," I said, ready to leap from the boat so I could fold my boy in my arms.

"Tom! Tom!" I shouted. We were still too far away to be heard above the noise of the water, and I was not even sure that Tom could see it was me in the boat coming towards him, but I could not stop myself from standing up in the boat and calling to him. "Tom! It's your mother!" I shouted.

My rising rocked the boat precipitously, and for a moment I thought I might fall into the water as Sutton Norman had. "Sit down, Madame Crousseau, or we will all be in the drink," Colin said gently. I knew this was sensible advice, but it was very difficult for me to keep my seat. I kept waving and shouting Tom's name, and when the boat was about fifty feet from shore, Tom recognized me and I heard his voice above the breeze. "Mama! Mama! My mama!" he cried and ran down the beach and into the sea towards us. I could no longer restrain myself. I pulled off my boots, tore off my hat and leaped out of the boat, shouting, "I'm coming, Tom, darling!"

I swam with all my might and the waves propelled me forward as well, until very close to the shore one picked me up and threw me forcefully onto the pebbled beach just as Tom reached the same place. We stood up and clutched each other amidst the swirl of the retreating wave. "Oh Mama, Mama, you've come back," he said clinging to me with all his might. "Yes, dear," I said, holding his head against my breast. "I have come back." I held my beloved little boy!

Still clasping each other we struggled out of the water so that we would not be taken back into the ocean by the next wave. As soon as we were clear of it, I held him away from me and devoured him with my eyes. He seemed to have grown two inches since I'd gone; his face was slightly different, his hands and feet much larger. "You are more Tom than when I left you," I said, again drawing him to me. "But you are the same Mama," he said. "I missed you so much. Where did you go?" he said and then his body began to tremble and shake with sobs. "There, there," I said. "It's all right now. I am back and will never leave you again." At this Tom's thundershower of crying went off as quickly as it had come, and he looked eagerly towards the boat that had now breasted the waves and was landing nearby. The men jumped out of it and dragged it up the beach.

"You did not wait for the grand landing we had planned for you, Madame Crousseau," Harry said, approaching Tom and me with his father. "I could not help myself. I'm sorry if I frightened you," I said. "This is my son Tom," I said as proudly as any mother could. "Hello, Tom," Harry said. "Hello," Tom said shyly, though his face was shining with curiosity, at which Colin lifted him up and swung him about, Tom laughing with delight. "Where is your father?" I asked when he alit. "Working in the garden," Tom answered. "Let us go and find him," I said, taking his hand.

I led the Mosebys up the path to the cave, Tom capering before us. As we passed the places that had marked my life for ten years I felt indescribably happy to see everything looking well cared for, and yet I saw everywhere subtle differences. This bred a slight unease that vied with my pride to hear the exclamations the men made over our arrangements.

At the top of the hill I saw the caramel circle of fur that was Roger lying in a sunny spot. He heard us and raised his head, his ears assuming their most alert posture. Suddenly, he bounded towards us and, when he reached me, jumped upon me with an ecstasy of barking. "Yes, Roger, it is I," I said, holding on to our good dog. I had seen Miss Higgins close by as well. She had not sullied her catly dignity with Roger's enthusiasm, but slowly rose, stretched, and sauntered over to wrap herself about my ankles. "Oh you are a silky beauty," I said, rubbing her ears at which she set up a loud purr. "Some kittens will join you soon," I warned her.

When we reached our house, I said, "Will you make yourselves comfortable and wait while I go further up to find my husband? When I come back I will find refreshments." I could barely contain myself enough to be courteous. "Of course," Colin Mosby said. "Don't be thinking of us at a time like this. Go to your man."

I went off immediately, Tom with me as he was not prepared to let me out of his sight, nor was Roger who ran ahead, though, I saw with a pang that he was slower than he used to be. As we walked I mused on Freeman doing garden work, which he had shown little inclination to do before.

When I first saw him he was bent over a plant, but he heard the noise on the path, rose and turned towards us, putting his hand to his eyes. There he was in the flesh, to me the most handsome man on earth. His body sang to me of grace, just as it had the first time I'd seen him. When he saw it was me he smiled most gloriously. I sprinted towards him and he to me. I felt so propelled towards him that I thought our impact might extinguish us both, but just before we met we stopped and looked at each other, our eyes rapidly communicating what could not have been said so quickly in words.

"Your errand took rather a long time," he said in a combination of our languages, then groaned and drew me to him, kissing me all over my face, running one hand through my hair then over my back and slipping the other around my waist, while Tom hugged us both about the legs. "I have missed you so, my darlings," I said, and then began to cry. We all sank to the ground amidst the stout bean stalks and carrot tops. Freeman held me against his chest and caressed my head until I stopped crying out all the year's worth of longing and sorrow.

When I was calmer, I looked more closely upon Freeman's broad face; his lively brown eyes were as lovely as ever, but I saw a weariness around them and saw how my mysterious absence had written its pain upon him. I caressed his face and ran my hands over his long soft black hair and his golden brown body that had pleasured my own so many times. I halted at a great scar upon his left arm. "Ah, some awkward sport upon the rocks," he said to my silent inquiry. "It was my fault, Mama," Tom said. "I went out too far and the tide came in, so Papa had to rescue me." I drew Tom to me; his anguish at having caused his father injury apparently preyed heavily upon him. "We all make mistakes, Tom," I said. Sometime soon I would tell of Richard.

"For so many hours I have looked at the horizon, wondering where you were, believing and not believing that you would come back, trying to comfort Tom and myself. Tell me what happened." Freeman said. I explained how Herbert Crent had taken me. "I thought it was something like that because of the man's ugly talk," he said, adding gravely, "I wanted to kill him." "He was punished," I assured him. I briefly told him of my journey to England and back. "But I must tell you more later," I said, "because I have not come back alone. Two fine seaman brought me here from the ship." At this Freeman looked interested, but I saw wariness as well. Before I had never seen suspicion harden his features in this way.

And then, just at that moment I was very startled to see something that must have put the same look upon my face. Walking down the path above the garden was a very beautiful young woman, her skin a golden brown, her hair as black and lustrous as Freeman's.

She was wearing a strip of cloth around her hips and a ring of flowers around her neck draped over her entirely bare bosom. Seeing my alarm, Freeman said, "It is Tulava. I found her as you found me—about to be killed by our tribesmen. When I last saw her she was a little girl, the daughter of my uncle."

She shyly approached us, looking very frightened and flabbergasted by the sight of me. Freeman spoke to her in their language, which I understood well enough to understand, "This is my wife. She has returned to us." At this the girl's face softened to a lovely smile. She took off the ring of flowers and offered it to me, saying "Thank you for the refuge of your home."

I was very much amazed. "Let us go and greet the seamen," Freeman said, still holding me close to him. I pulled myself away from the line of thoughts that came with the appearance of Tulava and looked at Freeman. "Yes, of course." I thought then how these Englishmen would respond to the unclothed Tulava. "It would be better for Tulava to cover her breasts or the men will stare at her endlessly," I said, "for in their country women never bare their breasts to strangers, or even sometimes to their intimates." I hated to say this as it put me immediately in a repressive role, but I felt I had no choice. We tore off a piece of the garden awning and fashioned a wrap for her. "Thank you," she said with downcast eyes, as though she had done something wrong.

The nasty beast of jealousy crouched in my heart, and I could not help but wonder what sort of relation had been established between Tulava and Freeman in my absence, even though they were cousins, especially since he could not know if I lived or would return to him and she was so very beautiful. I hated this feeling, coming as it did to shadow my happiness.

As we walked the path, I reasoned with myself. I had seen nothing to make me think they were lovers and Freeman's greeting to me was everything I could have wished. He remained as close to me as the path would allow and whenever it was wide enough he held me around the waist or took my hand. "I have missed you so much I thought my heart would break," he murmured. "If it had not been for Tom, I would not have been able to carry on." "You have taken good care of him, dear. I can tell," I said. "Tulava was a help," he said. I scanned his face closely as he said this and again found no reason to doubt that he was as devoted to me as I was to him. And then, it burst upon my mind that I didn't care if they were lovers. If she had comforted him, I was glad. Obviously, he still wanted me. I wish I could say I was able to maintain such equanimity, but I could do so only intermittently.

When they heard us coming, the Mosebys rose from their seats around the fireplace and came to meet us. The mutual greetings between them and Freeman were as warm and cordial as such beginnings can be between men from such different worlds. Harry Mosby was most happy to meet Tulava and attended her throughout the evening.

After we had all sat and talked for a good long time, and I had gazed about and got my bearings, I offered to prepare a meal. I suggested that Freeman and Tom might show the men around a bit while I did so. Tulava stayed to help me and I found her skillful, efficient and tactful. The kitchen seemed to have been her domain for some time, but she yielded it to me quite graciously, though from time to time I had to ask her where things were. I had retained most of what I had learned of Freeman's language so we were able to converse. She asked many questions about England, expressing herself in such a delightful way that I found myself liking her. She told me that, like Freeman, she had been banished by her tribe for refusing to marry as the tribal chief had commanded and felt herself extremely fortunate to have been saved by her cousin Freeman.

When the men came back, and while the meat roasted, I went to the waterfall to bathe. As the gentle water fell over me, I looked down at my body and could not help comparing it to Tulava's. I was older certainly, but I was also stronger. I rubbed my skin with the emollient Lady Evelyn had given me and felt my body tremble and my being grow hot when I thought how Freeman would soon caress me. I had waited so long for it!

When I came back, we all ate heartily of roast goat and fruit. How happy I was to taste again the yellow tube fruit that I now knew were called bananas! Despite the pleasure of the meal, however, I was most eager for the evening to end so that I might be alone with Freeman. All evening we had sat closely together. From time to time he would stroke my arm or smooth my hair, his arm around me. On the other side Tom pressed against me, and I caressed his head, remembering the many times of misery when I had longed to do so. I had given him Rachel's drawings which he pored over with immense interest. "Will I ever see my cousins?" he asked. "I don't know, dear. Perhaps," I said.

As the evening wore on, we made sleeping arrangements. It seems Tulava had as her room the loom enclosure that Freeman had inhabited when he first came to me. We made beds for the Mosebys under a shelter we had built for storing our tools. "Might Tom sleep with us?" Colin asked very considerately, I thought, as a way to allow Freeman and I some privacy. "Oh, yes," Tom said, "May I?" "Thank you, Colin," I said to his grinning face.

At last Freeman and I were alone, lying together in the marvelous island air. We lay for some time holding hands and talking, stroking each other as if making sure that we were really here together. We looked long into each other's eyes, as if reading the suffering that had changed us both. He told me how worried he had been that I had been hurt, but more how he warred within himself about whether or not I would come back. "But at last, I knew you would. I knew if there were any way to do it, you would find it," he said, clasping me to him. I exulted at his faith in me.

Then I told him about Richard. "He was so young and eager. And they will blame me at home for his death, and I cannot rid myself of the idea that it is so," I said and began to sob as if Richard's death were again new in my heart. "I am sorry that I will not meet him," Freeman said. "We will build a cairn for his memory." He didn't tell me not to sorrow or worry, but he held me very closely and seemed to say with his body that he would share my sorrow. It seemed then that that which had ravaged me would be less strong against us both.

Then Freeman began to kiss me very gently, over and over, each kiss laden with communication for which I had thirsted for more than a year. Gradually, I moved away from my island of sorrow and joined him, matching his increased tempo with my own. He slowly undressed me and kissed me over my entire body, and I was hungry to kiss him all over as well. When he drew aside his loincloth, his lovely sex rose to meet me and I opened myself to him with all my heart.

We lay talking late into the night. Freeman told me of Tom's doings during the year. He told me how the goats had fared and how he had fared as a farmer. "There is too much I didn't know. I needed you ten times a day," he said, kissing my face. "Freeman, dear," I said, "our island can never be taken from us. "Of course not," he said. "What I mean is, a country in the old world has claimed all this region as its own and so I went to their king and asked to buy this island, but instead he gave it to me." "How odd," Freeman said. "How could one across the ocean give you an island he has never seen nor trod upon?" "Yes, it is odd, but the important thing is that it is ours now," I said. "Perhaps someday we will visit the old world and you will see all its oddities," I said. "Perhaps so," he said with interest "Tom would like that, but you are what I crave now," and he again began to embrace me. All the things I wanted to tell him swam before my eyes, but I knew I had time. We would absorb each other's changes, and I had faith we could. I was at last at home.

Acknowledgements

Daniel Defoe's masterpiece *Robinson Crusoe* has been my inspiration. How Robinson made a household for himself alone on an island fascinated me. Robinson was also exasperating—in a beautiful place, he noticed very little about it that was unconnected to his material survival. He was always frightened and lonely, but when another human being turns up, Robinson makes a slave of him. I wanted to do it differently.

Ann Decker suggested I add sewn illustrations, conceiving the idea that it was the title character, Roberta, who would make textile pictures of her life. So I began a five year sewing project, with lots of encouragement along the way, especially from Jessie Lawson and Angela Botelho. Veronica Casares-Lee was enthusiastic and gave me some very good ideas; Jerry Engelbach was helpful too. My husband Butch Waller contributed his fine eye, design advice and excellent company as I stitched away. I'm grateful for the photography of Reed Cooper and Eduardo Solér. Ann Decker was there every step of the way with her artistry and counsel; this book would not exist without her. How lucky I am to have such friends.

Corless Smith is Professor Emerita of Broadcast and Communication Arts at San Francisco State University, where she taught dramatic writing and criticism of popular culture. She lives in Oakland, California with her husband Butch Waller and two cats—the graceful sweetheart Nikki and the handsome thug Marco. Contact her at: casmith@sfsu.edu